image® comics presents

Wayward

Volume Four: Threads and Portents

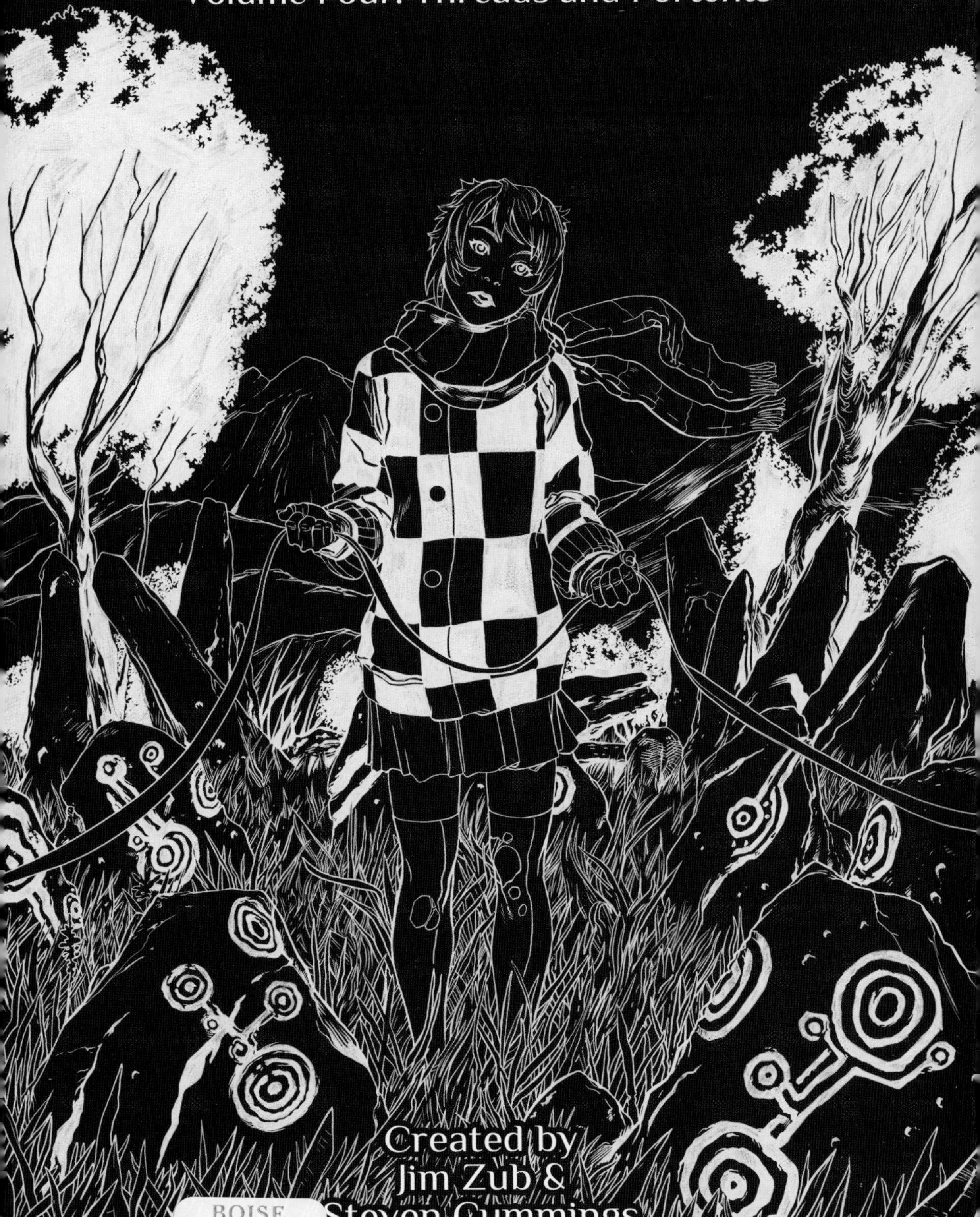

Created by
Jim Zub &
Steven Cummings

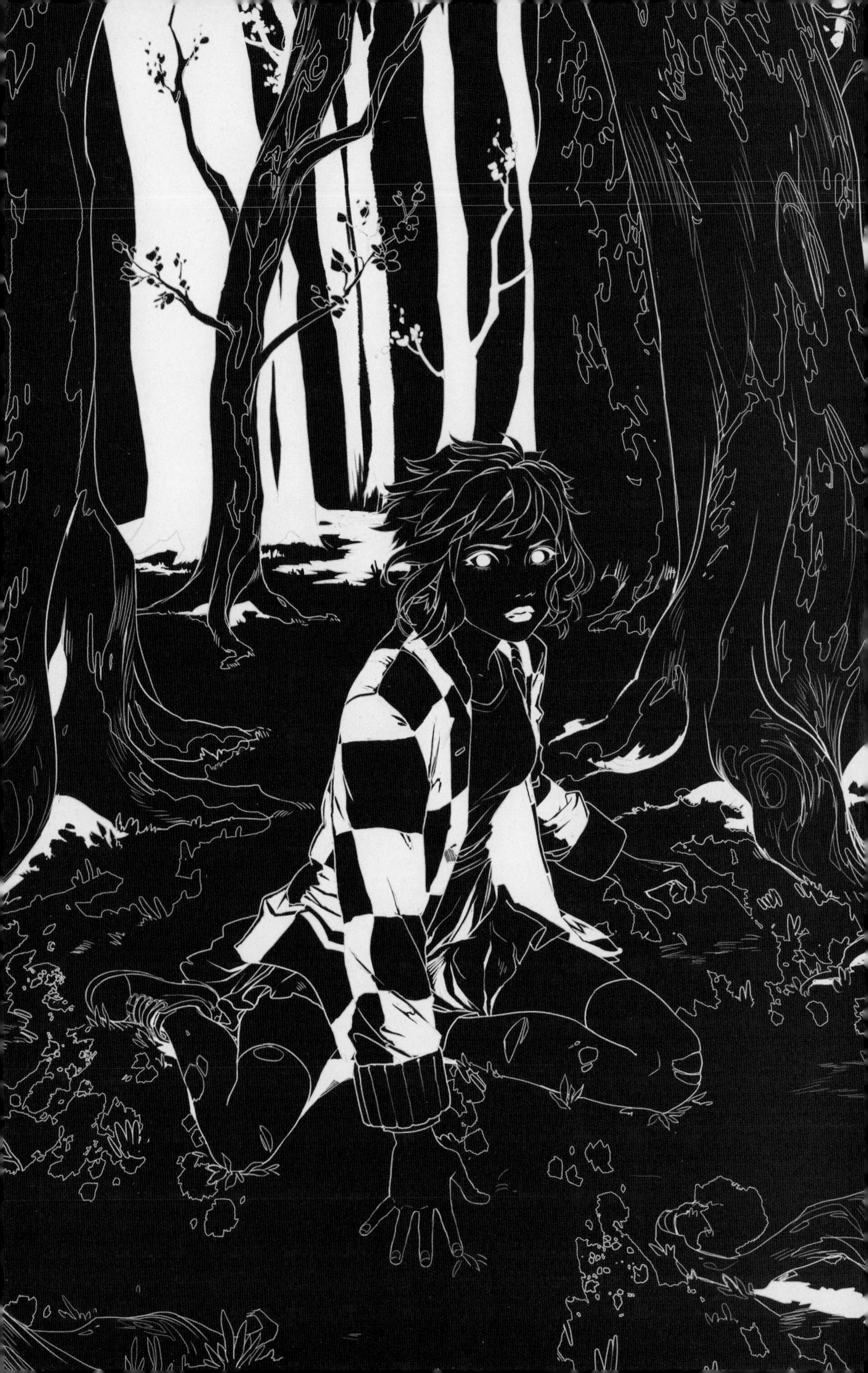

Previously

A group of teenagers in Japan discover they have strange supernatural powers. **Emi Ohara** can alter the form of manmade objects and change her body to match them. **Nikaido** controls emotions. **Shirai** feeds on spirit energy to sustain and empower him. **Ayane** is not a teen at all, she's a shape shifter formed from energy channeled through generations of cats. At the center is **Rori Lane**, a half-Japanese half-Irish girl called a 'Weaver', a powerful conduit for the strings of fate that define power and destiny.

Soon after these powers emerge, the teens are hunted by **Yokai**, mythical Japanese creatures and spirits. The Yokai sense these striplings are the next generation of the supernatural in Japan, but they're not willing to relinquish the control they've built over the centuries.

Manipulated by the **Nurarihyon**, a powerful Yokai, the Japanese Self-Defense Force attacked Meguro, a temple the teens were using as their base of operations. During that battle, **Dermot Lane**, Rori's father, grabbed his daughter and teleported them both home to Ireland, and Ayane was pulled along for the ride...

story
Jim Zub

line art
Steven Cummings

color art
Tamra Bonvillain

color assist
Brittany Peer

color flats
Ludwig Olimba

letters
Marshall Dillon

back matter
Zack Davisson
Ann O'Regan

special thanks
Olivia Ngai
Ryan Brewer
Jonathan Chan
Amanda Schank

IMAGE COMICS, INC.
Robert Kirkman—Chief Operating Officer
Erik Larsen—Chief Financial Officer
Todd McFarlane—President
Marc Silvestri—Chief Executive Officer
Jim Valentino—Vice-President

Eric Stephenson—Publisher
Corey Murphy—Director of Sales
Jeff Boison—Director of Publishing Planning & Book Trade Sales
Chris Ross—Director of Digital Sales
Kat Salazar—Director of PR & Marketing
Branwyn Bigglestone—Controller
Susan Korpela—Accounts Manager
Drew Gill—Art Director
Brett Warnock—Production Manager
Meredith Wallace—Print Manager
Briah Skelly—Publicist
Aly Hoffman—Conventions & Events Coordinator
Sasha Head—Sales & Marketing Production Designer
David Brothers—Branding Manager
Melissa Gifford—Content Manager
Erika Schnatz—Production Artist
Ryan Brewer—Production Artist
Shanna Matuszak—Production Artist
Tricia Ramos—Production Artist
Vincent Kukua—Production Artist
Jeff Stang—Direct Market Sales Representative
Emilio Bautista—Digital Sales Associate
Leanna Caunter—Accounting Assistant
Chloe Ramos-Peterson—Library Market Sales Representative
IMAGECOMICS.COM

WAYWARD VOL. 4: THREADS AND PORTENTS.
ISBN: 978-1-5343-0053-8. First Printing. MARCH 2017.
Published by Image Comics, Inc. Office of publication: 2701 NW
Vaughn St., Suite 780, Portland, OR 97210. Copyright © 2017
Jim Zub and Steven Cummings. All rights reserved. Originally
published in single magazine form as WAYWARD #16-20.
WAYWARD™ (including all prominent characters featured herein),
its logo and all character likenesses are trademarks of Jim Zub
and Steven Cummings, unless otherwise noted. Image Comics®
and its logos are registered trademarks of Image Comics, Inc.
No part of this publication may be reproduced or transmitted, in
any form or by any means (except for short excerpts for review
purposes) without the express written permission of Image
Comics, Inc. All names, characters, events and locales in this
publication are entirely fictional. Any resemblance to actual
persons (living or dead), events or places, without satiric intent,
is coincidental. PRINTED IN THE USA. For information regarding
the CPSIA on this printed material call: 203-595-3636 and provide
reference # RICH – 726083.

For international rights contact: foreignlicensing@imagecomics.com.

Chapter Sixteen

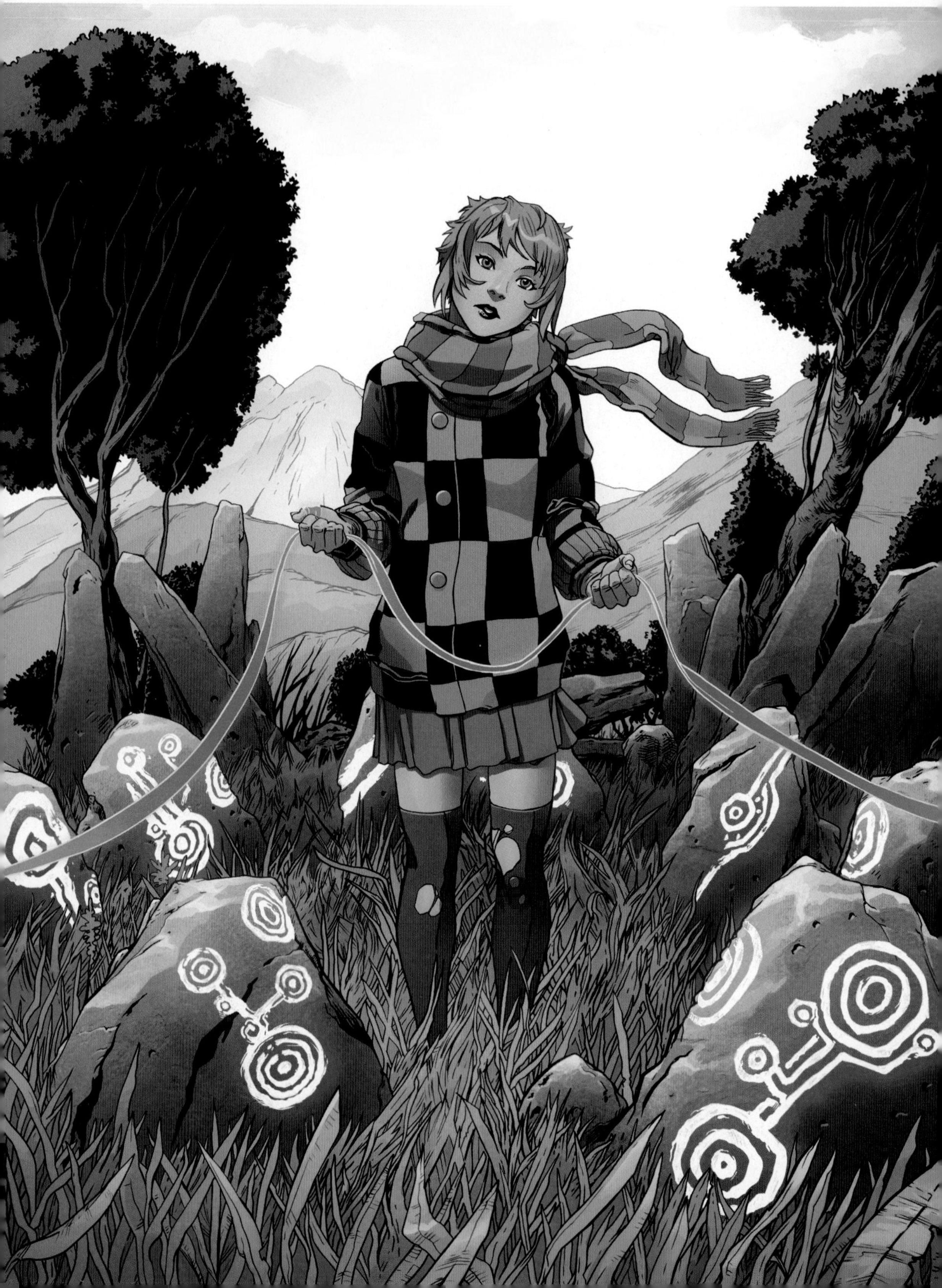

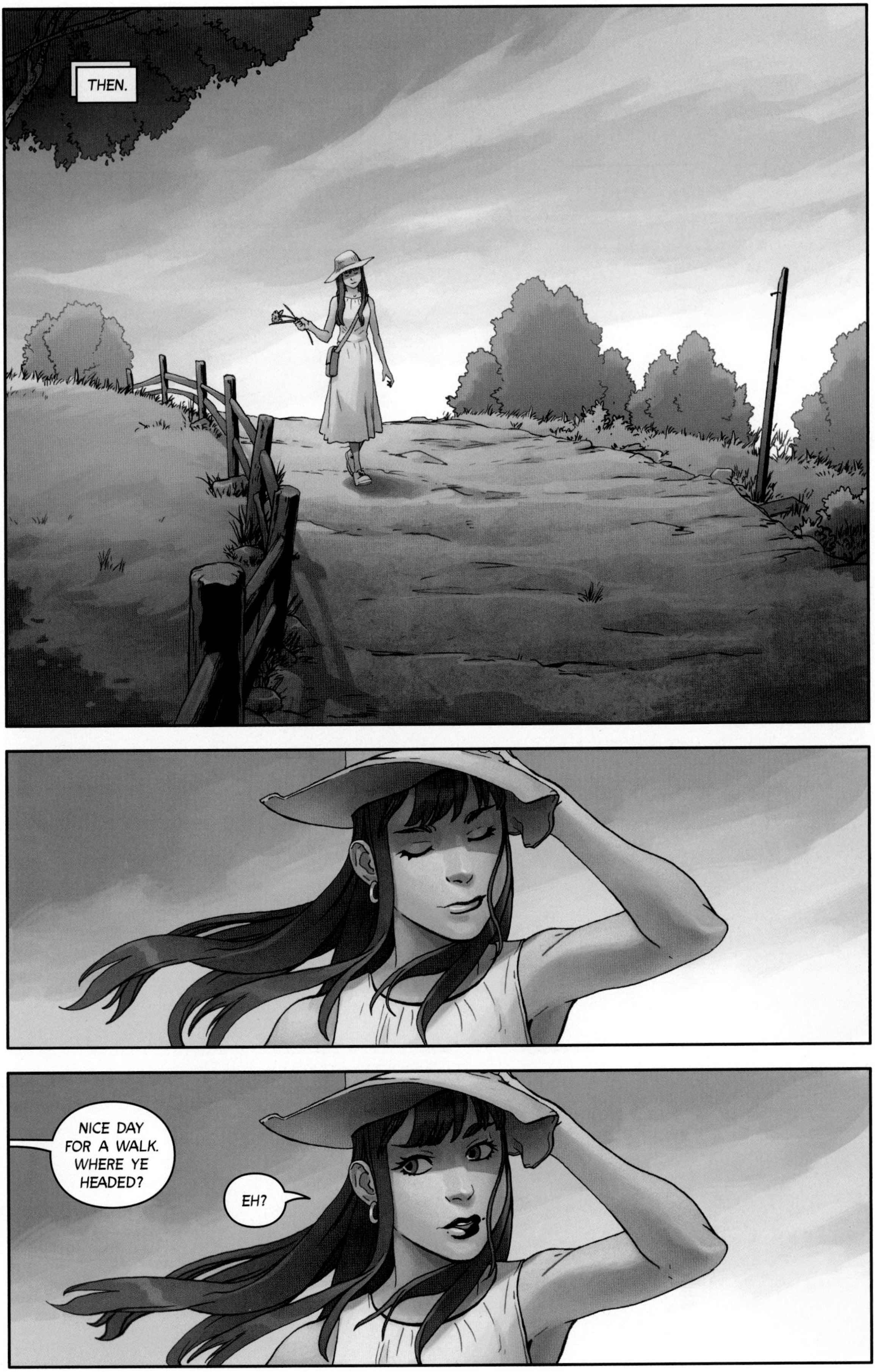
THEN.
NICE DAY FOR A WALK. WHERE YE HEADED?
EH?

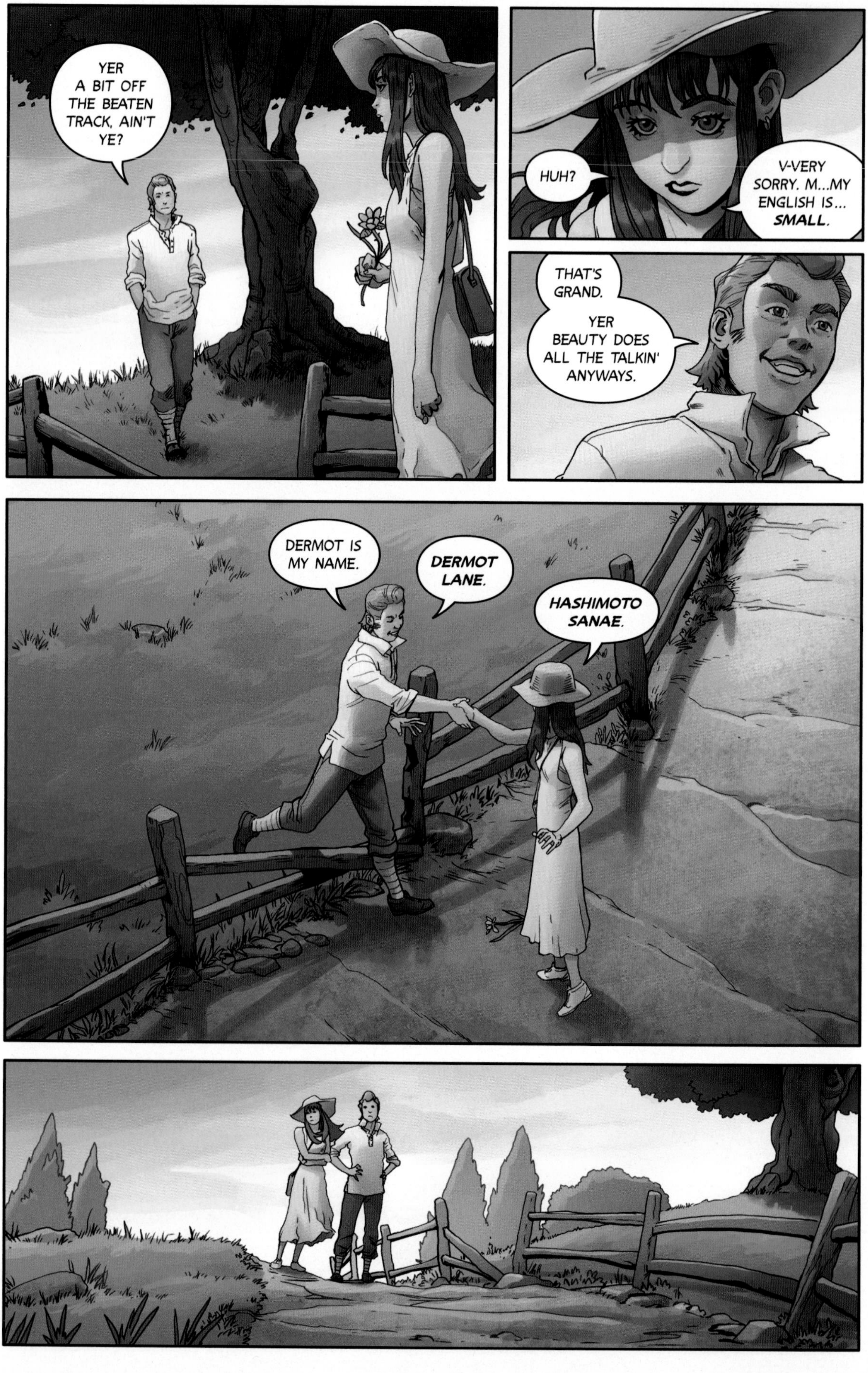
YER A BIT OFF THE BEATEN TRACK, AIN'T YE?
HUH?
V-VERY SORRY. M...MY ENGLISH IS... **SMALL.**
THAT'S GRAND.
YER BEAUTY DOES ALL THE TALKIN' ANYWAYS.
DERMOT IS MY NAME.
DERMOT LANE.
HASHIMOTO SANAE.

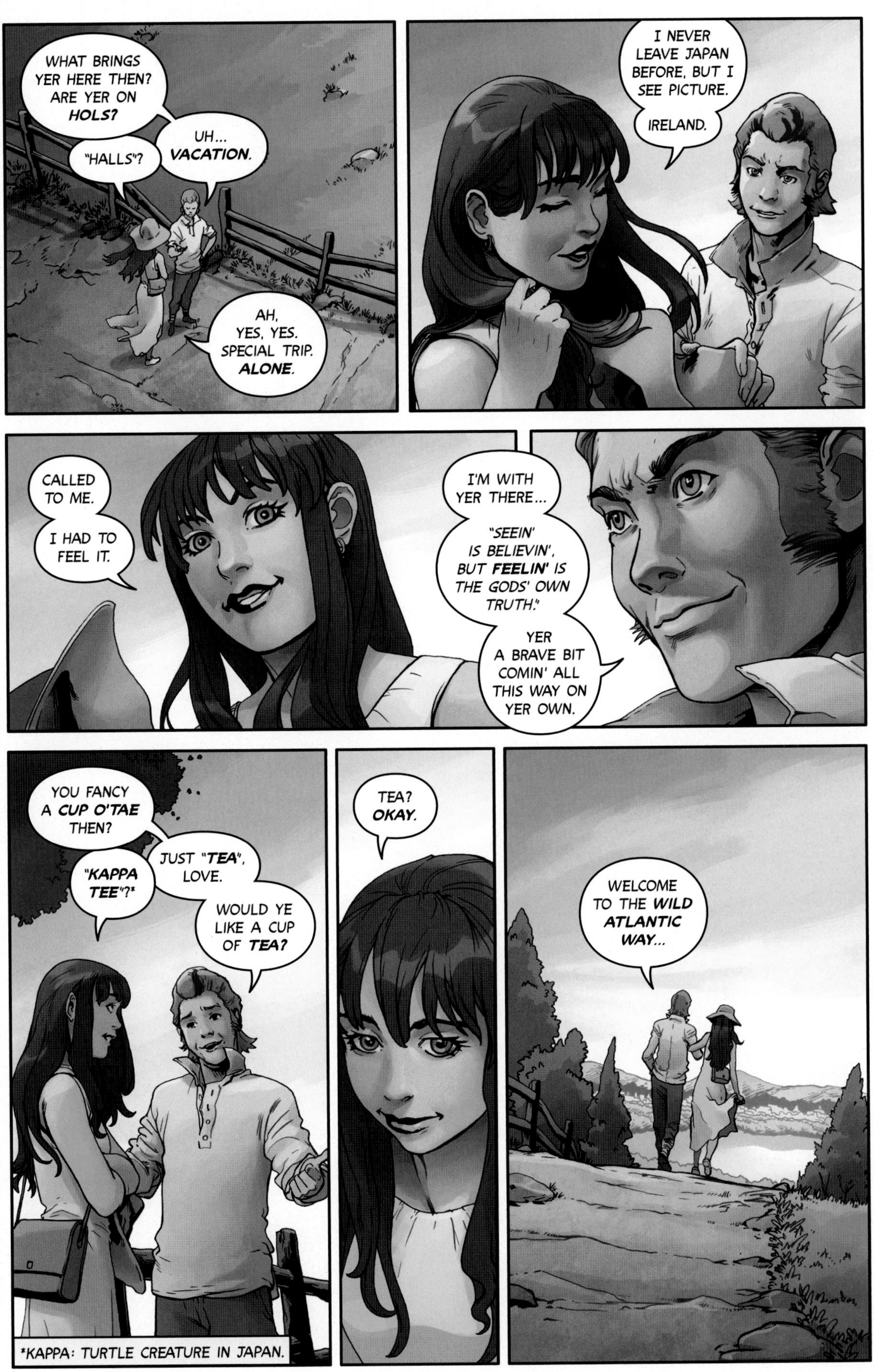
WHAT BRINGS YER HERE THEN? ARE YER ON **HOLS?**
"HALLS"?
UH... **VACATION.**
AH, YES, YES. SPECIAL TRIP. **ALONE.**
I NEVER LEAVE JAPAN BEFORE, BUT I SEE PICTURE.
IRELAND.
CALLED TO ME.
I HAD TO FEEL IT.
I'M WITH YER THERE...
"SEEIN' IS BELIEVIN', BUT **FEELIN'** IS THE GODS' OWN TRUTH."
YER A BRAVE BIT COMIN' ALL THIS WAY ON YER OWN.
YOU FANCY A **CUP O'TAE** THEN?
"**KAPPA TEE**"?*
JUST "**TEA**", LOVE.
WOULD YE LIKE A CUP OF **TEA?**
*KAPPA: TURTLE CREATURE IN JAPAN.
TEA? **OKAY.**
WELCOME TO THE **WILD ATLANTIC WAY...**

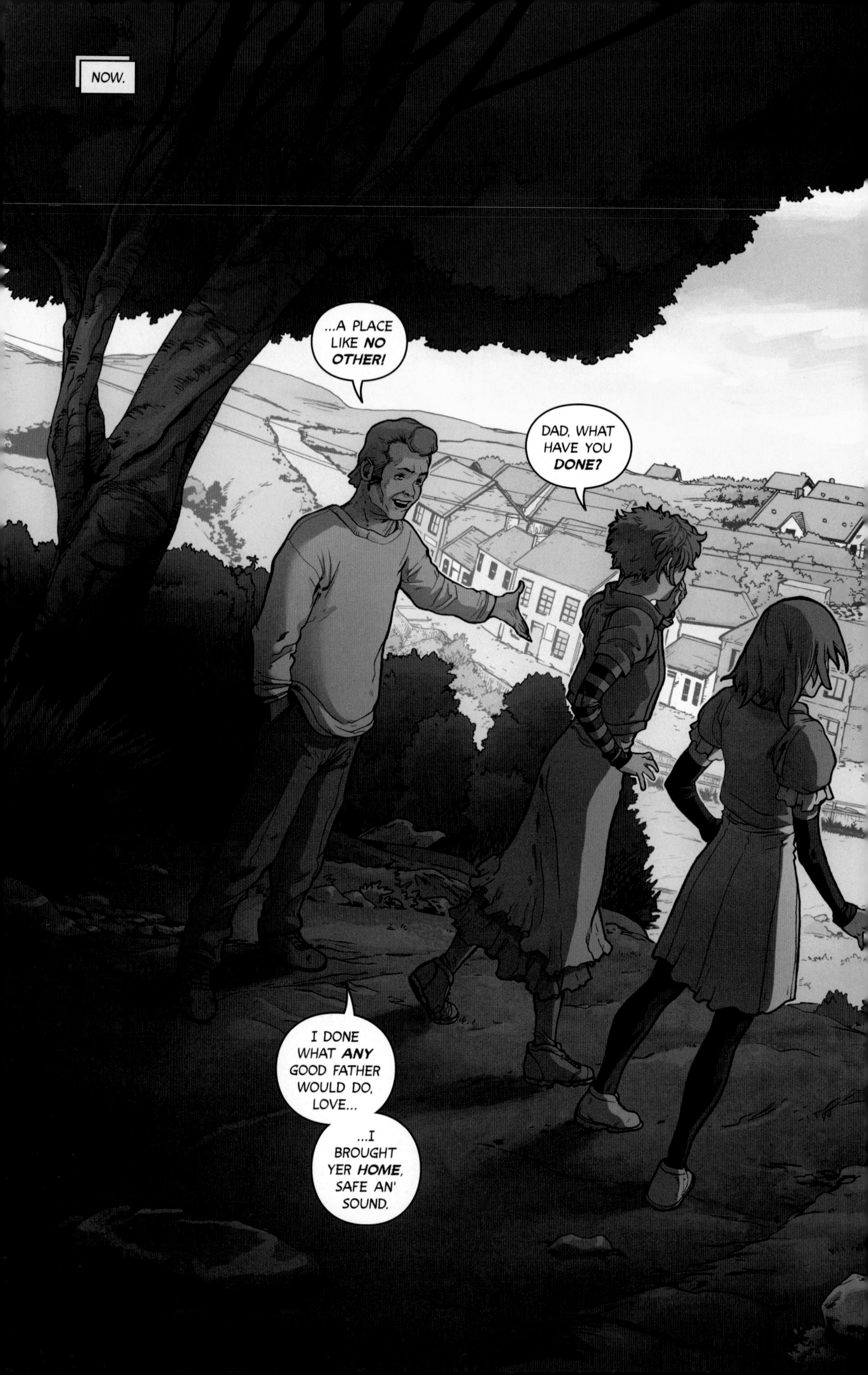
NOW.
...A PLACE LIKE **NO OTHER!**
DAD, WHAT HAVE YOU **DONE?**
I DONE WHAT **ANY** GOOD FATHER WOULD DO, LOVE...
...I BROUGHT YER **HOME**, SAFE AN' SOUND.

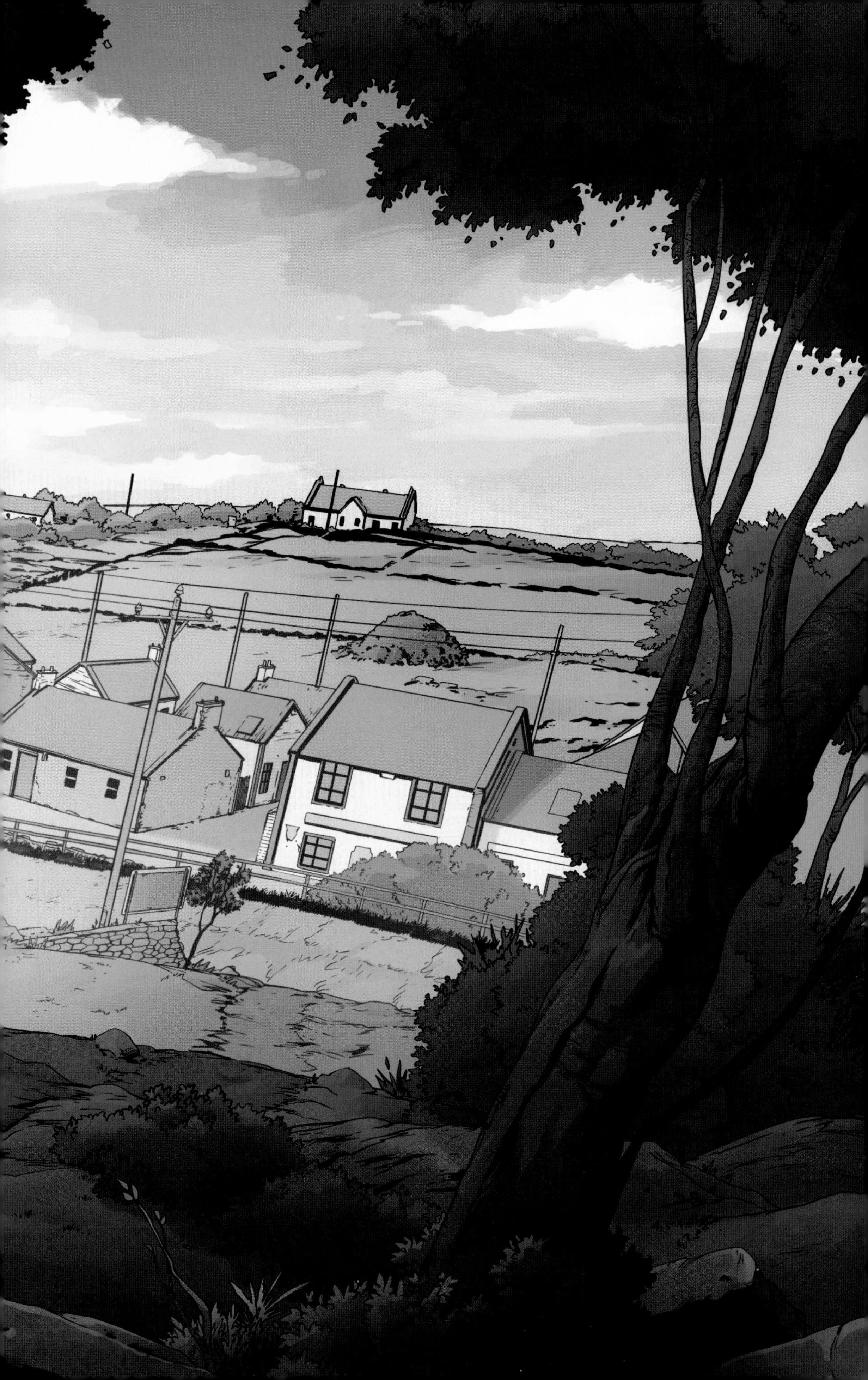

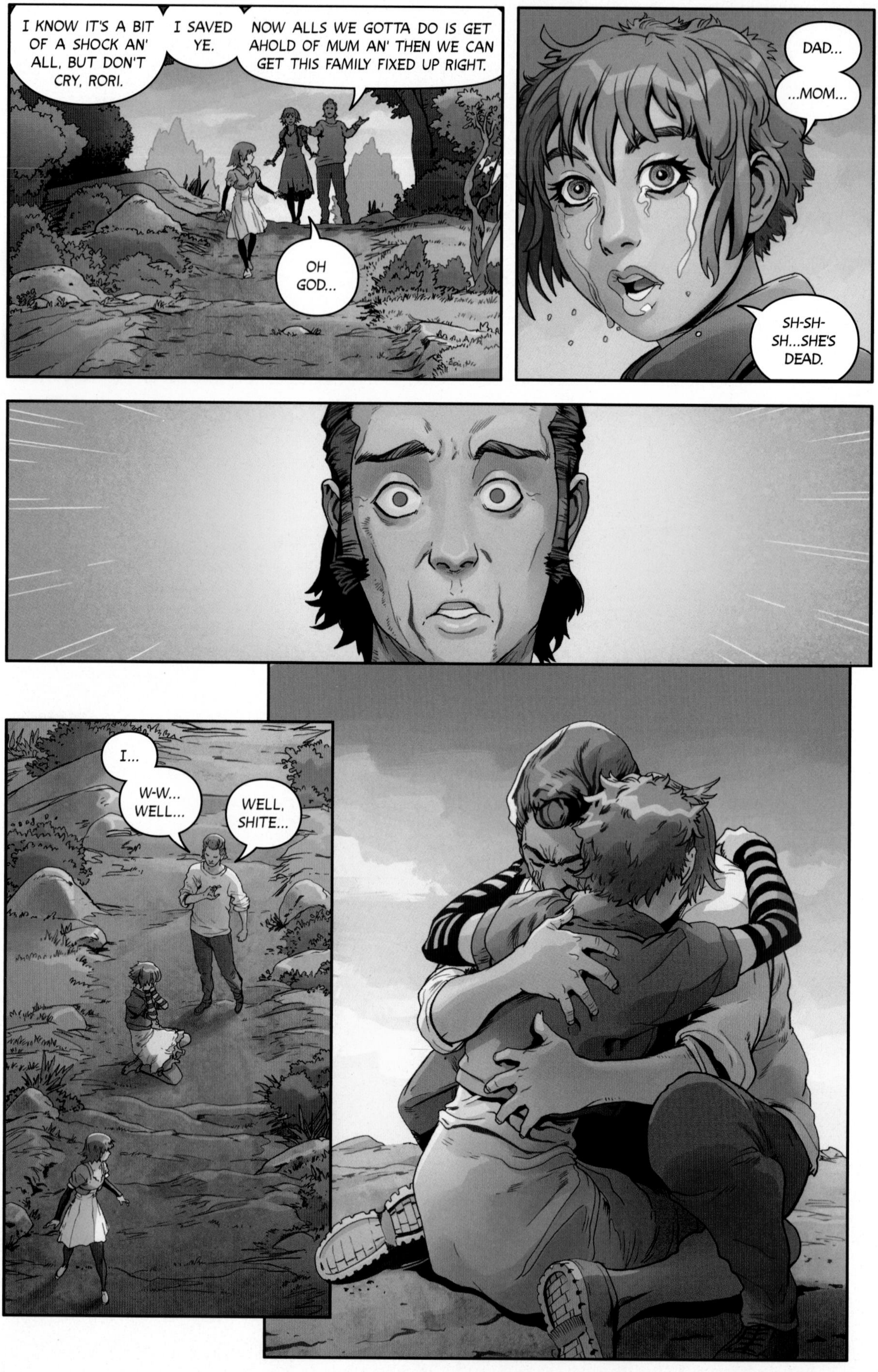
I KNOW IT'S A BIT OF A SHOCK AN' ALL, BUT DON'T CRY, RORI.
I SAVED YE.
NOW ALLS WE GOTTA DO IS GET AHOLD OF MUM AN' THEN WE CAN GET THIS FAMILY FIXED UP RIGHT.
OH GOD...
DAD...
...MOM...
SH-SH-SH...SHE'S DEAD.
I...
W-W... WELL...
WELL, SHITE...

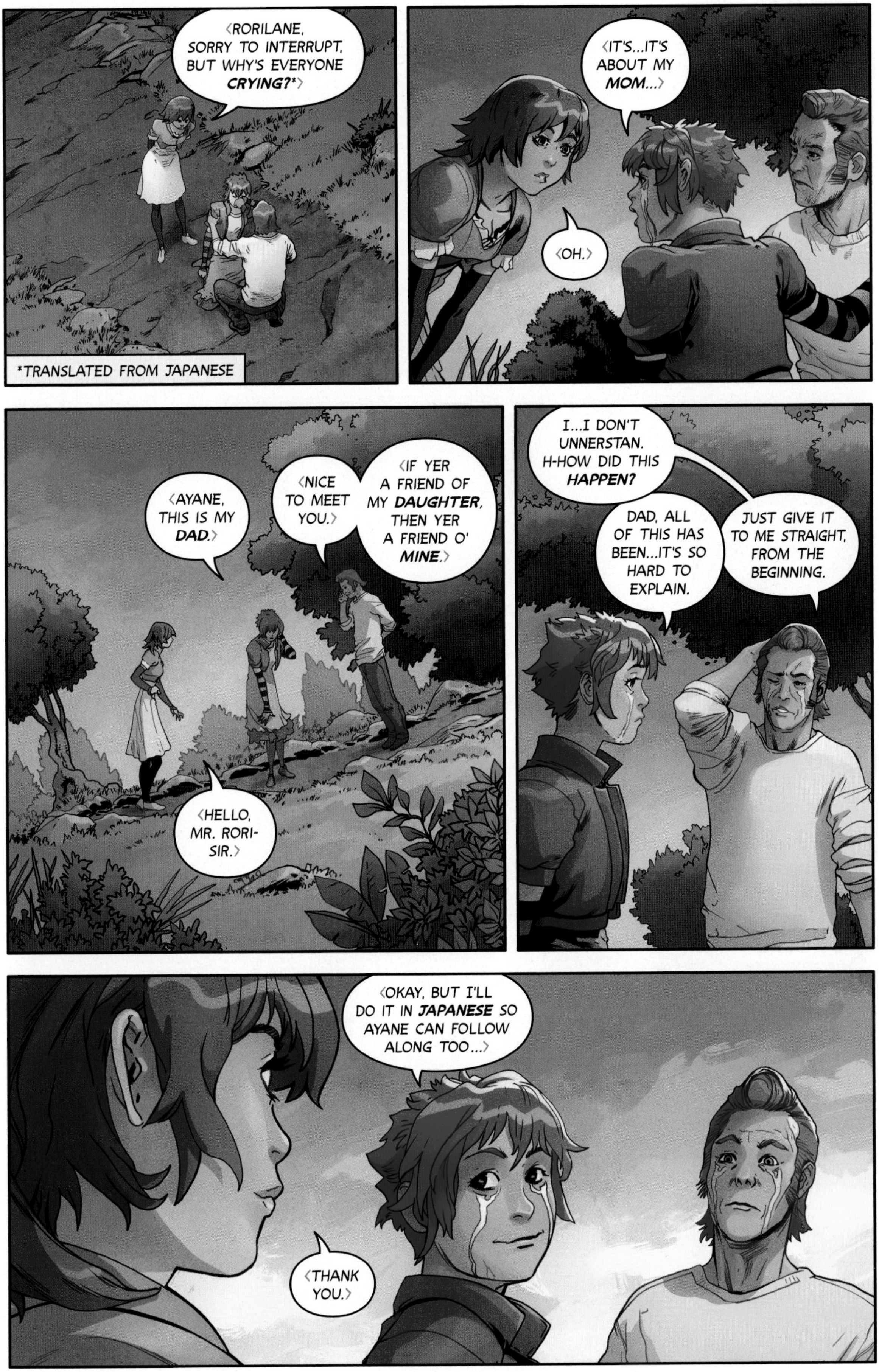
⟨RORILANE, SORRY TO INTERRUPT, BUT WHY'S EVERYONE CRYING?*⟩
*TRANSLATED FROM JAPANESE
⟨IT'S...IT'S ABOUT MY MOM...⟩
⟨OH.⟩
⟨AYANE, THIS IS MY DAD.⟩
⟨NICE TO MEET YOU.⟩
⟨IF YER A FRIEND OF MY DAUGHTER, THEN YER A FRIEND O' MINE.⟩
⟨HELLO, MR. RORI-SIR.⟩
I...I DON'T UNNERSTAN. H-HOW DID THIS HAPPEN?
DAD, ALL OF THIS HAS BEEN...IT'S SO HARD TO EXPLAIN.
JUST GIVE IT TO ME STRAIGHT, FROM THE BEGINNING.
⟨OKAY, BUT I'LL DO IT IN JAPANESE SO AYANE CAN FOLLOW ALONG TOO...⟩
⟨THANK YOU.⟩

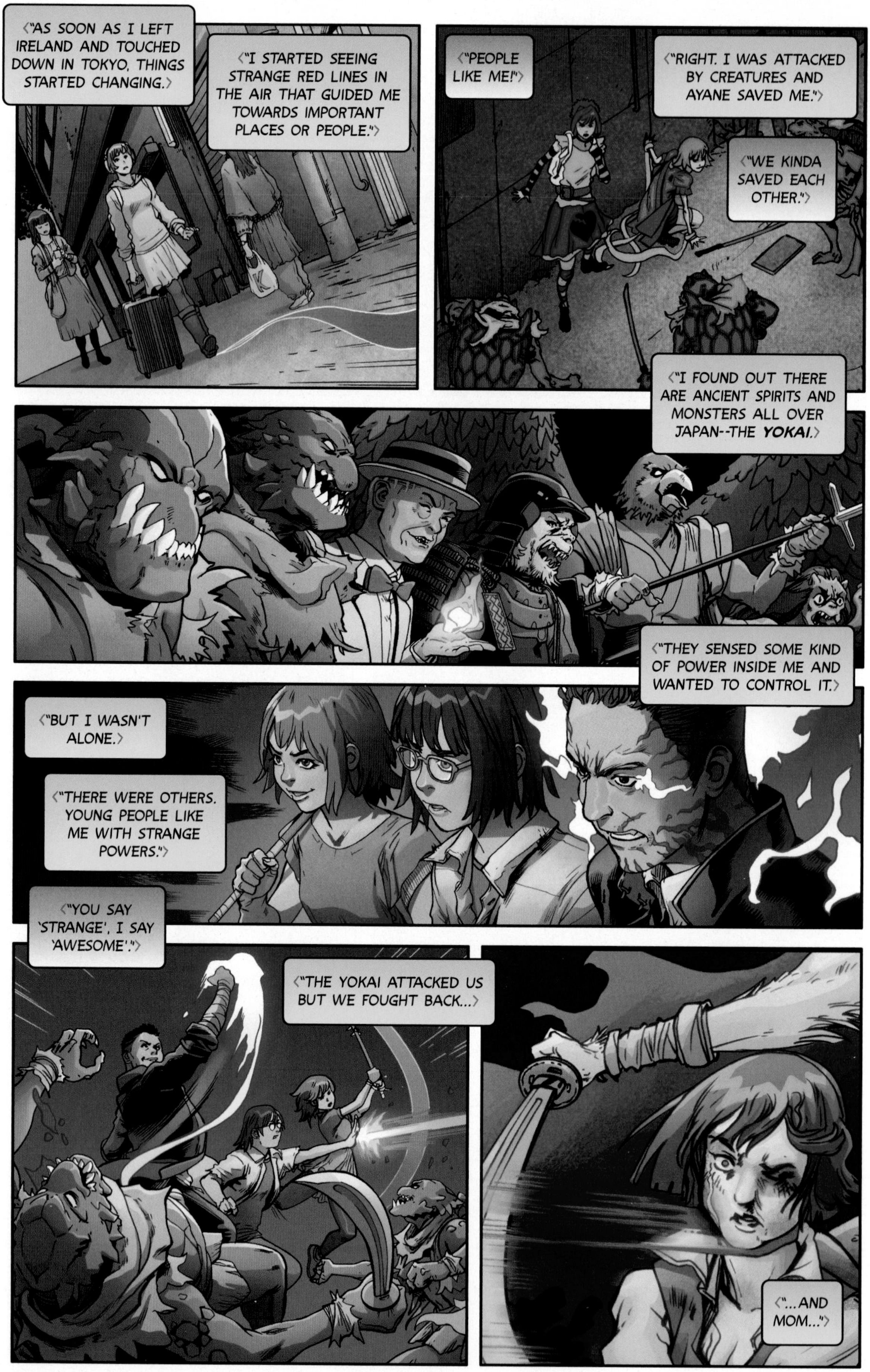
<"AS SOON AS I LEFT IRELAND AND TOUCHED DOWN IN TOKYO, THINGS STARTED CHANGING.>
<"I STARTED SEEING STRANGE RED LINES IN THE AIR THAT GUIDED ME TOWARDS IMPORTANT PLACES OR PEOPLE.">
<"PEOPLE LIKE ME!">
<"RIGHT. I WAS ATTACKED BY CREATURES AND AYANE SAVED ME.">
<"WE KINDA SAVED EACH OTHER.">
<"I FOUND OUT THERE ARE ANCIENT SPIRITS AND MONSTERS ALL OVER JAPAN--THE ***YOKAI***.>
<"THEY SENSED SOME KIND OF POWER INSIDE ME AND WANTED TO CONTROL IT.>
<"BUT I WASN'T ALONE.>
<"THERE WERE OTHERS. YOUNG PEOPLE LIKE ME WITH STRANGE POWERS.">
<"YOU SAY 'STRANGE', I SAY 'AWESOME'.">
<"THE YOKAI ATTACKED US BUT WE FOUGHT BACK...>
<"...AND MOM...">

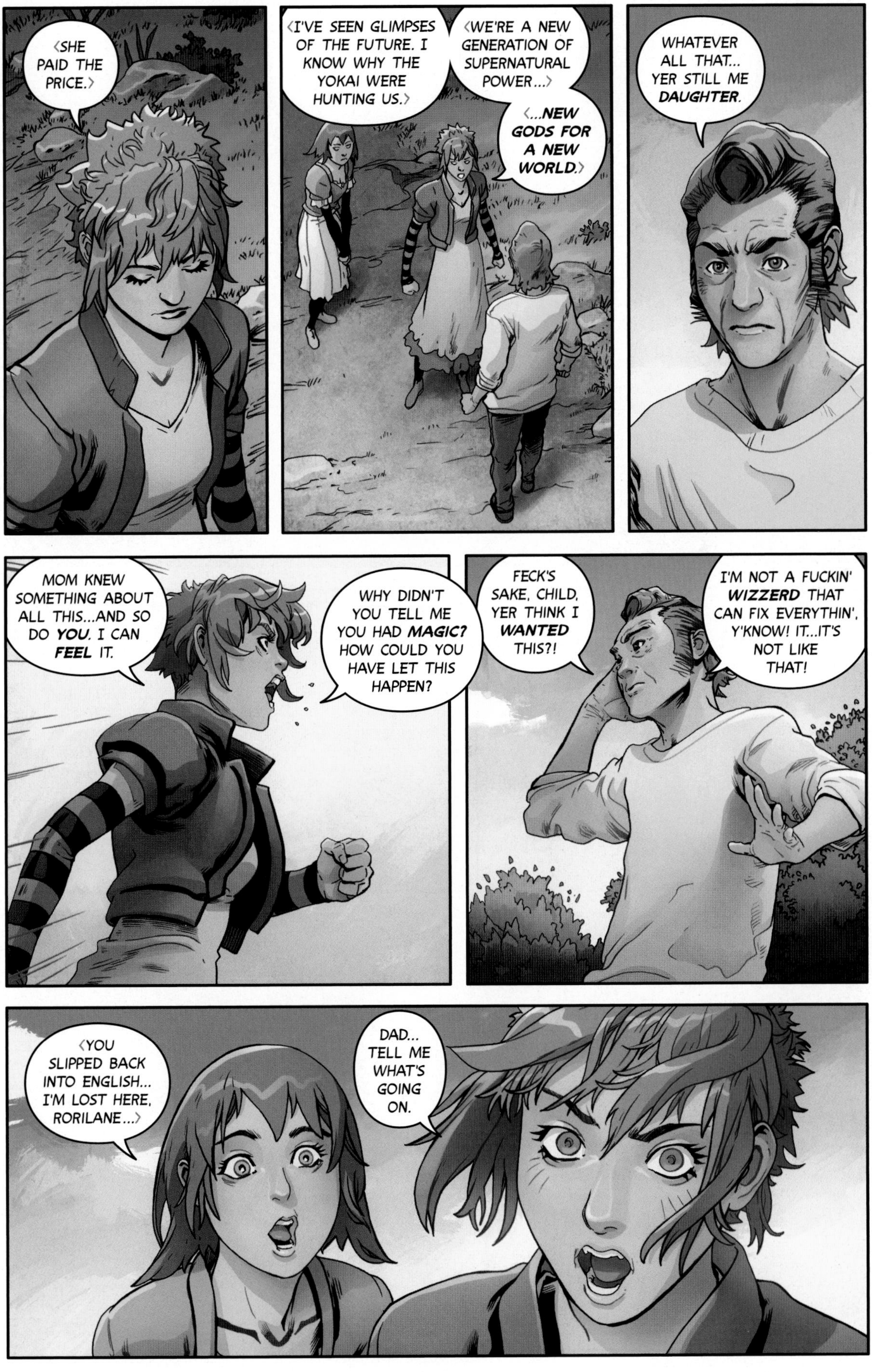
‹SHE PAID THE PRICE.›
‹I'VE SEEN GLIMPSES OF THE FUTURE. I KNOW WHY THE YOKAI WERE HUNTING US.›
‹WE'RE A NEW GENERATION OF SUPERNATURAL POWER...›
‹...***NEW GODS FOR A NEW WORLD.***›
WHATEVER ALL THAT... YER STILL ME ***DAUGHTER.***
MOM KNEW SOMETHING ABOUT ALL THIS...AND SO DO ***YOU.*** I CAN ***FEEL*** IT.
WHY DIDN'T YOU TELL ME YOU HAD ***MAGIC?*** HOW COULD YOU HAVE LET THIS HAPPEN?
FECK'S SAKE, CHILD, YER THINK I ***WANTED*** THIS?!
I'M NOT A FUCKIN' ***WIZZERD*** THAT CAN FIX EVERYTHIN', Y'KNOW! IT...IT'S NOT LIKE THAT!
‹YOU SLIPPED BACK INTO ENGLISH... I'M LOST HERE, RORILANE...›
DAD... TELL ME WHAT'S GOING ON.

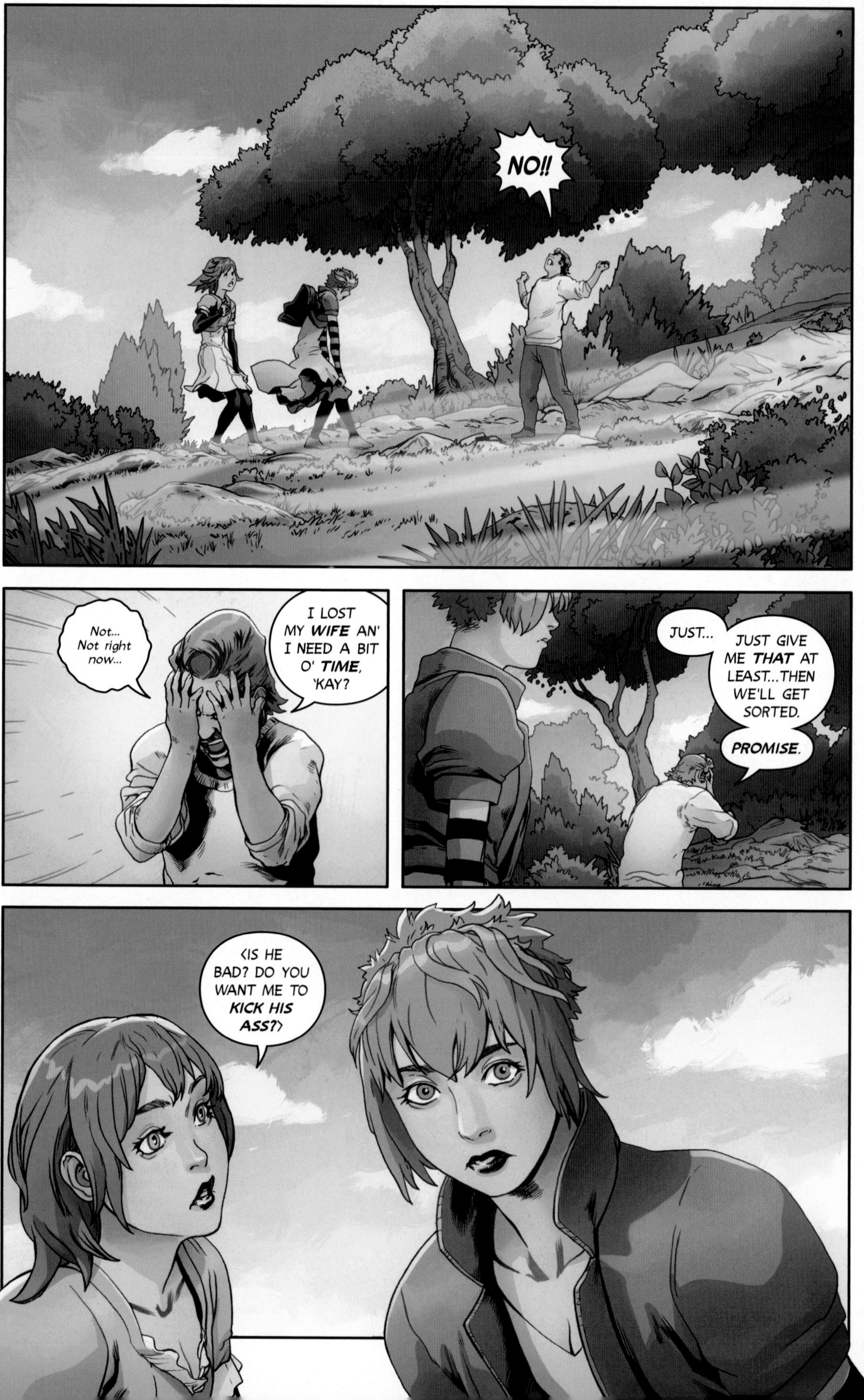
NO!!
Not... Not right now...
I LOST MY WIFE AN' I NEED A BIT O' TIME, 'KAY?
JUST...
JUST GIVE ME THAT AT LEAST...THEN WE'LL GET SORTED.
PROMISE.
<IS HE BAD? DO YOU WANT ME TO KICK HIS ASS?>

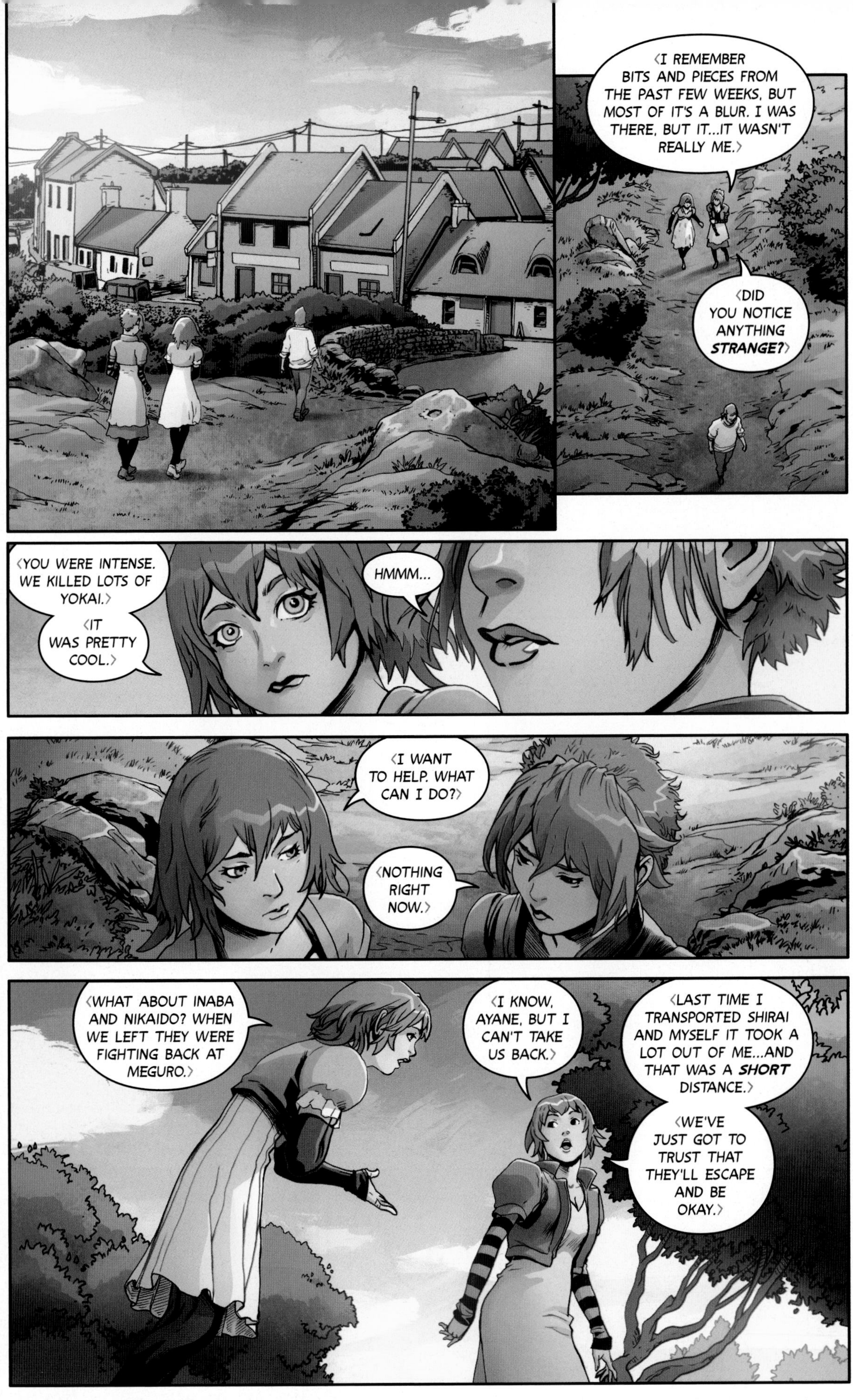

<I REMEMBER BITS AND PIECES FROM THE PAST FEW WEEKS, BUT MOST OF IT'S A BLUR. I WAS THERE, BUT IT...IT WASN'T REALLY ME.>
<DID YOU NOTICE ANYTHING ***STRANGE?***>
<YOU WERE INTENSE. WE KILLED LOTS OF YOKAI.>
<IT WAS PRETTY COOL.>
HMMM...
<I WANT TO HELP. WHAT CAN I DO?>
<NOTHING RIGHT NOW.>
<WHAT ABOUT INABA AND NIKAIDO? WHEN WE LEFT THEY WERE FIGHTING BACK AT MEGURO.>
<I KNOW, AYANE, BUT I CAN'T TAKE US BACK.>
<LAST TIME I TRANSPORTED SHIRAI AND MYSELF IT TOOK A LOT OUT OF ME...AND THAT WAS A ***SHORT*** DISTANCE.>
<WE'VE JUST GOT TO TRUST THAT THEY'LL ESCAPE AND BE OKAY.>

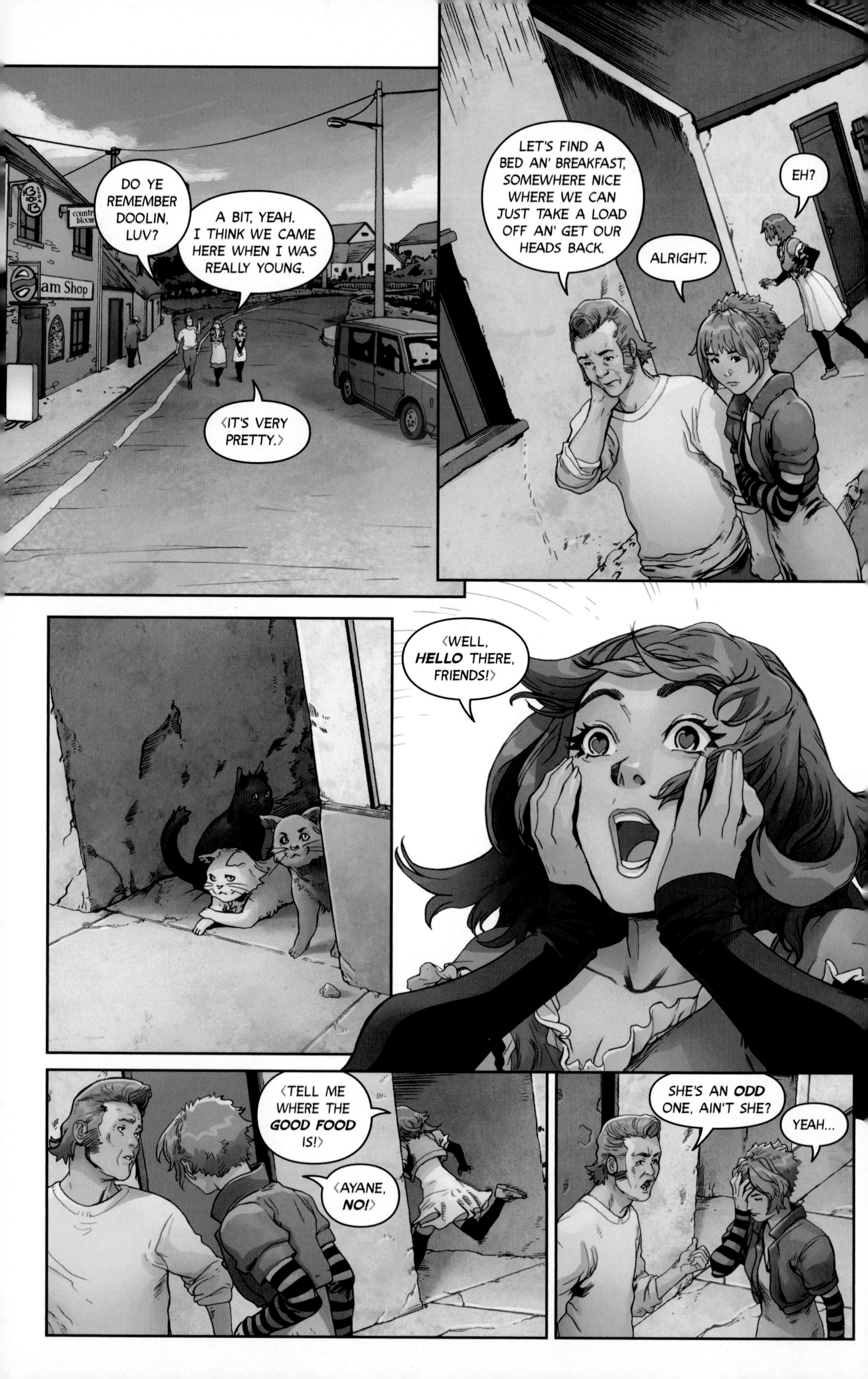

DO YE REMEMBER DOOLIN, LUV?
A BIT, YEAH. I THINK WE CAME HERE WHEN I WAS REALLY YOUNG.
⟨IT'S VERY PRETTY.⟩
am Shop
LET'S FIND A BED AN' BREAKFAST, SOMEWHERE NICE WHERE WE CAN JUST TAKE A LOAD OFF AN' GET OUR HEADS BACK.
ALRIGHT.
EH?
⟨WELL, **HELLO** THERE, FRIENDS!⟩
⟨TELL ME WHERE THE ***GOOD FOOD*** IS!⟩
⟨AYANE, ***NO!***⟩
SHE'S AN ***ODD*** ONE, AIN'T SHE?
YEAH...

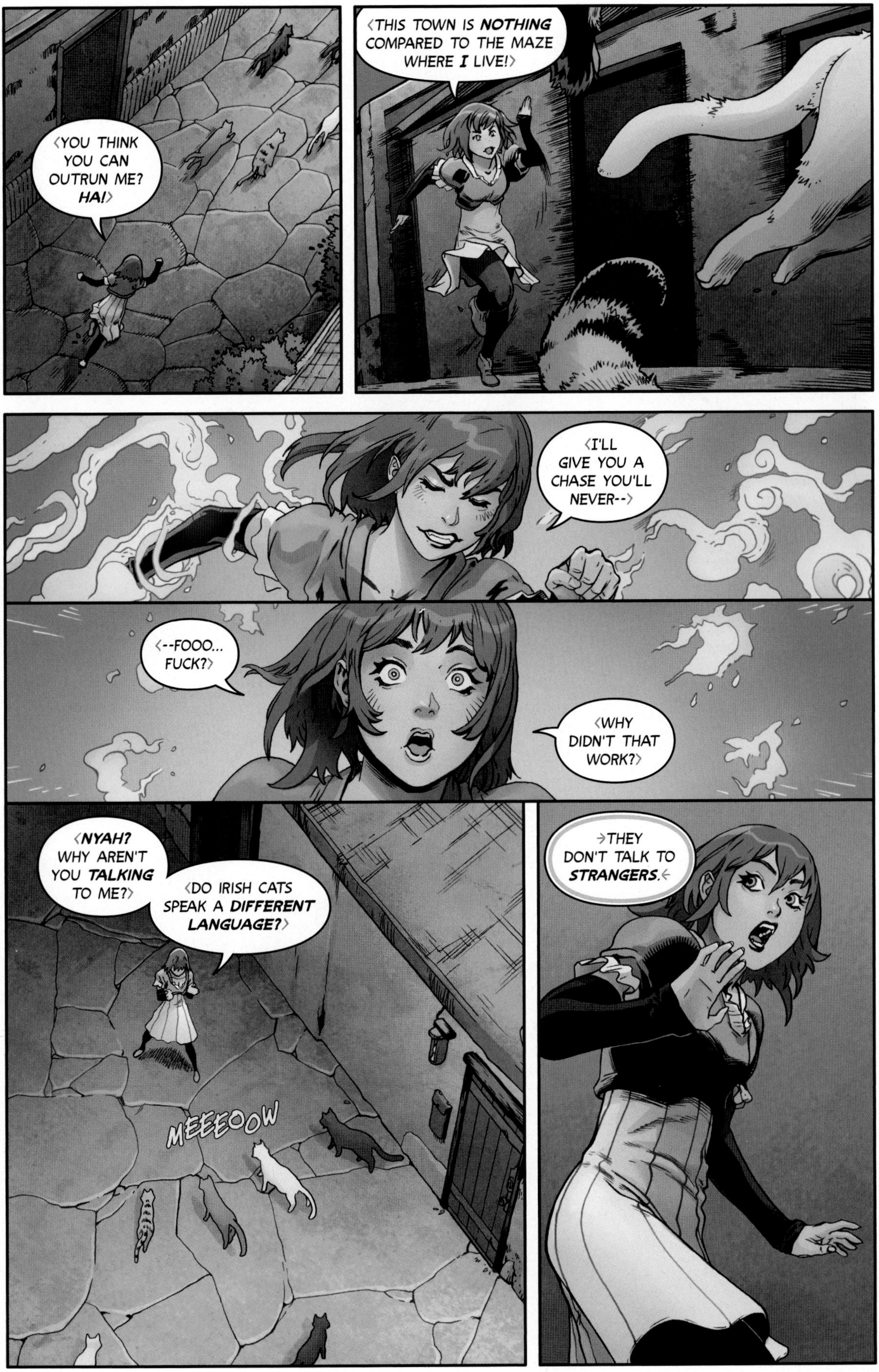

<YOU THINK YOU CAN OUTRUN ME? **HA!**>
<THIS TOWN IS **NOTHING** COMPARED TO THE MAZE WHERE **I** LIVE!>
<I'LL GIVE YOU A CHASE YOU'LL NEVER-->
<--FOOO... FUCK?>
<WHY DIDN'T THAT WORK?>
<**NYAH?** WHY AREN'T YOU **TALKING** TO ME?>
<DO IRISH CATS SPEAK A **DIFFERENT LANGUAGE?**>
MEEEOOW
→THEY DON'T TALK TO **STRANGERS**.←

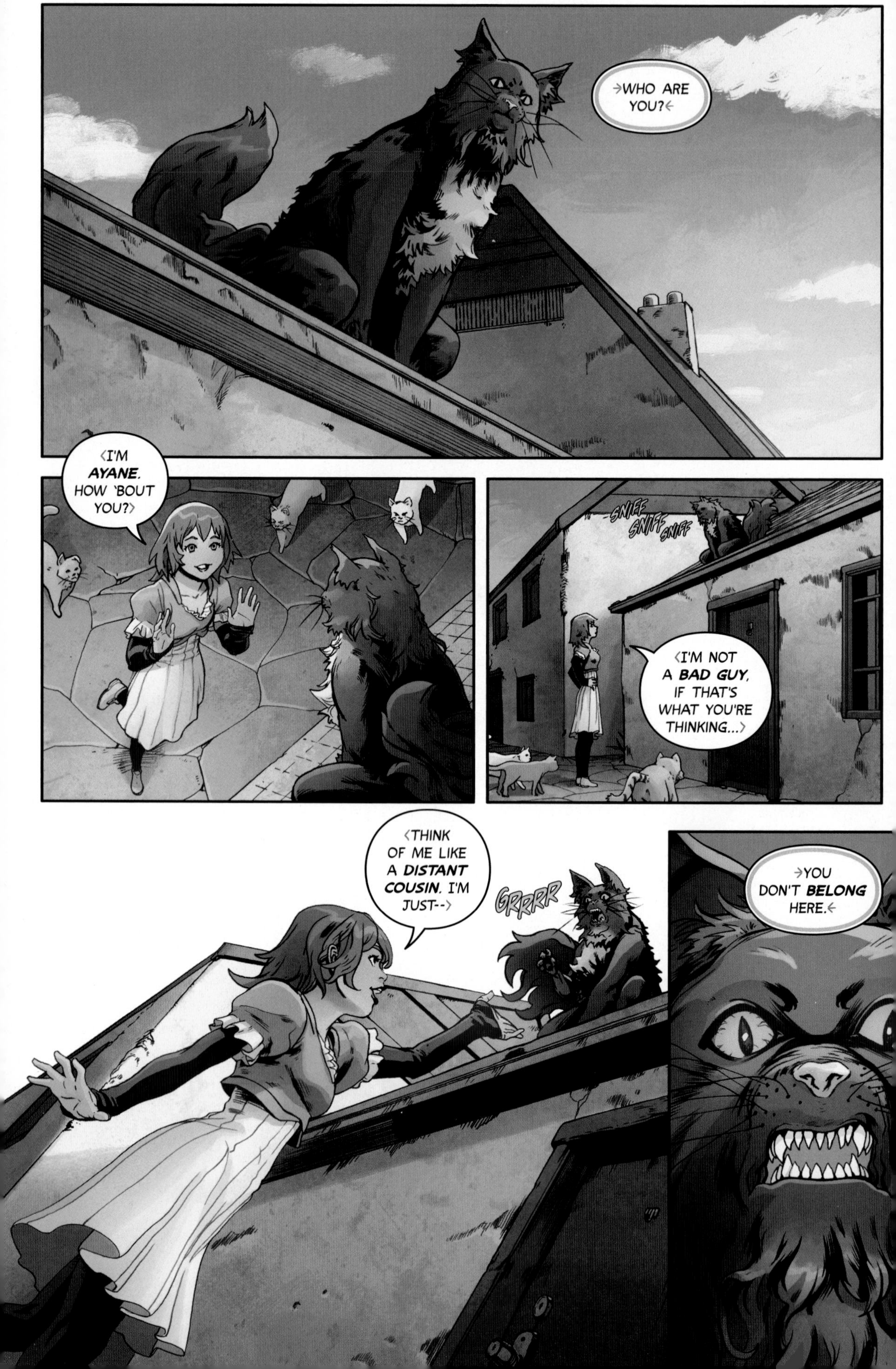
→WHO ARE YOU?←
‹I'M AYANE. HOW 'BOUT YOU?›
SNIFF SNIFF SNIFF
‹I'M NOT A BAD GUY, IF THAT'S WHAT YOU'RE THINKING...›
‹THINK OF ME LIKE A DISTANT COUSIN. I'M JUST--›
GRRRR
→YOU DON'T BELONG HERE.←

⟨AYANE!⟩

⟨AYANE, WHERE'D YOU GO?!⟩

⟨I'M OVER HERE!⟩

⟨LOOK, RORILANE, IT'S A CAT-FRIEND!⟩

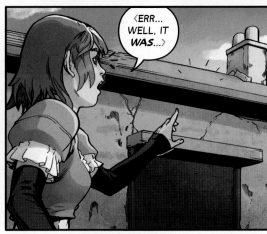

⟨ERR... WELL, IT WAS...⟩

⟨C'MON. WE NEED TO STAY TOGETHER. I DON'T WANT TO LOSE YOU HERE.⟩

⟨O-OKAY...⟩

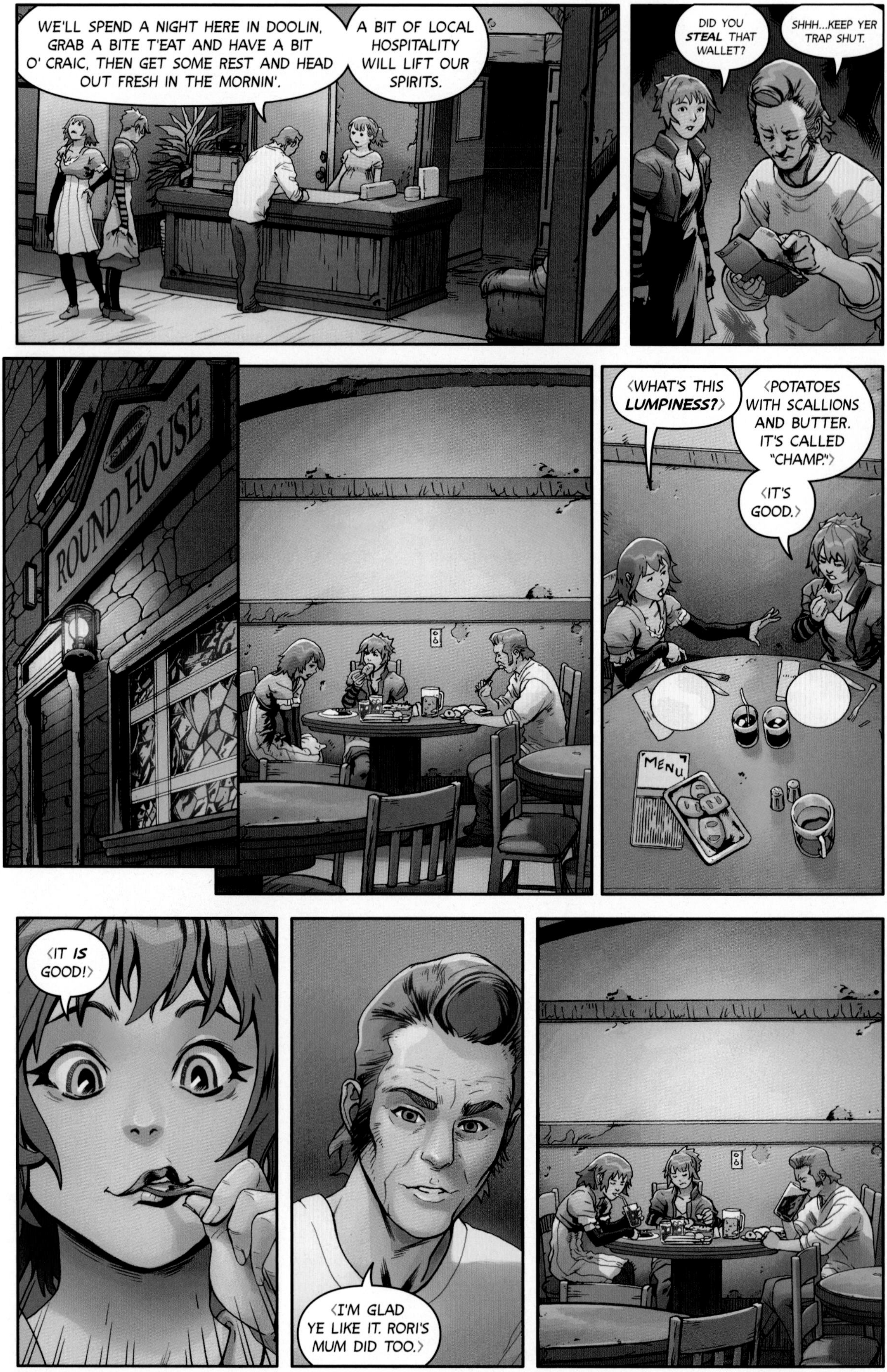
WE'LL SPEND A NIGHT HERE IN DOOLIN, GRAB A BITE T'EAT AND HAVE A BIT O' CRAIC, THEN GET SOME REST AND HEAD OUT FRESH IN THE MORNIN'.
A BIT OF LOCAL HOSPITALITY WILL LIFT OUR SPIRITS.
DID YOU STEAL THAT WALLET?
SHHH...KEEP YER TRAP SHUT.
ROUND HOUSE
‹WHAT'S THIS LUMPINESS?›
‹POTATOES WITH SCALLIONS AND BUTTER. IT'S CALLED "CHAMP."›
‹IT'S GOOD.›
MENU
‹IT IS GOOD!›
‹I'M GLAD YE LIKE IT. RORI'S MUM DID TOO.›

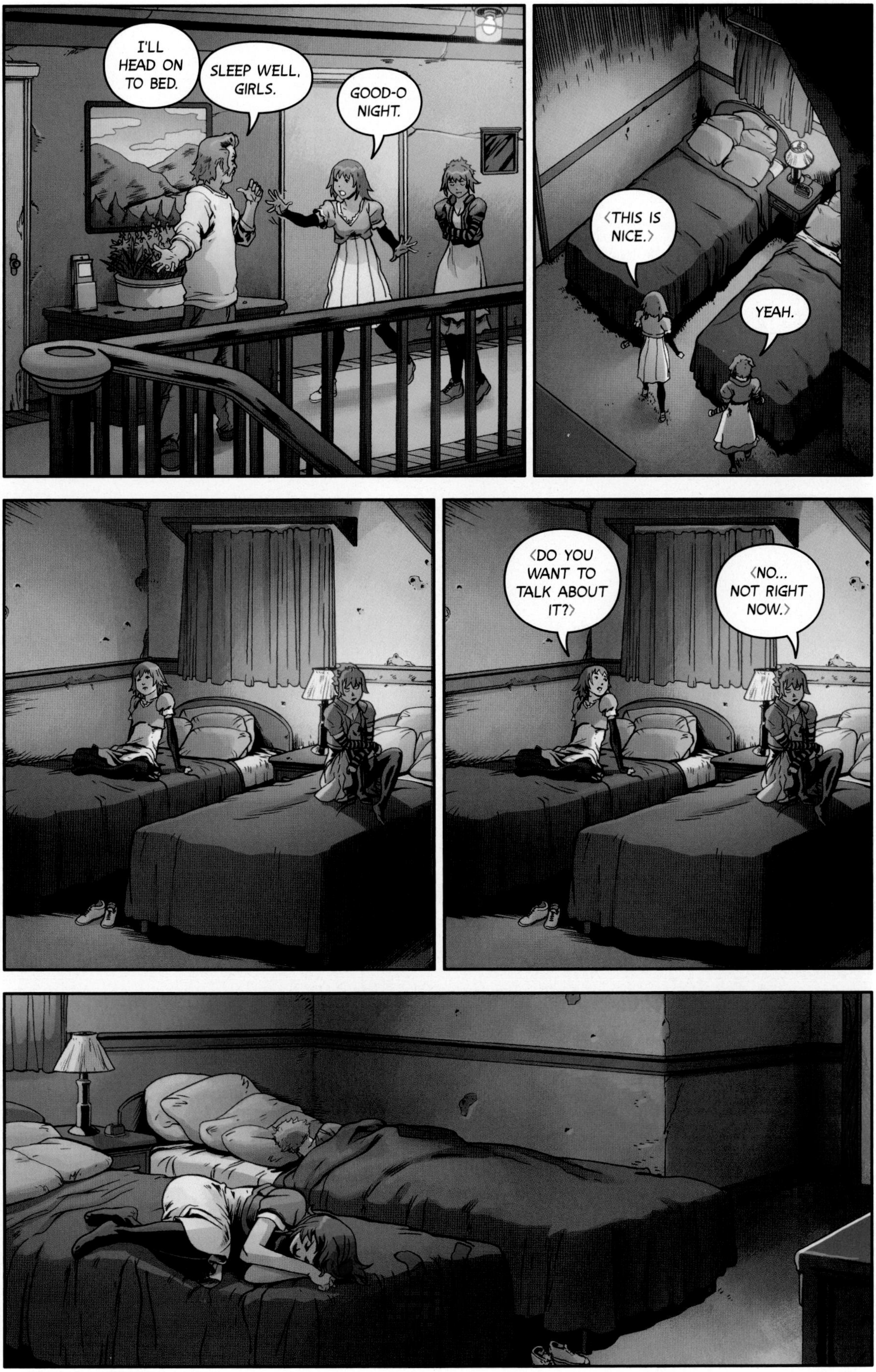
I'LL HEAD ON TO BED.
SLEEP WELL, GIRLS.
GOOD-O NIGHT.
<THIS IS NICE.>
YEAH.
<DO YOU WANT TO TALK ABOUT IT?>
<NO... NOT RIGHT NOW.>

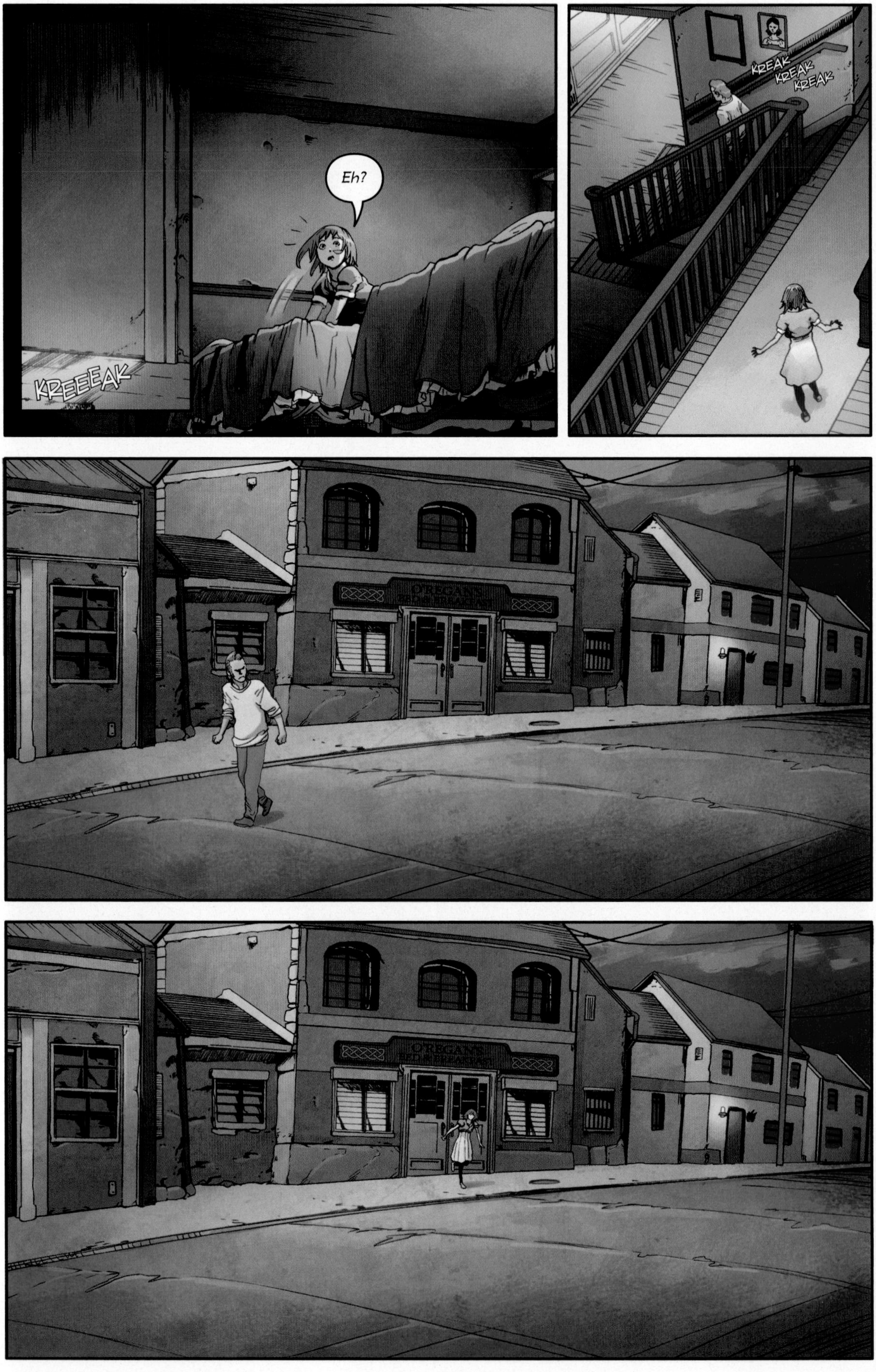
KREEEEAK
Eh?
KREAK
KREAK
KREAK

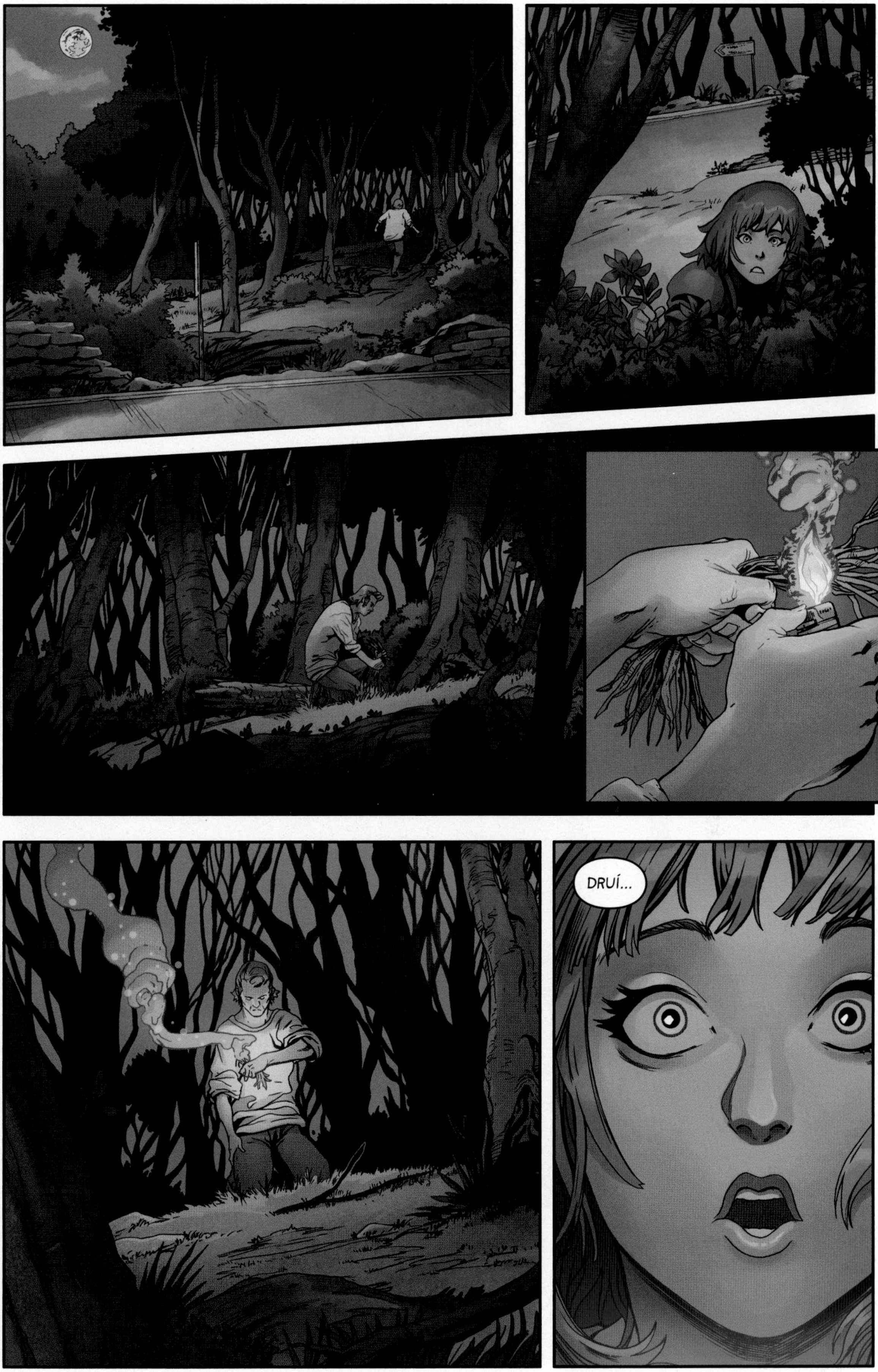
DRUÍ...

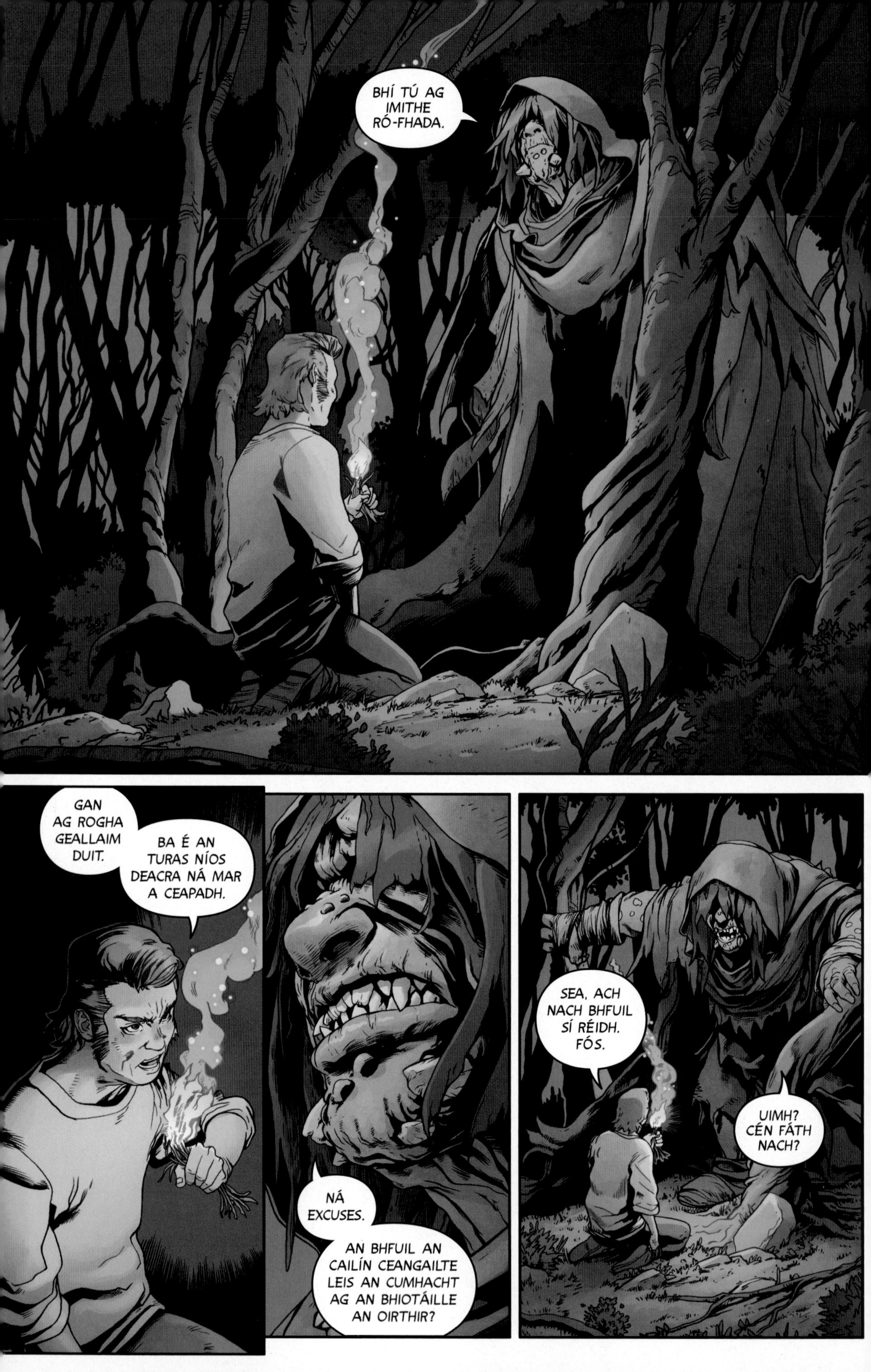
BHÍ TÚ AG IMITHE RÓ-FHADA.
GAN AG ROGHA GEALLAIM DUIT.
BA É AN TURAS NÍOS DEACRA NÁ MAR A CEAPADH.
NÁ EXCUSES.
AN BHFUIL AN CAILÍN CEANGAILTE LEIS AN CUMHACHT AG AN BHIOTÁILLE AN OIRTHIR?
SEA, ACH NACH BHFUIL SÍ RÉIDH. FÓS.
UIMH? CÉN FÁTH NACH?

MAR TÁ SÍ MO INÍON.

DHÍTH ORM LE BEAGÁN AMA CHUN SLÁN A FHÁGÁIL.

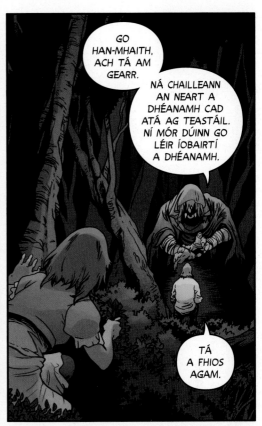

GO HAN-MHAITH, ACH TÁ AM GEARR.

NÁ CHAILLEANN AN NEART A DHÉANAMH CAD ATÁ AG TEASTÁIL. NÍ MÓR DÚINN GO LÉIR ÍOBAIRTÍ A DHÉANAMH.

TÁ A FHIOS AGAM.

⟨RORILANE, WAKE UP!⟩

⟨I JUST SAW YOUR--⟩

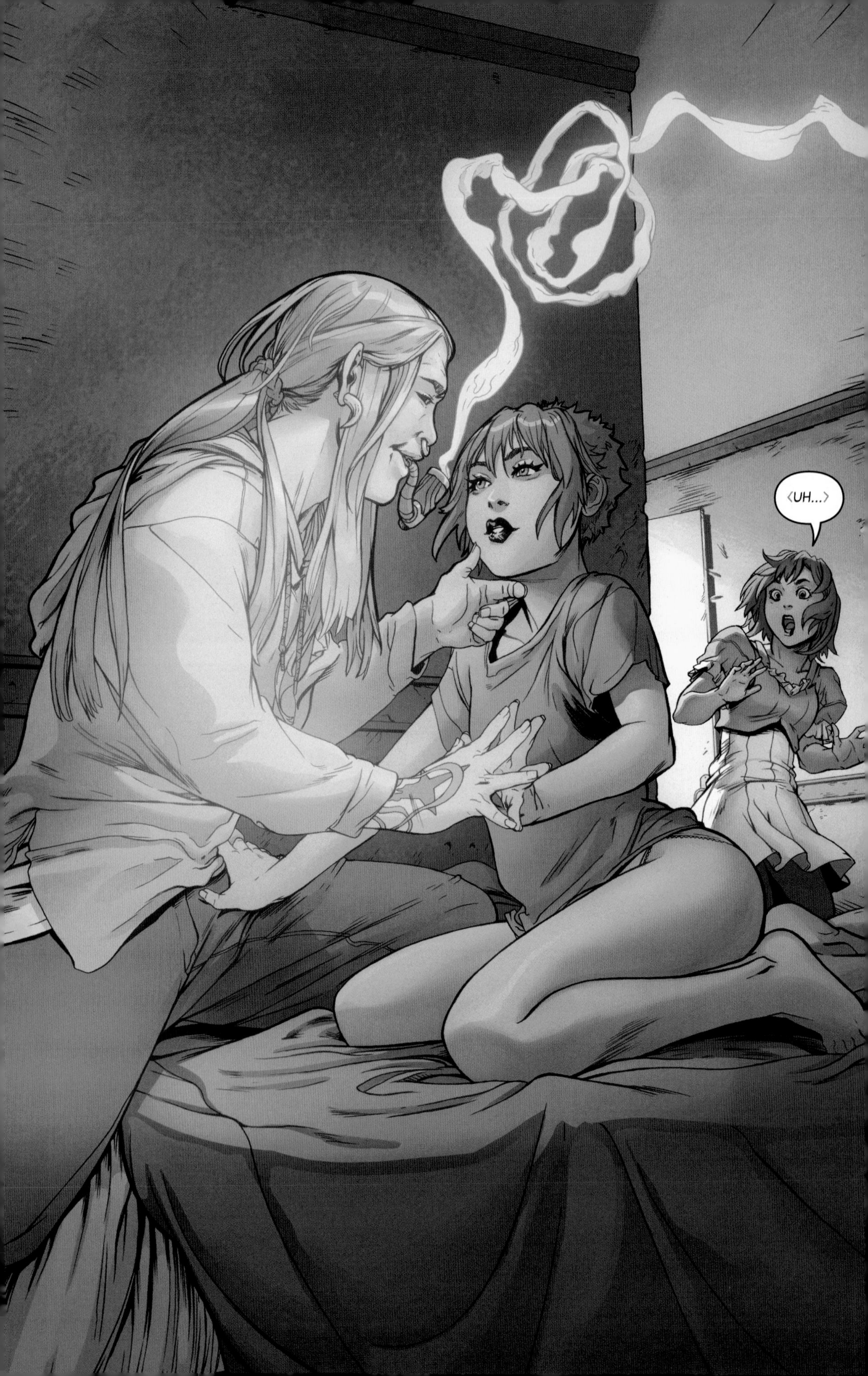
<UH...>

Chapter Seventeen

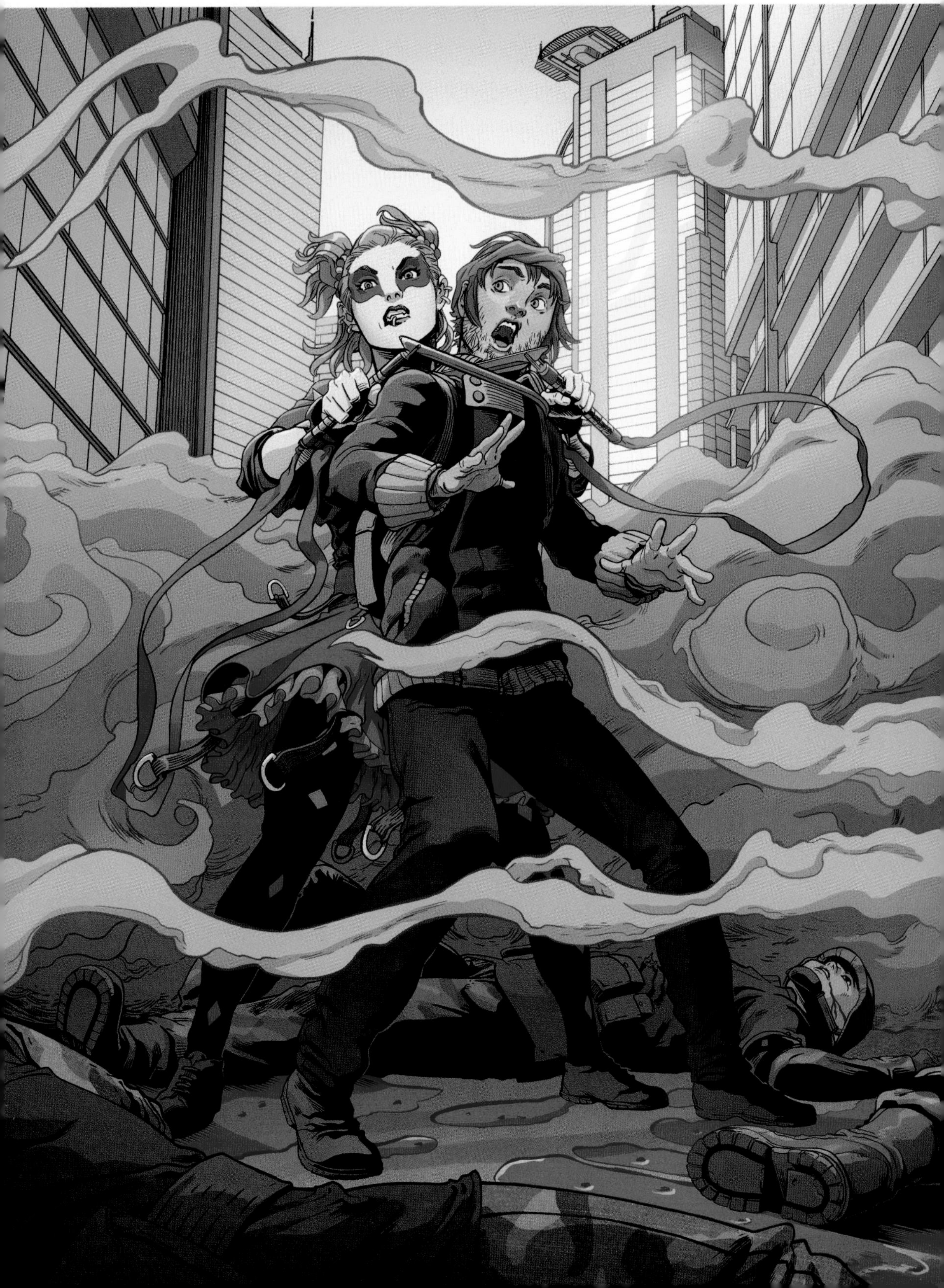

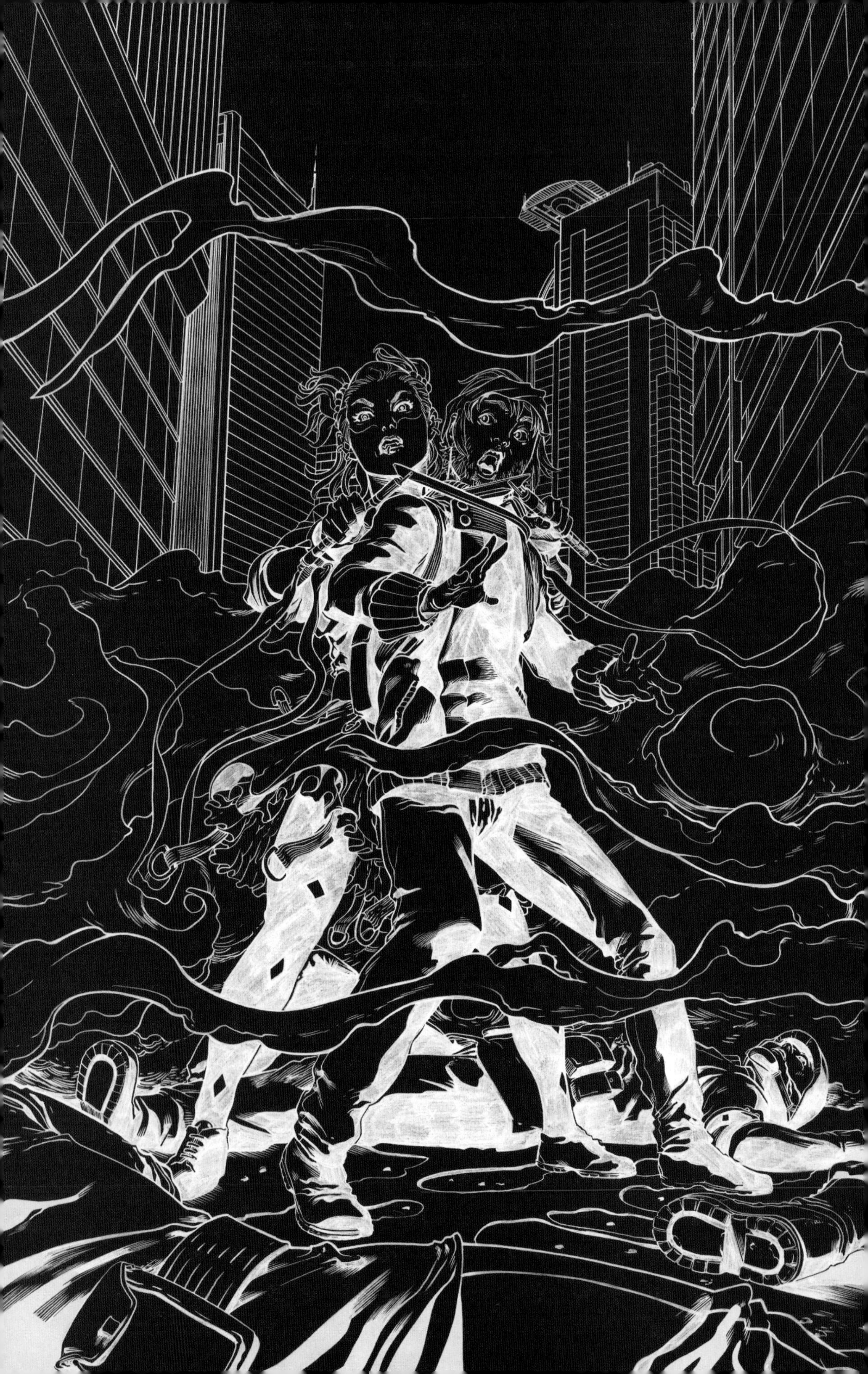

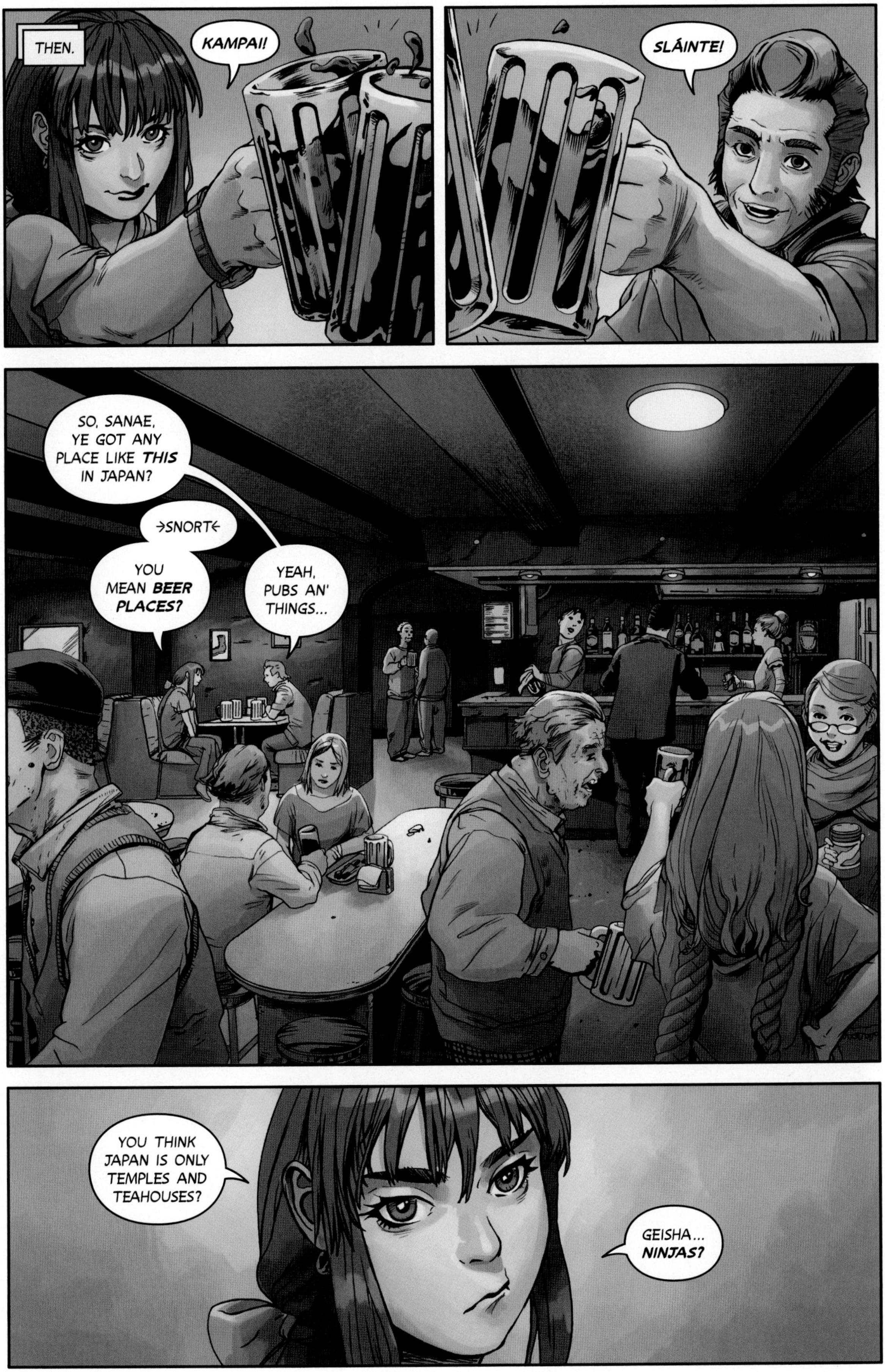
THEN.
KAMPAI!
SLÁINTE!
SO, SANAE, YE GOT ANY PLACE LIKE THIS IN JAPAN?
→SNORT←
YOU MEAN BEER PLACES?
YEAH, PUBS AN' THINGS...
YOU THINK JAPAN IS ONLY TEMPLES AND TEAHOUSES?
GEISHA... NINJAS?

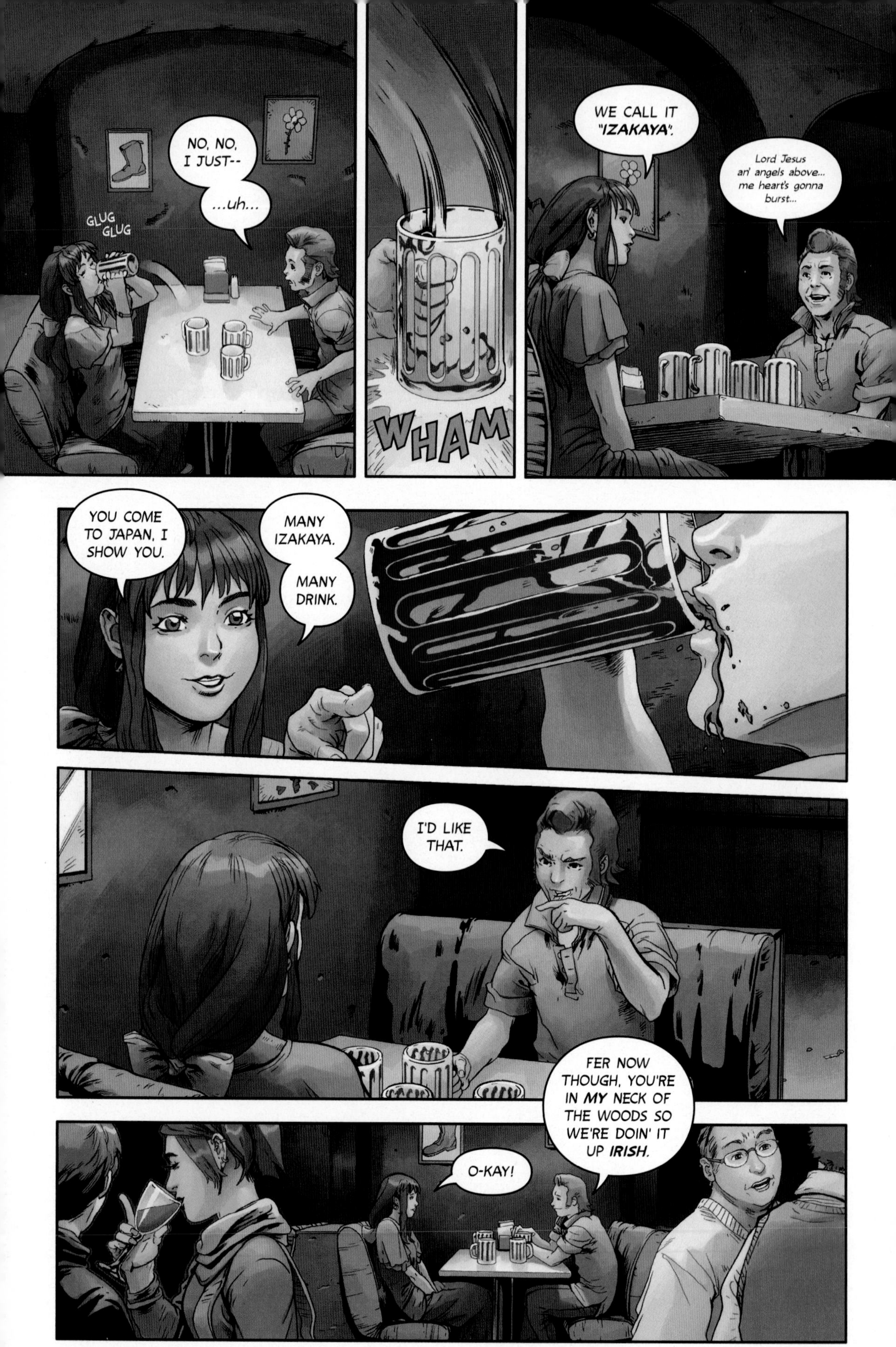
NO, NO, I JUST--
...uh...
GLUG GLUG
WHAM
WE CALL IT "IZAKAYA".
Lord Jesus an' angels above... me heart's gonna burst...
YOU COME TO JAPAN, I SHOW YOU.
MANY IZAKAYA.
MANY DRINK.
I'D LIKE THAT.
FER NOW THOUGH, YOU'RE IN MY NECK OF THE WOODS SO WE'RE DOIN' IT UP IRISH.
O-KAY!

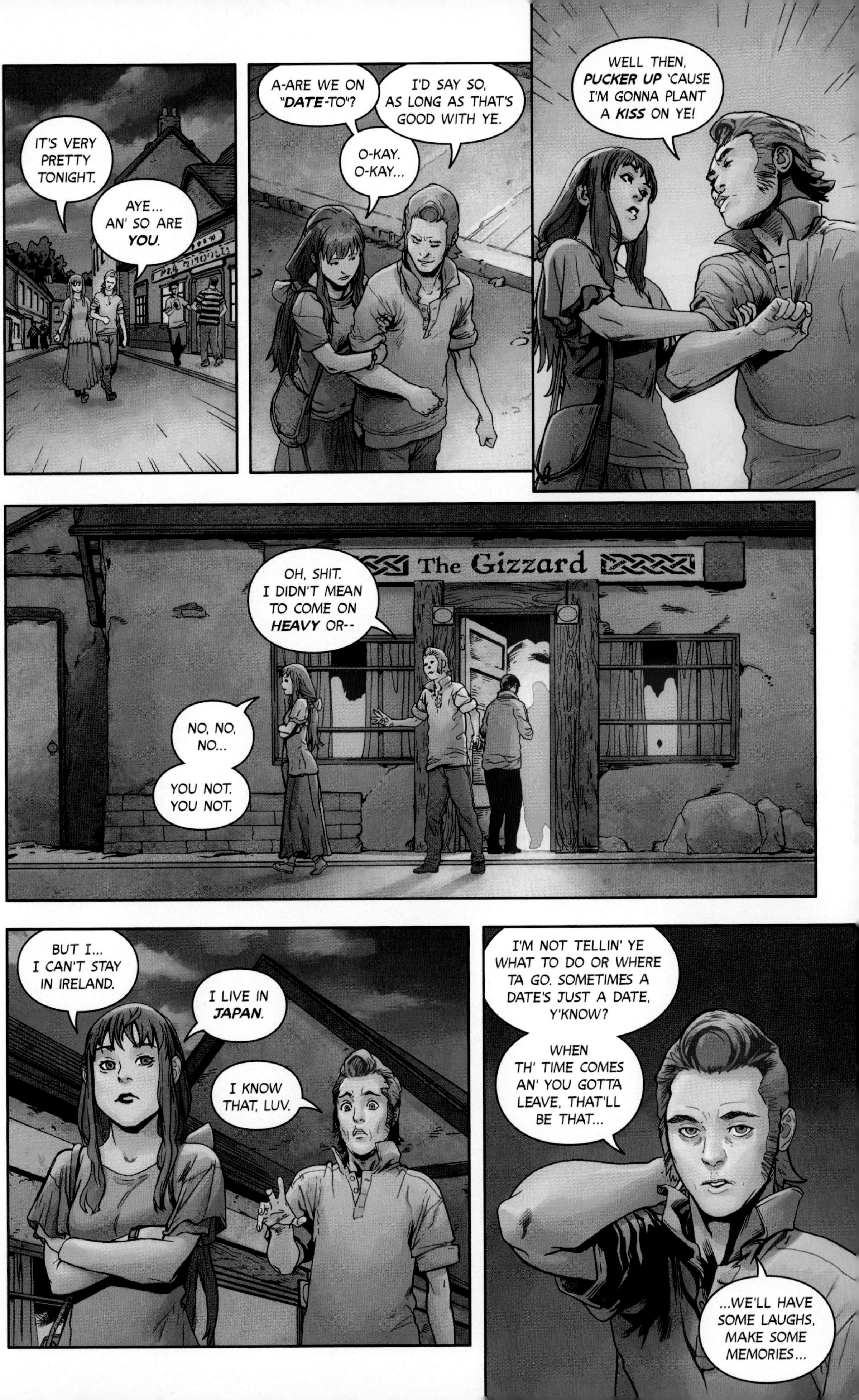
IT'S VERY PRETTY TONIGHT.
AYE... AN' SO ARE YOU.
A-ARE WE ON "DATE-TO"?
I'D SAY SO, AS LONG AS THAT'S GOOD WITH YE.
O-KAY. O-KAY...
WELL THEN, PUCKER UP 'CAUSE I'M GONNA PLANT A KISS ON YE!
The Gizzard
OH, SHIT. I DIDN'T MEAN TO COME ON HEAVY OR--
NO, NO, NO...
YOU NOT. YOU NOT.
BUT I... I CAN'T STAY IN IRELAND.
I LIVE IN JAPAN.
I KNOW THAT, LUV.
I'M NOT TELLIN' YE WHAT TO DO OR WHERE TA GO. SOMETIMES A DATE'S JUST A DATE, Y'KNOW?
WHEN TH' TIME COMES AN' YOU GOTTA LEAVE, THAT'LL BE THAT...
...WE'LL HAVE SOME LAUGHS, MAKE SOME MEMORIES...

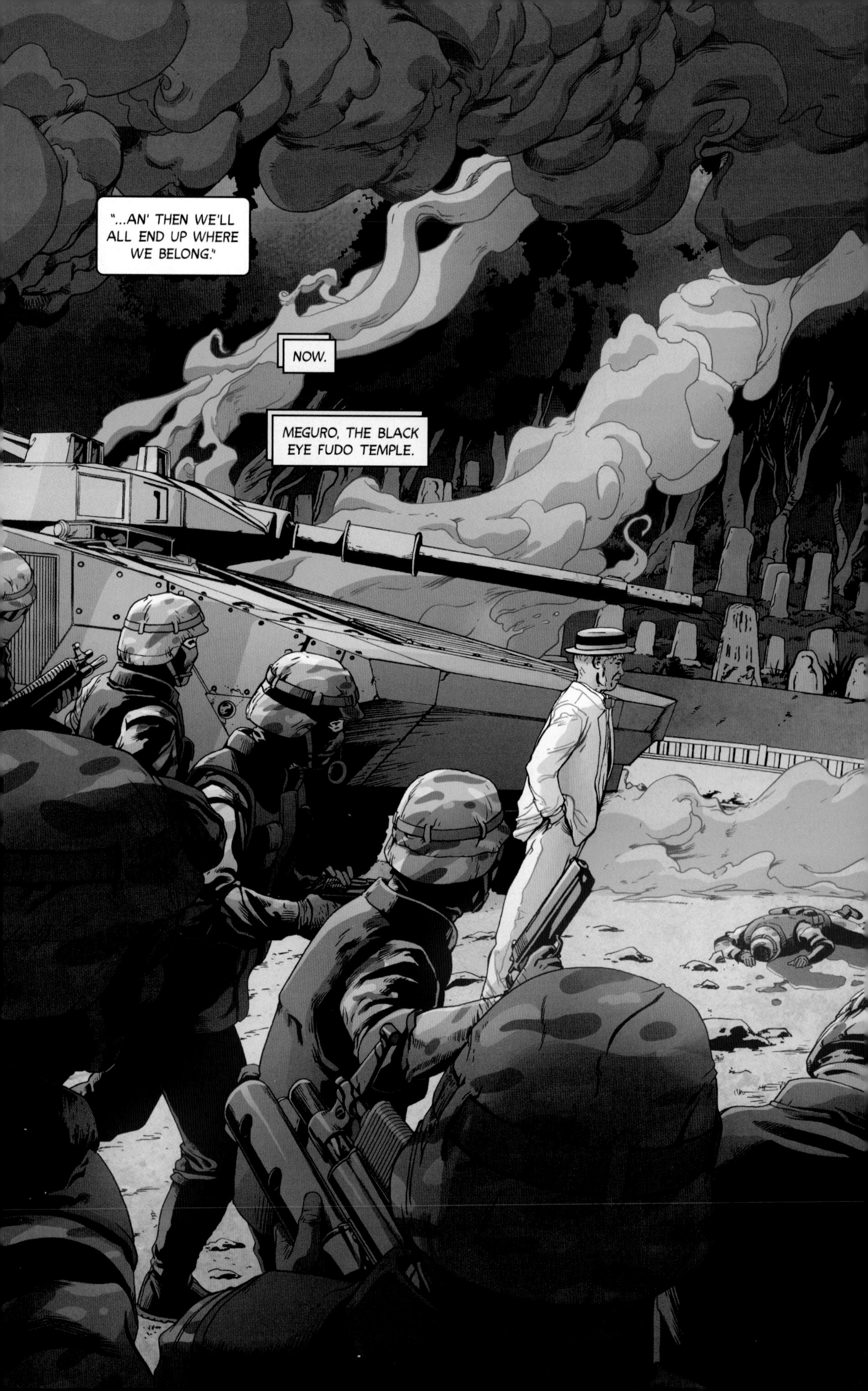
"...AN' THEN WE'LL ALL END UP WHERE WE BELONG."
NOW.
MEGURO, THE BLACK EYE FUDO TEMPLE.

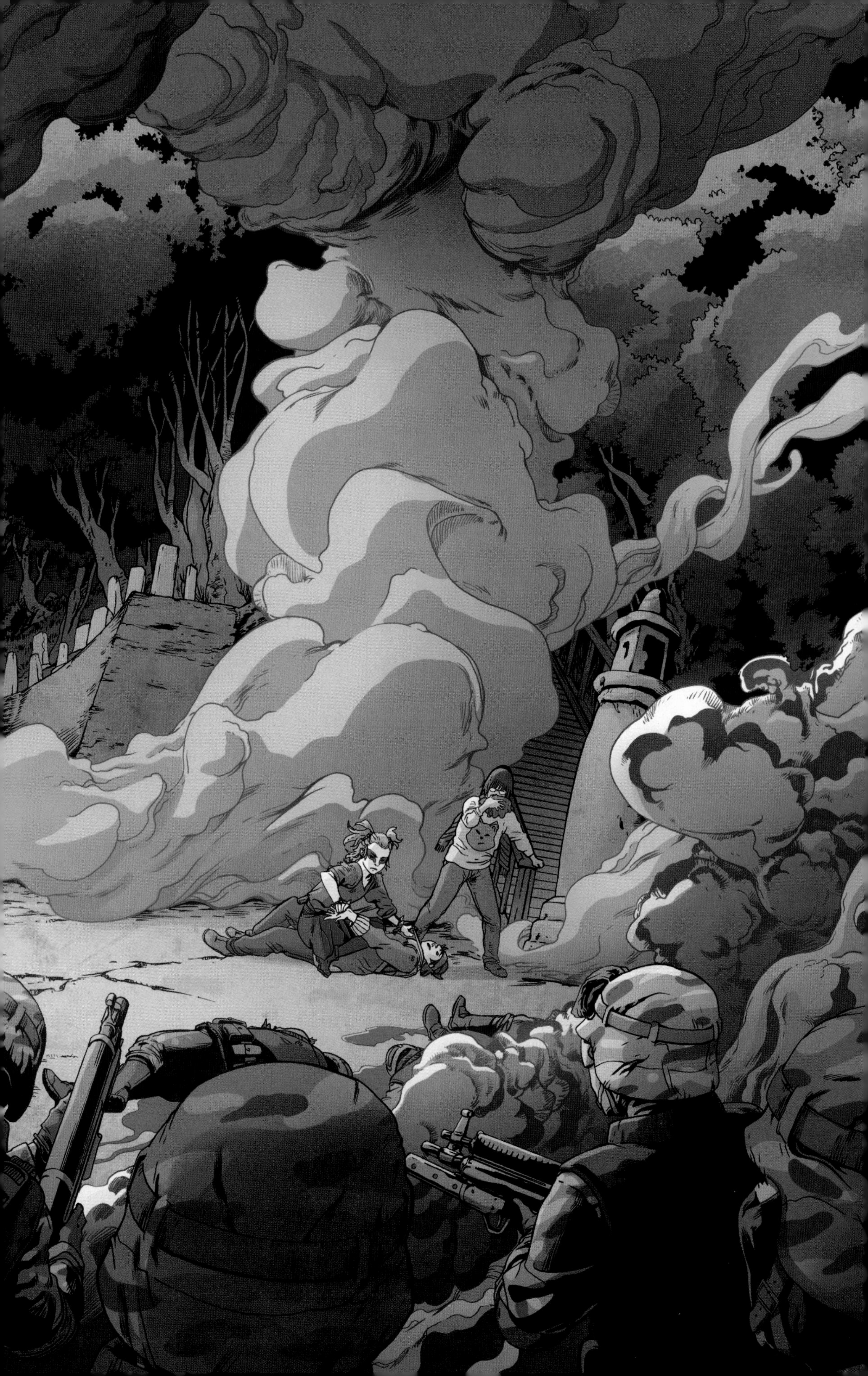

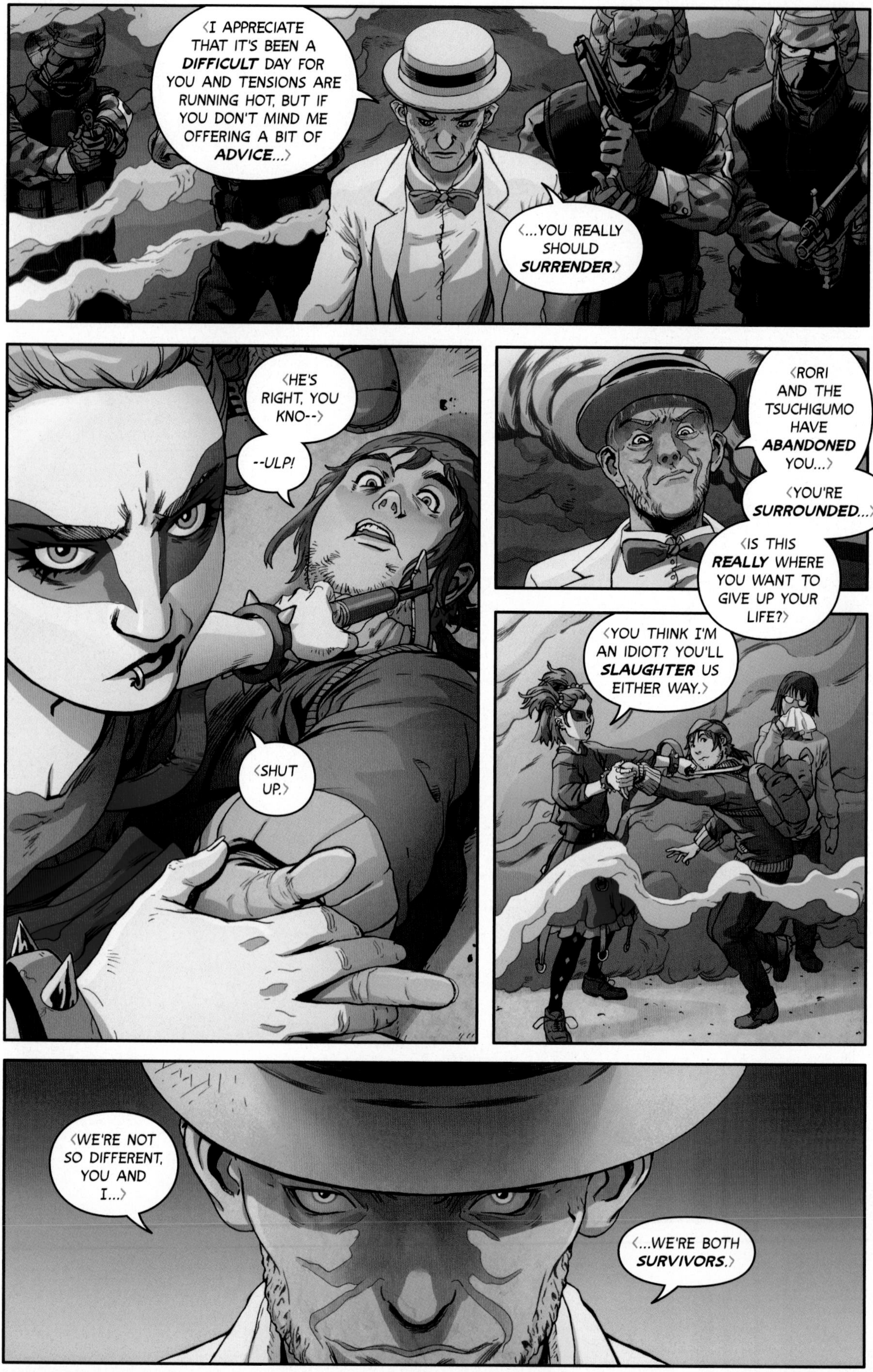
⟨I APPRECIATE THAT IT'S BEEN A ***DIFFICULT*** DAY FOR YOU AND TENSIONS ARE RUNNING HOT, BUT IF YOU DON'T MIND ME OFFERING A BIT OF ***ADVICE***...⟩
⟨...YOU REALLY SHOULD ***SURRENDER***.⟩
⟨HE'S RIGHT, YOU KNO--⟩
--ULP!
⟨SHUT UP.⟩
⟨RORI AND THE TSUCHIGUMO HAVE ***ABANDONED*** YOU...⟩
⟨YOU'RE ***SURROUNDED***...⟩
⟨IS THIS ***REALLY*** WHERE YOU WANT TO GIVE UP YOUR LIFE?⟩
⟨YOU THINK I'M AN IDIOT? YOU'LL ***SLAUGHTER*** US EITHER WAY.⟩
⟨WE'RE NOT SO DIFFERENT, YOU AND I...⟩
⟨...WE'RE BOTH ***SURVIVORS***.⟩

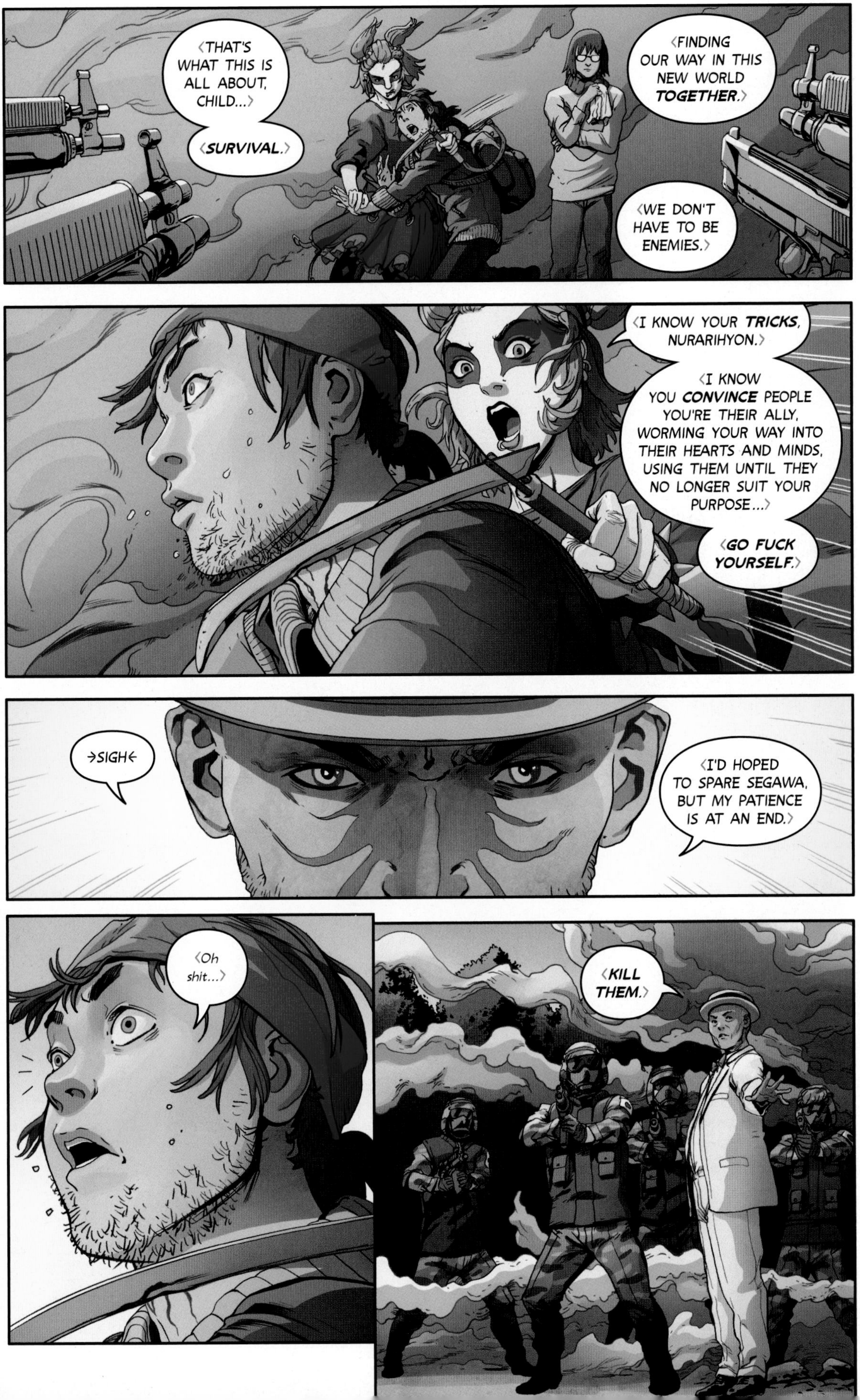
〈THAT'S WHAT THIS IS ALL ABOUT, CHILD...〉
〈SURVIVAL.〉
〈FINDING OUR WAY IN THIS NEW WORLD TOGETHER.〉
〈WE DON'T HAVE TO BE ENEMIES.〉
〈I KNOW YOUR TRICKS, NURARIHYON.〉
〈I KNOW YOU CONVINCE PEOPLE YOU'RE THEIR ALLY, WORMING YOUR WAY INTO THEIR HEARTS AND MINDS, USING THEM UNTIL THEY NO LONGER SUIT YOUR PURPOSE...〉
〈GO FUCK YOURSELF.〉
→SIGH←
〈I'D HOPED TO SPARE SEGAWA, BUT MY PATIENCE IS AT AN END.〉
〈Oh shit...〉
〈KILL THEM.〉

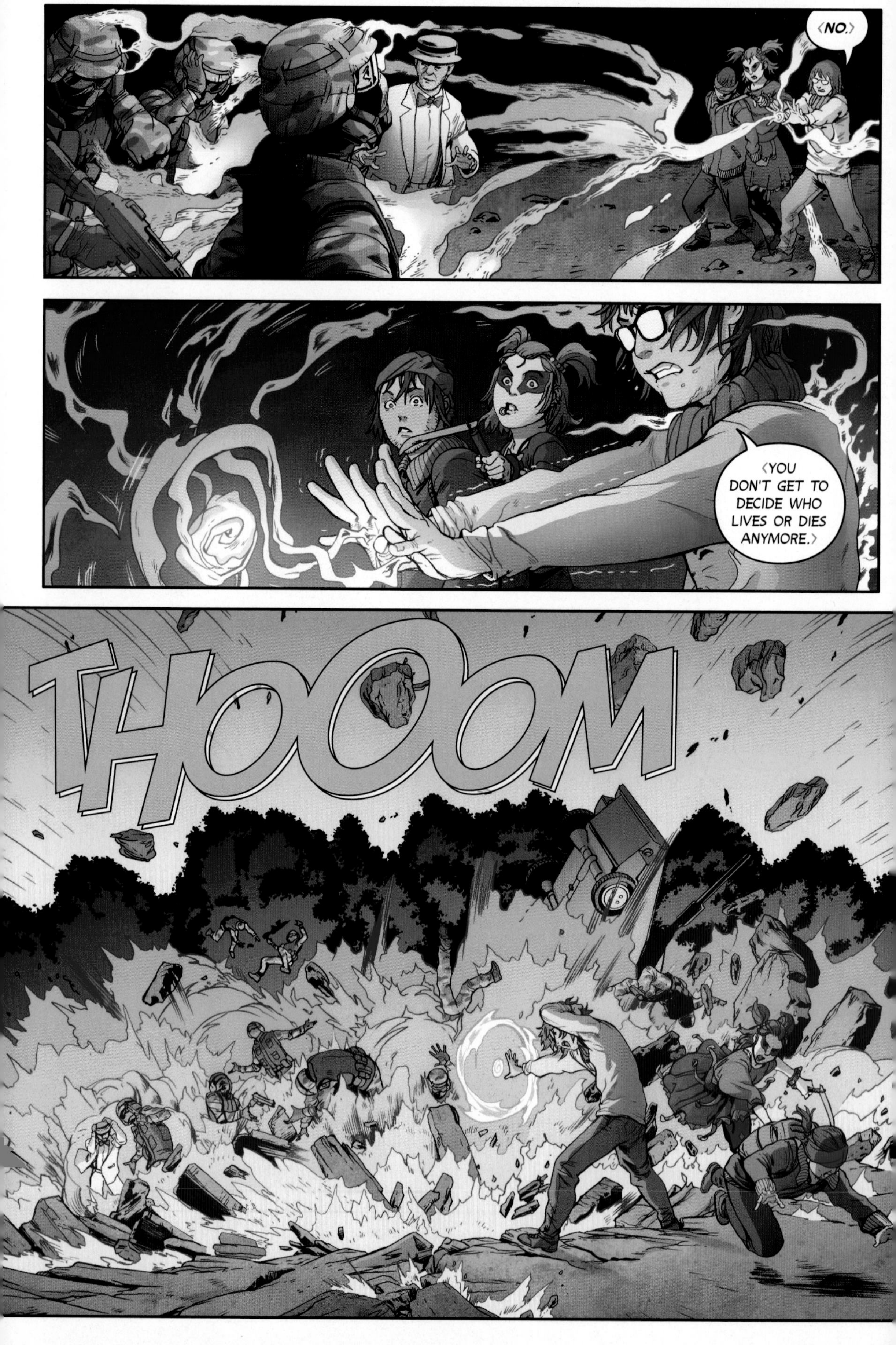

‹NO.›
‹YOU DON'T GET TO DECIDE WHO LIVES OR DIES ANYMORE.›
THOOOM

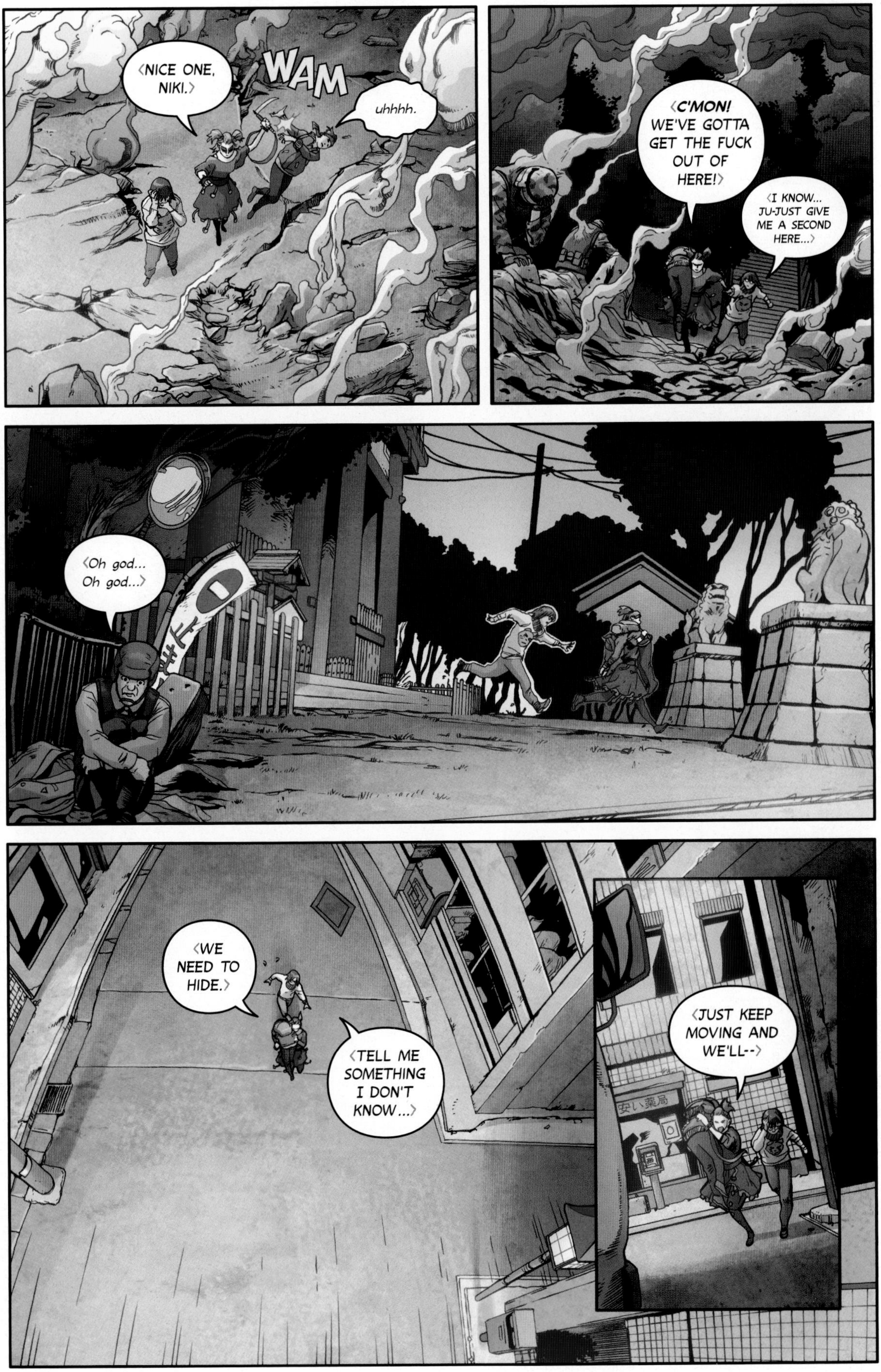
WAM
⟨NICE ONE, NIKI.⟩
uhhhh.
⟨C'MON! WE'VE GOTTA GET THE FUCK OUT OF HERE!⟩
⟨I KNOW... JU-JUST GIVE ME A SECOND HERE...⟩
⟨Oh god... Oh god...⟩
⟨WE NEED TO HIDE.⟩
⟨TELL ME SOMETHING I DON'T KNOW...⟩
⟨JUST KEEP MOVING AND WE'LL--⟩
安い薬局

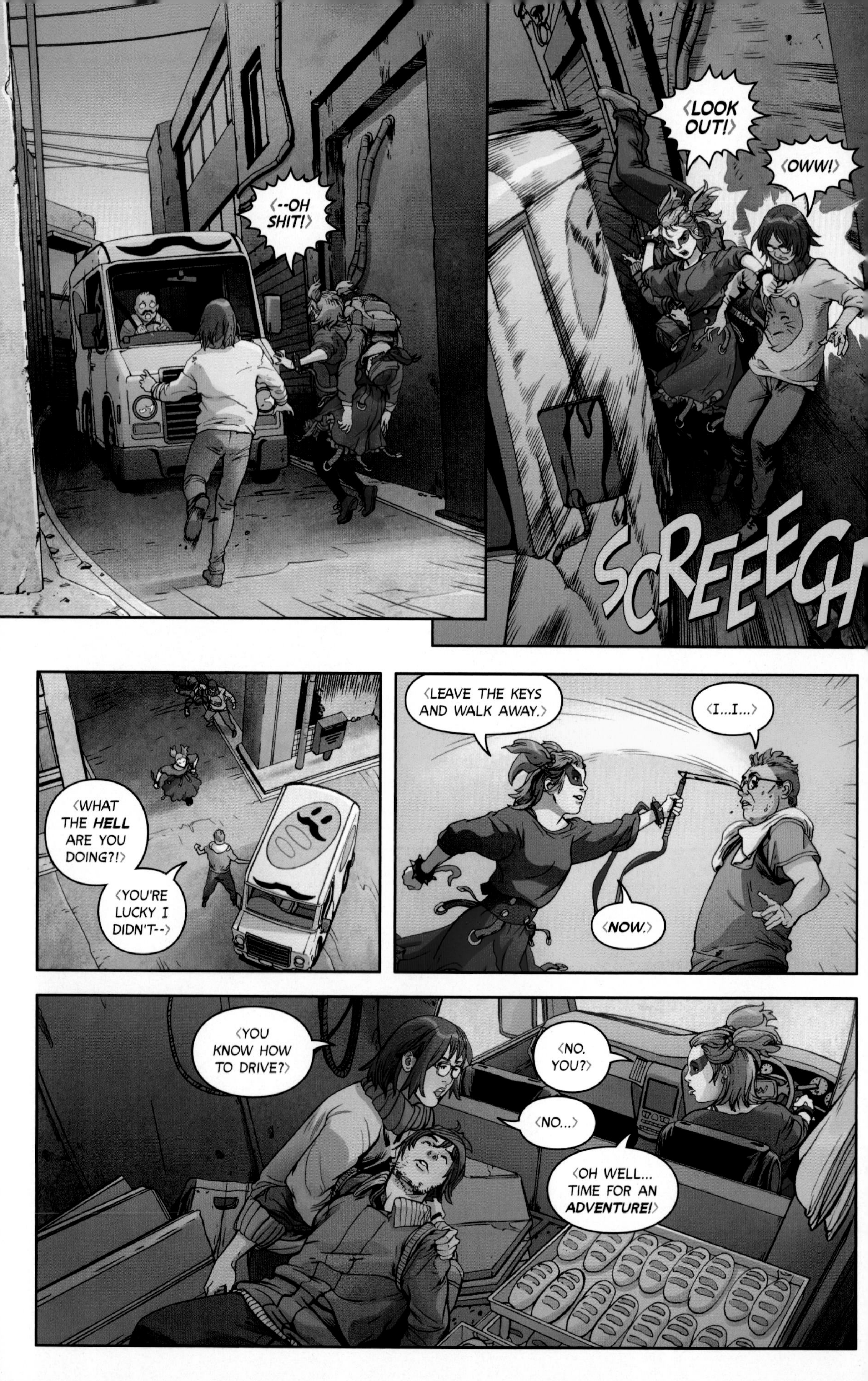
‹--OH SHIT!›
‹LOOK OUT!›
‹OWW!›
SCREEECH
‹WHAT THE HELL ARE YOU DOING?!›
‹YOU'RE LUCKY I DIDN'T--›
‹LEAVE THE KEYS AND WALK AWAY.›
‹I...I...›
‹NOW.›
‹YOU KNOW HOW TO DRIVE?›
‹NO. YOU?›
‹NO...›
‹OH WELL... TIME FOR AN ADVENTURE!›

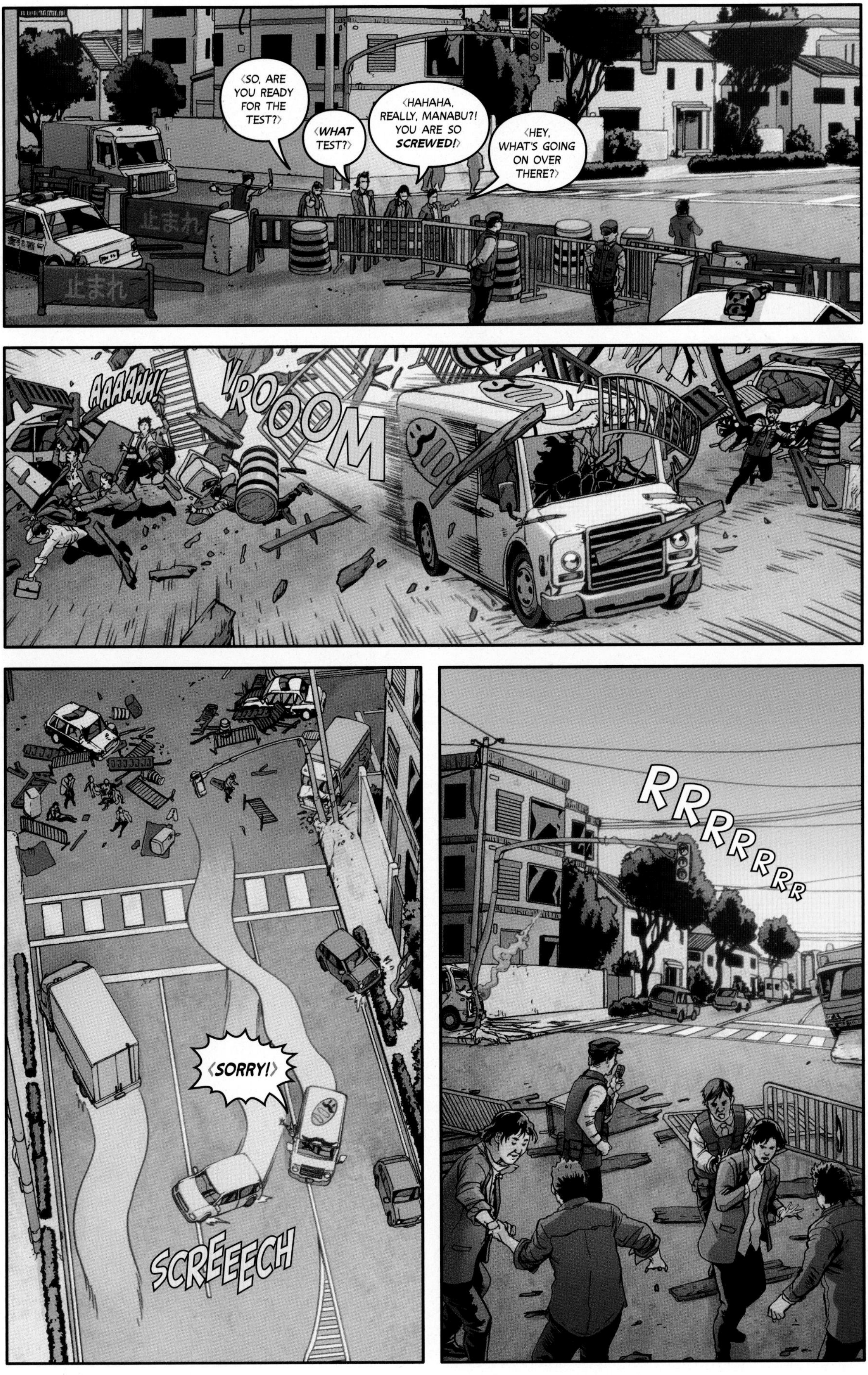
‹SO, ARE YOU READY FOR THE TEST?›
‹WHAT TEST?›
‹HAHAHA, REALLY, MANABU?! YOU ARE SO SCREWED!›
‹HEY, WHAT'S GOING ON OVER THERE?›
止まれ
止まれ
AAAAHH!
VROOOM
‹SORRY!›
SCREEECH
RRRRRRRR

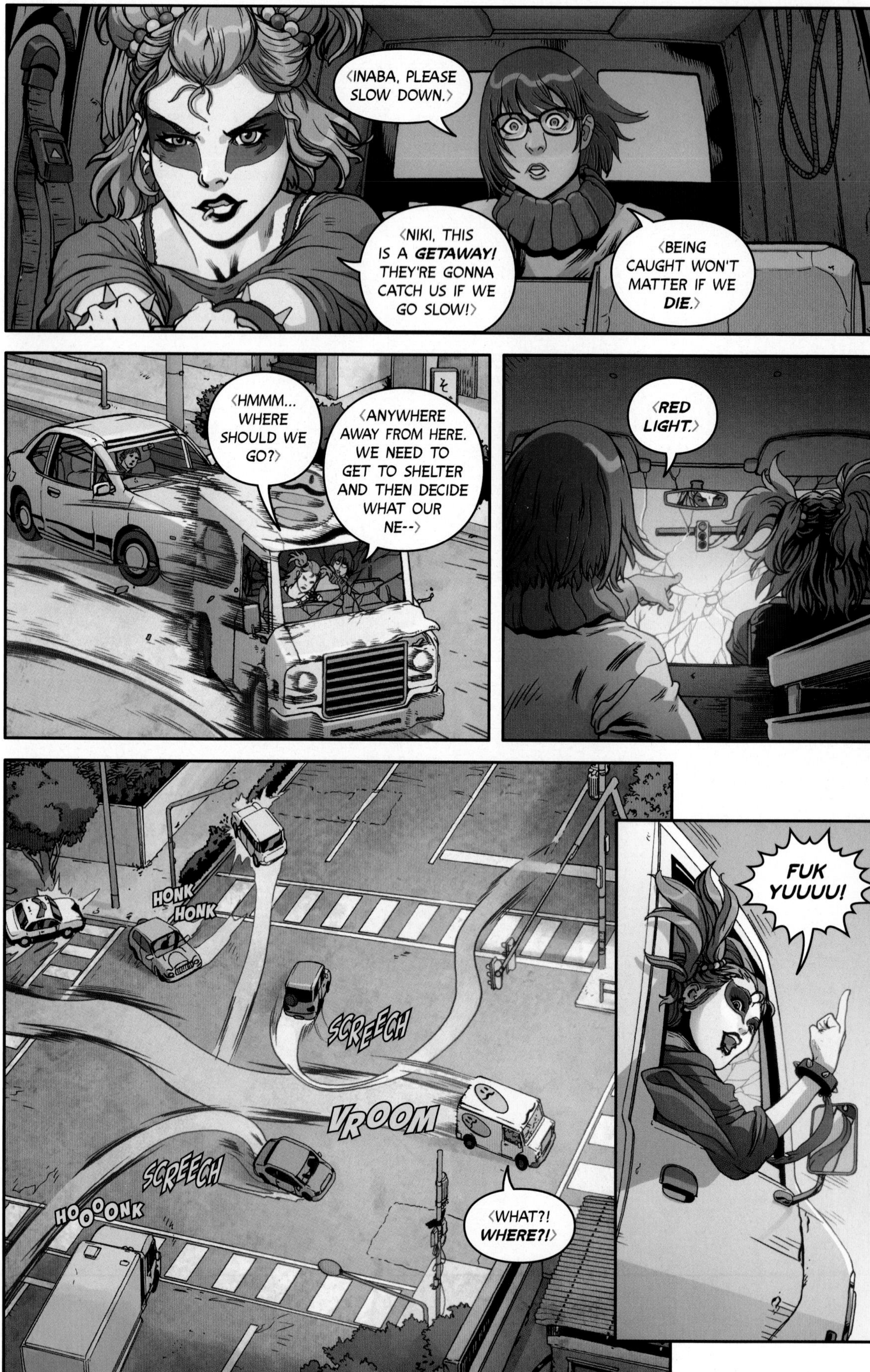

‹INABA, PLEASE SLOW DOWN.›
‹NIKI, THIS IS A **GETAWAY!** THEY'RE GONNA CATCH US IF WE GO SLOW!›
‹BEING CAUGHT WON'T MATTER IF WE **DIE.**›
‹HMMM... WHERE SHOULD WE GO?›
‹ANYWHERE AWAY FROM HERE. WE NEED TO GET TO SHELTER AND THEN DECIDE WHAT OUR NE--›
‹**RED LIGHT.**›
HONK
HONK
SCREECH
VROOM
SCREECH
HOOOONK
‹WHAT?! **WHERE?!**›
FUK YUUUU!

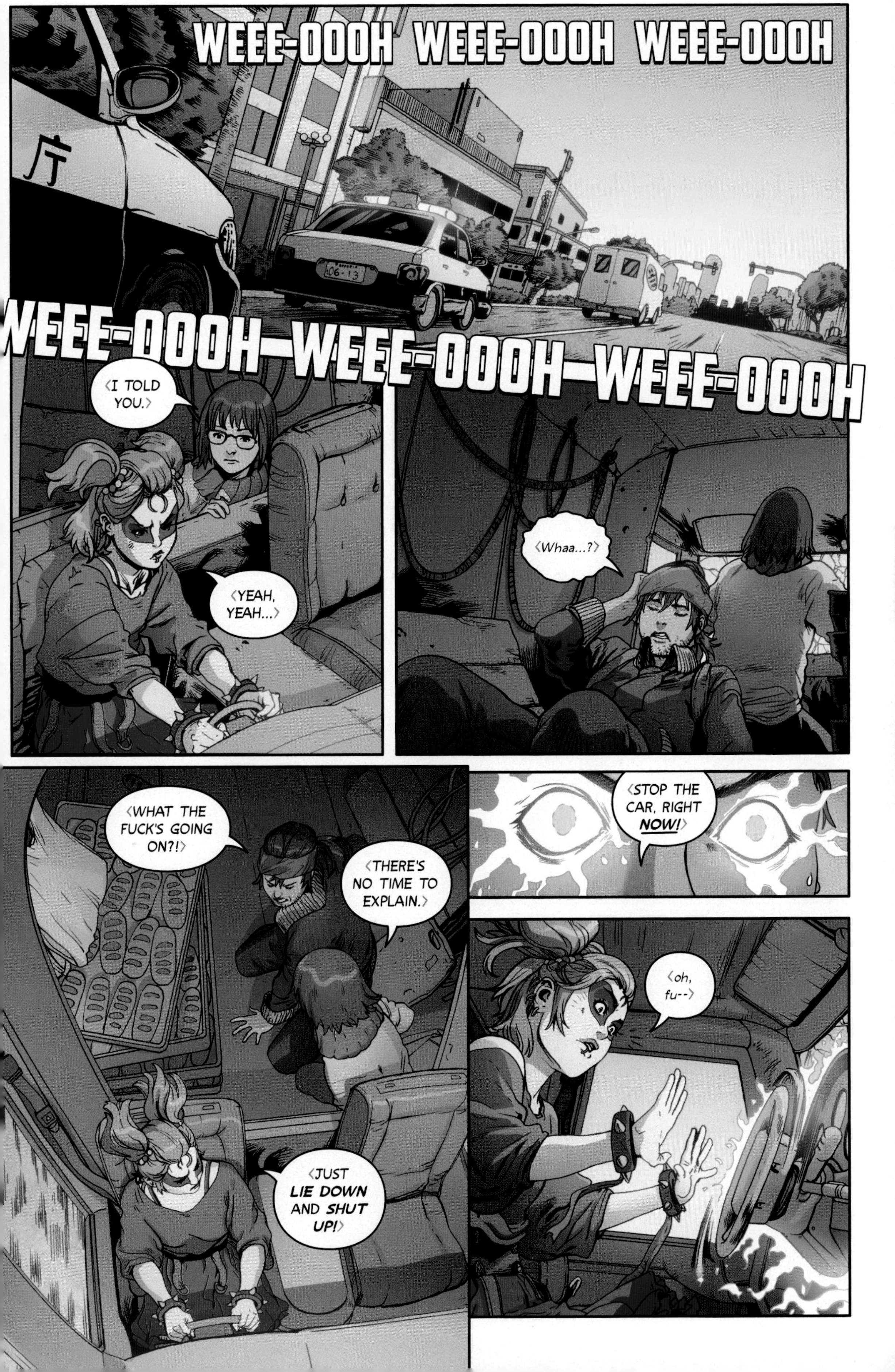
WEEE-OOOH WEEE-OOOH WEEE-OOOH
庁
WEEE-OOOH WEEE-OOOH WEEE-OOOH
⟨I TOLD YOU.⟩
⟨YEAH, YEAH...⟩
⟨Whaa...?⟩
⟨WHAT THE FUCK'S GOING ON?!⟩
⟨THERE'S NO TIME TO EXPLAIN.⟩
⟨JUST **LIE DOWN** AND **SHUT UP!**⟩
⟨STOP THE CAR, RIGHT **NOW!**⟩
⟨oh, fu--⟩

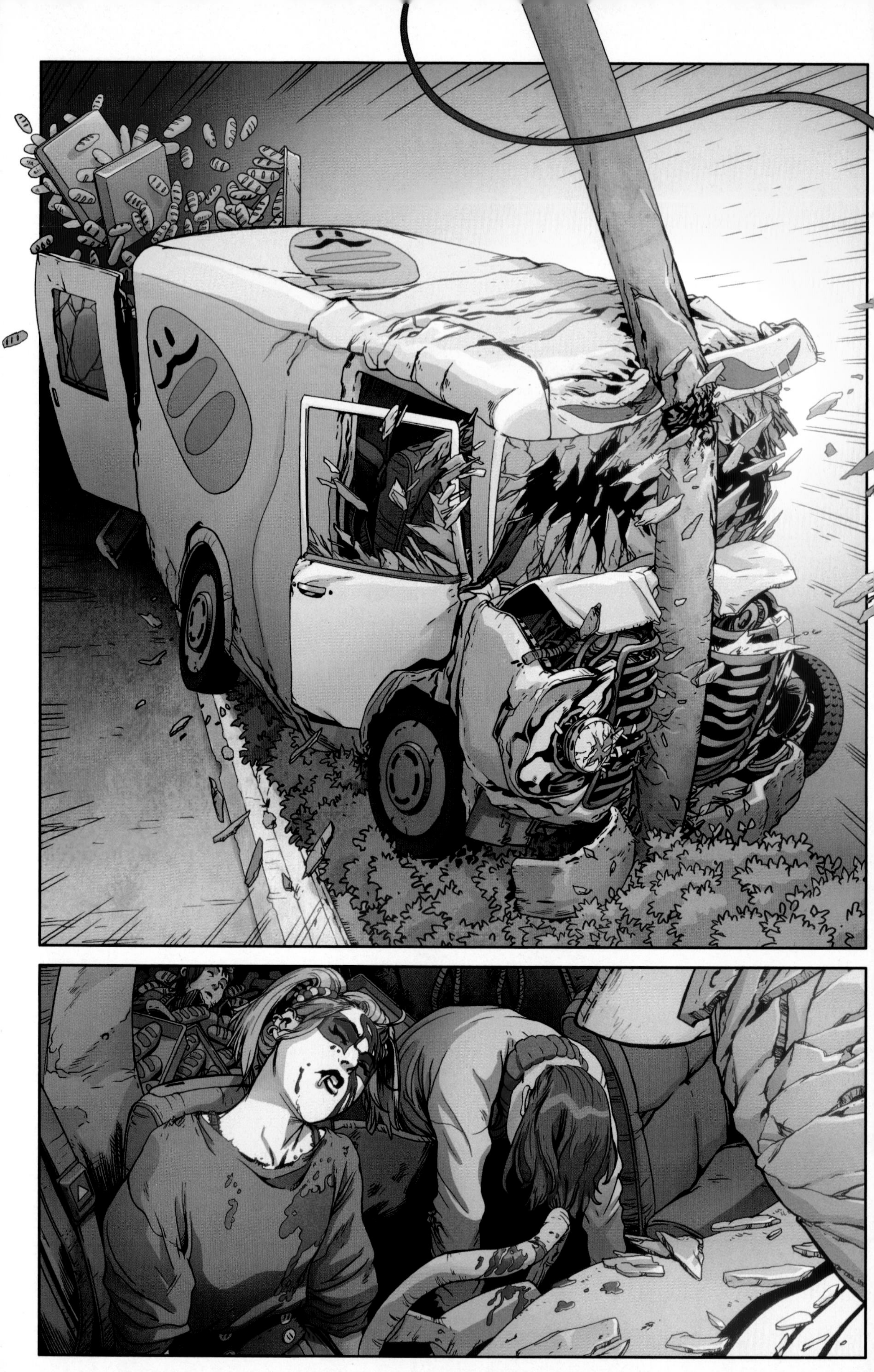

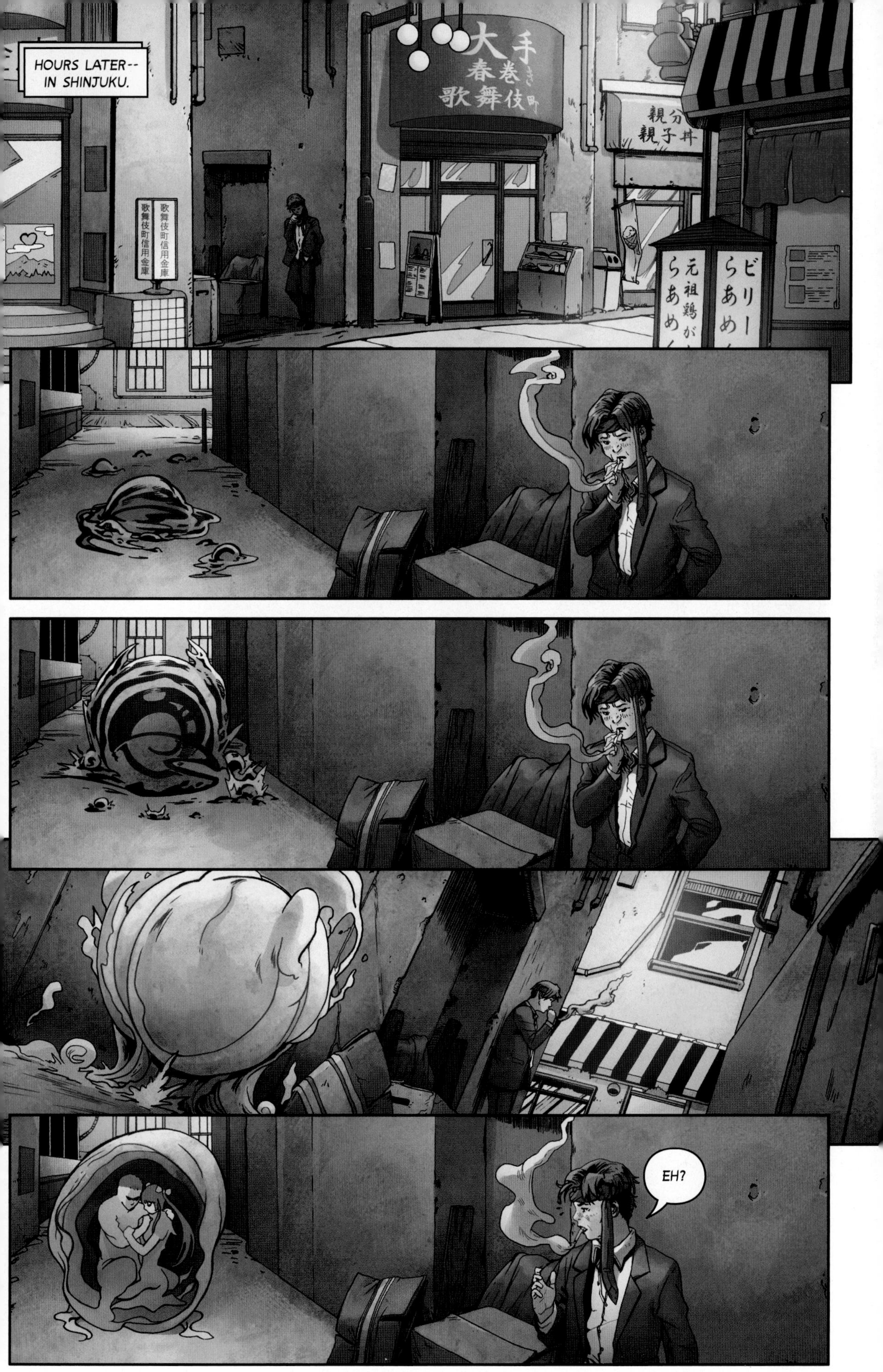
HOURS LATER-- IN SHINJUKU.
大手
春巻き
歌舞伎町
親分
親子丼
歌舞伎町信用金庫
EH?

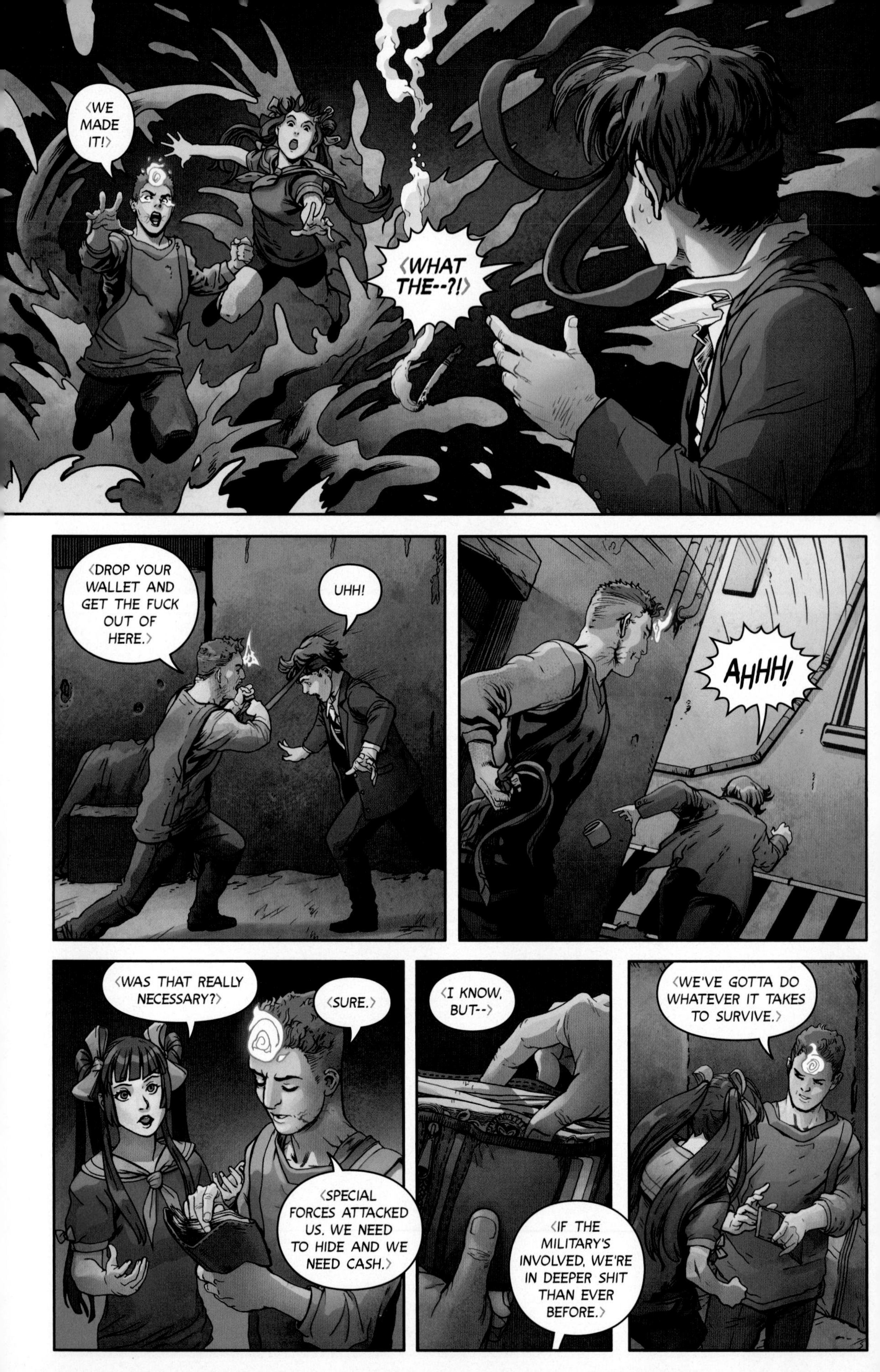

<WE MADE IT!>
<WHAT THE--?!>
<DROP YOUR WALLET AND GET THE FUCK OUT OF HERE.>
UHH!
AHHH!
<WAS THAT REALLY NECESSARY?>
<SURE.>
<SPECIAL FORCES ATTACKED US. WE NEED TO HIDE AND WE NEED CASH.>
<I KNOW, BUT-->
<IF THE MILITARY'S INVOLVED, WE'RE IN DEEPER SHIT THAN EVER BEFORE.>
<WE'VE GOTTA DO WHATEVER IT TAKES TO SURVIVE.>

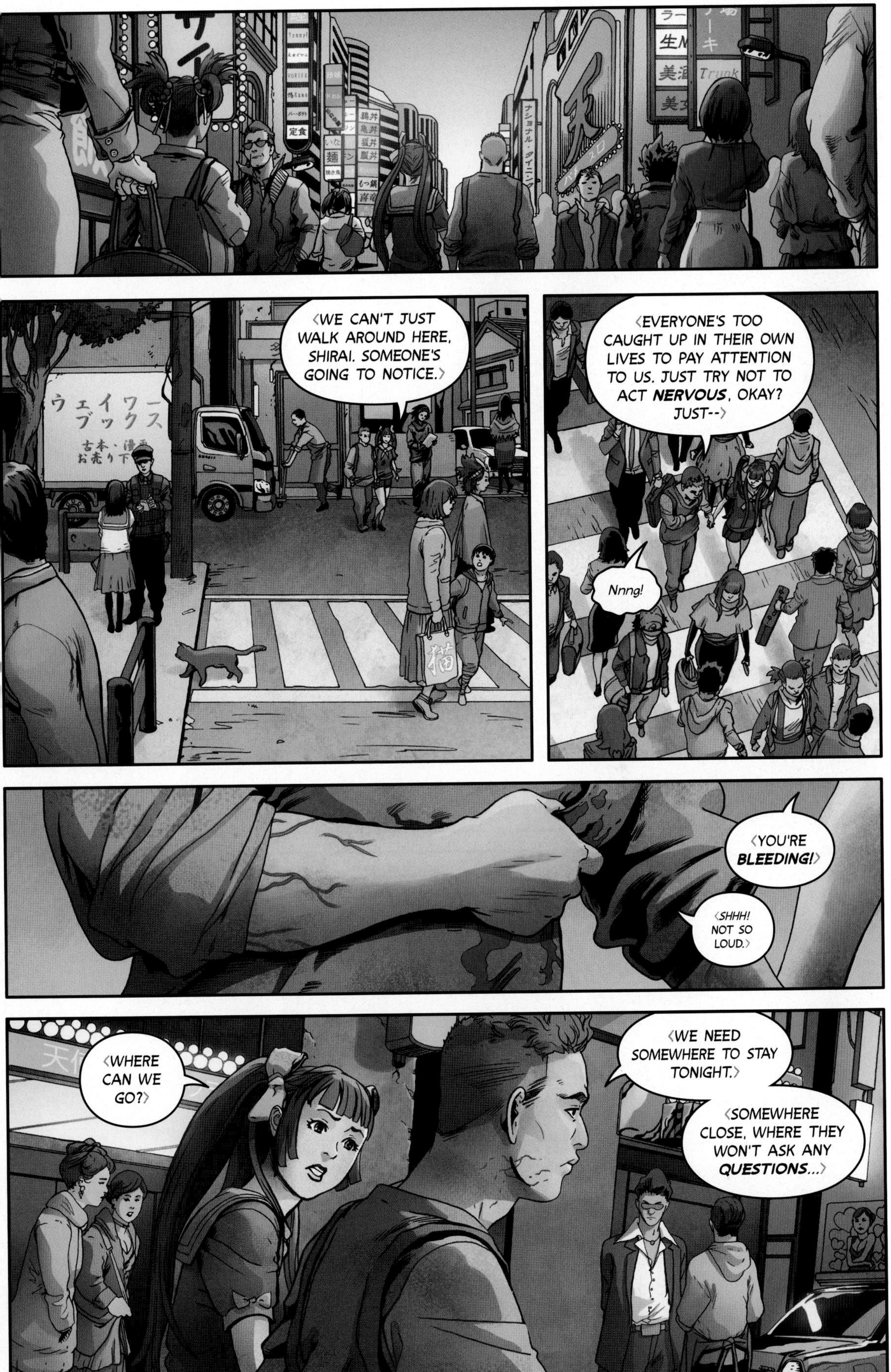
〈WE CAN'T JUST WALK AROUND HERE, SHIRAI. SOMEONE'S GOING TO NOTICE.〉
〈EVERYONE'S TOO CAUGHT UP IN THEIR OWN LIVES TO PAY ATTENTION TO US. JUST TRY NOT TO ACT **NERVOUS**, OKAY? JUST--〉
Nnng!
〈YOU'RE **BLEEDING!**〉
〈*SHHH!* NOT SO LOUD.〉
〈WHERE CAN WE GO?〉
〈WE NEED SOMEWHERE TO STAY TONIGHT.〉
〈SOMEWHERE CLOSE, WHERE THEY WON'T ASK ANY **QUESTIONS**...〉

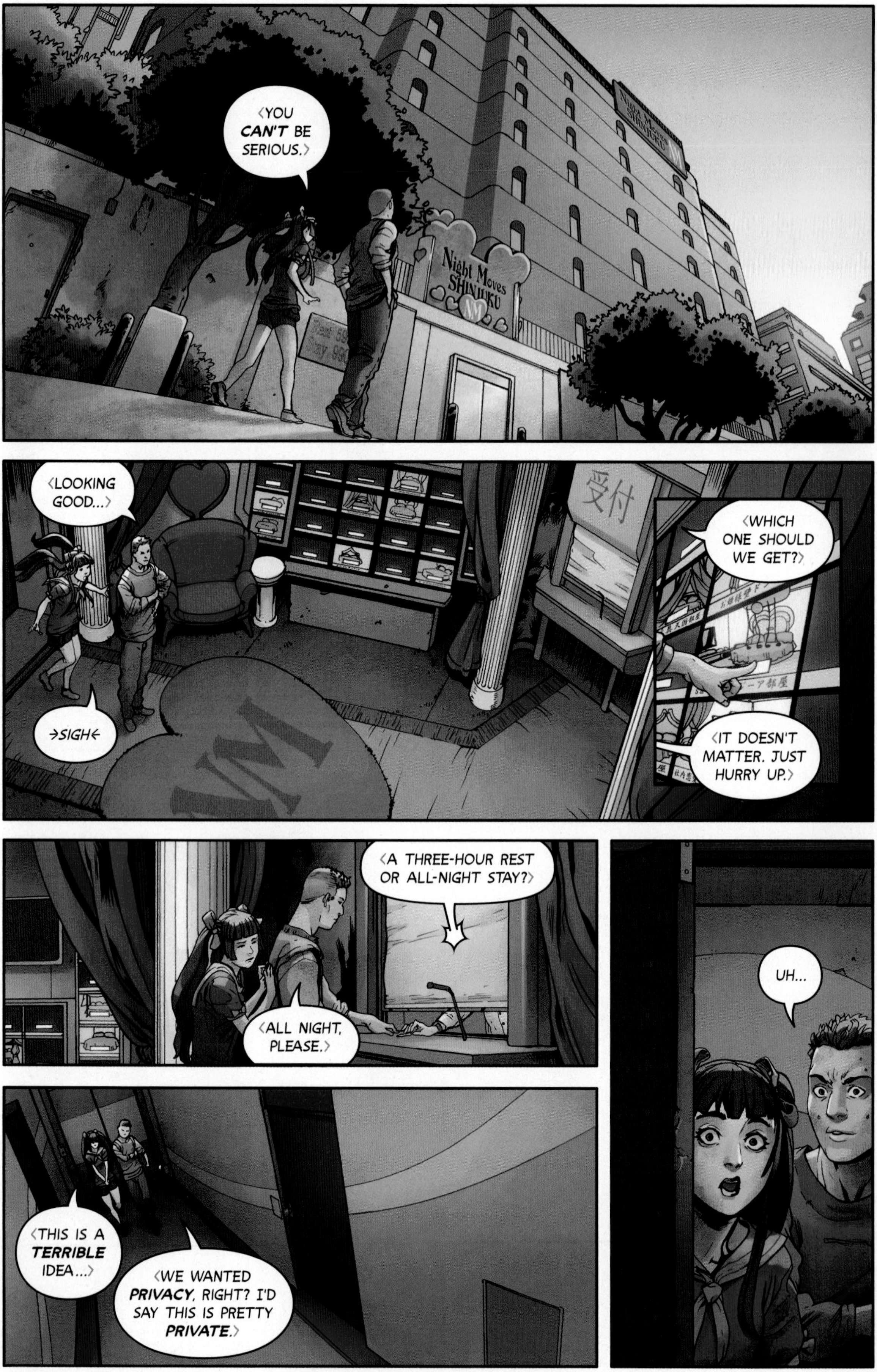
Night Moves SHINJUKU
⟨YOU CAN'T BE SERIOUS.⟩
⟨LOOKING GOOD...⟩
→SIGH←
受付
⟨WHICH ONE SHOULD WE GET?⟩
⟨IT DOESN'T MATTER. JUST HURRY UP.⟩
⟨A THREE-HOUR REST OR ALL-NIGHT STAY?⟩
⟨ALL NIGHT, PLEASE.⟩
⟨THIS IS A TERRIBLE IDEA...⟩
⟨WE WANTED PRIVACY, RIGHT? I'D SAY THIS IS PRETTY PRIVATE.⟩
UH...

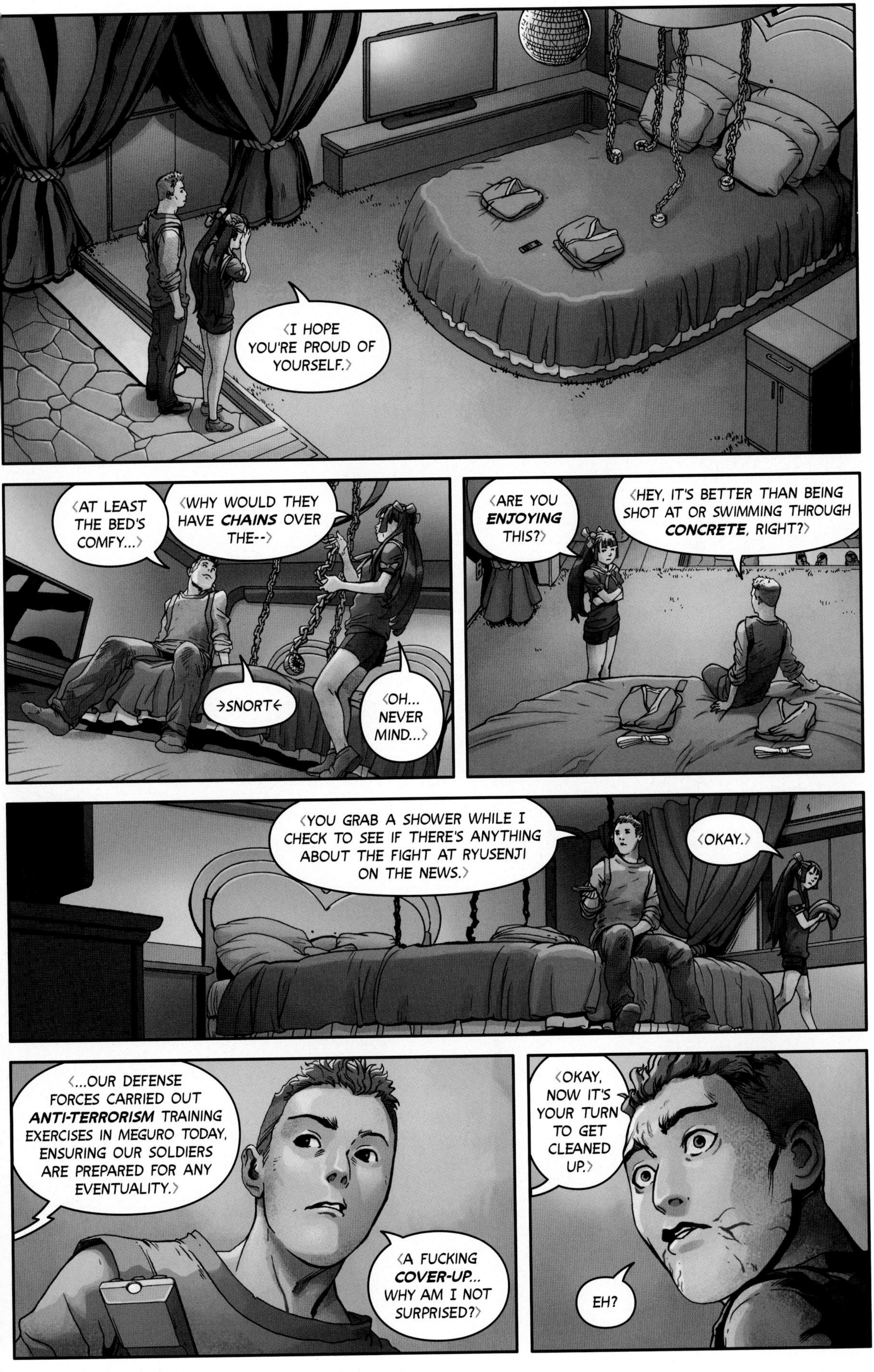

⟨I HOPE YOU'RE PROUD OF YOURSELF.⟩
⟨AT LEAST THE BED'S COMFY...⟩
⟨WHY WOULD THEY HAVE CHAINS OVER THE--⟩
→SNORT←
⟨OH... NEVER MIND...⟩
⟨ARE YOU ENJOYING THIS?⟩
⟨HEY, IT'S BETTER THAN BEING SHOT AT OR SWIMMING THROUGH CONCRETE, RIGHT?⟩
⟨YOU GRAB A SHOWER WHILE I CHECK TO SEE IF THERE'S ANYTHING ABOUT THE FIGHT AT RYUSENJI ON THE NEWS.⟩
⟨OKAY.⟩
⟨...OUR DEFENSE FORCES CARRIED OUT ANTI-TERRORISM TRAINING EXERCISES IN MEGURO TODAY, ENSURING OUR SOLDIERS ARE PREPARED FOR ANY EVENTUALITY.⟩
⟨A FUCKING COVER-UP... WHY AM I NOT SURPRISED?⟩
⟨OKAY, NOW IT'S YOUR TURN TO GET CLEANED UP.⟩
EH?

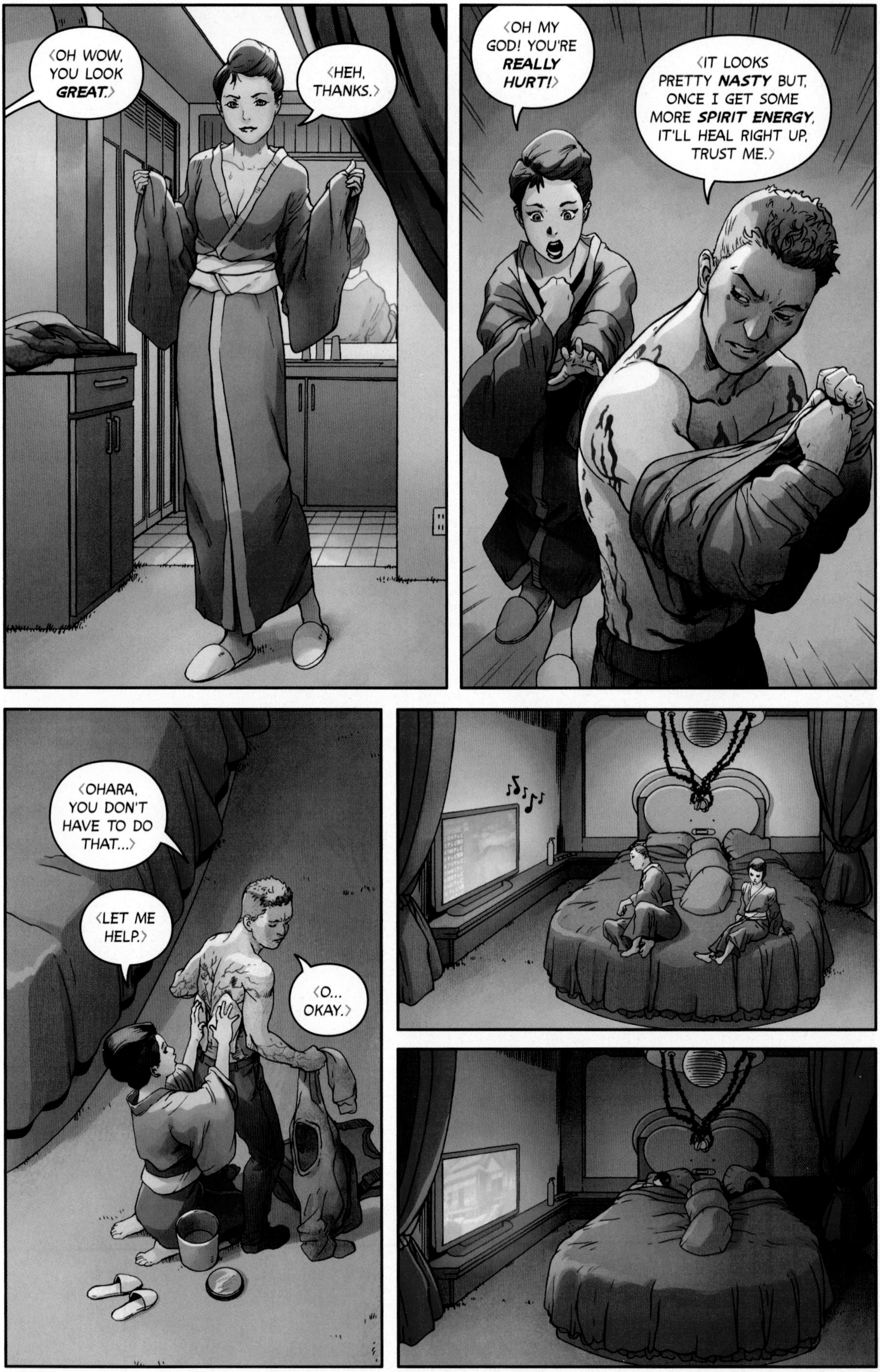

〈OH WOW, YOU LOOK GREAT.〉
〈HEH, THANKS.〉
〈OH MY GOD! YOU'RE REALLY HURT!〉
〈IT LOOKS PRETTY NASTY BUT, ONCE I GET SOME MORE SPIRIT ENERGY, IT'LL HEAL RIGHT UP, TRUST ME.〉
〈OHARA, YOU DON'T HAVE TO DO THAT...〉
〈LET ME HELP.〉
〈O... OKAY.〉

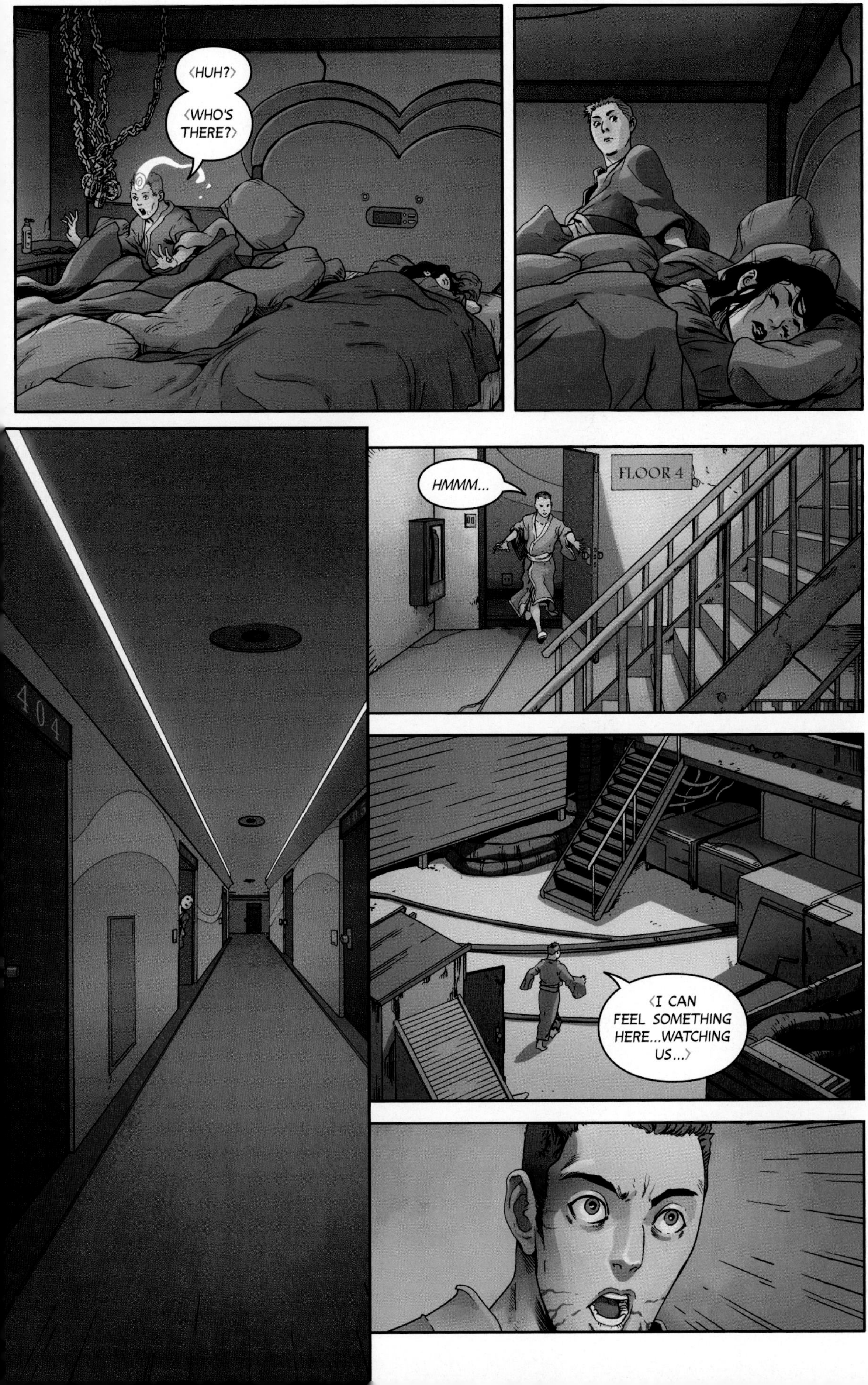

⟨HUH?⟩
⟨WHO'S THERE?⟩
404
FLOOR 4
HMMM...
⟨I CAN FEEL SOMETHING HERE...WATCHING US...⟩

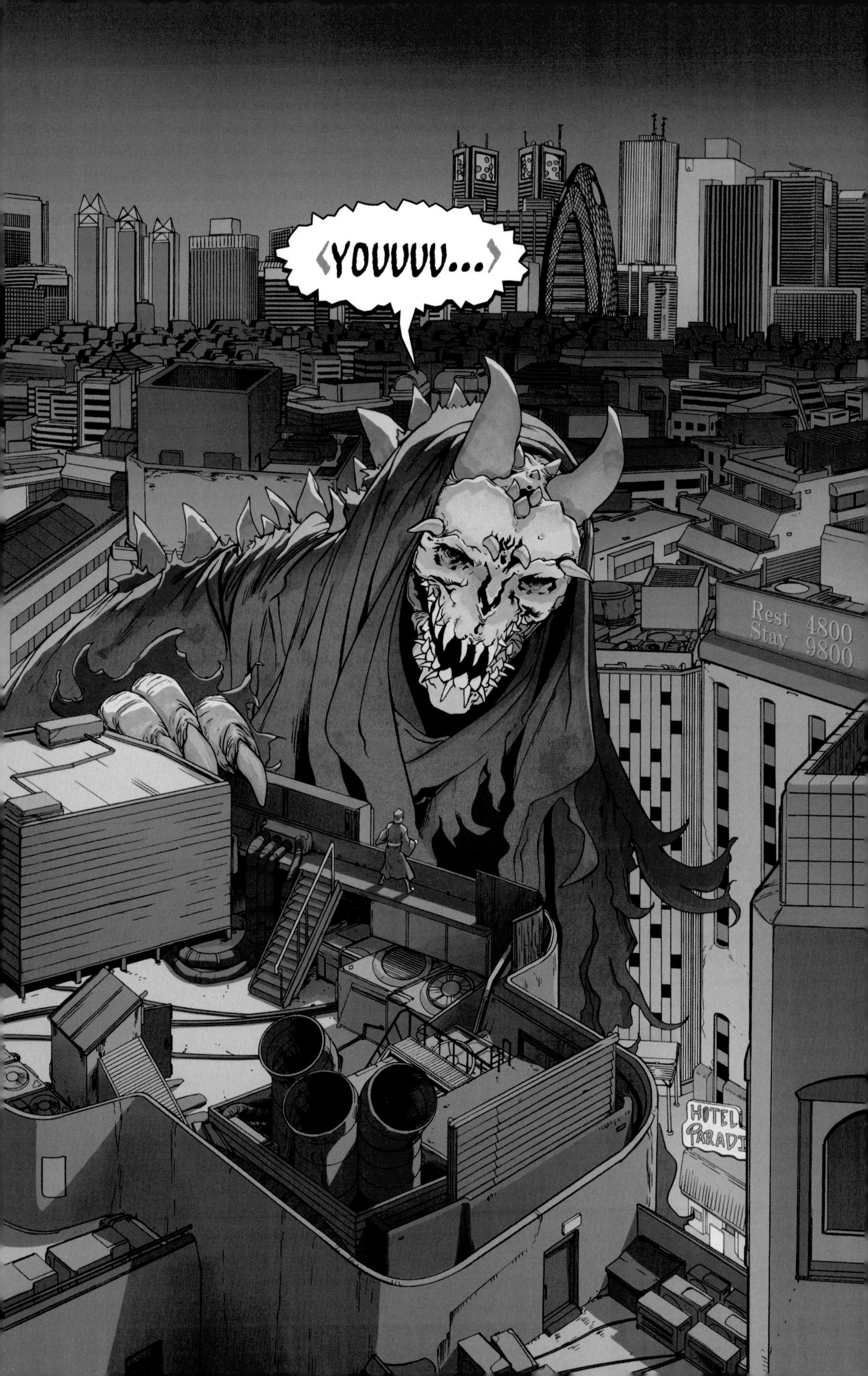
‹YOUUUU...›
Rest 4800
Stay 9800
HOTEL
PARADI

Chapter Eighteen

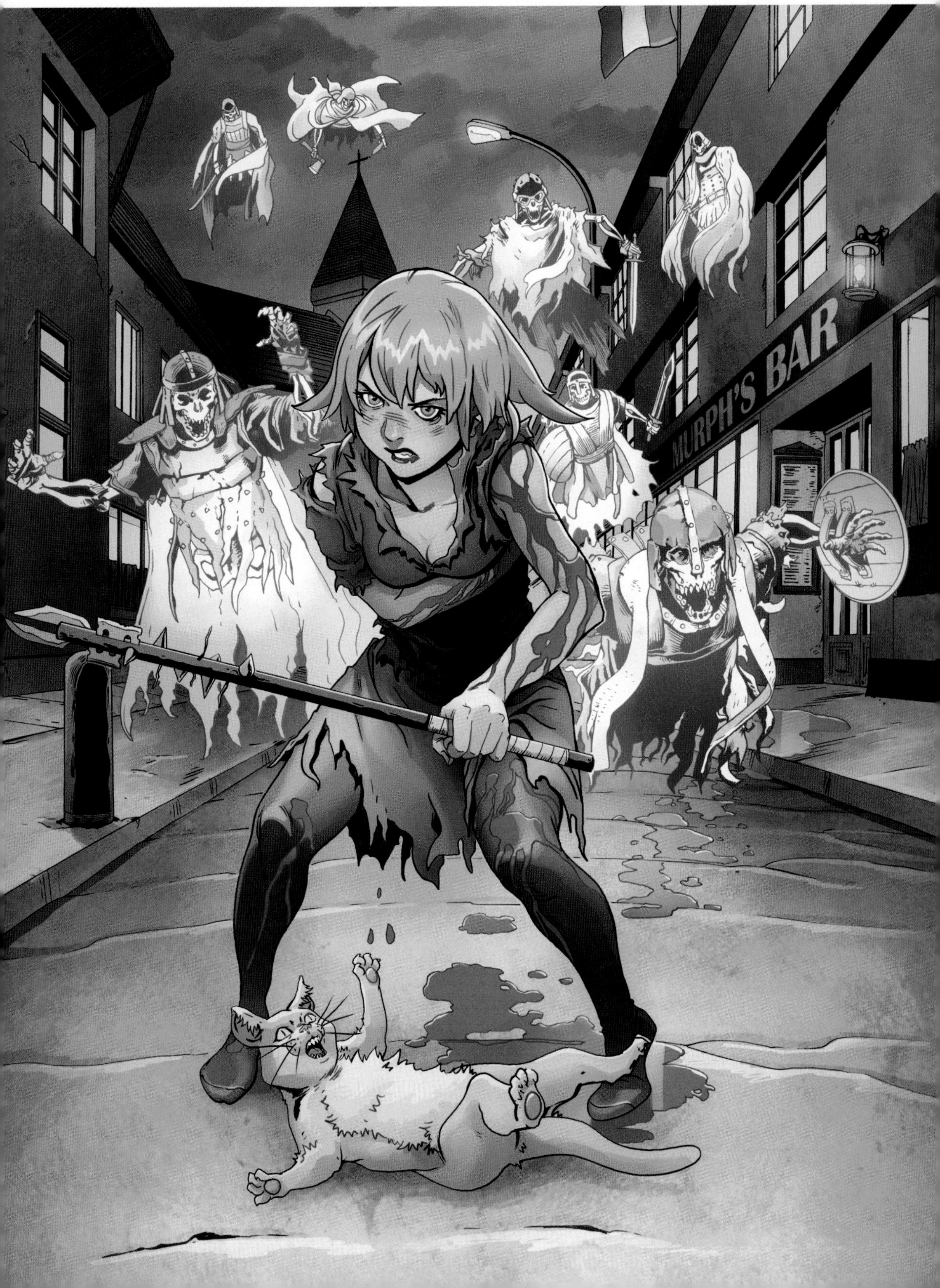
MURPH'S BAR

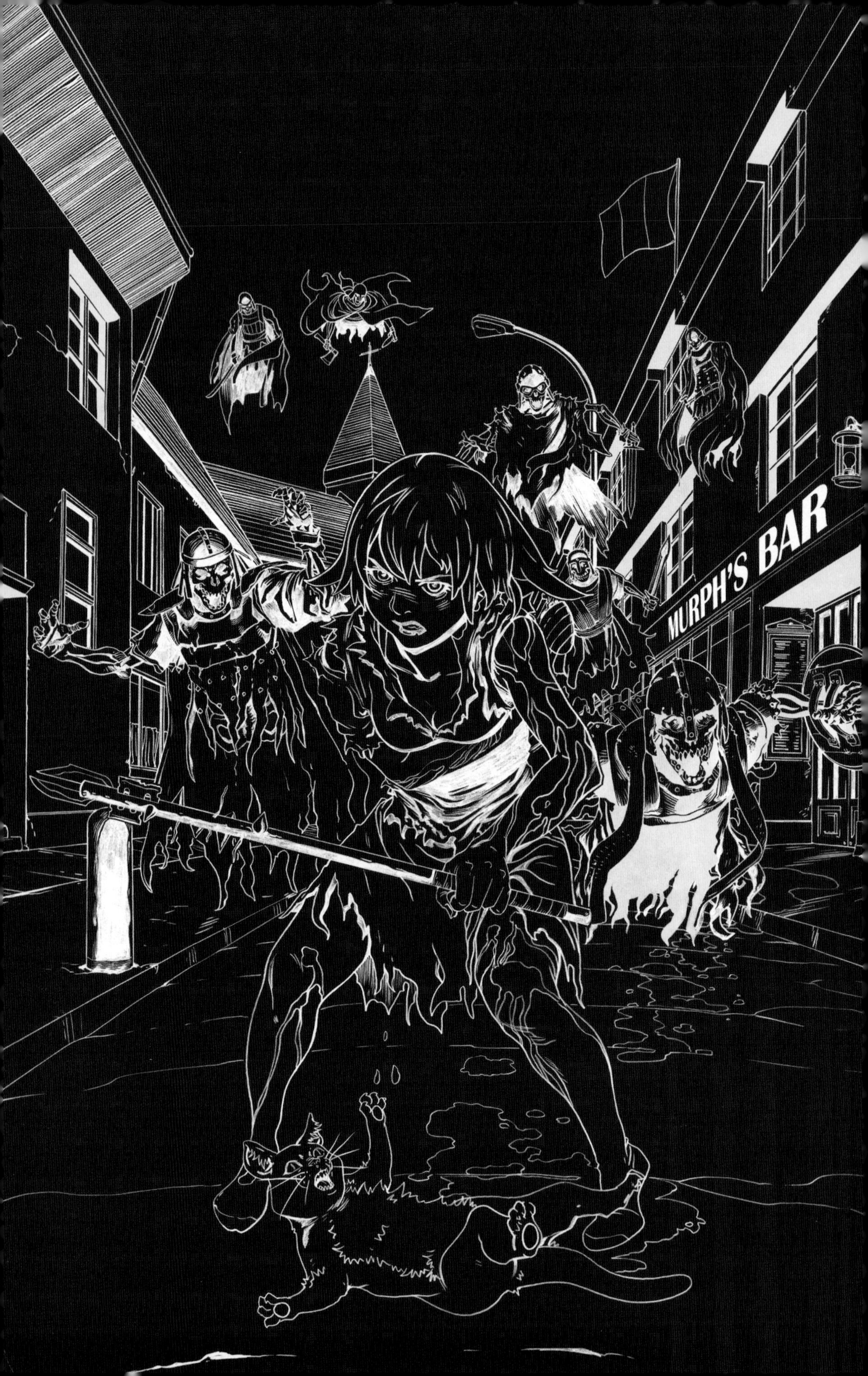
MURPH'S BAR

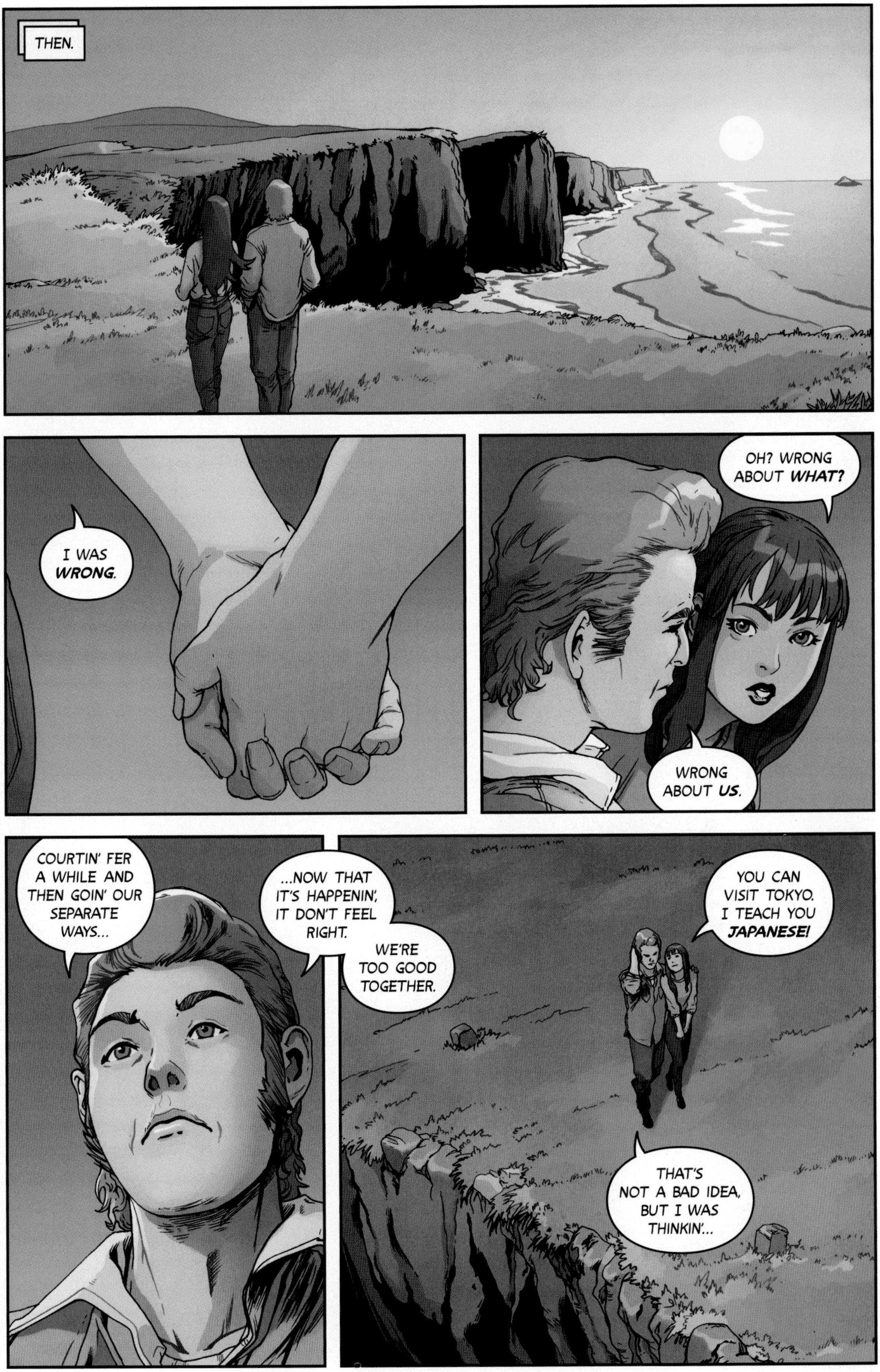
THEN.
I WAS **WRONG.**
OH? WRONG ABOUT **WHAT?**
WRONG ABOUT **US.**
COURTIN' FER A WHILE AND THEN GOIN' OUR SEPARATE WAYS...
...NOW THAT IT'S HAPPENIN', IT DON'T FEEL RIGHT.
WE'RE TOO GOOD TOGETHER.
YOU CAN VISIT TOKYO. I TEACH YOU **JAPANESE!**
THAT'S NOT A BAD IDEA, BUT I WAS THINKIN'...

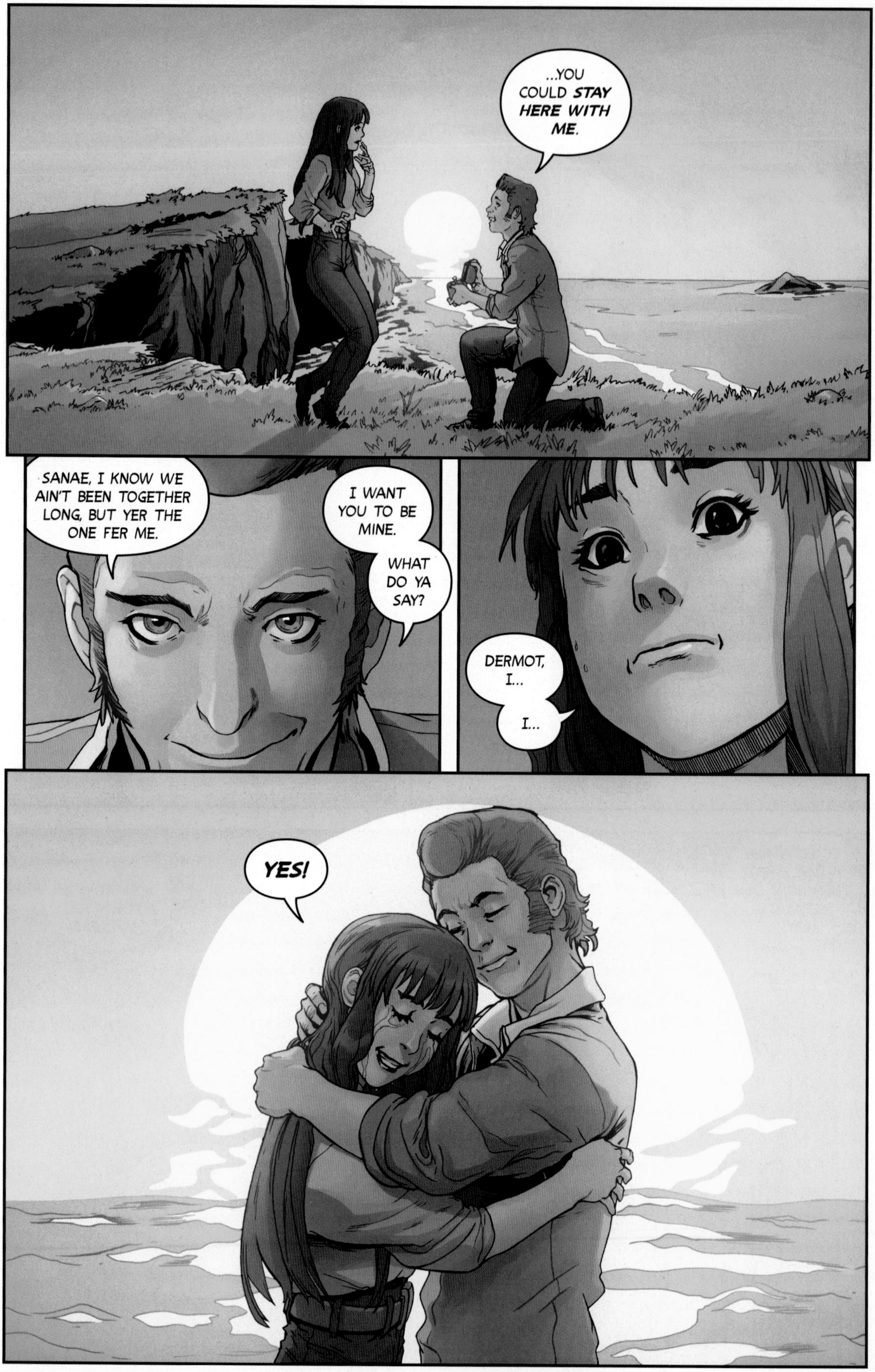
...YOU COULD STAY HERE WITH ME.
SANAE, I KNOW WE AIN'T BEEN TOGETHER LONG, BUT YER THE ONE FER ME.
I WANT YOU TO BE MINE.
WHAT DO YA SAY?
DERMOT, I...
I...
YES!

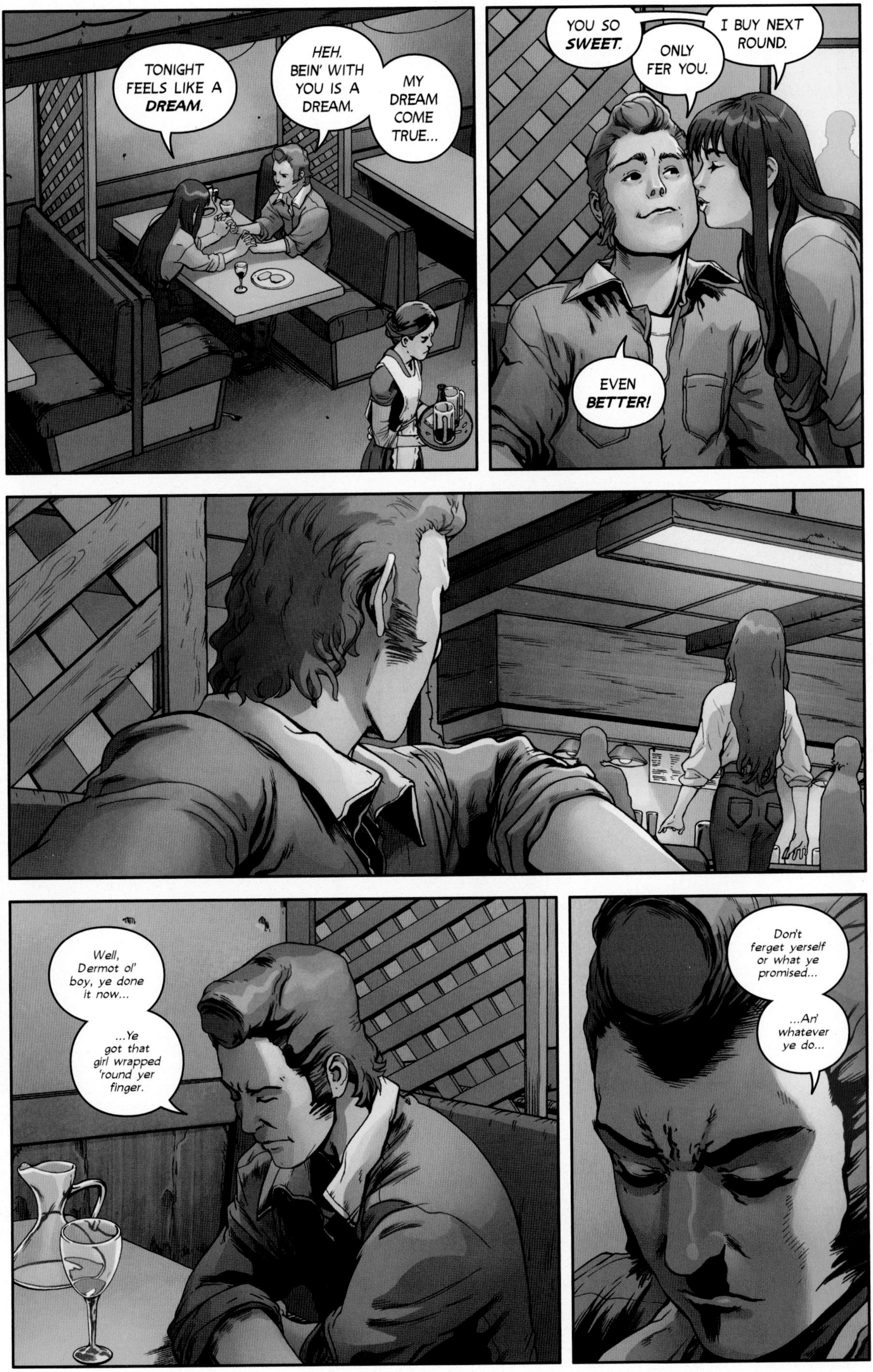
TONIGHT FEELS LIKE A **DREAM**.
HEH. BEIN' WITH YOU IS A DREAM.
MY DREAM COME TRUE...
YOU SO **SWEET**.
ONLY FER YOU.
I BUY NEXT ROUND.
EVEN **BETTER!**
Well, Dermot ol' boy, ye done it now...
...Ye got that girl wrapped 'round yer finger.
Don't ferget yerself or what ye promised...
...An' whatever ye do...

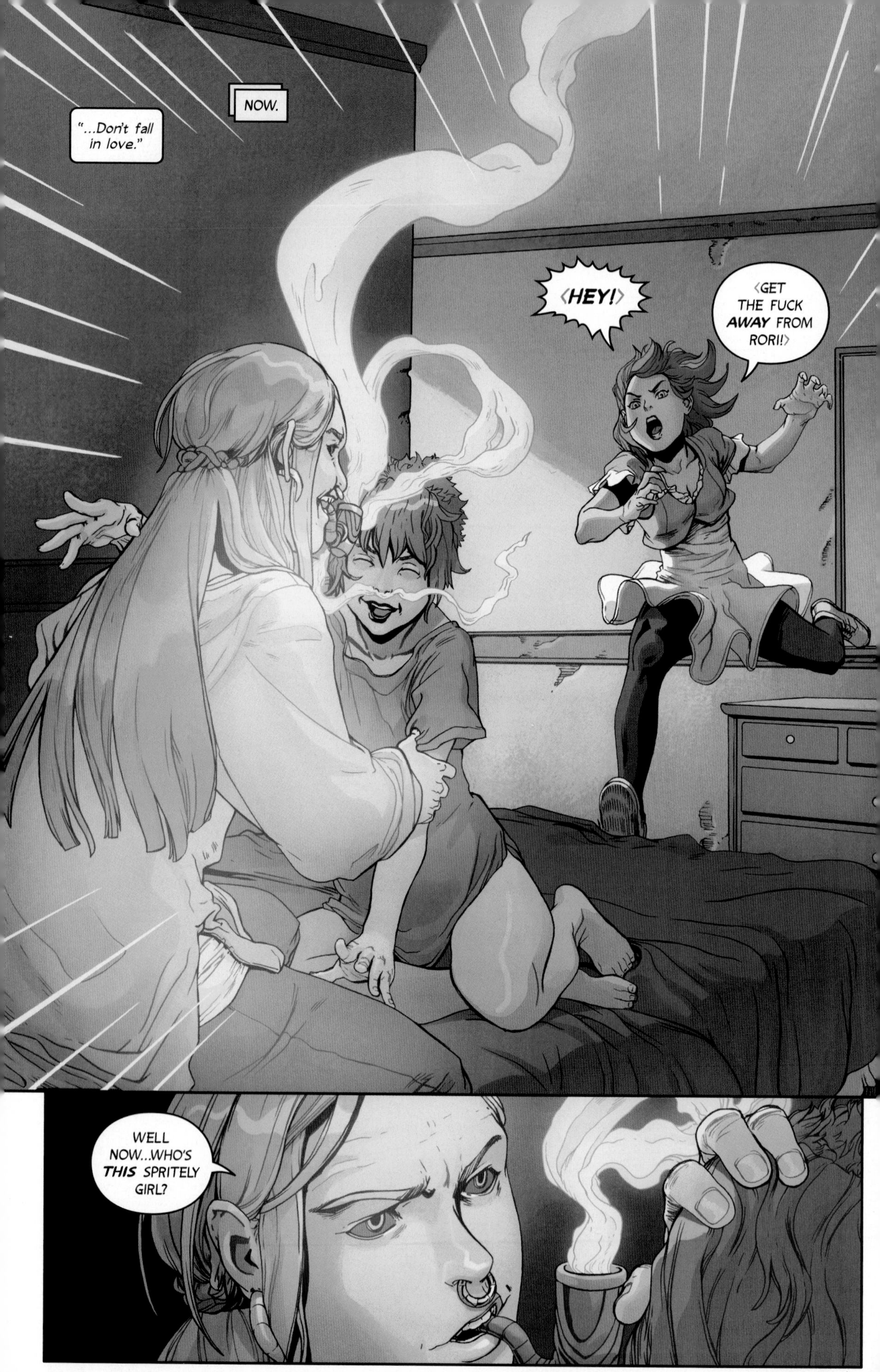
"...Don't fall in love."
NOW.
<**HEY!**>
<GET THE FUCK **AWAY** FROM RORI!>
WELL NOW...WHO'S **THIS** SPRITELY GIRL?

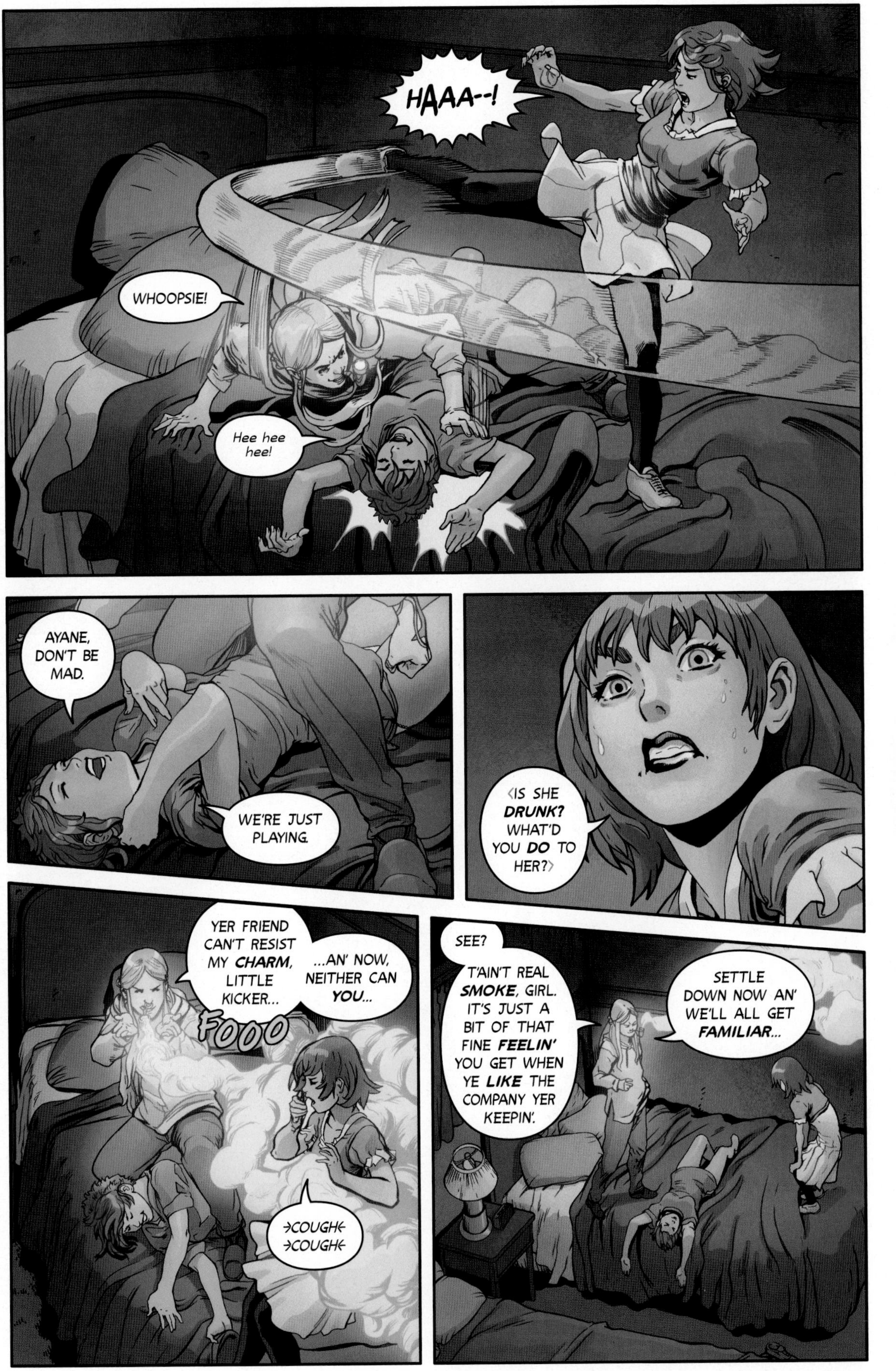
HAAA--!
WHOOPSIE!
Hee hee hee!
AYANE, DON'T BE MAD.
WE'RE JUST PLAYING.
‹IS SHE DRUNK? WHAT'D YOU DO TO HER?›
YER FRIEND CAN'T RESIST MY CHARM, LITTLE KICKER...
...AN' NOW, NEITHER CAN YOU...
FOOO
›COUGH‹ ›COUGH‹
SEE?
T'AIN'T REAL SMOKE, GIRL. IT'S JUST A BIT OF THAT FINE FEELIN' YOU GET WHEN YE LIKE THE COMPANY YER KEEPIN'.
SETTLE DOWN NOW AN' WE'LL ALL GET FAMILIAR...

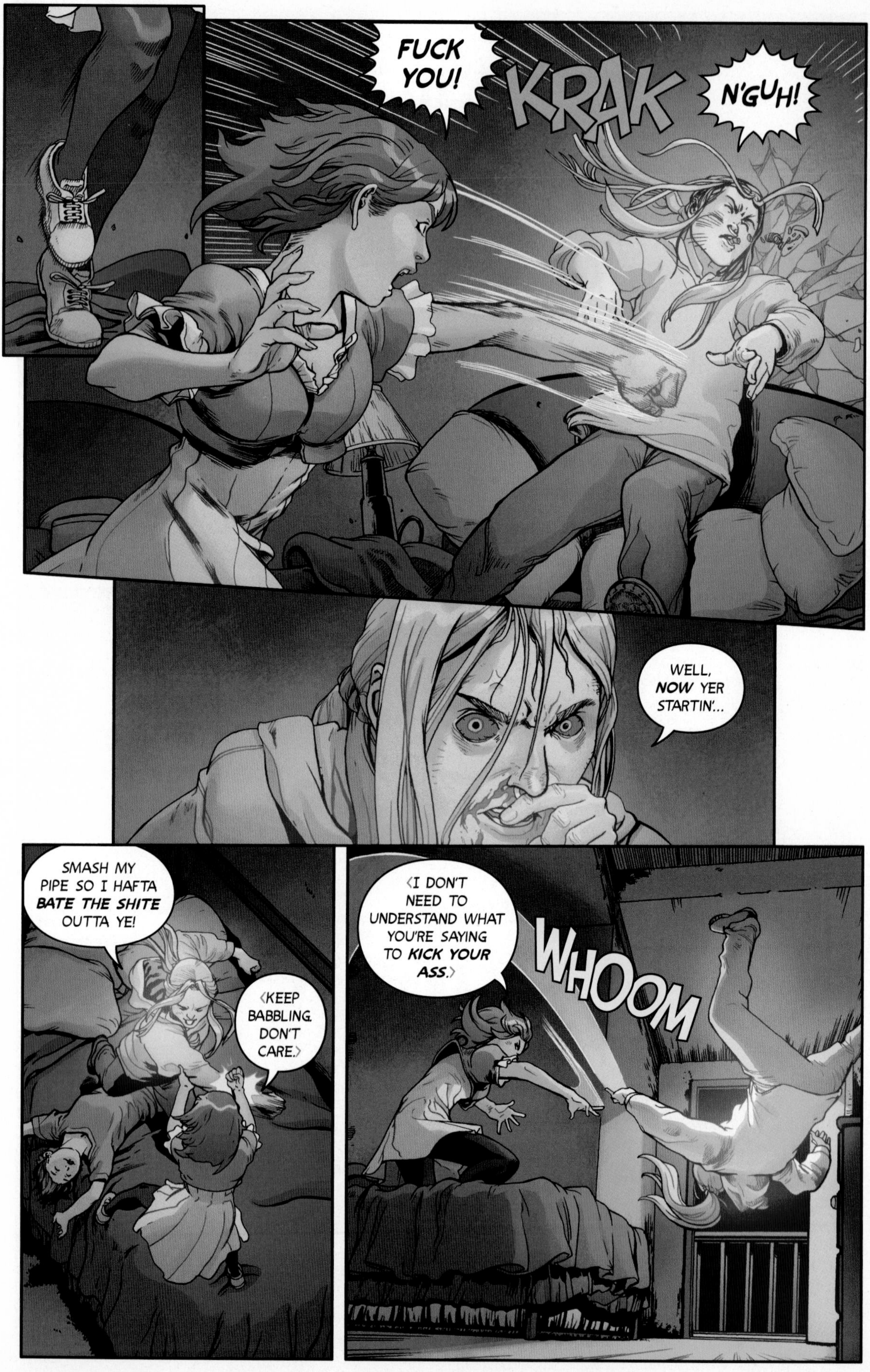
FUCK YOU!
KRAK
N'GUH!
WELL, NOW YER STARTIN'...
SMASH MY PIPE SO I HAFTA BATE THE SHITE OUTTA YE!
‹KEEP BABBLING. DON'T CARE.›
‹I DON'T NEED TO UNDERSTAND WHAT YOU'RE SAYING TO KICK YOUR ASS.›
WHOOM

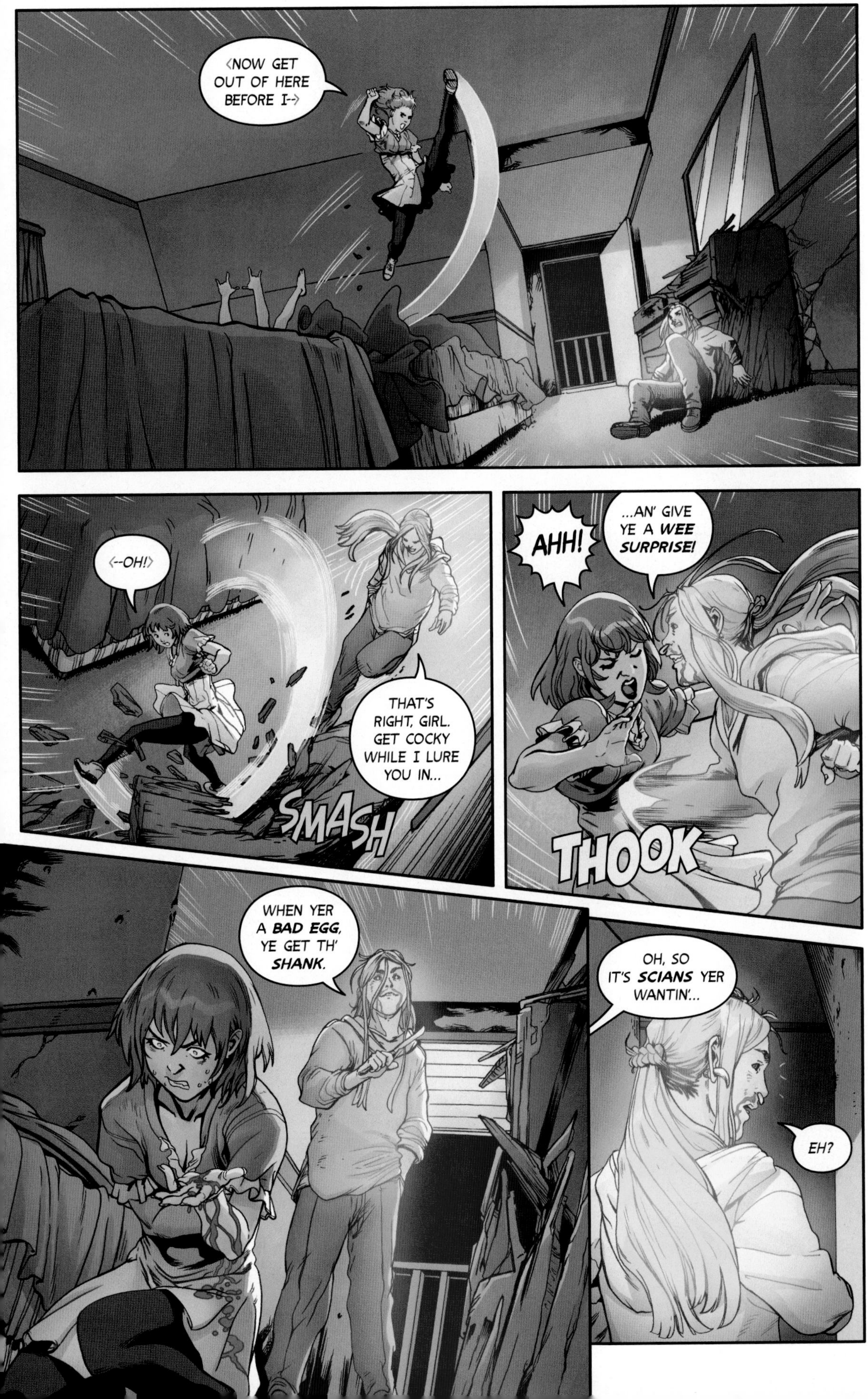
<NOW GET OUT OF HERE BEFORE I-->
<--OH!>
THAT'S RIGHT, GIRL. GET COCKY WHILE I LURE YOU IN...
SMASH
AHH!
...AN' GIVE YE A WEE SURPRISE!
THOOK
WHEN YER A BAD EGG, YE GET TH' SHANK.
OH, SO IT'S SCIANS YER WANTIN'...
EH?

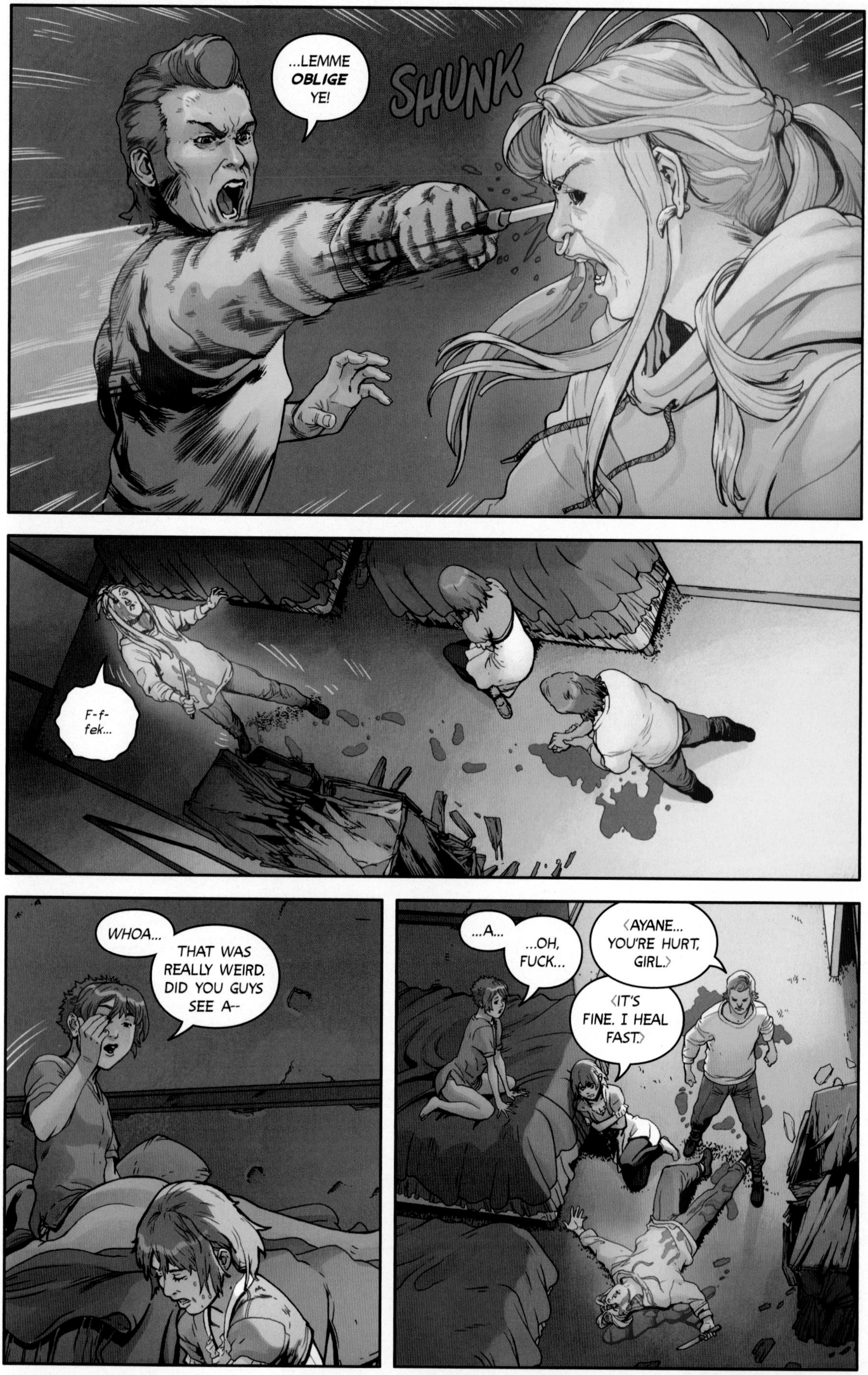

...LEMME OBLIGE YE!
SHUNK
F-f- fek...
WHOA...
THAT WAS REALLY WEIRD. DID YOU GUYS SEE A--
...A...
...OH, FUCK...
‹AYANE... YOU'RE HURT, GIRL.›
‹IT'S FINE. I HEAL FAST.›

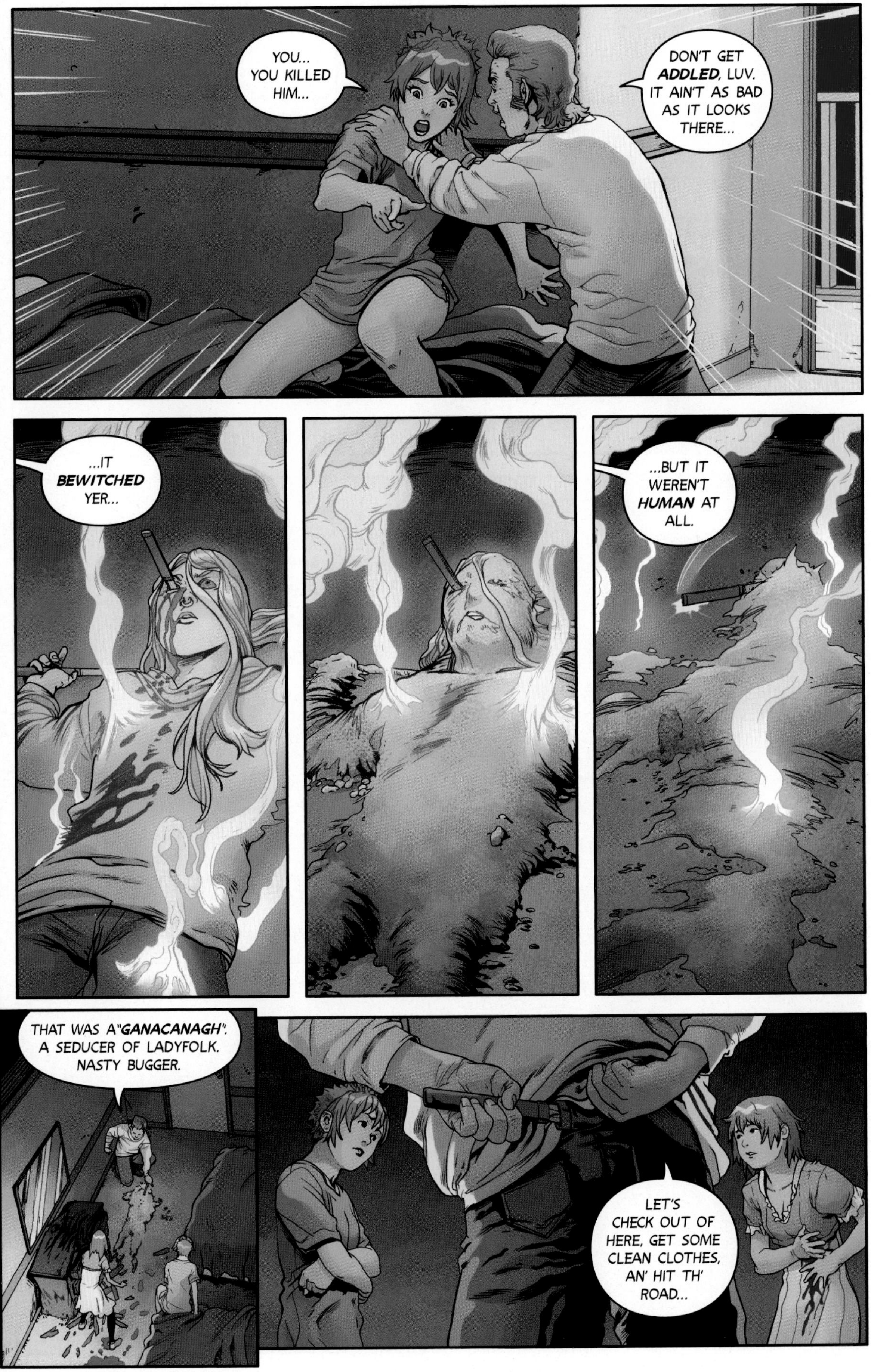
YOU... YOU KILLED HIM...
DON'T GET ADDLED, LUV. IT AIN'T AS BAD AS IT LOOKS THERE...
...IT BEWITCHED YER...
...BUT IT WEREN'T HUMAN AT ALL.
THAT WAS A "GANACANAGH". A SEDUCER OF LADYFOLK. NASTY BUGGER.
LET'S CHECK OUT OF HERE, GET SOME CLEAN CLOTHES, AN' HIT TH' ROAD...

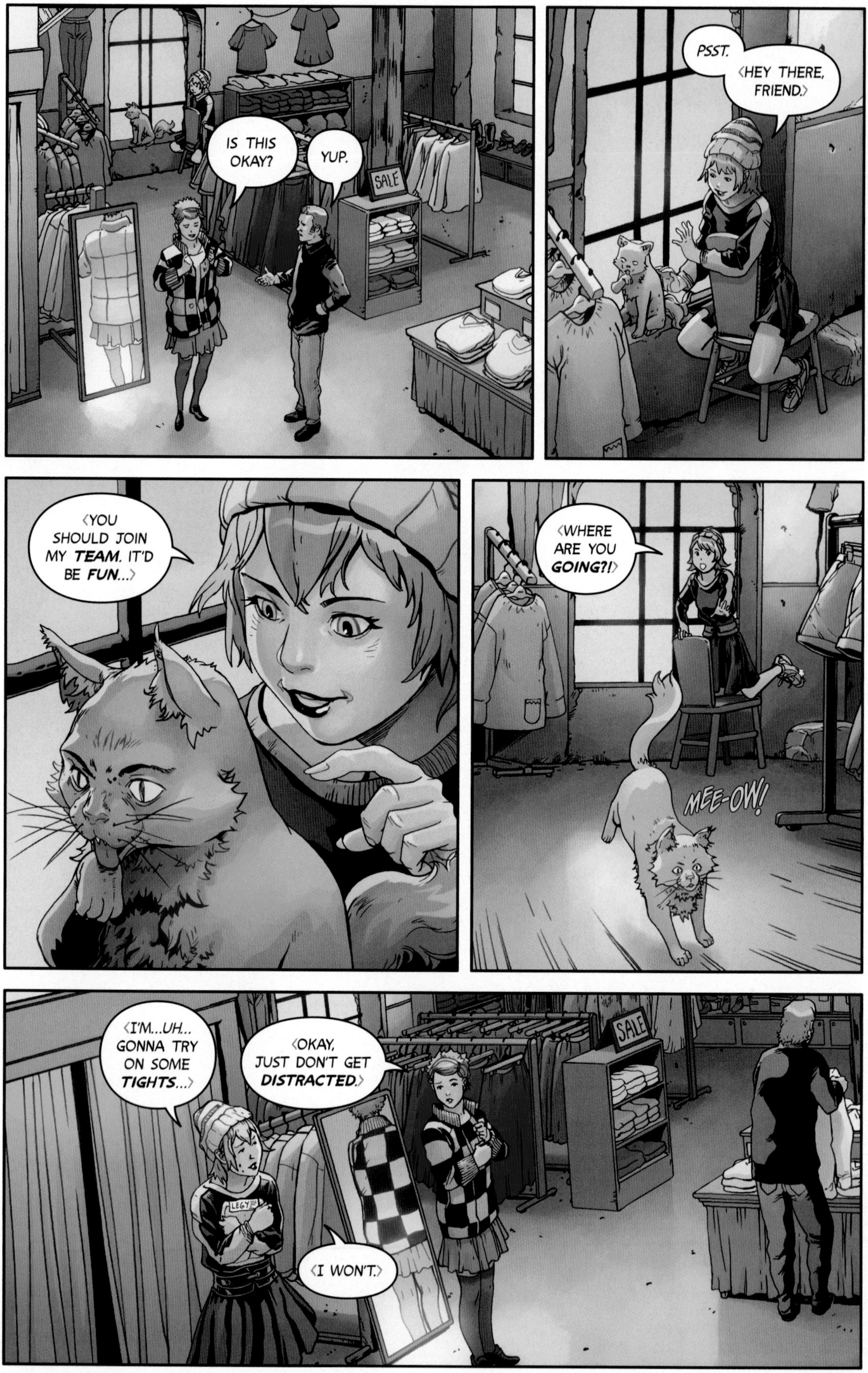
IS THIS OKAY?
YUP.
SALE
PSST.
‹HEY THERE, FRIEND.›
‹YOU SHOULD JOIN MY TEAM. IT'D BE FUN...›
‹WHERE ARE YOU GOING?!›
MEE-OW!
‹I'M...UH... GONNA TRY ON SOME TIGHTS...›
‹OKAY, JUST DON'T GET DISTRACTED.›
SALE
‹I WON'T.›

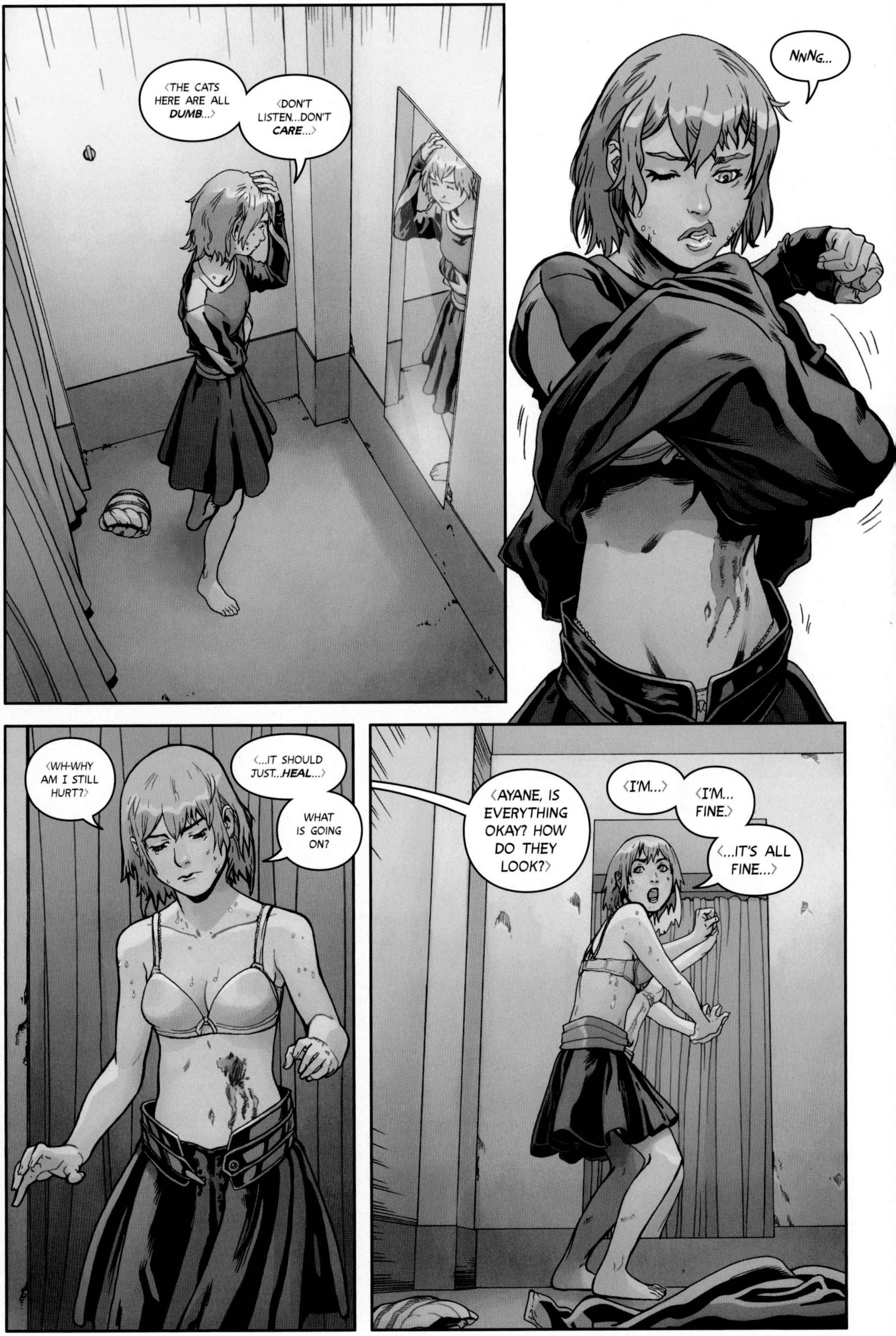

<THE CATS HERE ARE ALL DUMB...>
<DON'T LISTEN...DON'T CARE...>
NNNG...
<WH-WHY AM I STILL HURT?>
<...IT SHOULD JUST...HEAL...>
WHAT IS GOING ON?
<AYANE, IS EVERYTHING OKAY? HOW DO THEY LOOK?>
<I'M...>
<I'M... FINE.>
<...IT'S ALL FINE...>

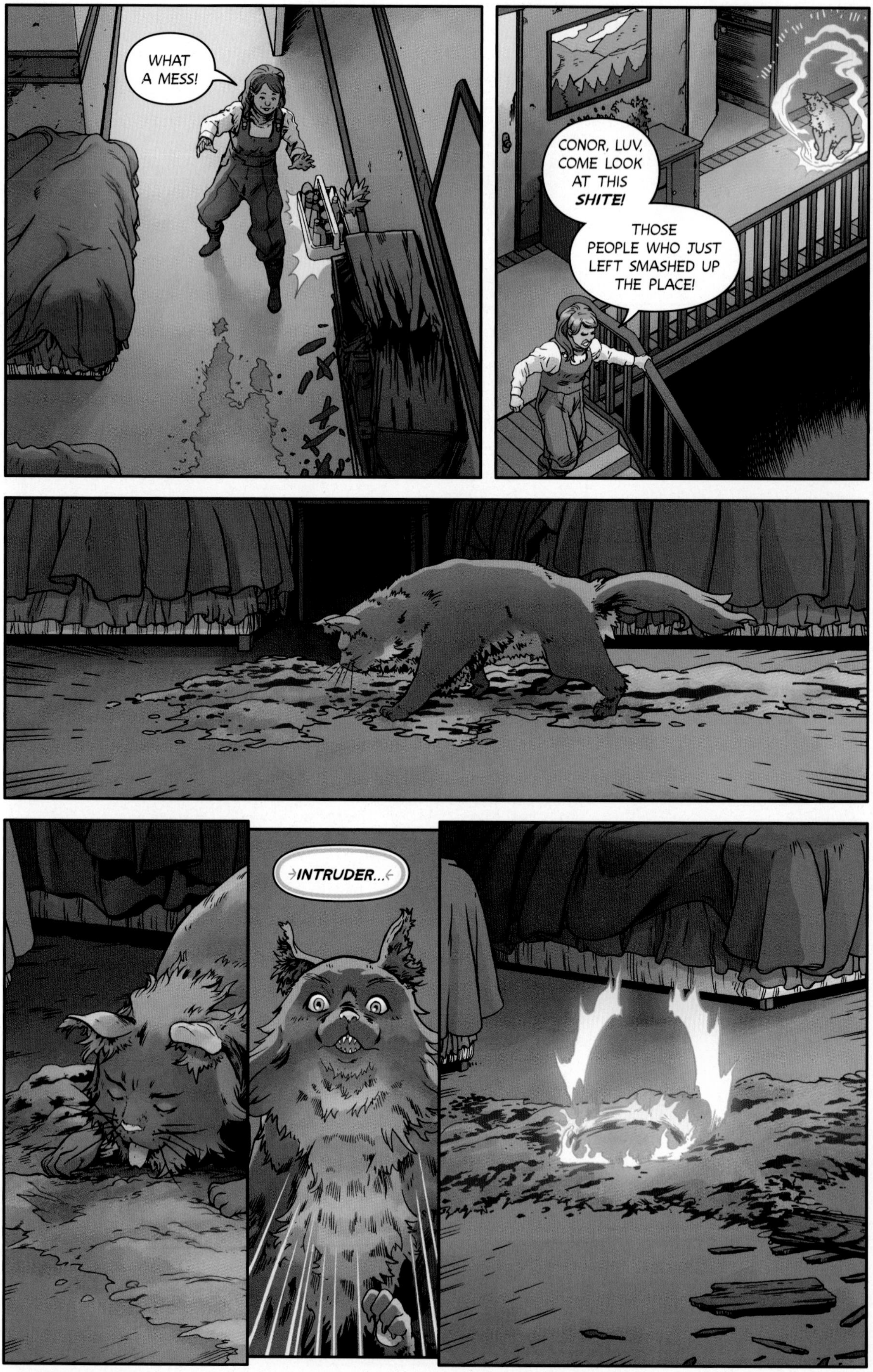
WHAT A MESS!
CONOR, LUV, COME LOOK AT THIS **SHITE!**
THOSE PEOPLE WHO JUST LEFT SMASHED UP THE PLACE!
INTRUDER...

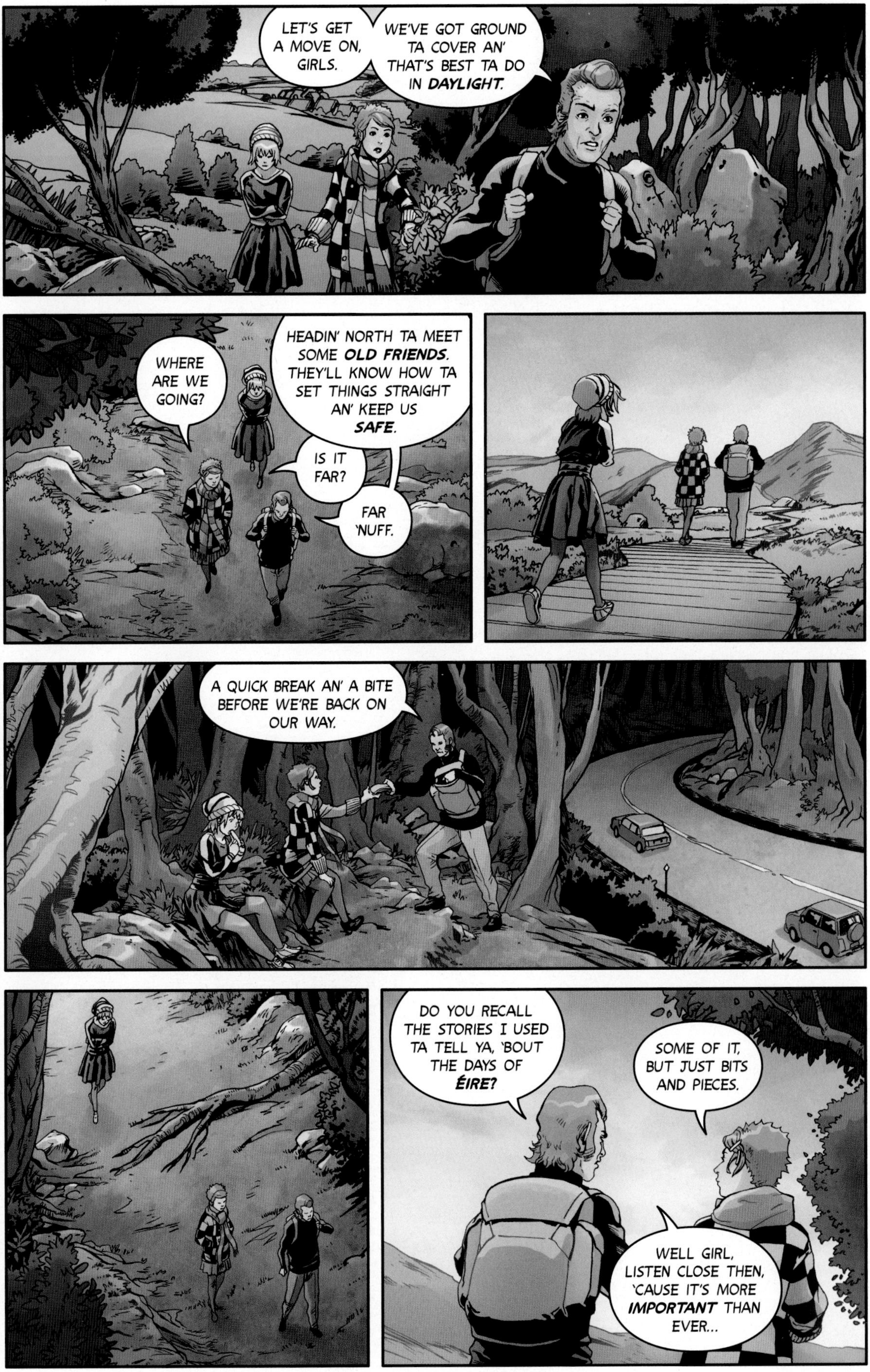
LET'S GET A MOVE ON, GIRLS.
WE'VE GOT GROUND TA COVER AN' THAT'S BEST TA DO IN **DAYLIGHT.**
WHERE ARE WE GOING?
HEADIN' NORTH TA MEET SOME **OLD FRIENDS.** THEY'LL KNOW HOW TA SET THINGS STRAIGHT AN' KEEP US **SAFE.**
IS IT FAR?
FAR 'NUFF.
A QUICK BREAK AN' A BITE BEFORE WE'RE BACK ON OUR WAY.
DO YOU RECALL THE STORIES I USED TA TELL YA, 'BOUT THE DAYS OF **ÉIRE?**
SOME OF IT, BUT JUST BITS AND PIECES.
WELL GIRL, LISTEN CLOSE THEN, 'CAUSE IT'S MORE **IMPORTANT** THAN EVER...

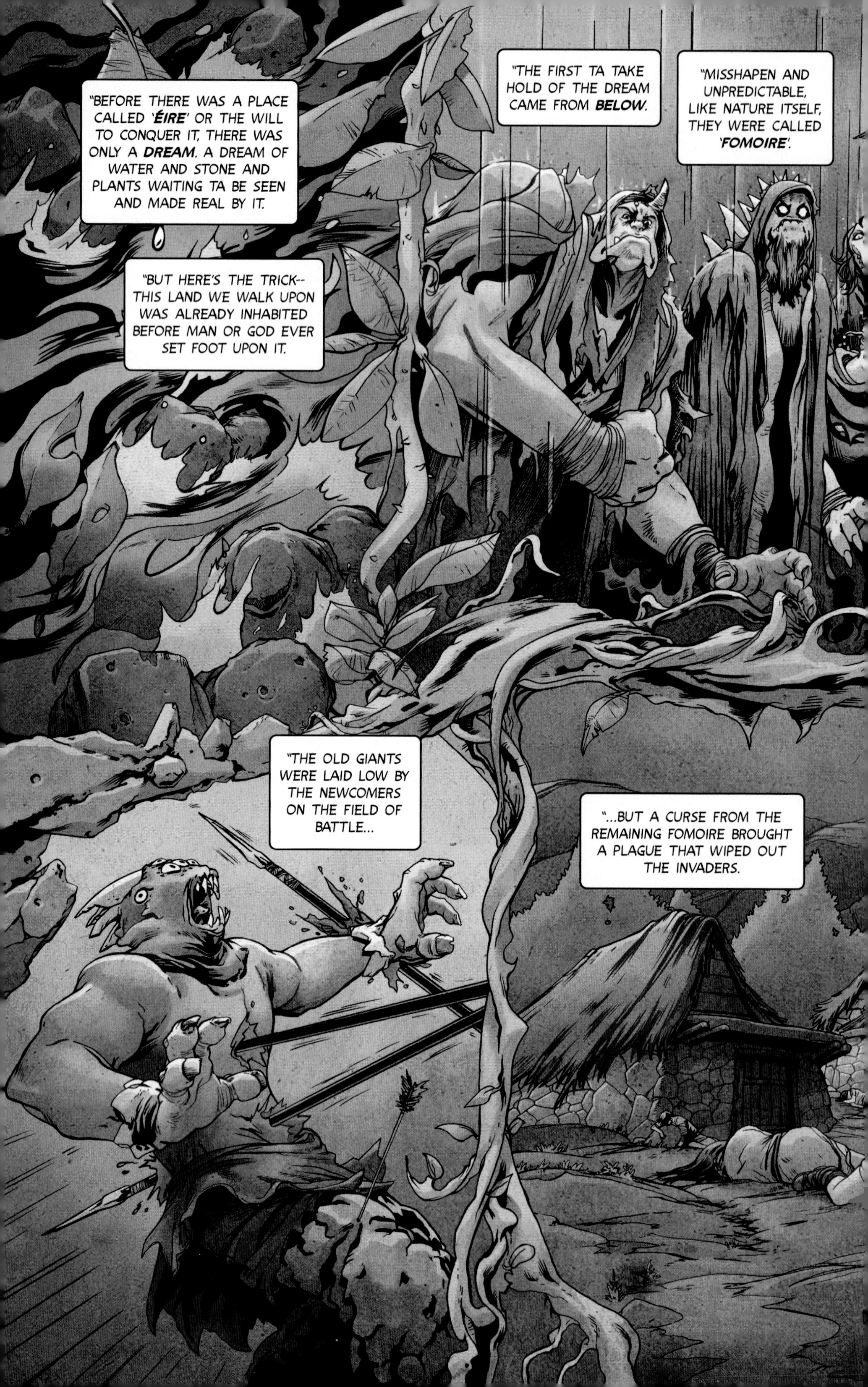
"BEFORE THERE WAS A PLACE CALLED '**ÉIRE**' OR THE WILL TO CONQUER IT, THERE WAS ONLY A **DREAM**. A DREAM OF WATER AND STONE AND PLANTS WAITING TA BE SEEN AND MADE REAL BY IT.
"THE FIRST TA TAKE HOLD OF THE DREAM CAME FROM **BELOW**.
"MISSHAPEN AND UNPREDICTABLE, LIKE NATURE ITSELF, THEY WERE CALLED '**FOMOIRE**'.
"BUT HERE'S THE TRICK-- THIS LAND WE WALK UPON WAS ALREADY INHABITED BEFORE MAN OR GOD EVER SET FOOT UPON IT.
"THE OLD GIANTS WERE LAID LOW BY THE NEWCOMERS ON THE FIELD OF BATTLE...
"...BUT A CURSE FROM THE REMAINING FOMOIRE BROUGHT A PLAGUE THAT WIPED OUT THE INVADERS.

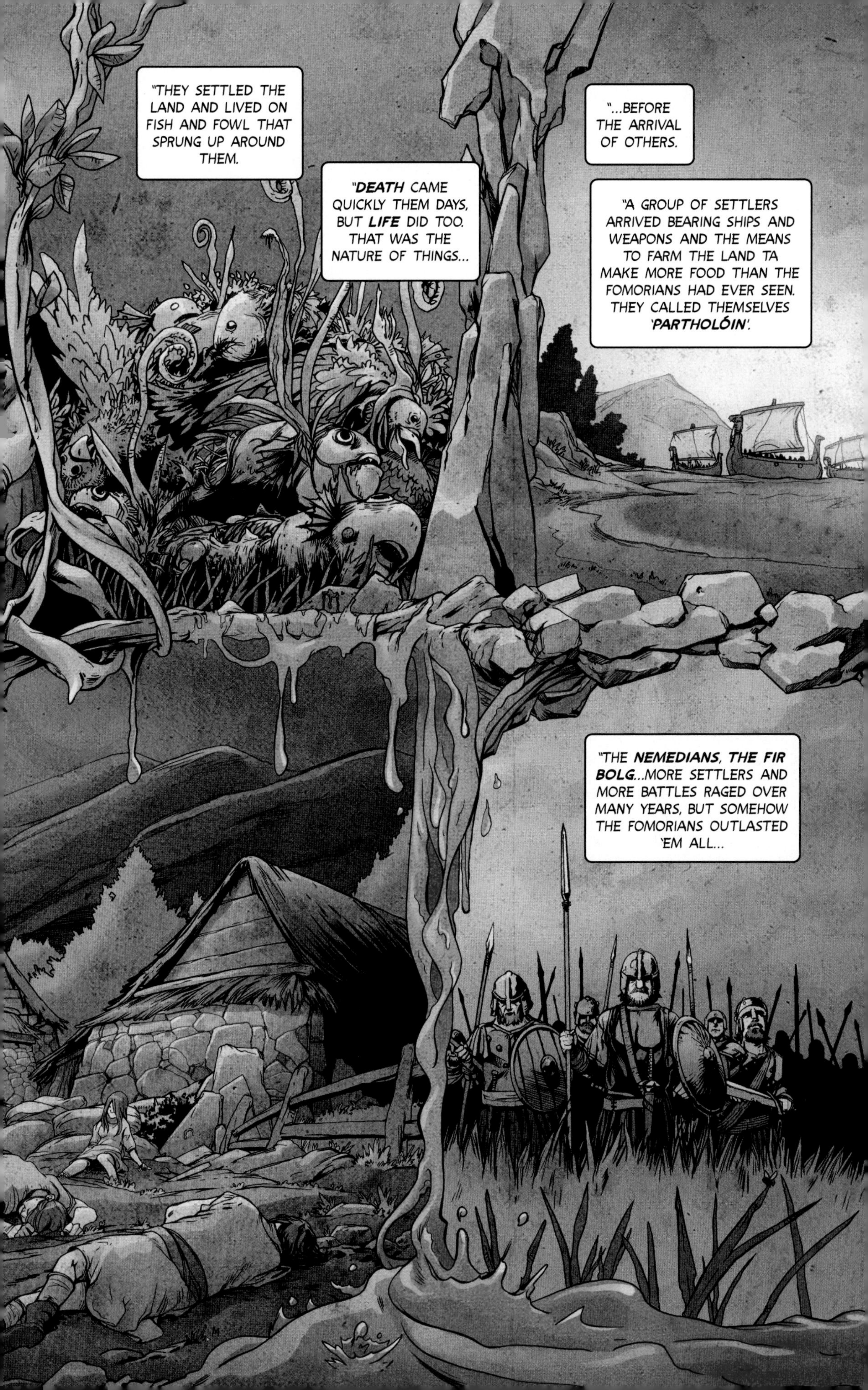
"THEY SETTLED THE LAND AND LIVED ON FISH AND FOWL THAT SPRUNG UP AROUND THEM.
"DEATH CAME QUICKLY THEM DAYS, BUT LIFE DID TOO. THAT WAS THE NATURE OF THINGS...
"...BEFORE THE ARRIVAL OF OTHERS.
"A GROUP OF SETTLERS ARRIVED BEARING SHIPS AND WEAPONS AND THE MEANS TO FARM THE LAND TA MAKE MORE FOOD THAN THE FOMORIANS HAD EVER SEEN. THEY CALLED THEMSELVES 'PARTHOLÓIN'.
"THE NEMEDIANS, THE FIR BOLG...MORE SETTLERS AND MORE BATTLES RAGED OVER MANY YEARS, BUT SOMEHOW THE FOMORIANS OUTLASTED 'EM ALL...

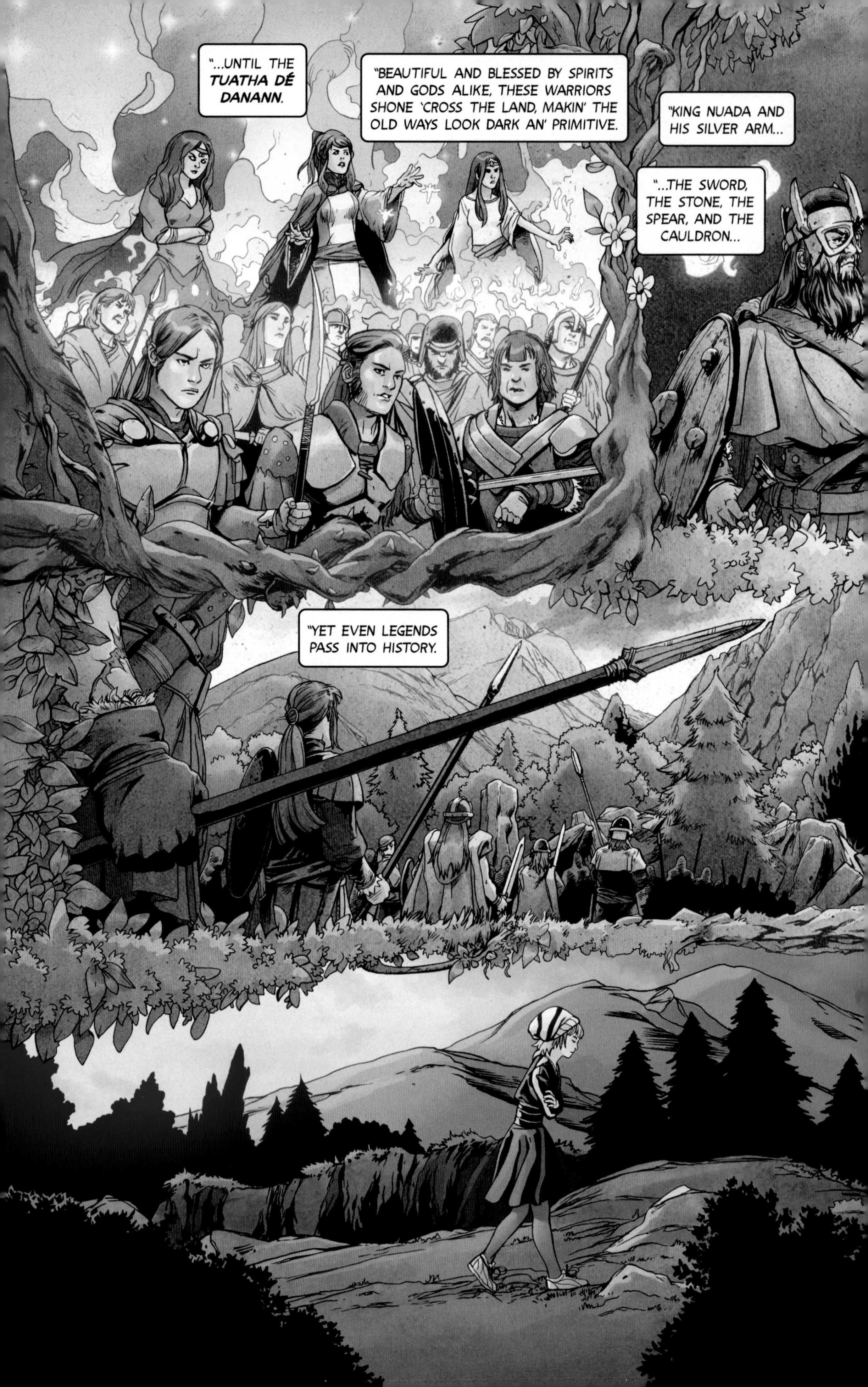
"...UNTIL THE *TUATHA DÉ DANANN.*
"BEAUTIFUL AND BLESSED BY SPIRITS AND GODS ALIKE, THESE WARRIORS SHONE 'CROSS THE LAND, MAKIN' THE OLD WAYS LOOK DARK AN' PRIMITIVE.
"KING NUADA AND HIS SILVER ARM...
"...THE SWORD, THE STONE, THE SPEAR, AND THE CAULDRON...
"YET EVEN LEGENDS PASS INTO HISTORY.

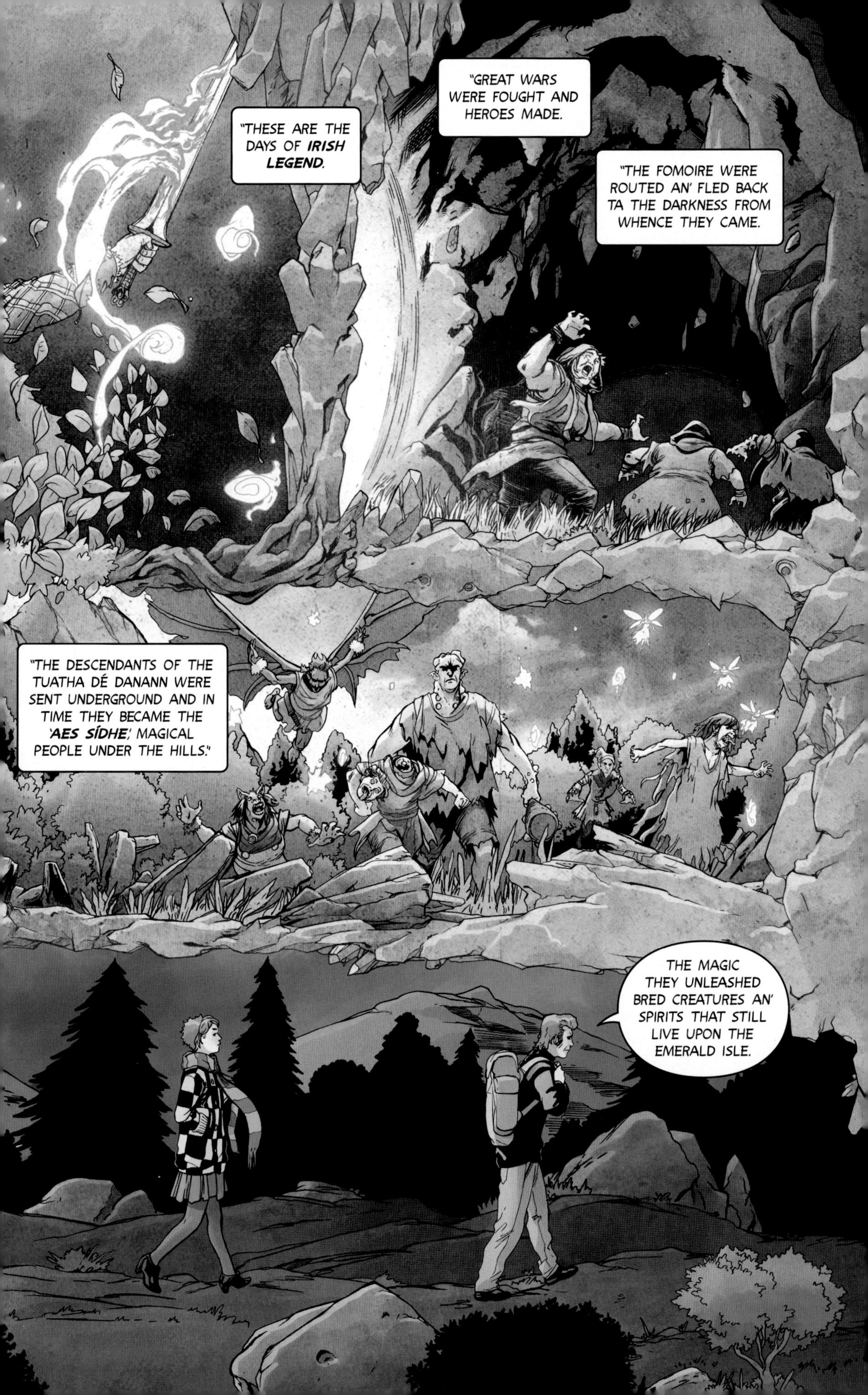
"THESE ARE THE DAYS OF *IRISH LEGEND*.
"GREAT WARS WERE FOUGHT AND HEROES MADE.
"THE FOMOIRE WERE ROUTED AN' FLED BACK TA THE DARKNESS FROM WHENCE THEY CAME.
"THE DESCENDANTS OF THE TUATHA DÉ DANANN WERE SENT UNDERGROUND AND IN TIME THEY BECAME THE '*AES SÍDHE*,' MAGICAL PEOPLE UNDER THE HILLS."
THE MAGIC THEY UNLEASHED BRED CREATURES AN' SPIRITS THAT STILL LIVE UPON THE EMERALD ISLE.

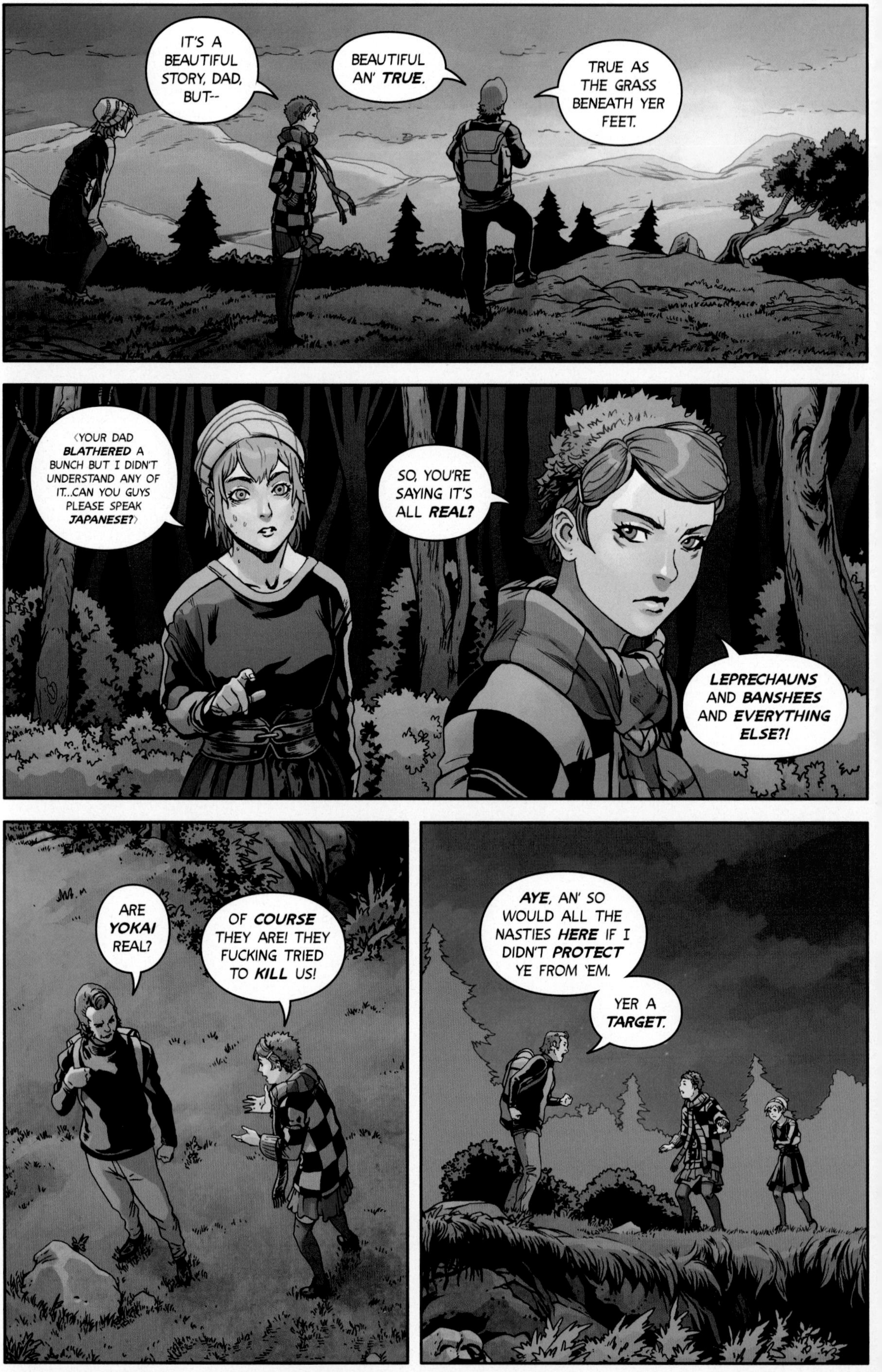
IT'S A BEAUTIFUL STORY, DAD, BUT--
BEAUTIFUL AN' TRUE.
TRUE AS THE GRASS BENEATH YER FEET.
‹YOUR DAD BLATHERED A BUNCH BUT I DIDN'T UNDERSTAND ANY OF IT...CAN YOU GUYS PLEASE SPEAK JAPANESE?›
SO, YOU'RE SAYING IT'S ALL REAL?
LEPRECHAUNS AND BANSHEES AND EVERYTHING ELSE?!
ARE YOKAI REAL?
OF COURSE THEY ARE! THEY FUCKING TRIED TO KILL US!
AYE, AN' SO WOULD ALL THE NASTIES HERE IF I DIDN'T PROTECT YE FROM 'EM.
YER A TARGET.

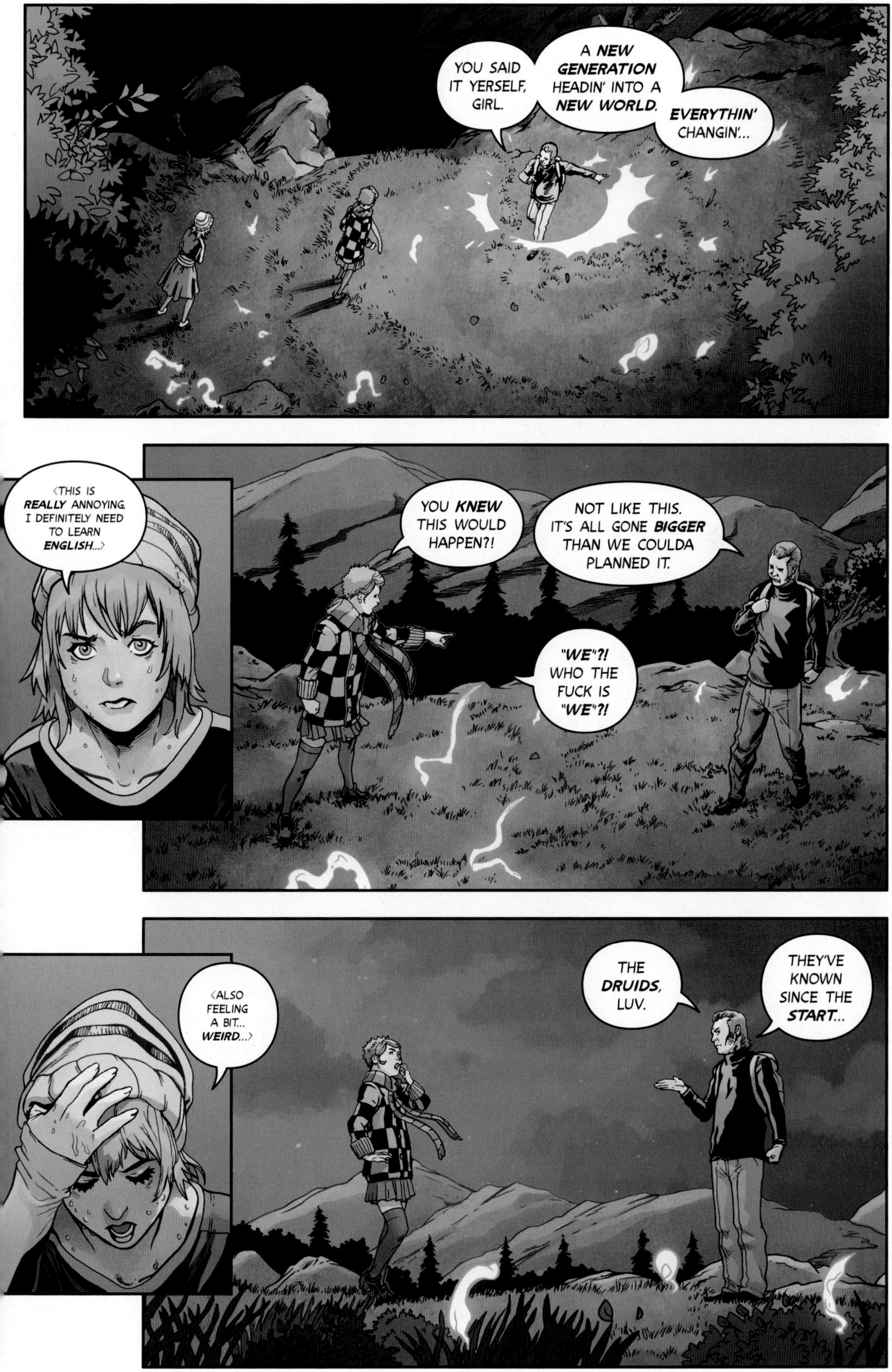
YOU SAID IT YERSELF, GIRL.
A NEW GENERATION HEADIN' INTO A NEW WORLD.
EVERYTHIN' CHANGIN'...
‹THIS IS REALLY ANNOYING. I DEFINITELY NEED TO LEARN ENGLISH...›
YOU KNEW THIS WOULD HAPPEN?!
NOT LIKE THIS. IT'S ALL GONE BIGGER THAN WE COULDA PLANNED IT.
"WE"?! WHO THE FUCK IS "WE"?!
‹ALSO FEELING A BIT... WEIRD...›
THE DRUIDS, LUV.
THEY'VE KNOWN SINCE THE START...

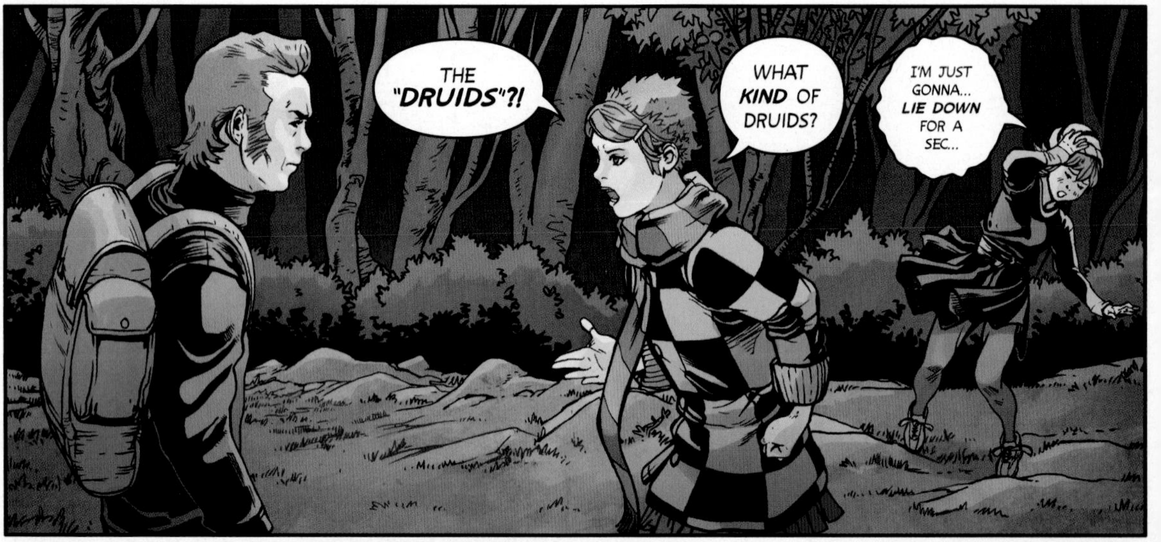
THE "DRUIDS"?!
WHAT KIND OF DRUIDS?
I'M JUST GONNA... LIE DOWN FOR A SEC...

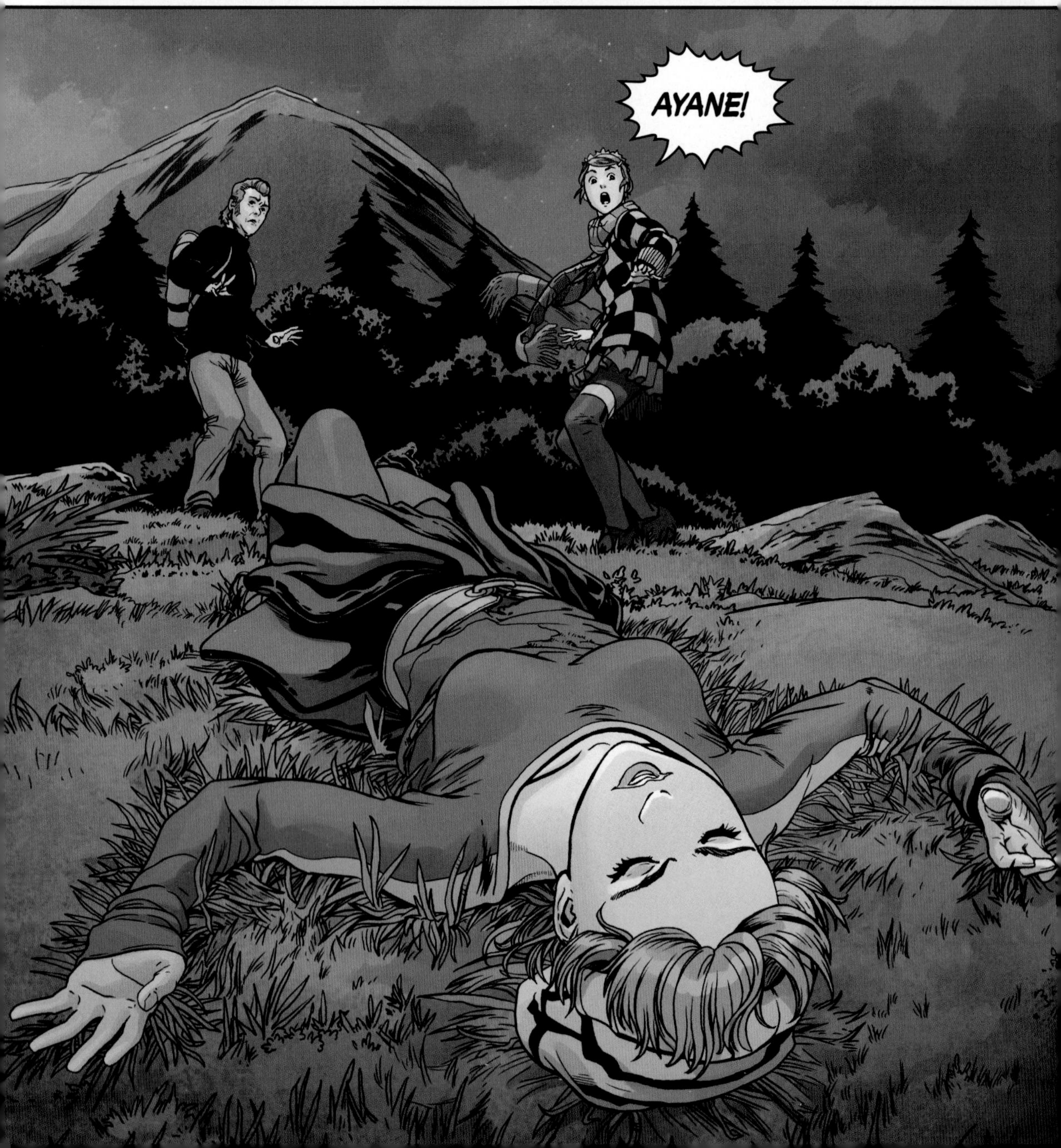
AYANE!

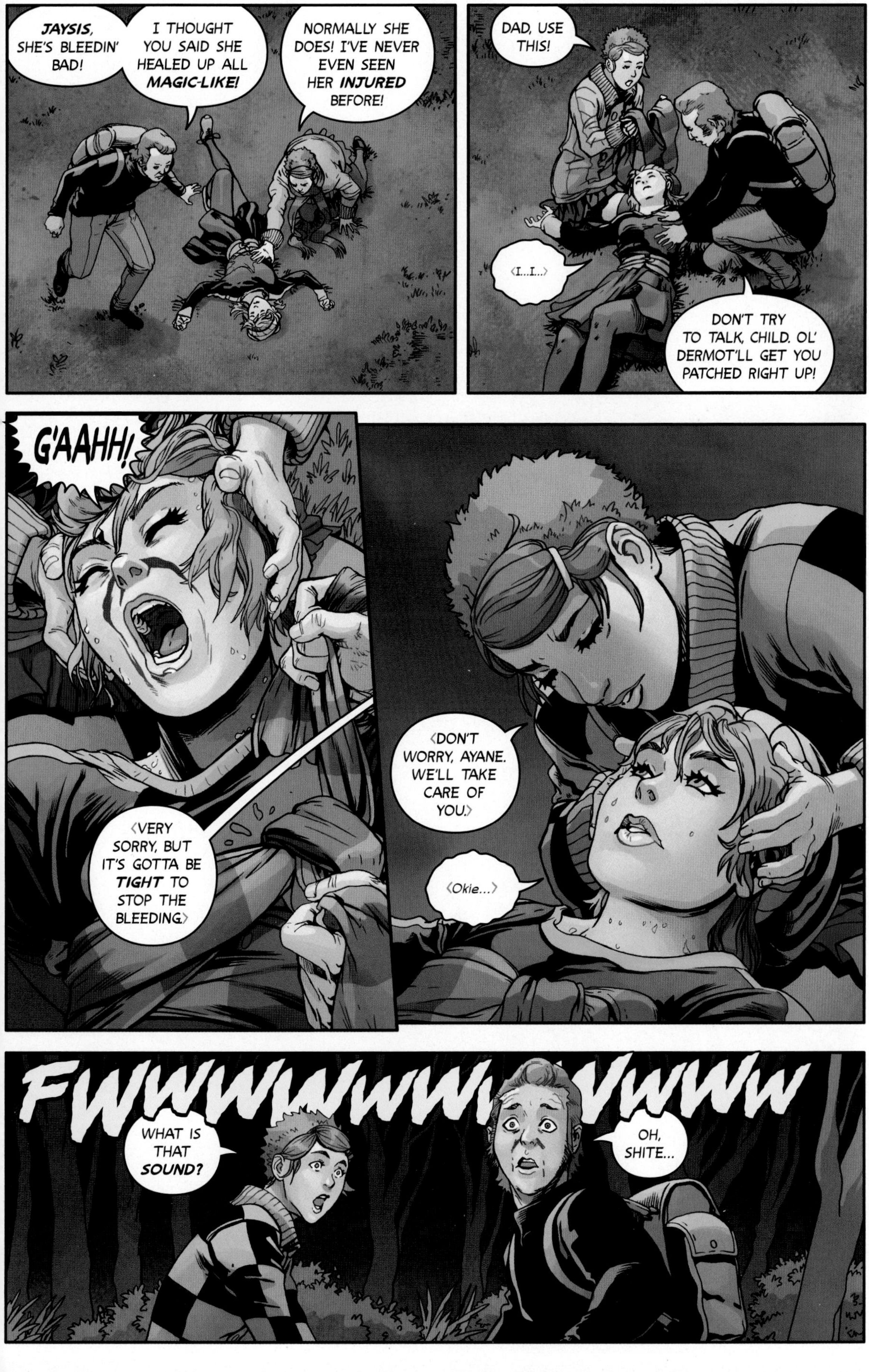

JAYSIS, SHE'S BLEEDIN' BAD!
I THOUGHT YOU SAID SHE HEALED UP ALL MAGIC-LIKE!
NORMALLY SHE DOES! I'VE NEVER EVEN SEEN HER INJURED BEFORE!
DAD, USE THIS!
‹I...I...›
DON'T TRY TO TALK, CHILD. OL' DERMOT'LL GET YOU PATCHED RIGHT UP!
G'AAHH!
‹VERY SORRY, BUT IT'S GOTTA BE TIGHT TO STOP THE BLEEDING.›
‹DON'T WORRY, AYANE. WE'LL TAKE CARE OF YOU.›
‹Okie...›
FWWWWWWWWWWWWWW
WHAT IS THAT SOUND?
OH, SHITE...

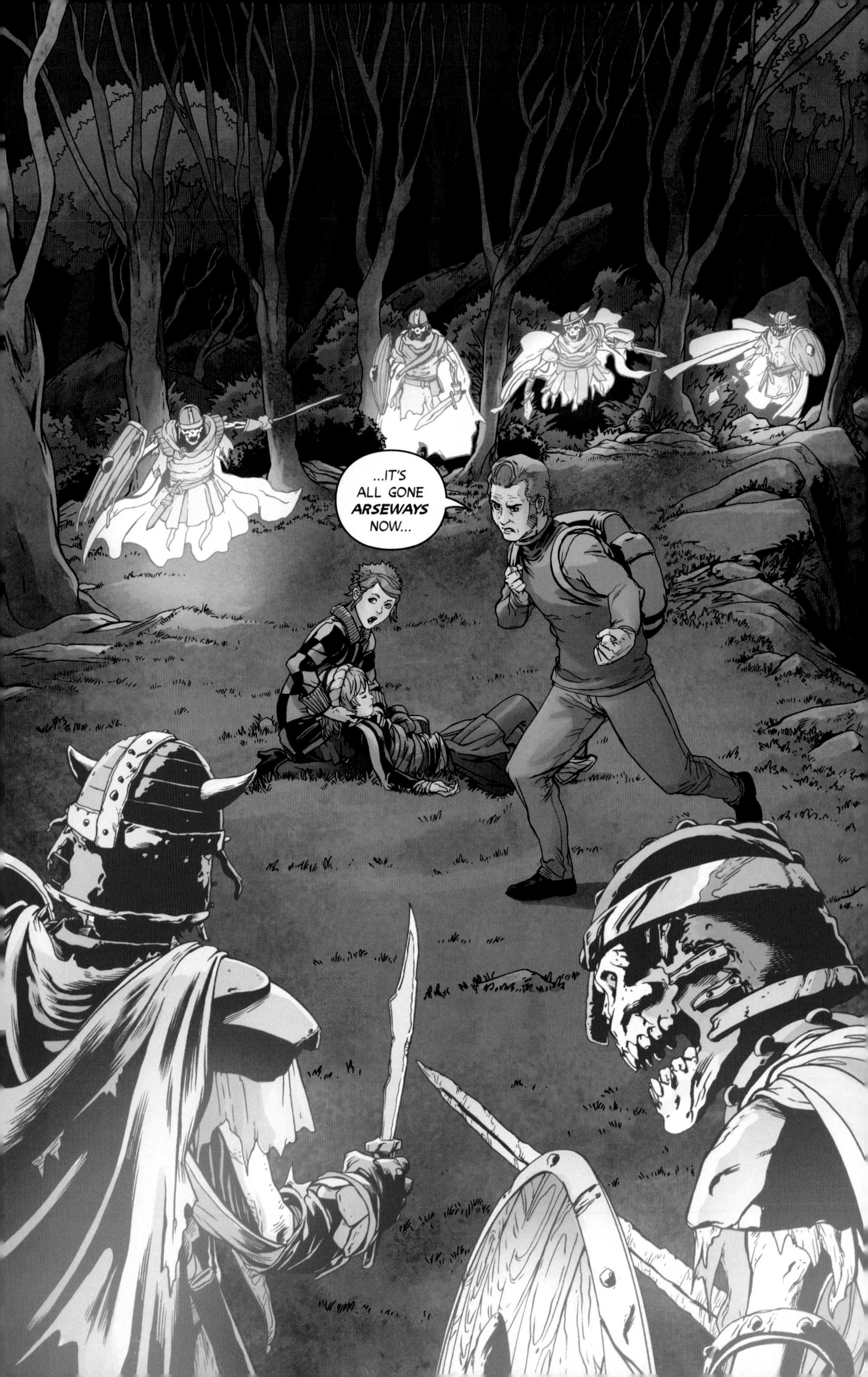
...IT'S ALL GONE ARSEWAYS NOW...

Chapter Nineteen

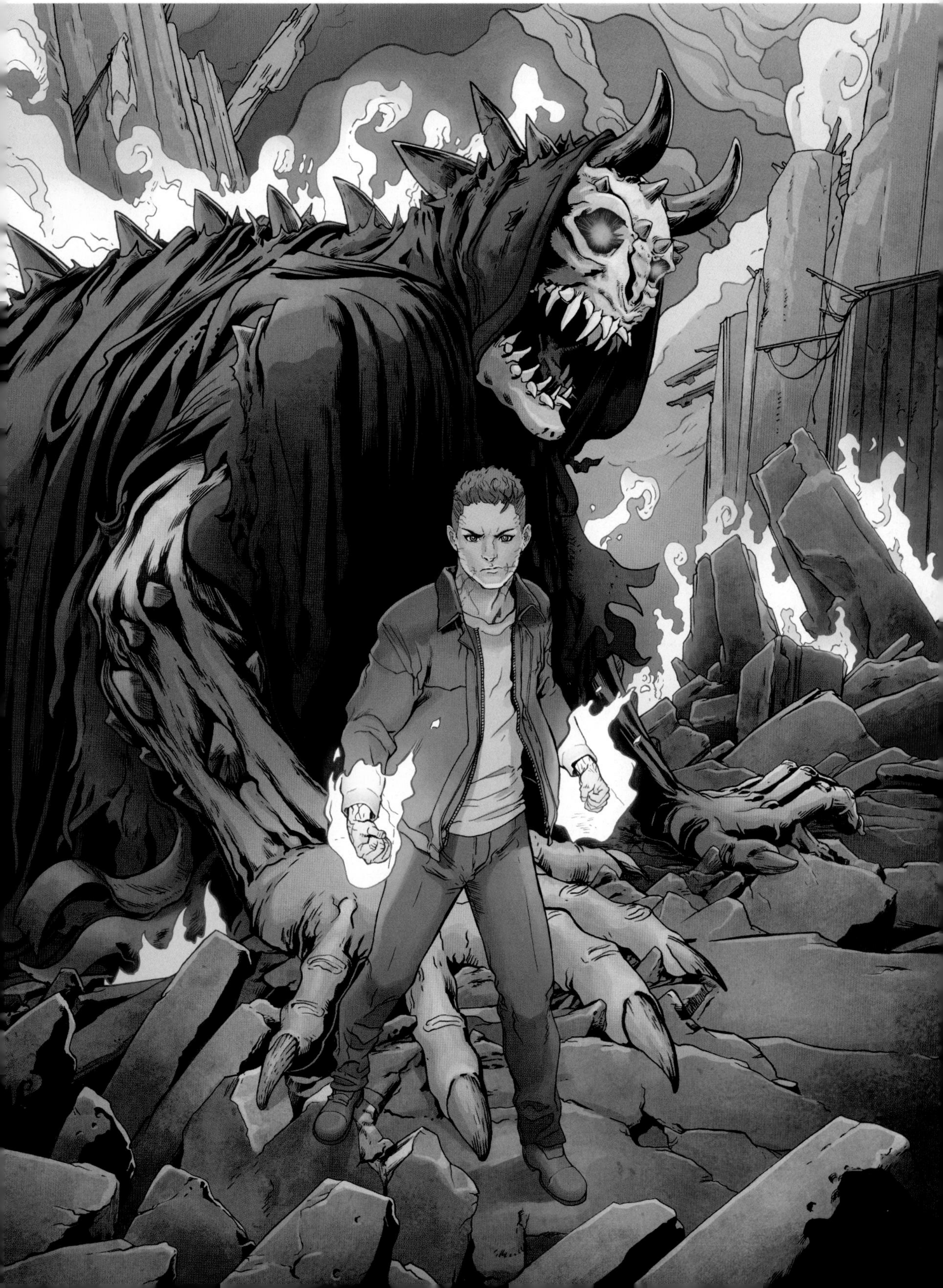

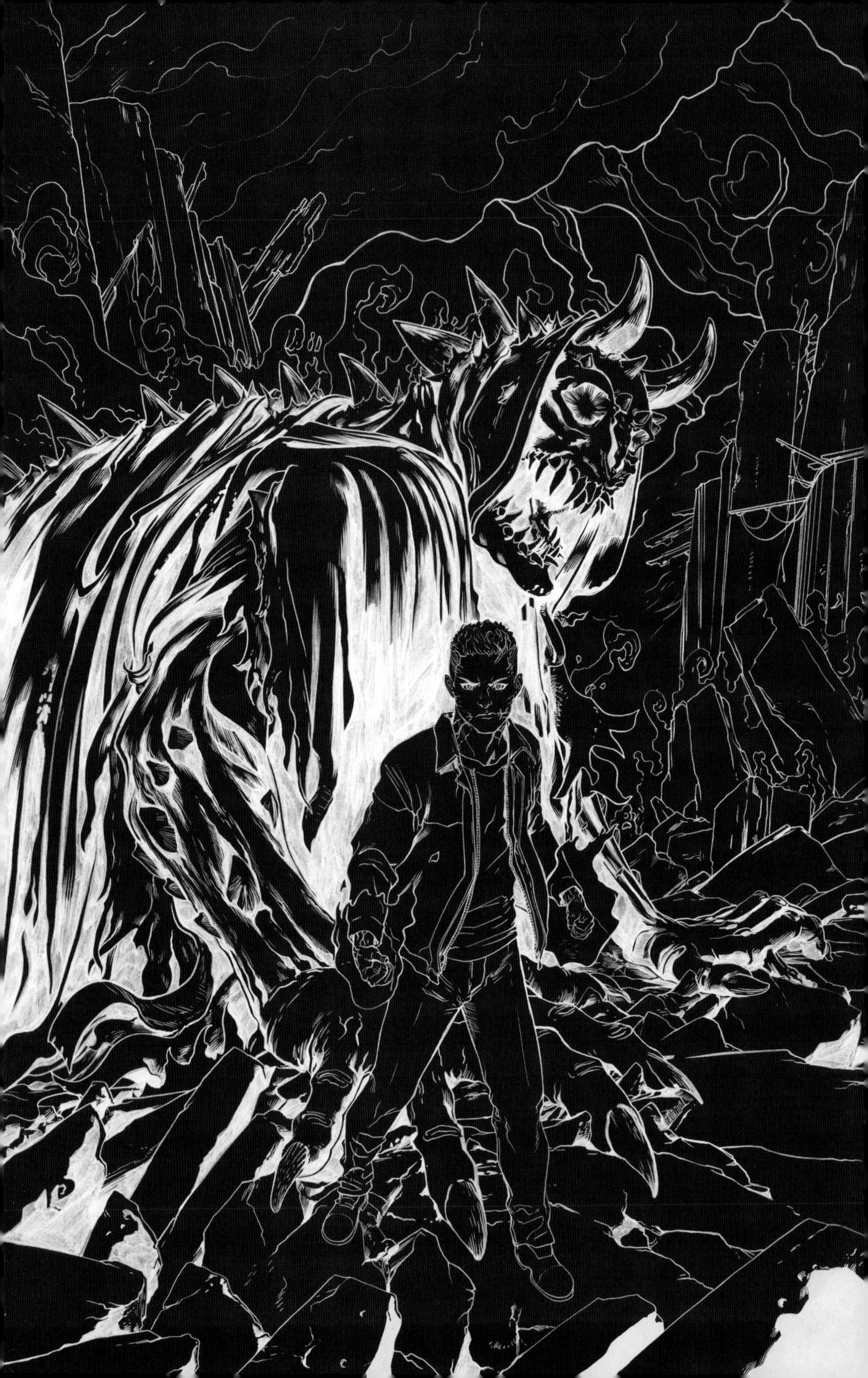

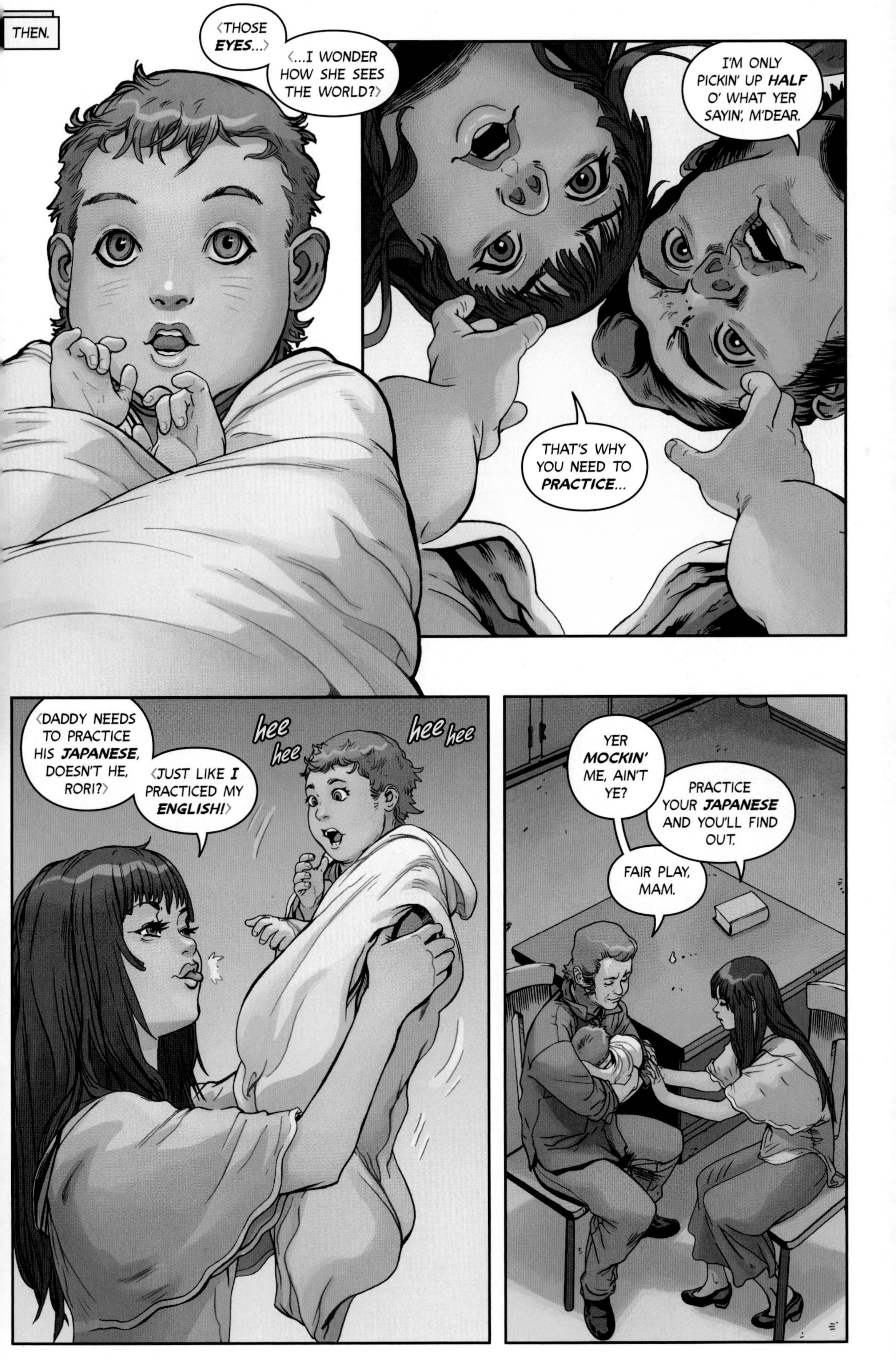
THEN.
⟨THOSE EYES...⟩
⟨...I WONDER HOW SHE SEES THE WORLD?⟩
I'M ONLY PICKIN' UP HALF O' WHAT YER SAYIN', M'DEAR.
THAT'S WHY YOU NEED TO PRACTICE...
⟨DADDY NEEDS TO PRACTICE HIS JAPANESE, DOESN'T HE, RORI?⟩
⟨JUST LIKE I PRACTICED MY ENGLISH!⟩
hee hee
hee hee
YER MOCKIN' ME, AIN'T YE?
PRACTICE YOUR JAPANESE AND YOU'LL FIND OUT.
FAIR PLAY, MAM.

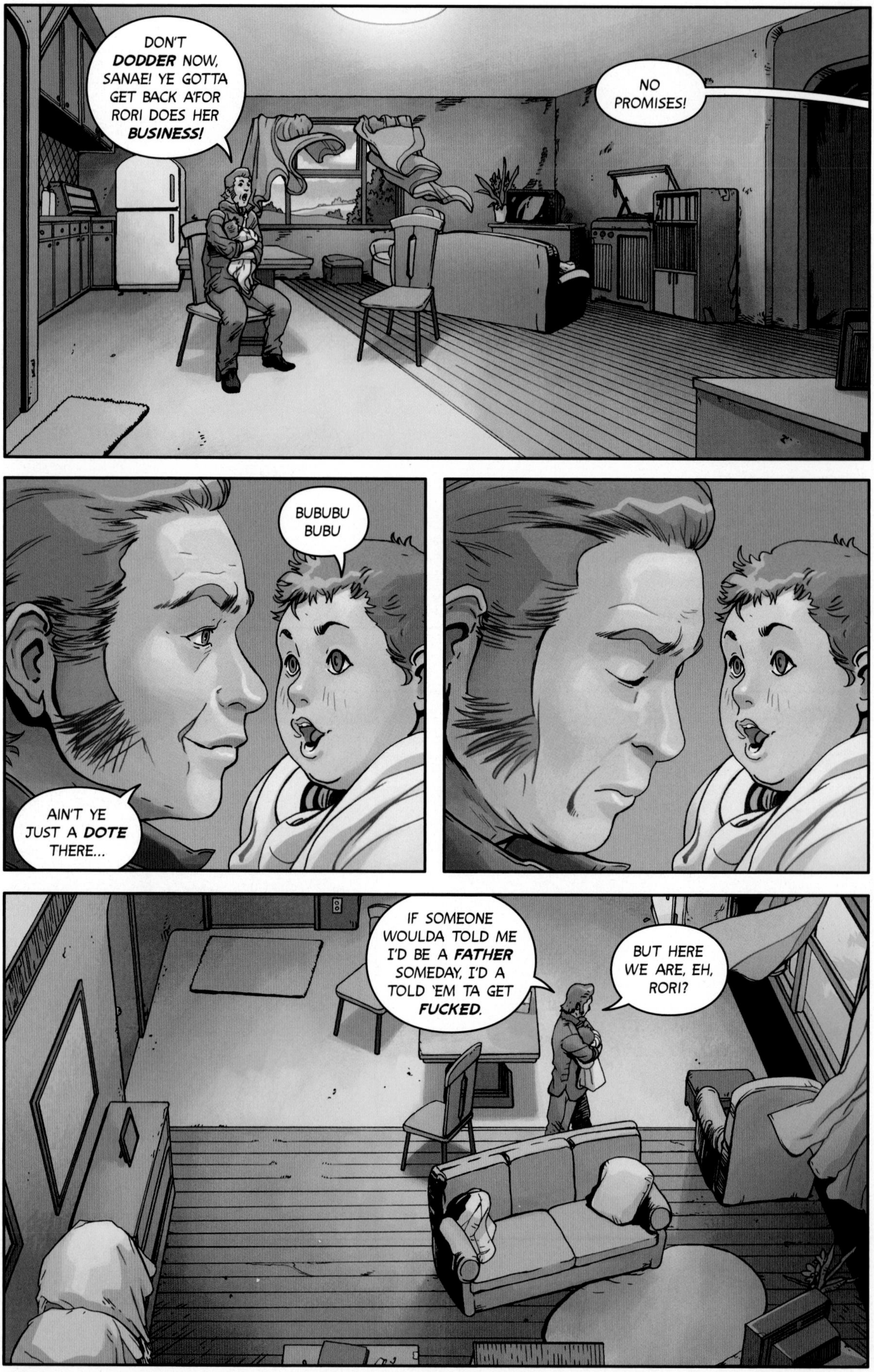
DON'T DODDER NOW, SANAE! YE GOTTA GET BACK A'FOR RORI DOES HER BUSINESS!
NO PROMISES!
BUBUBU BUBU
AIN'T YE JUST A DOTE THERE...
IF SOMEONE WOULDA TOLD ME I'D BE A FATHER SOMEDAY, I'D A TOLD 'EM TA GET FUCKED.
BUT HERE WE ARE, EH, RORI?

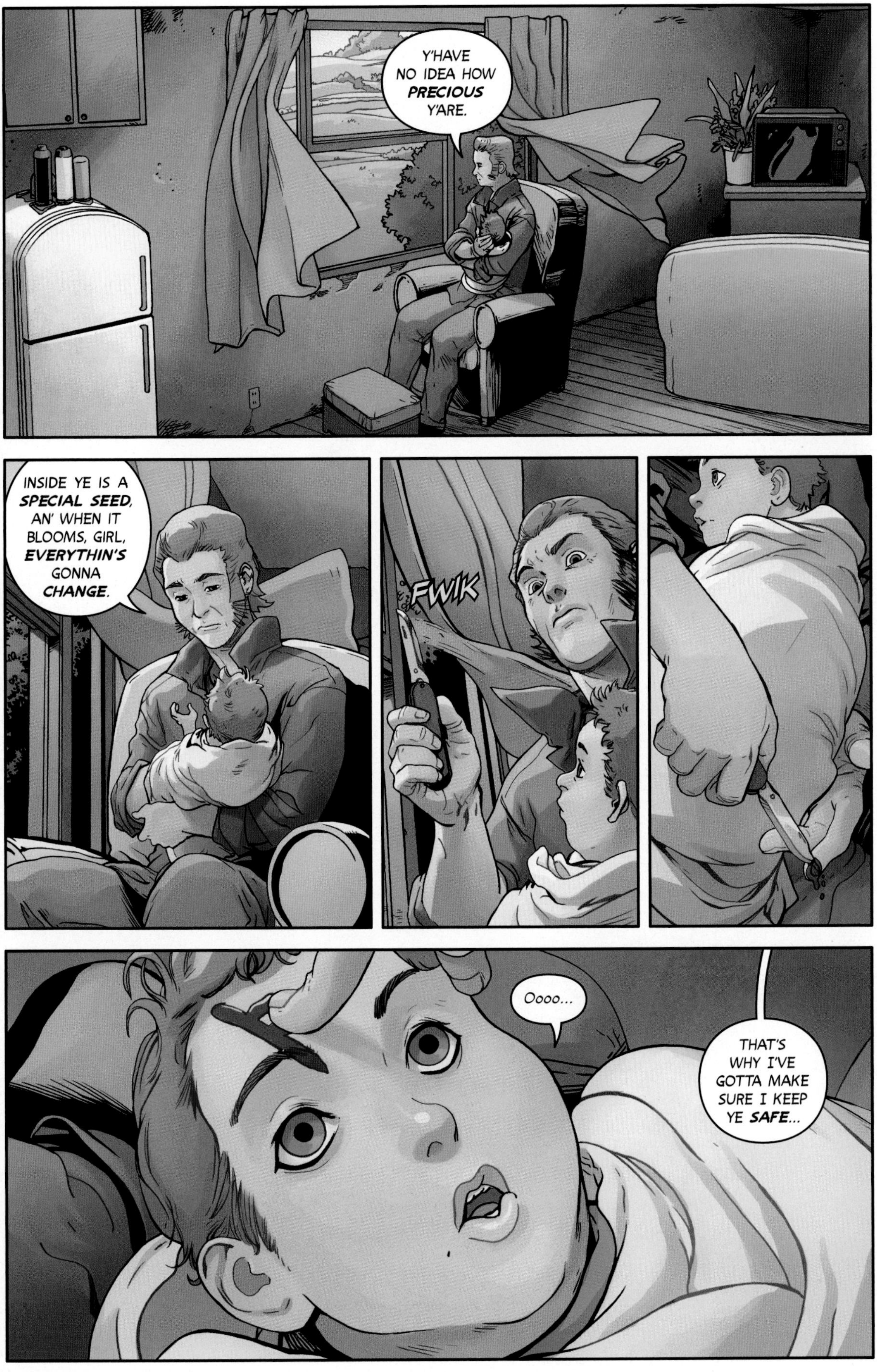
Y'HAVE NO IDEA HOW PRECIOUS Y'ARE.
INSIDE YE IS A SPECIAL SEED, AN' WHEN IT BLOOMS, GIRL, EVERYTHIN'S GONNA CHANGE.
FWIK
Oooo...
THAT'S WHY I'VE GOTTA MAKE SURE I KEEP YE SAFE...

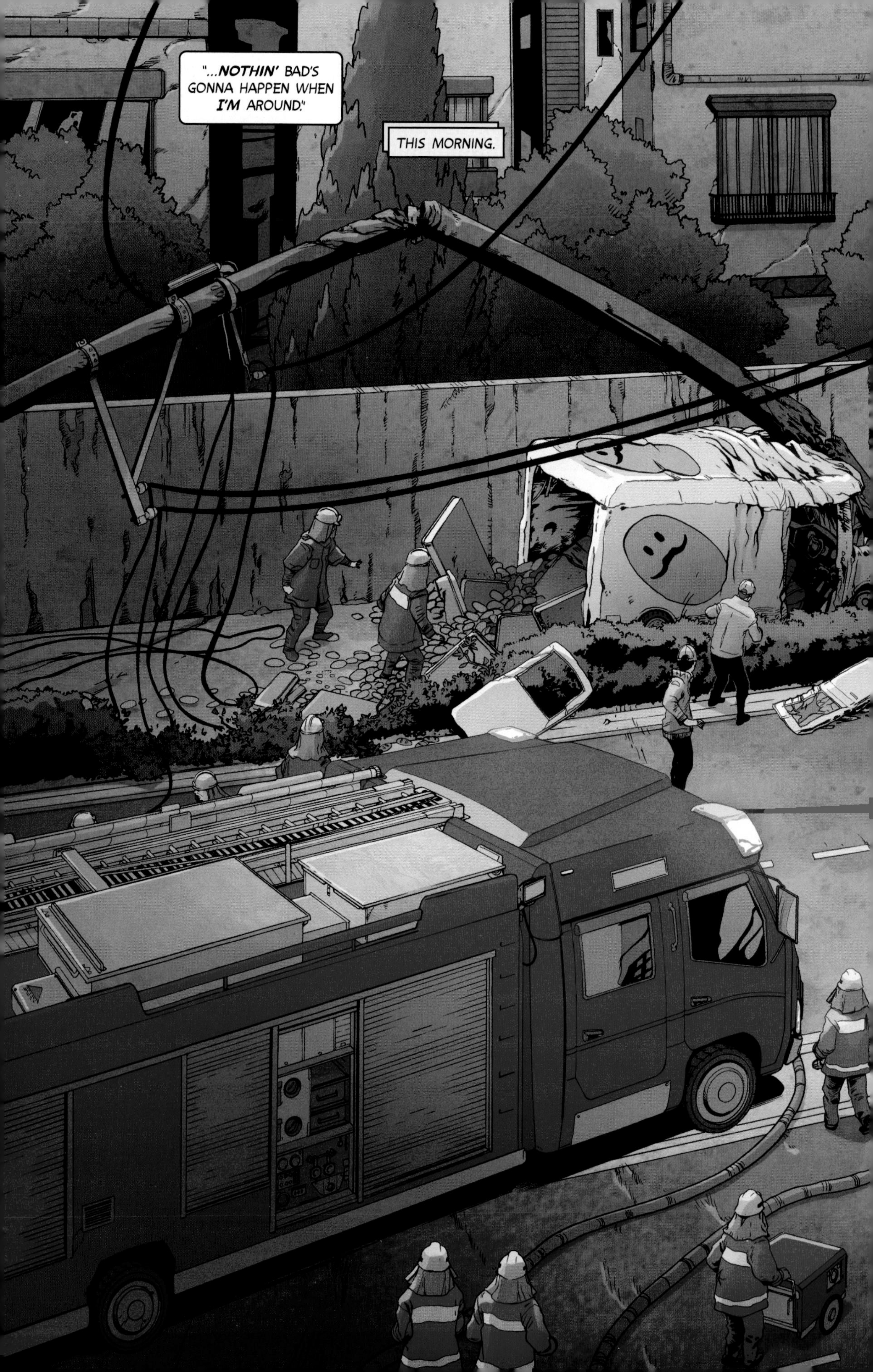
"...NOTHIN' BAD'S GONNA HAPPEN WHEN I'M AROUND."
THIS MORNING.

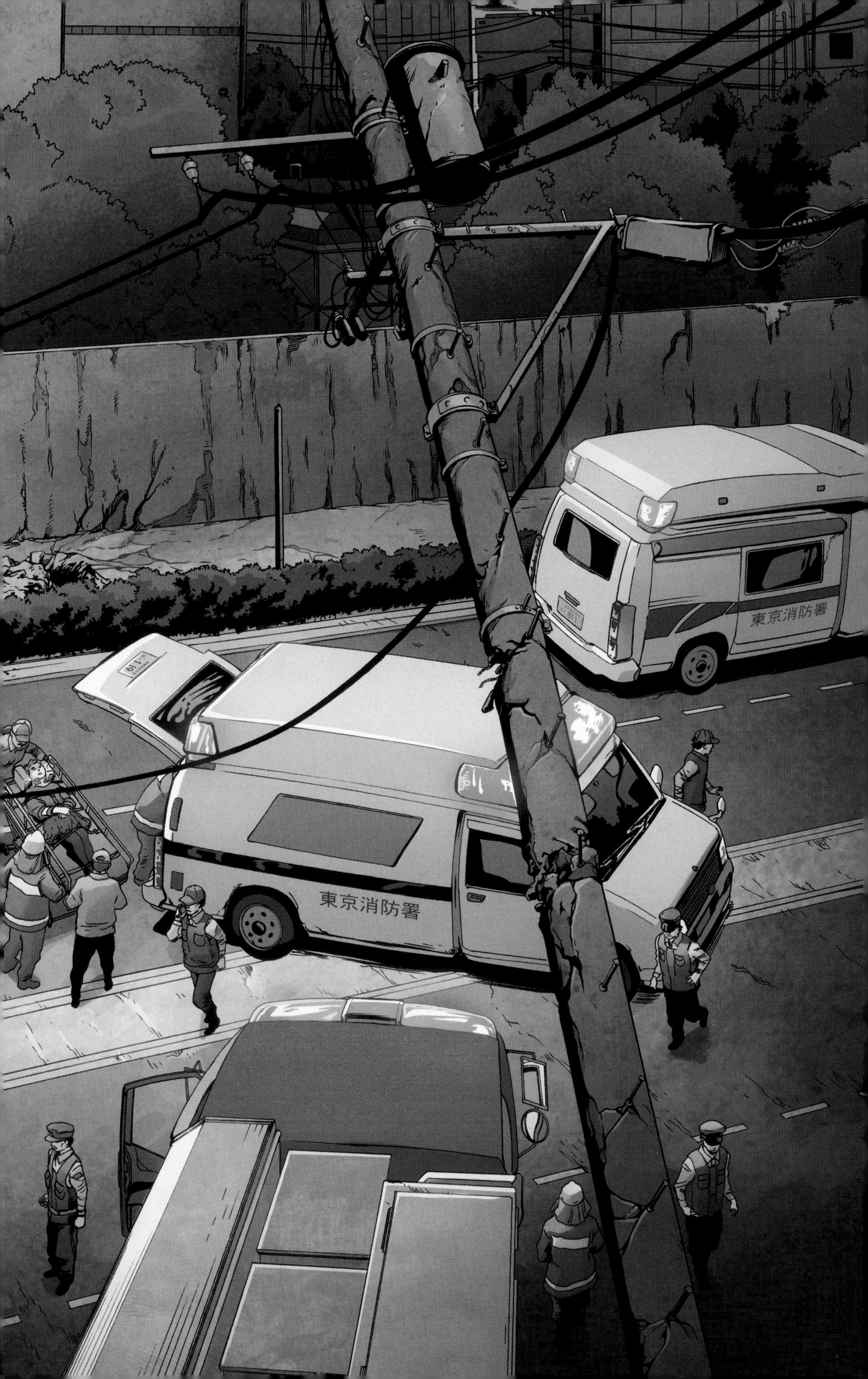
東京消防署
東京消防署

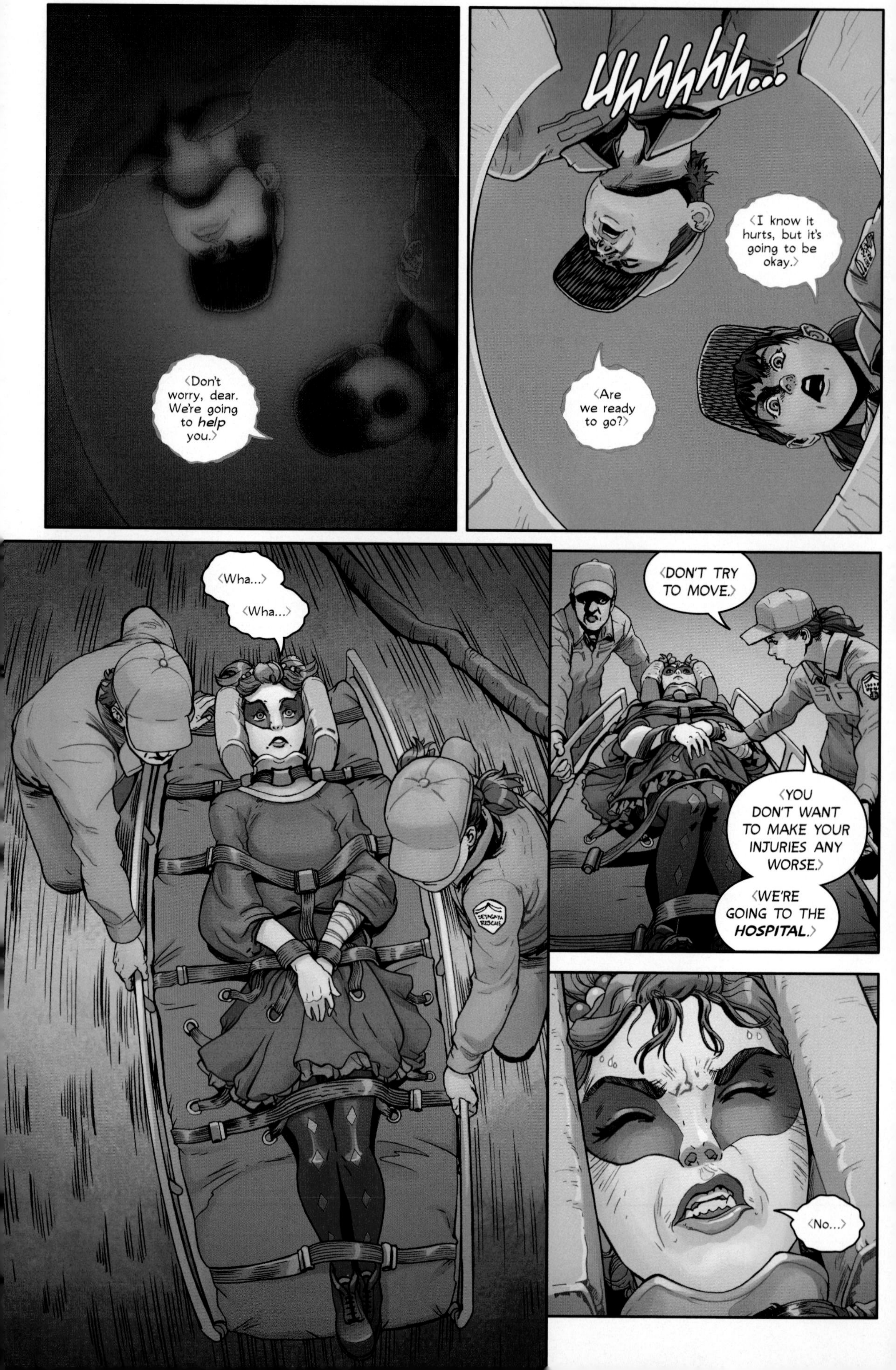

‹Don't worry, dear. We're going to *help* you.›
Uhhhhh...
‹I know it hurts, but it's going to be okay.›
‹Are we ready to go?›
‹Wha...›
‹Wha...›
SETAGAYA RESCUE
‹DON'T TRY TO MOVE.›
‹YOU DON'T WANT TO MAKE YOUR INJURIES ANY WORSE.›
‹WE'RE GOING TO THE **HOSPITAL**.›
‹No...›

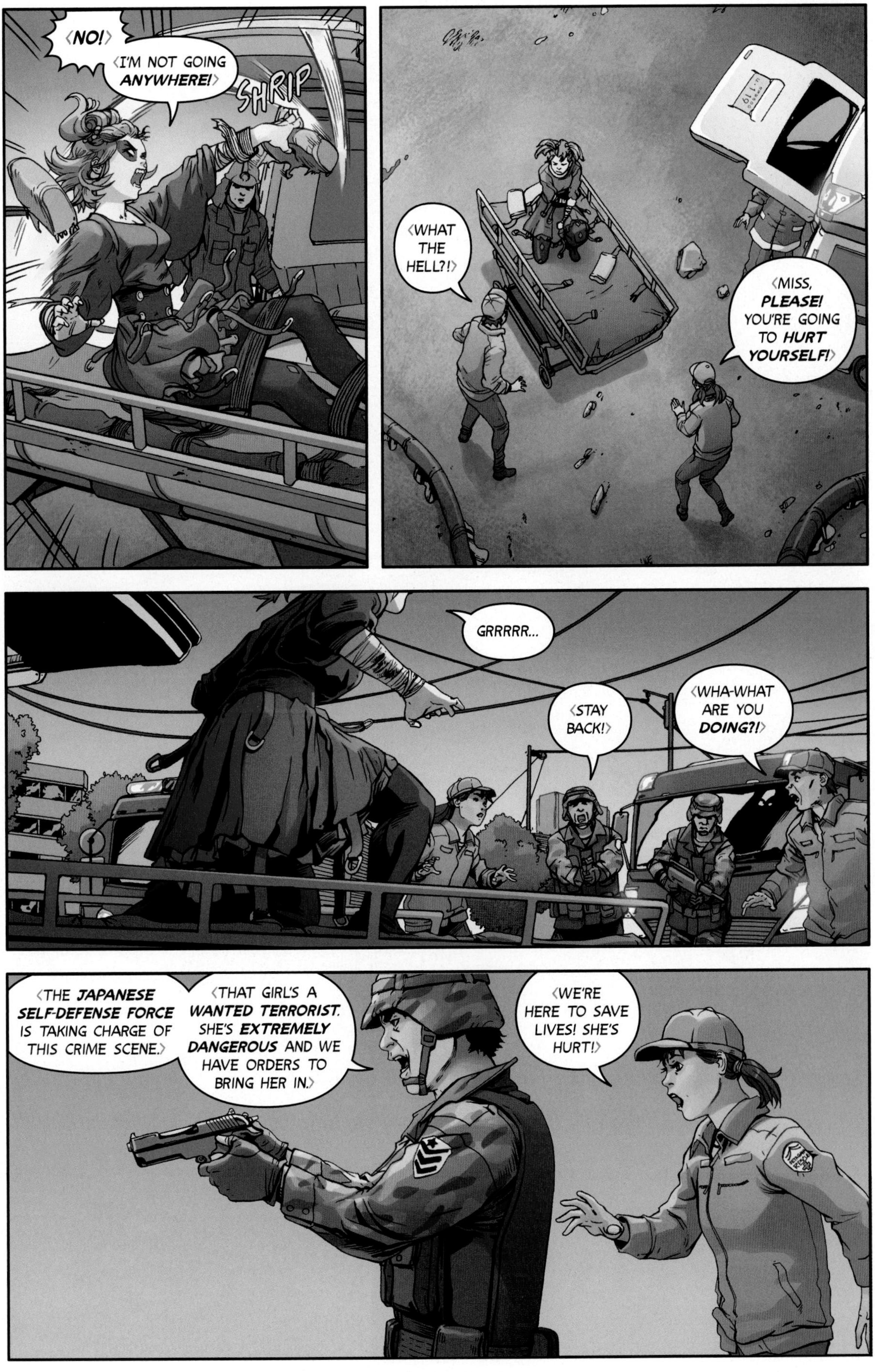

〈NO!〉
〈I'M NOT GOING ANYWHERE!〉
SHRIP
〈WHAT THE HELL?!〉
〈MISS, PLEASE! YOU'RE GOING TO HURT YOURSELF!〉
GRRRRR...
〈STAY BACK!〉
〈WHA-WHAT ARE YOU DOING?!〉
〈THE JAPANESE SELF-DEFENSE FORCE IS TAKING CHARGE OF THIS CRIME SCENE.〉
〈THAT GIRL'S A WANTED TERRORIST. SHE'S EXTREMELY DANGEROUS AND WE HAVE ORDERS TO BRING HER IN.〉
〈WE'RE HERE TO SAVE LIVES! SHE'S HURT!〉

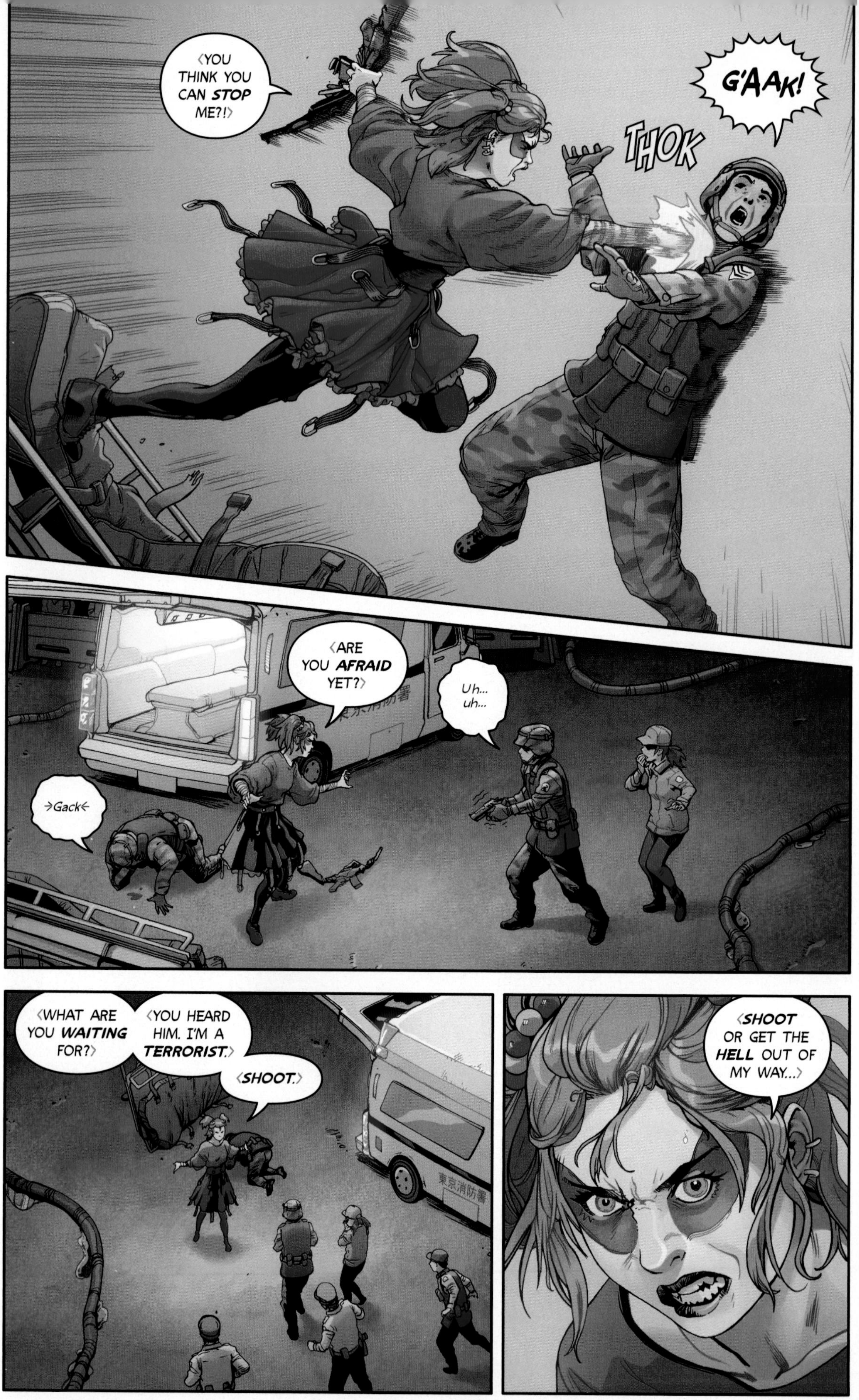

‹YOU THINK YOU CAN STOP ME?!›
THOK
G'AAK!
‹ARE YOU AFRAID YET?›
Uh... uh...
→Gack←
東京消防署
‹WHAT ARE YOU WAITING FOR?›
‹YOU HEARD HIM. I'M A TERRORIST.›
‹SHOOT.›
東京消防署
‹SHOOT OR GET THE HELL OUT OF MY WAY...›

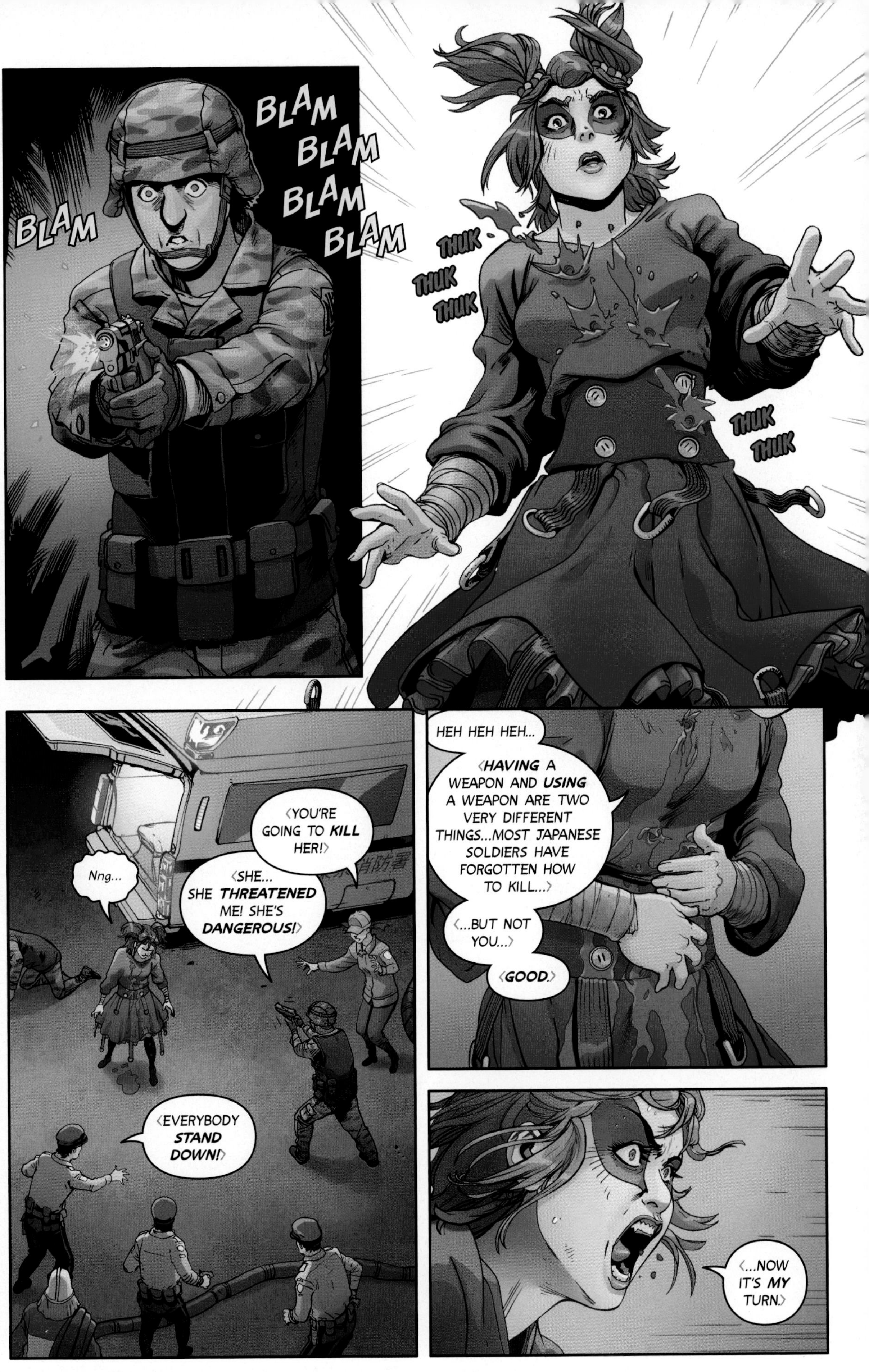
BLAM
BLAM
BLAM
BLAM
BLAM
THUK
THUK
THUK
THUK
THUK
Nng...
‹YOU'RE GOING TO **KILL** HER!›
‹SHE... SHE **THREATENED** ME! SHE'S **DANGEROUS!**›
‹EVERYBODY **STAND DOWN!**›
HEH HEH HEH...
‹**HAVING** A WEAPON AND **USING** A WEAPON ARE TWO VERY DIFFERENT THINGS...MOST JAPANESE SOLDIERS HAVE FORGOTTEN HOW TO KILL...›
‹...BUT NOT YOU...›
‹**GOOD.**›
‹...NOW IT'S **MY** TURN.›

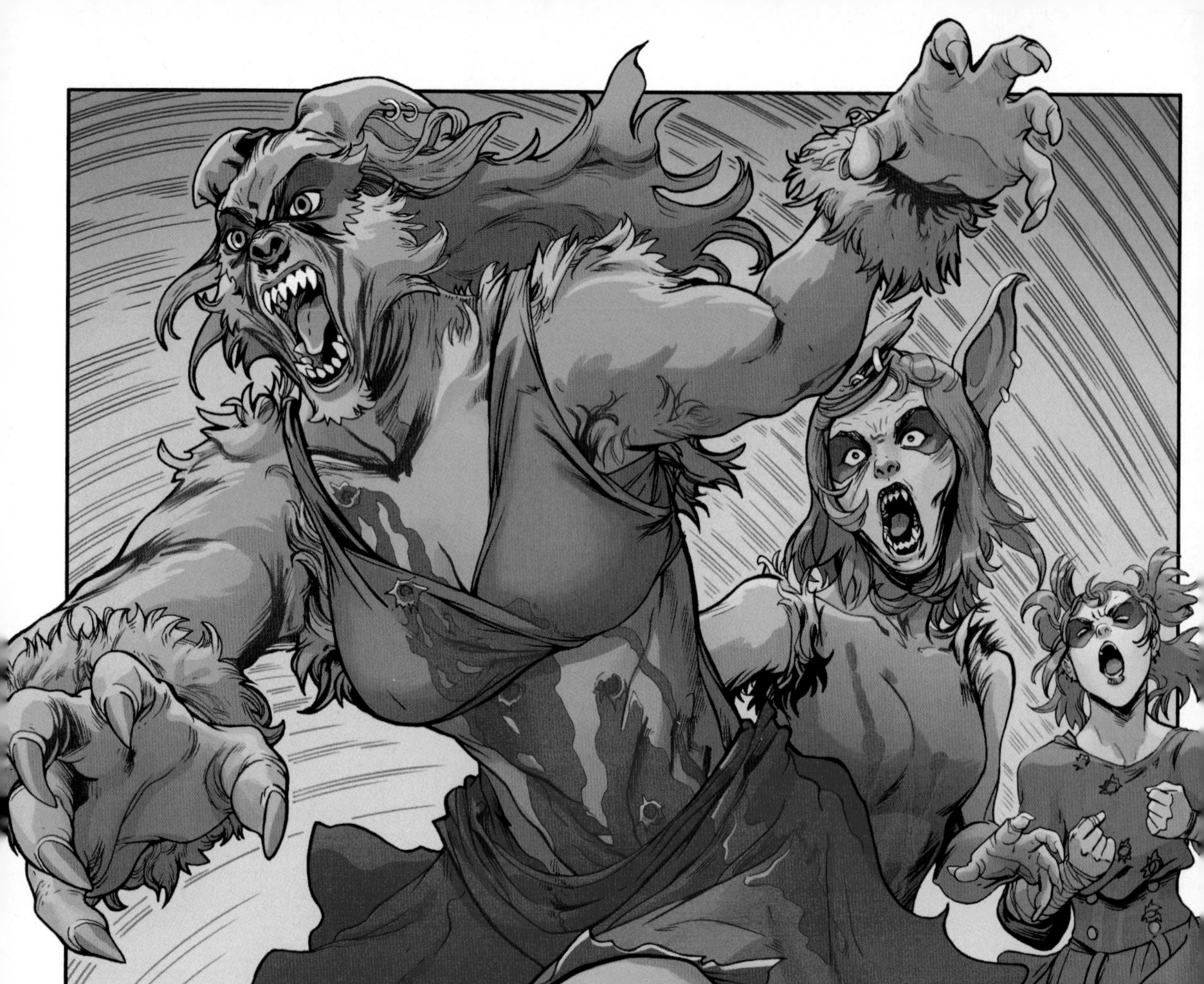

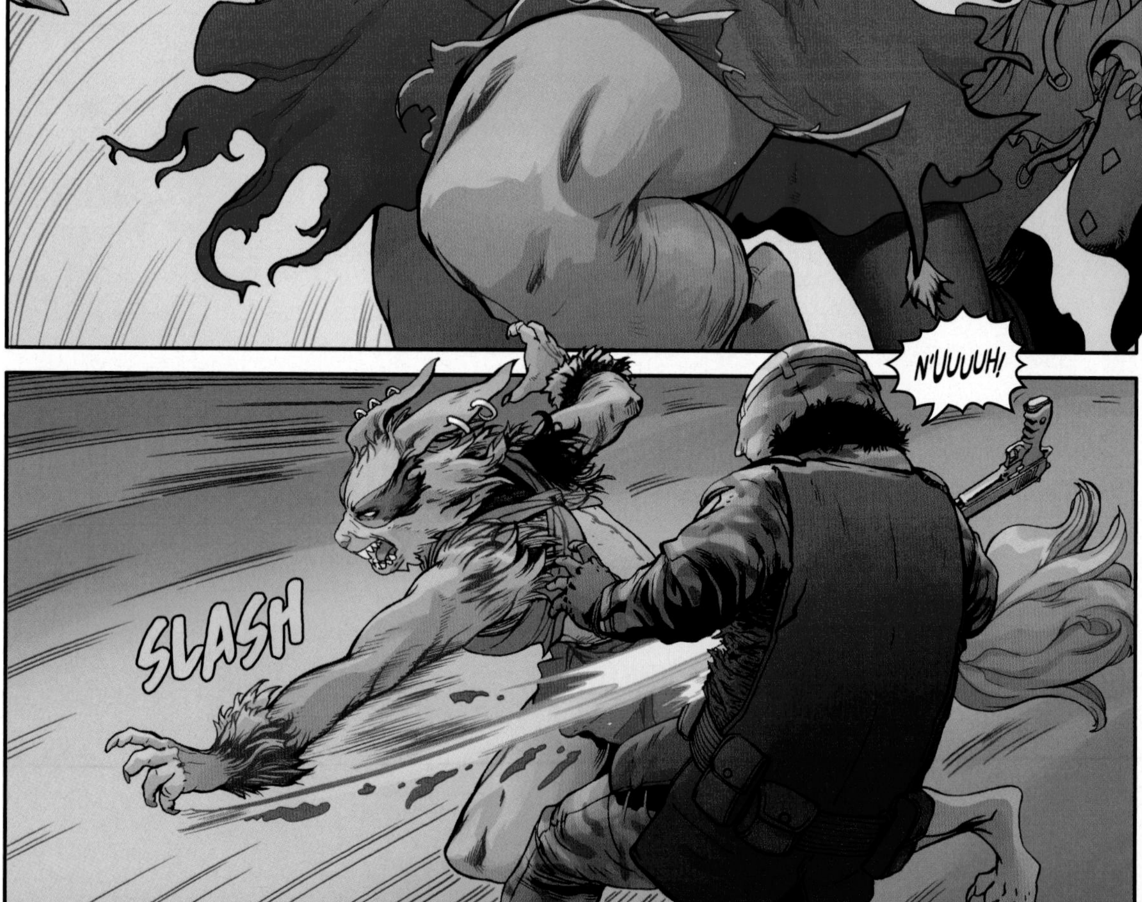
N'UUUUH!
SLASH

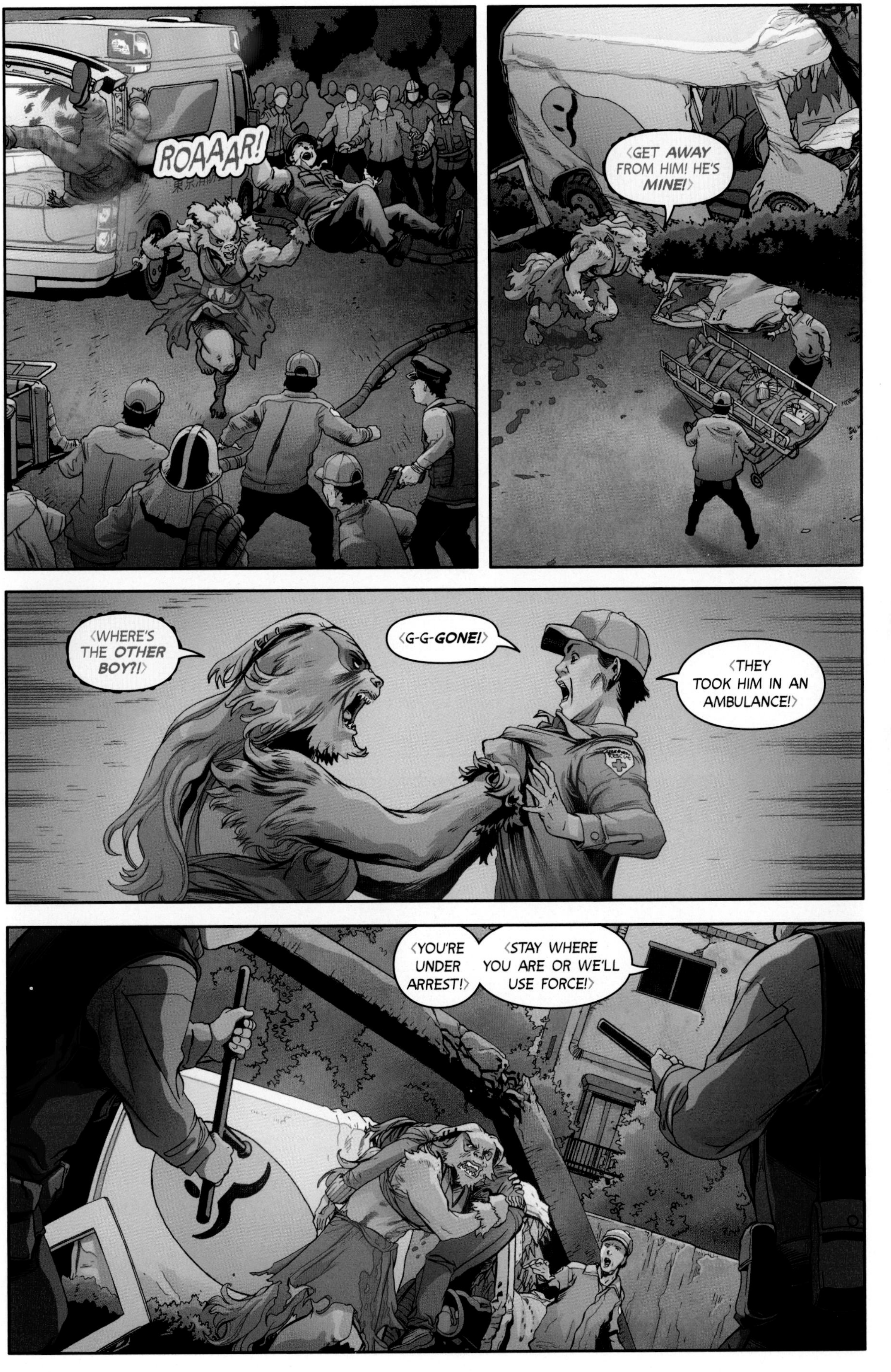
ROAAAR!
〈GET AWAY FROM HIM! HE'S MINE!〉
〈WHERE'S THE OTHER BOY?!〉
〈G-G-GONE!〉
〈THEY TOOK HIM IN AN AMBULANCE!〉
〈YOU'RE UNDER ARREST!〉
〈STAY WHERE YOU ARE OR WE'LL USE FORCE!〉

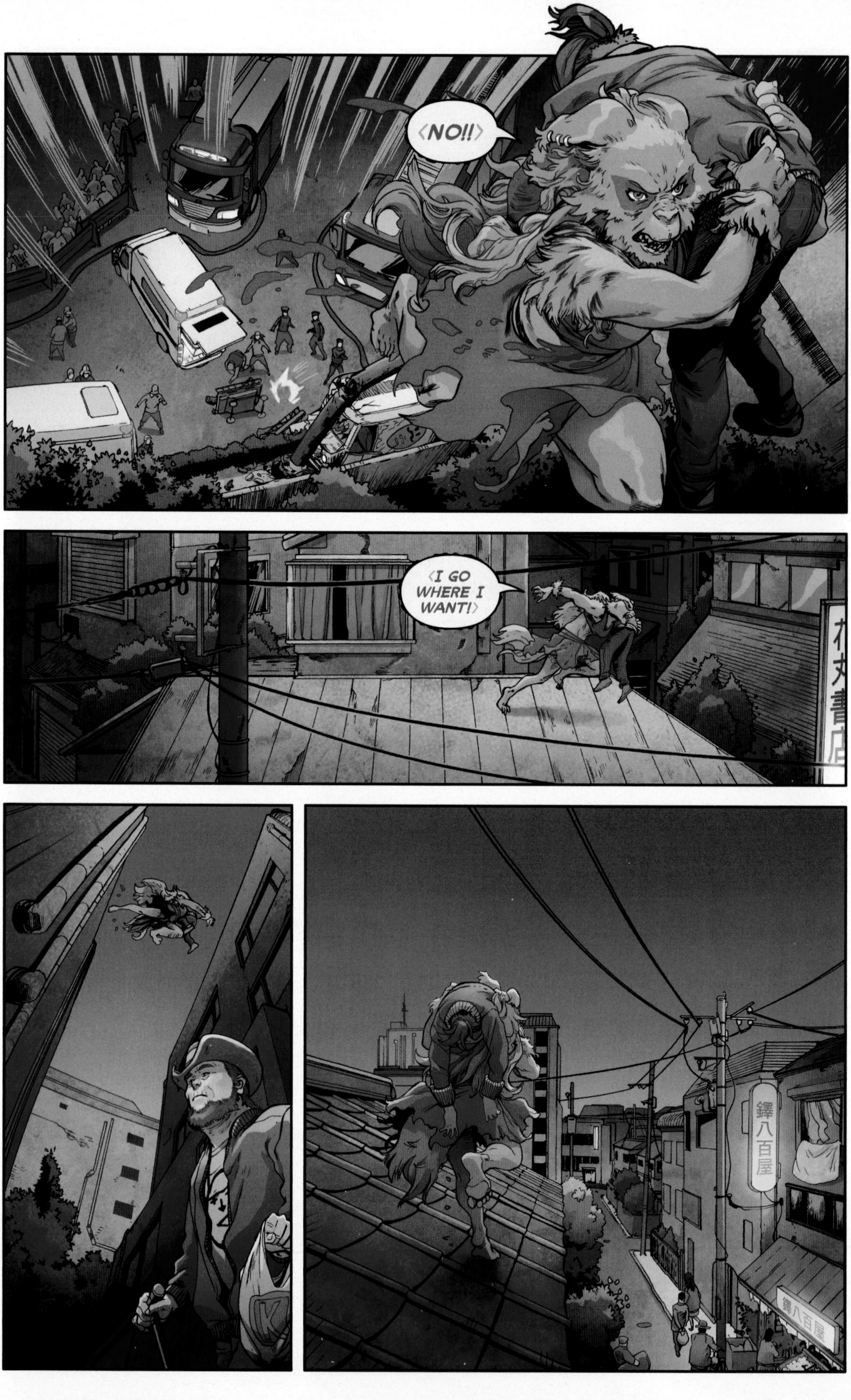
<NO!!>
<I GO WHERE I WANT!>

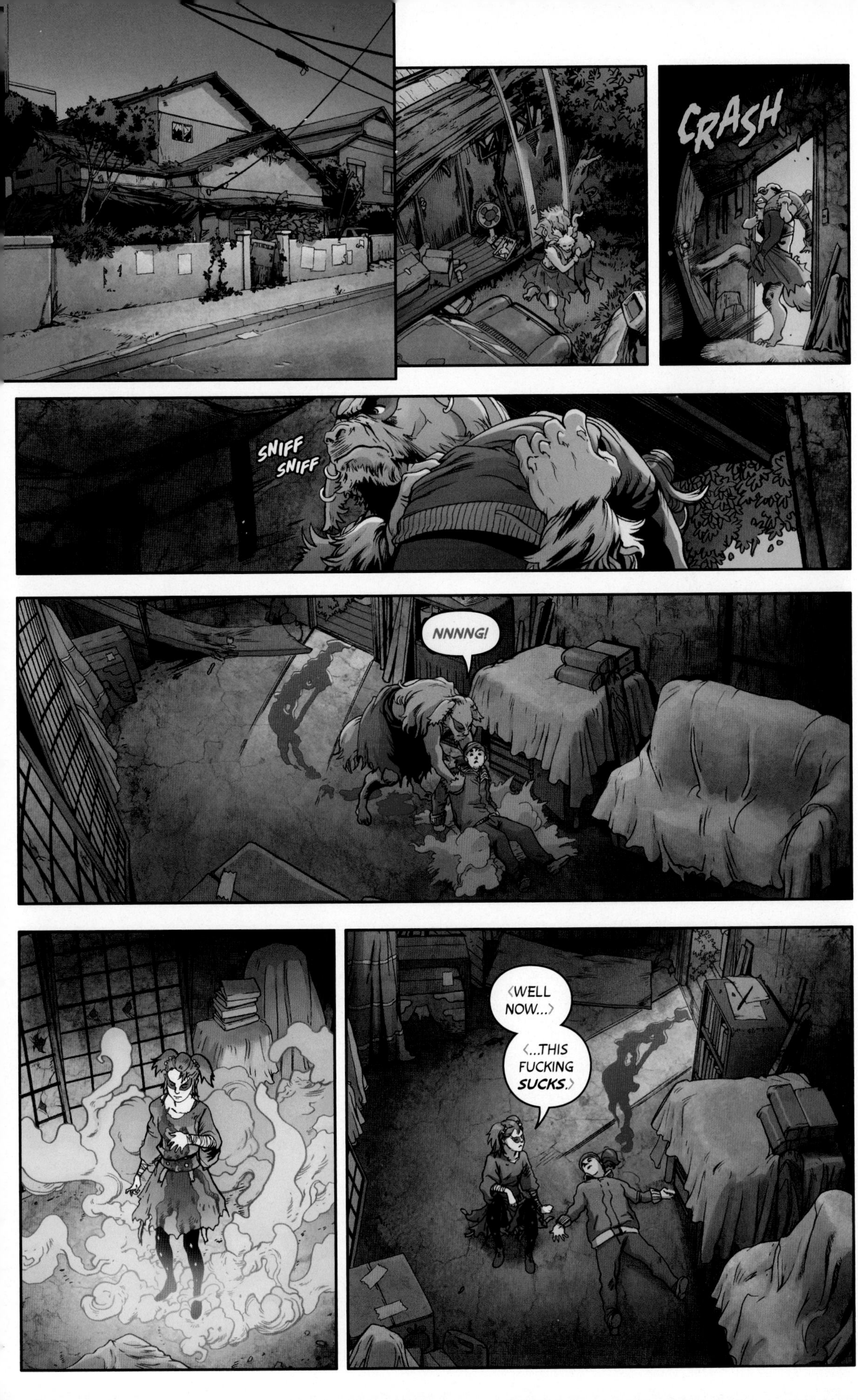
CRASH
SNIFF SNIFF
NNNNG!
‹WELL NOW...›
‹...THIS FUCKING SUCKS.›

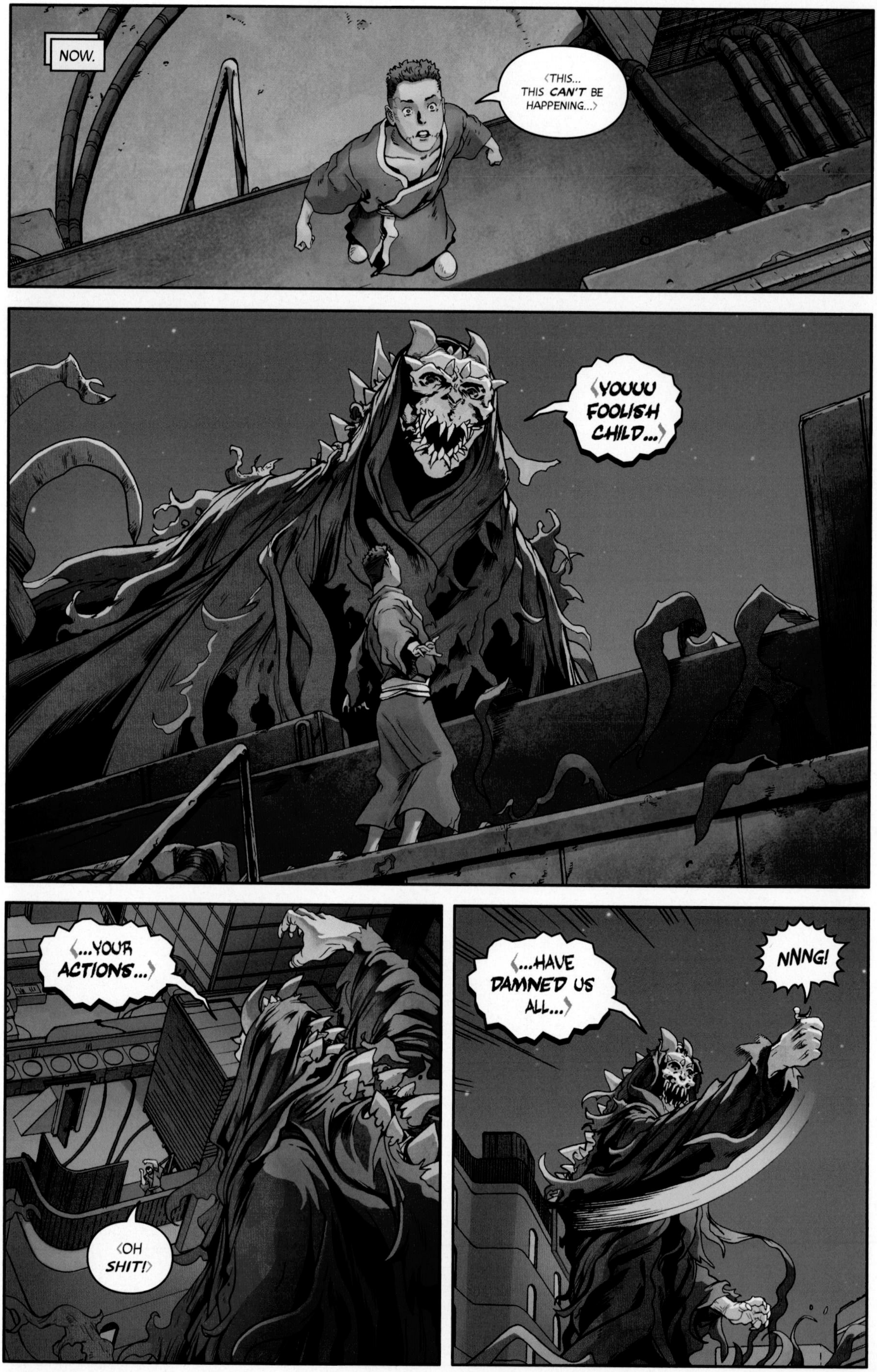
NOW.
‹THIS... THIS CAN'T BE HAPPENING...›
‹YOUUU FOOLISH CHILD...›
‹...YOUR ACTIONS...›
‹OH SHIT!›
‹...HAVE DAMNED US ALL...›
NNNG!

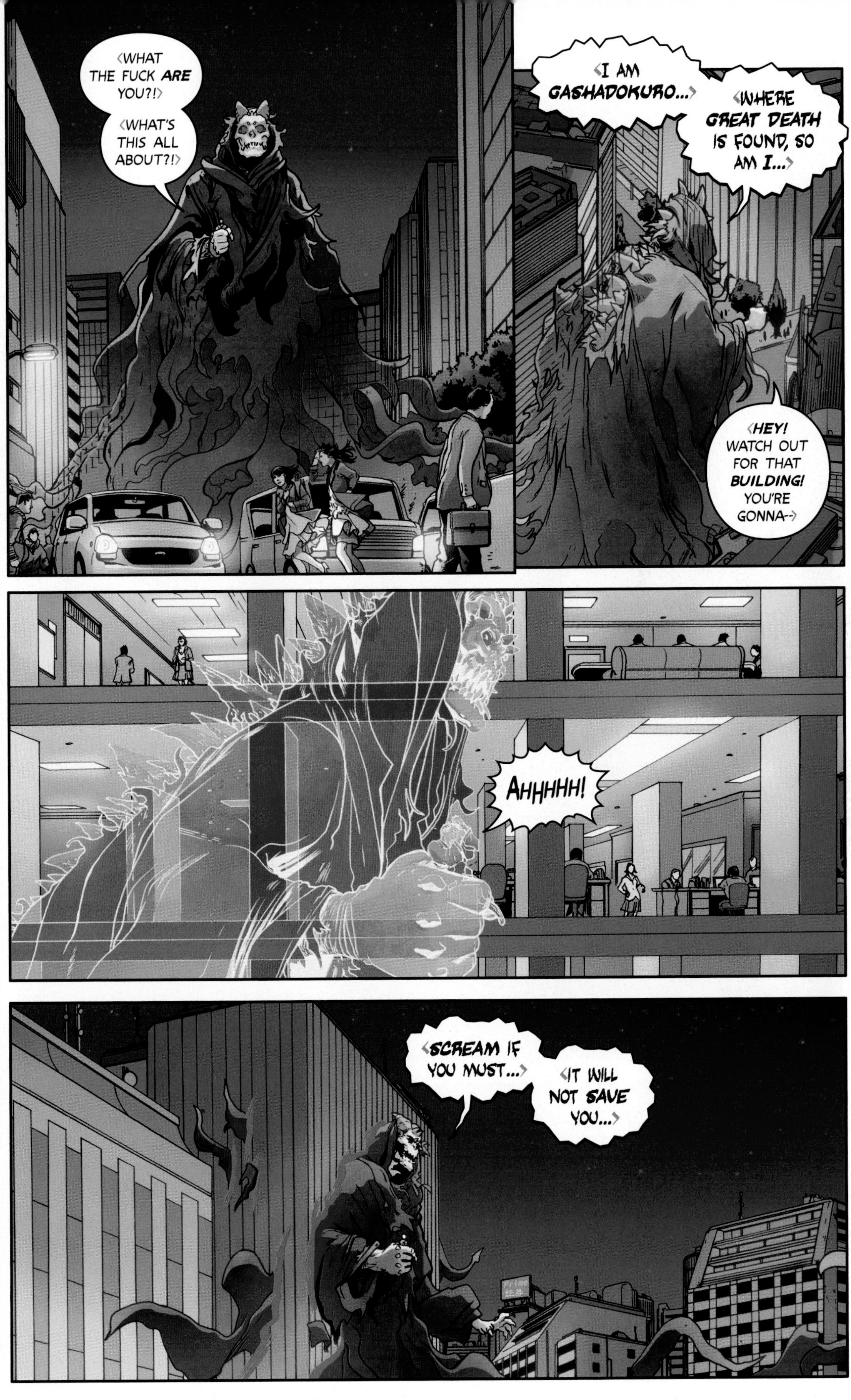

‹WHAT THE FUCK ARE YOU?!›
‹WHAT'S THIS ALL ABOUT?!›
‹I AM GASHADOKURO...›
‹WHERE GREAT DEATH IS FOUND, SO AM I...›
‹HEY! WATCH OUT FOR THAT BUILDING! YOU'RE GONNA--›
AHHHHH!
‹SCREAM IF YOU MUST...›
‹IT WILL NOT SAVE YOU...›

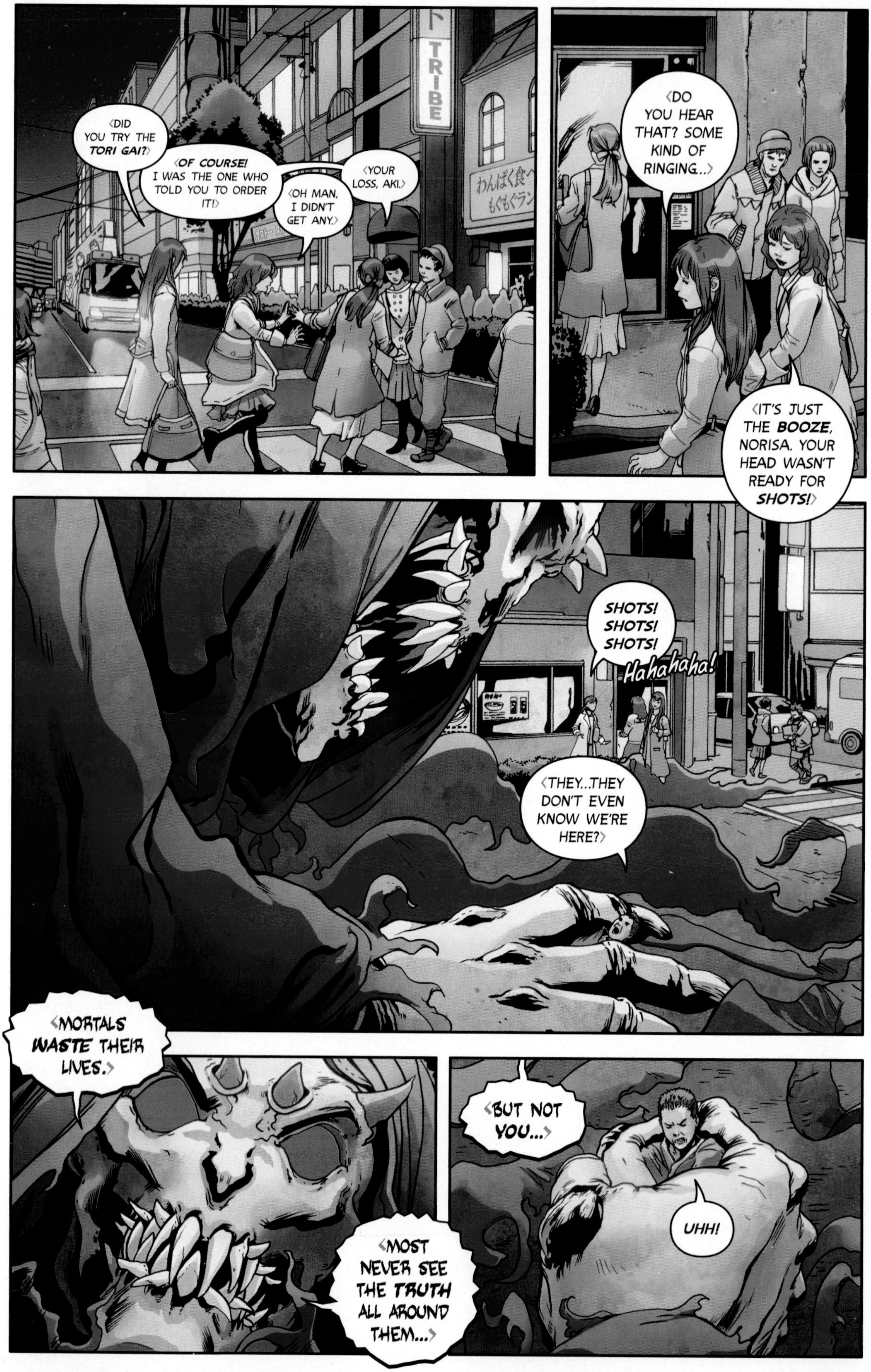
TRIBE
‹DID YOU TRY THE **TORI GAI?**›
‹**OF COURSE!** I WAS THE ONE WHO TOLD YOU TO ORDER IT!›
‹OH MAN, I DIDN'T GET ANY.›
‹YOUR LOSS, AKI.›
‹DO YOU HEAR THAT? SOME KIND OF RINGING...›
‹IT'S JUST THE **BOOZE**, NORISA. YOUR HEAD WASN'T READY FOR **SHOTS!**›
SHOTS! SHOTS! SHOTS!
Hahahaha!
‹THEY...THEY DON'T EVEN KNOW WE'RE HERE?›
‹MORTALS **WASTE** THEIR LIVES.›
‹MOST NEVER SEE THE **TRUTH** ALL AROUND THEM...›
‹BUT NOT **YOU...**›
UHH!

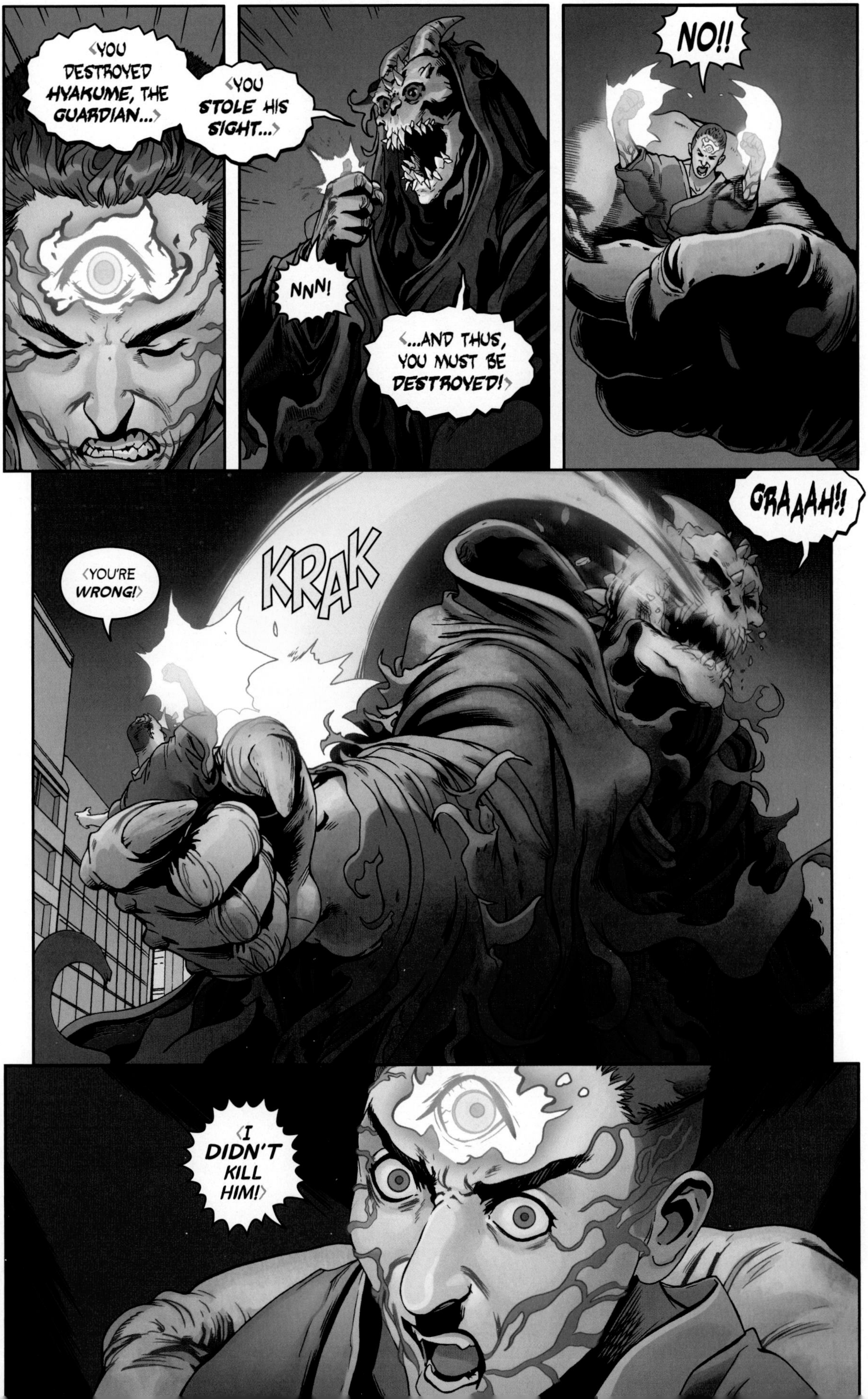
‹YOU DESTROYED HYAKUME, THE GUARDIAN...›
‹YOU STOLE HIS SIGHT...›
NNN!
‹...AND THUS, YOU MUST BE DESTROYED!›
NO!!
GRAAAH!!
‹YOU'RE WRONG!›
KRAK
‹I DIDN'T KILL HIM!›

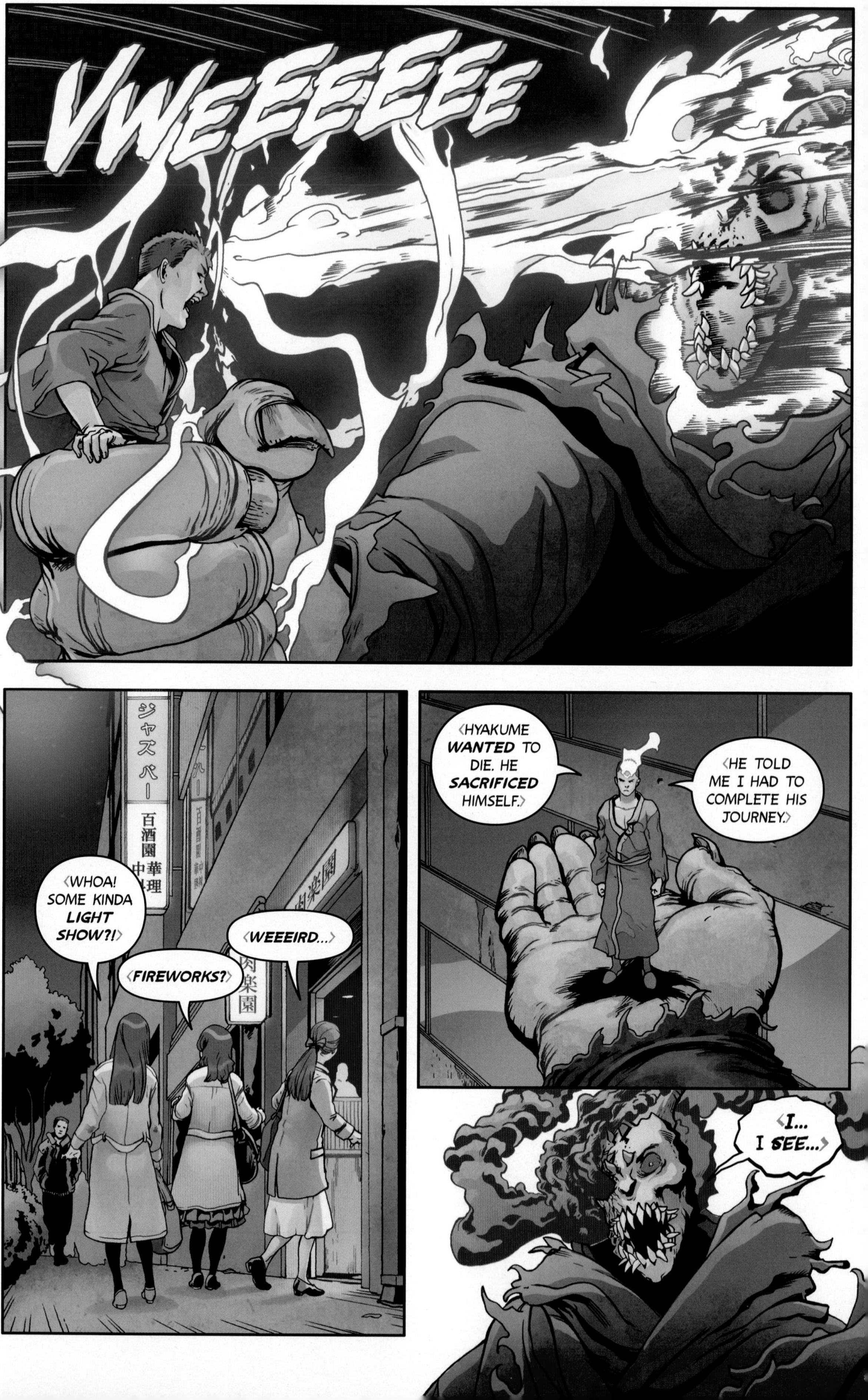
VWEEEEEEE
ジャズバー
百酒園
中華料理
肉楽園
‹WHOA! SOME KINDA LIGHT SHOW?!›
‹FIREWORKS?›
‹WEEEIRD...›
‹HYAKUME WANTED TO DIE. HE SACRIFICED HIMSELF.›
‹HE TOLD ME I HAD TO COMPLETE HIS JOURNEY.›
‹I... I SEE...›

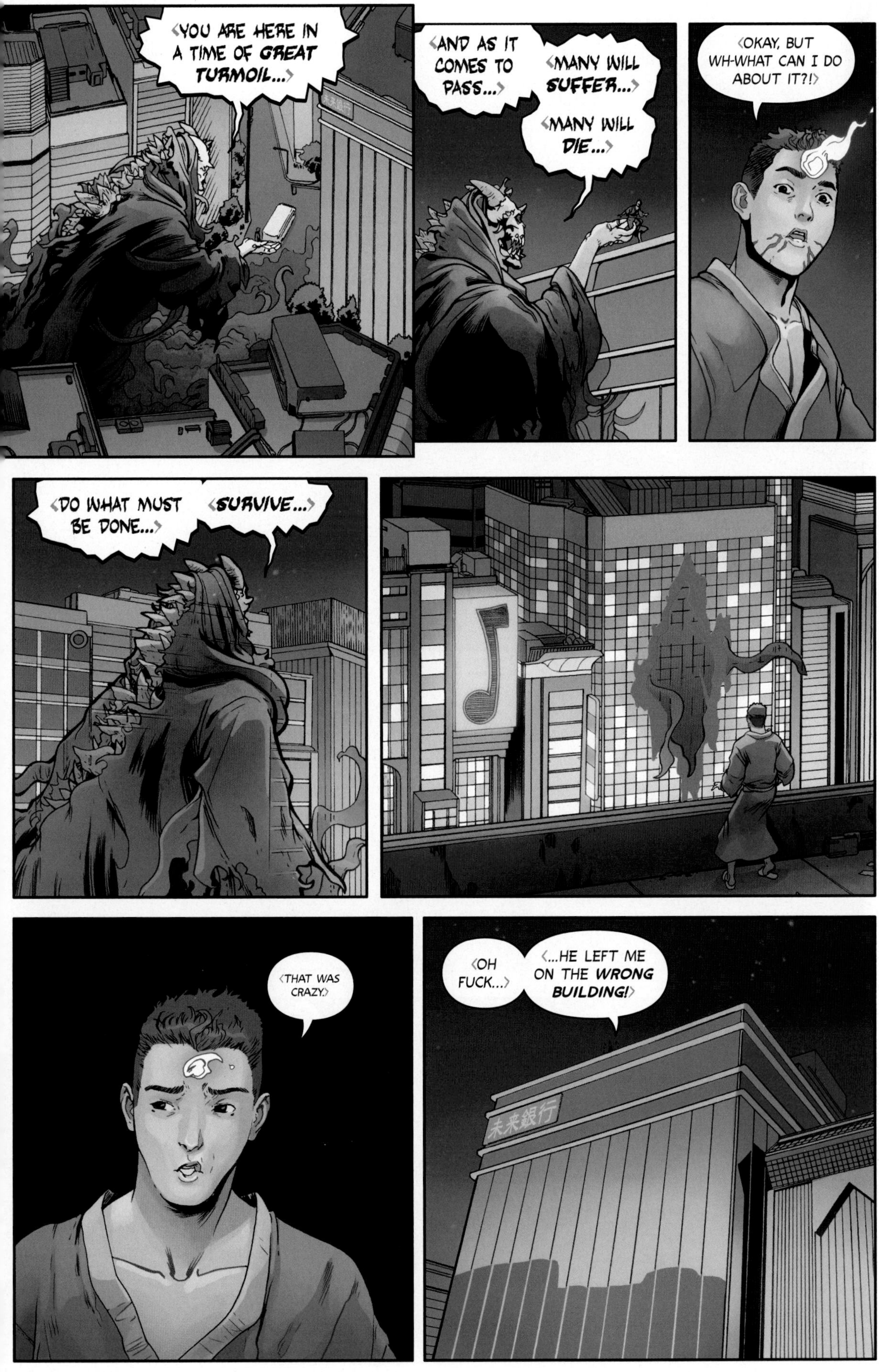
‹YOU ARE HERE IN A TIME OF GREAT TURMOIL...›
未来銀行
‹AND AS IT COMES TO PASS...›
‹MANY WILL SUFFER...›
‹MANY WILL DIE...›
‹OKAY, BUT WH-WHAT CAN I DO ABOUT IT?!›
‹DO WHAT MUST BE DONE...›
‹SURVIVE...›
‹THAT WAS CRAZY.›
‹OH FUCK...›
‹...HE LEFT ME ON THE WRONG BUILDING!›
未来銀行

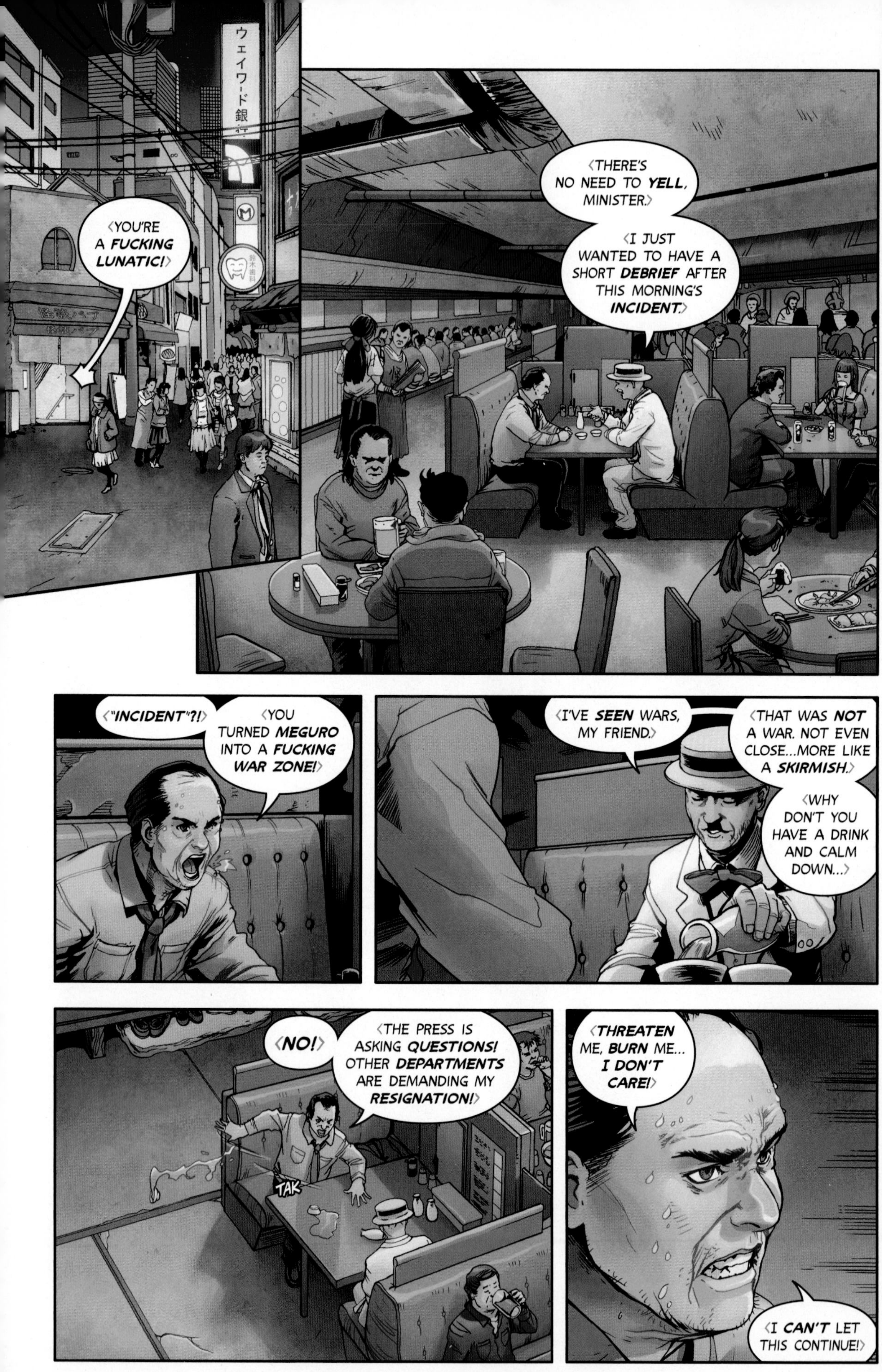

‹YOU'RE A FUCKING LUNATIC!›
‹THERE'S NO NEED TO YELL, MINISTER.›
‹I JUST WANTED TO HAVE A SHORT DEBRIEF AFTER THIS MORNING'S INCIDENT.›
‹"INCIDENT"?!›
‹YOU TURNED MEGURO INTO A FUCKING WAR ZONE!›
‹I'VE SEEN WARS, MY FRIEND.›
‹THAT WAS NOT A WAR. NOT EVEN CLOSE...MORE LIKE A SKIRMISH.›
‹WHY DON'T YOU HAVE A DRINK AND CALM DOWN...›
‹NO!›
‹THE PRESS IS ASKING QUESTIONS! OTHER DEPARTMENTS ARE DEMANDING MY RESIGNATION!›
TAK
‹THREATEN ME, BURN ME... I DON'T CARE!›
‹I CAN'T LET THIS CONTINUE!›

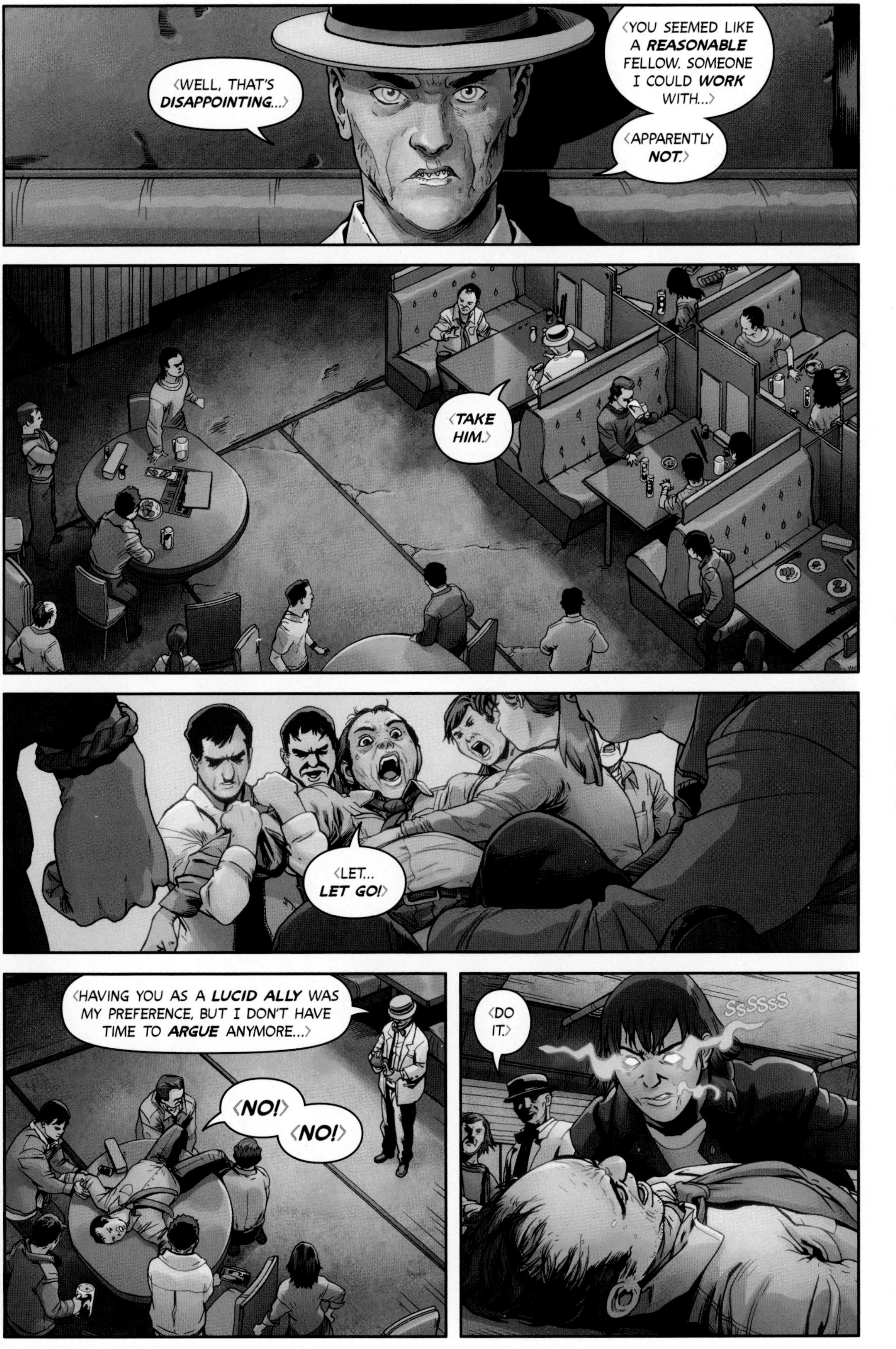

‹WELL, THAT'S DISAPPOINTING...›
‹YOU SEEMED LIKE A REASONABLE FELLOW. SOMEONE I COULD WORK WITH...›
‹APPARENTLY NOT.›
‹TAKE HIM.›
‹LET... LET GO!›
‹HAVING YOU AS A LUCID ALLY WAS MY PREFERENCE, BUT I DON'T HAVE TIME TO ARGUE ANYMORE...›
‹NO!›
‹NO!›
‹DO IT.›
SsSSSS

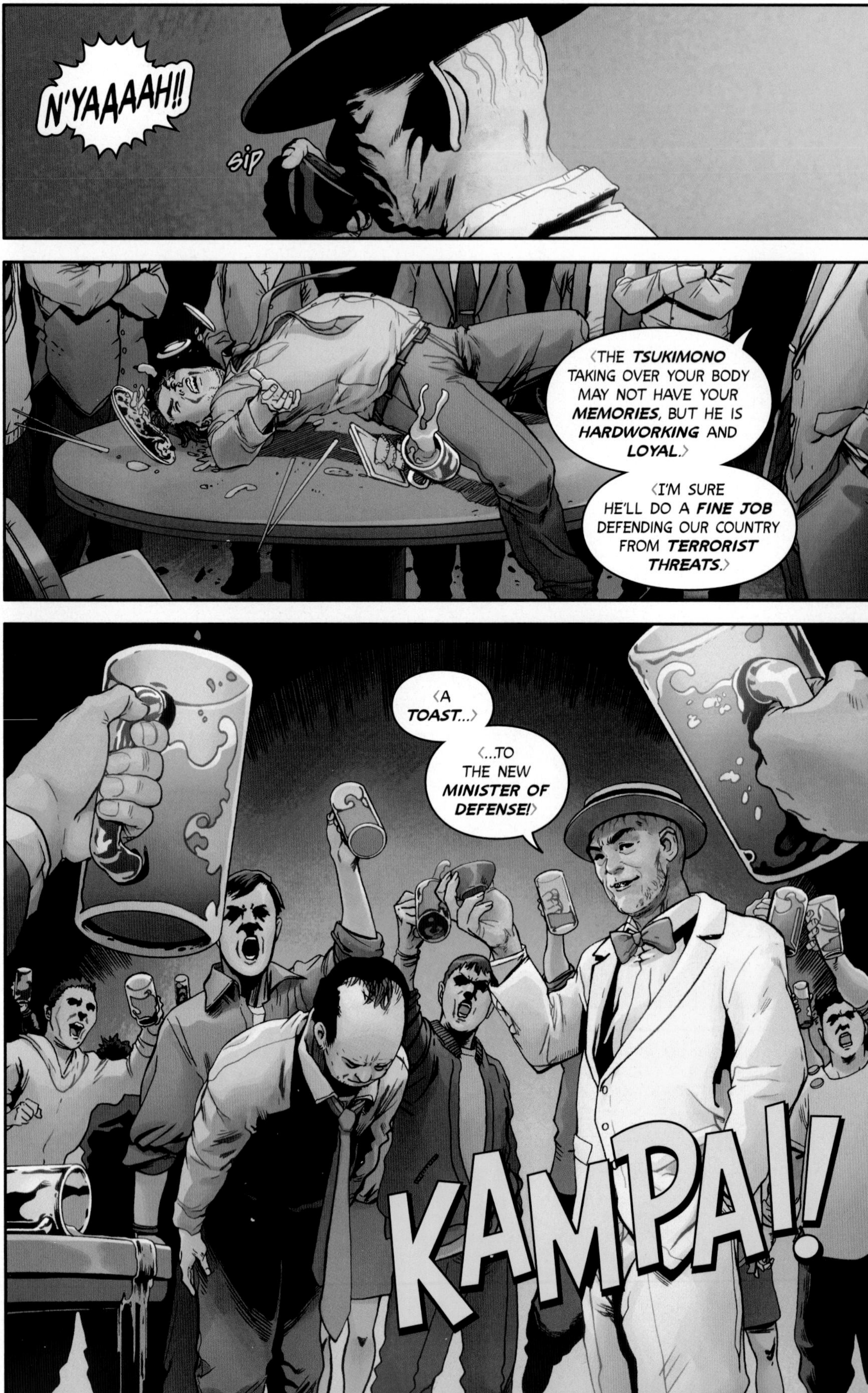
N'YAAAAH!!
sip
‹THE TSUKIMONO TAKING OVER YOUR BODY MAY NOT HAVE YOUR MEMORIES, BUT HE IS HARDWORKING AND LOYAL.›
‹I'M SURE HE'LL DO A FINE JOB DEFENDING OUR COUNTRY FROM TERRORIST THREATS.›
‹A TOAST...›
‹...TO THE NEW MINISTER OF DEFENSE!›
KAMPAI!

Chapter Twenty

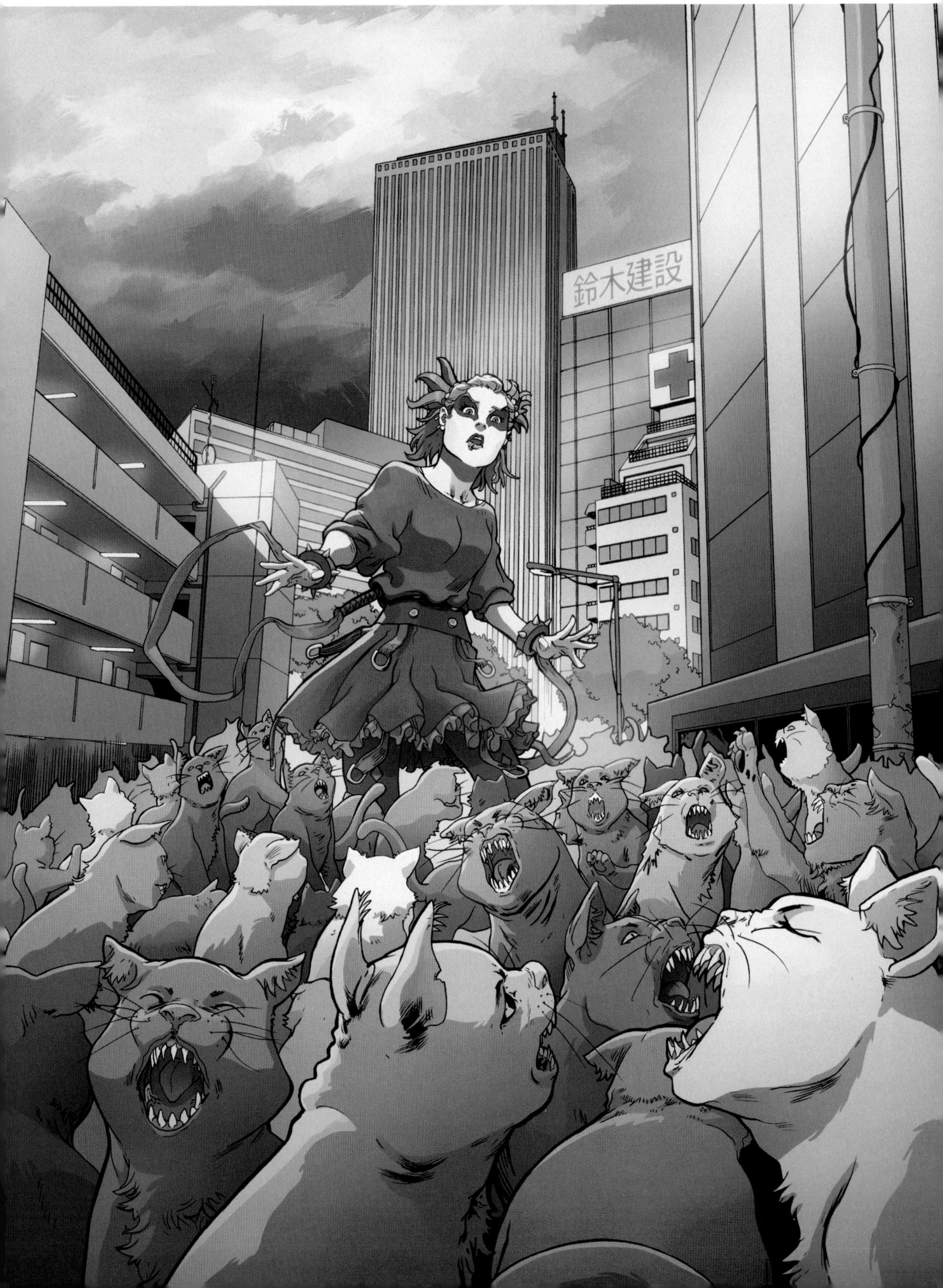

鈴木建設

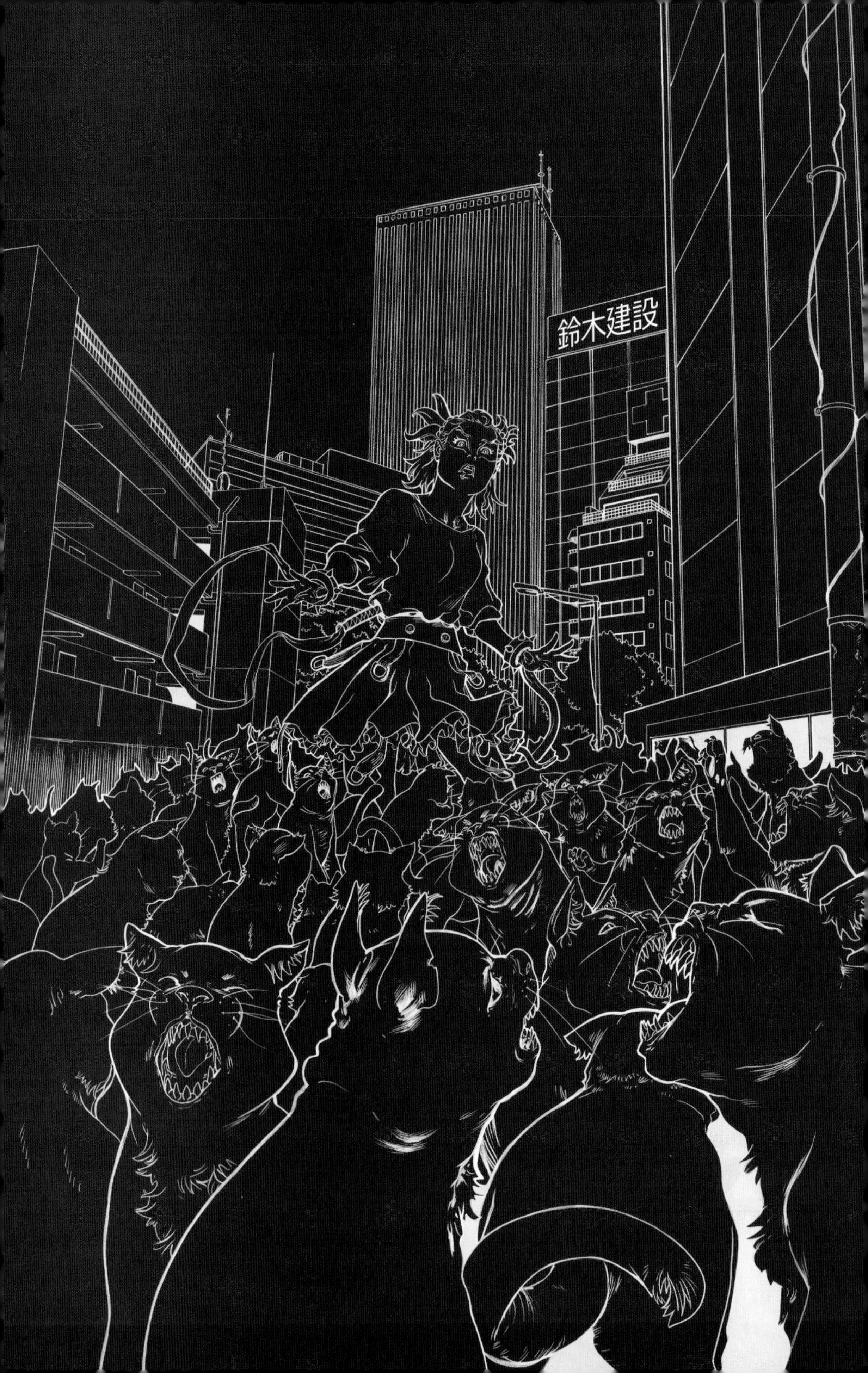
鈴木建設

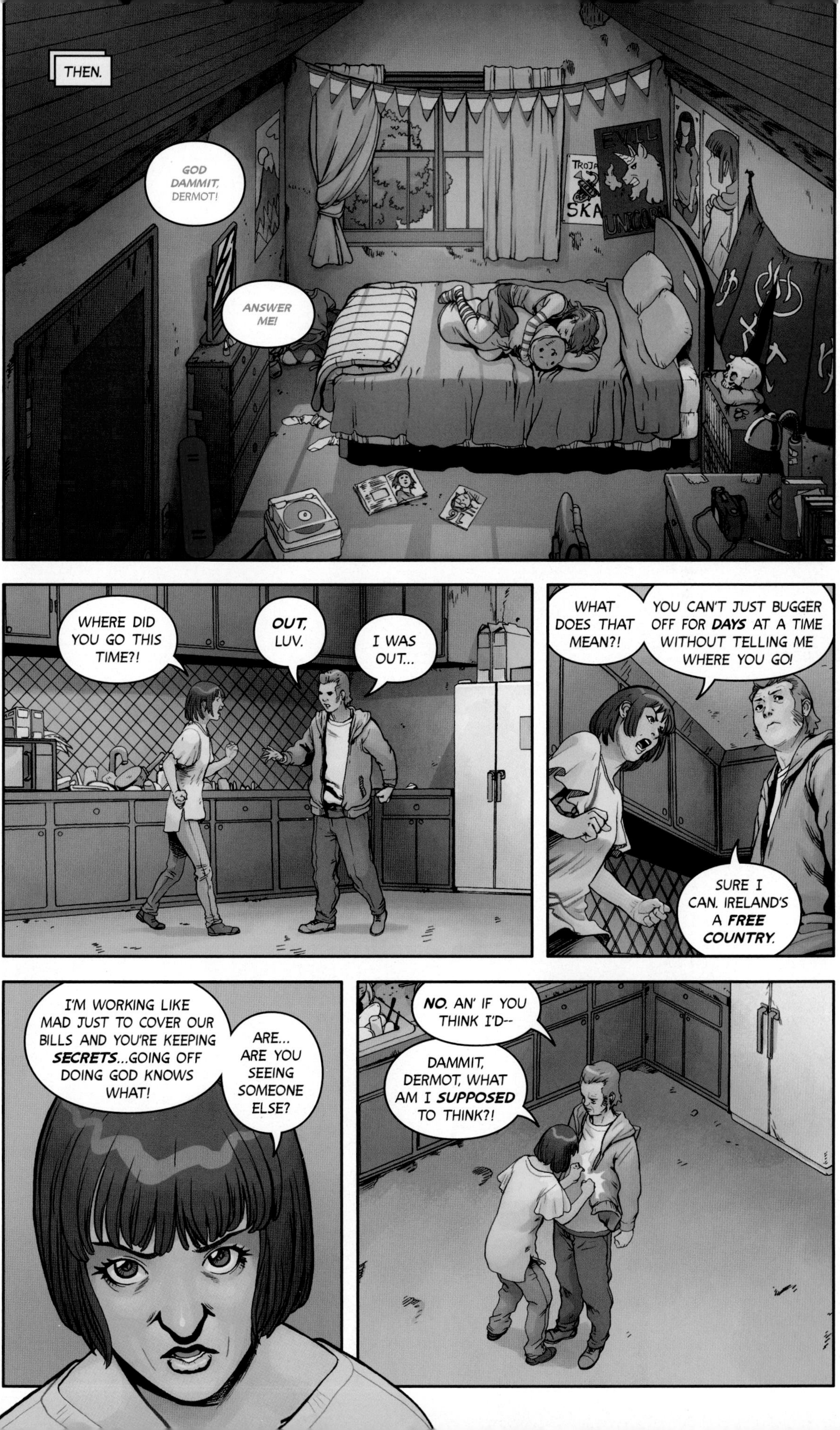
THEN.
GOD DAMMIT, DERMOT!
ANSWER ME!
WHERE DID YOU GO THIS TIME?!
OUT, LUV.
I WAS OUT...
WHAT DOES THAT MEAN?!
YOU CAN'T JUST BUGGER OFF FOR DAYS AT A TIME WITHOUT TELLING ME WHERE YOU GO!
SURE I CAN. IRELAND'S A FREE COUNTRY.
I'M WORKING LIKE MAD JUST TO COVER OUR BILLS AND YOU'RE KEEPING SECRETS...GOING OFF DOING GOD KNOWS WHAT!
ARE... ARE YOU SEEING SOMEONE ELSE?
NO. AN' IF YOU THINK I'D--
DAMMIT, DERMOT, WHAT AM I SUPPOSED TO THINK?!

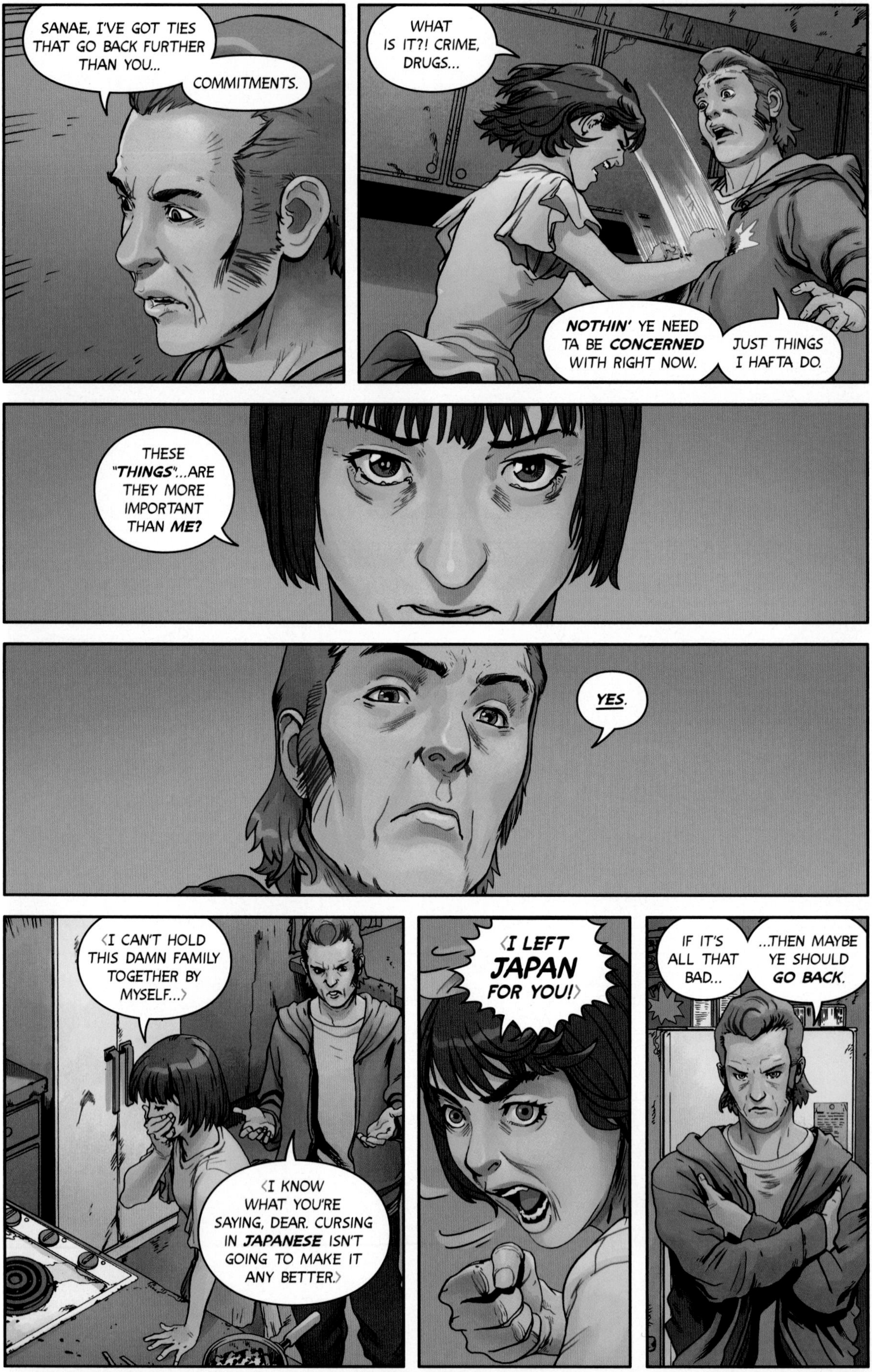
SANAE, I'VE GOT TIES THAT GO BACK FURTHER THAN YOU...
COMMITMENTS.
WHAT IS IT?! CRIME, DRUGS...
NOTHIN' YE NEED TA BE CONCERNED WITH RIGHT NOW.
JUST THINGS I HAFTA DO.
THESE "THINGS"...ARE THEY MORE IMPORTANT THAN ME?
YES.
‹I CAN'T HOLD THIS DAMN FAMILY TOGETHER BY MYSELF...›
‹I KNOW WHAT YOU'RE SAYING, DEAR. CURSING IN JAPANESE ISN'T GOING TO MAKE IT ANY BETTER.›
‹I LEFT JAPAN FOR YOU!›
IF IT'S ALL THAT BAD...
...THEN MAYBE YE SHOULD GO BACK.

I'M GOING OUT...

RORI, *WAIT!*

SLAM

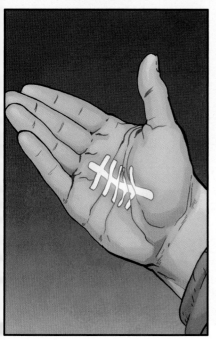

IT'S *DONE*, Y' BASTARDS.

MY FAMILY DESTROYED, JUST LIKE YE WANTED...

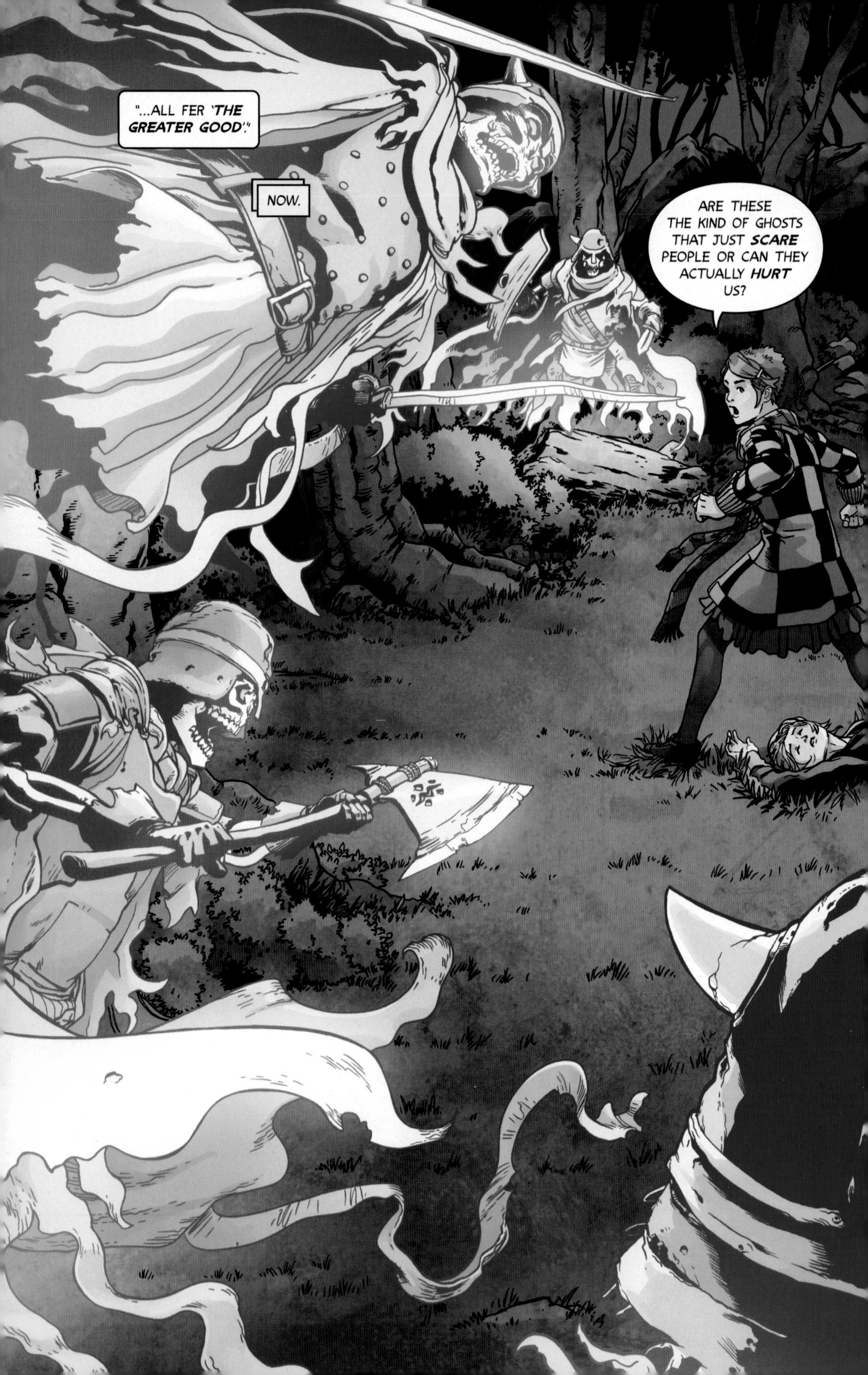
"...ALL FER 'THE GREATER GOOD'."
NOW.
ARE THESE THE KIND OF GHOSTS THAT JUST SCARE PEOPLE OR CAN THEY ACTUALLY HURT US?

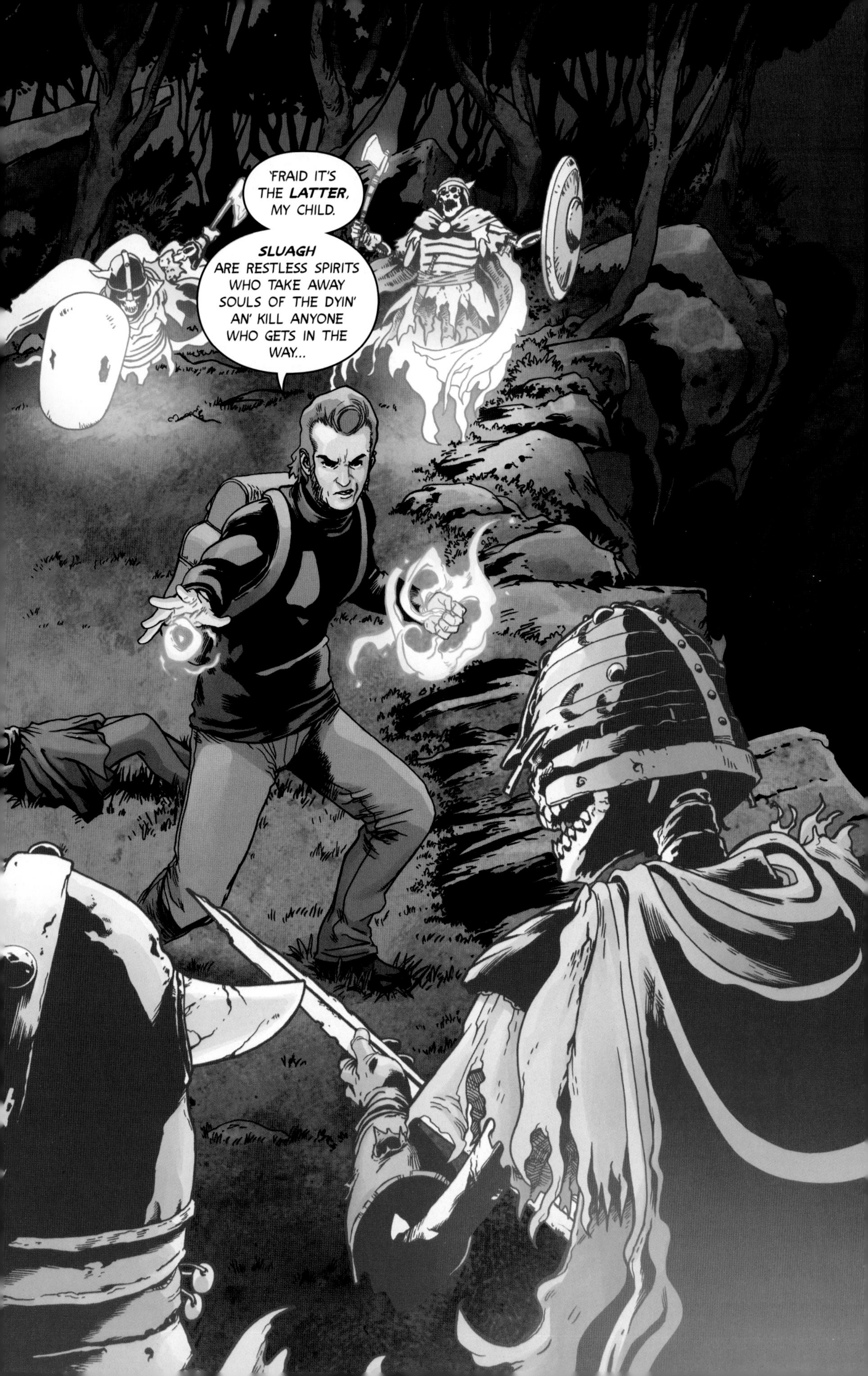
'FRAID IT'S THE **LATTER**, MY CHILD.
SLUAGH ARE RESTLESS SPIRITS WHO TAKE AWAY SOULS OF THE DYIN' AN' KILL ANYONE WHO GETS IN THE WAY...

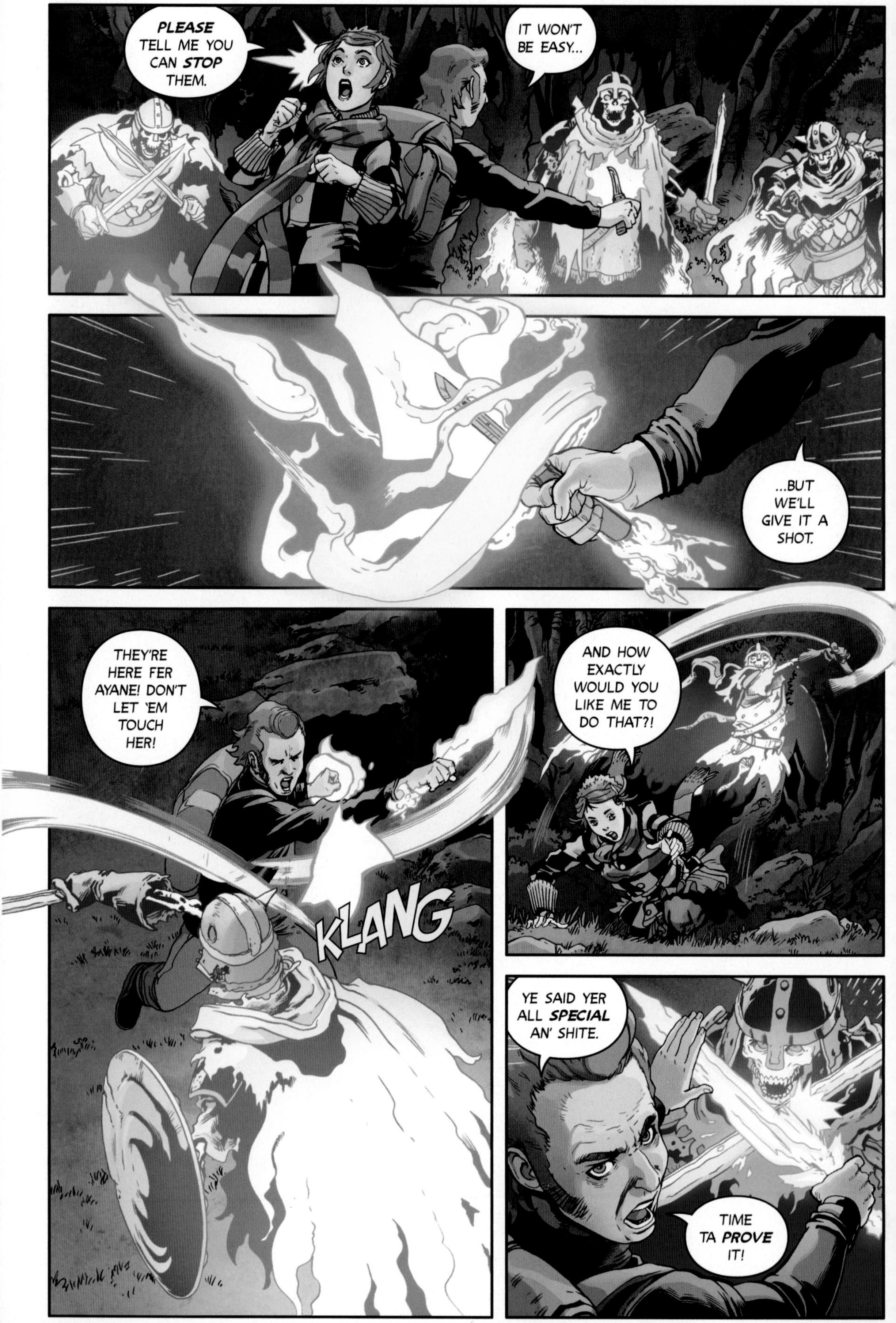
PLEASE TELL ME YOU CAN STOP THEM.
IT WON'T BE EASY...
...BUT WE'LL GIVE IT A SHOT.
THEY'RE HERE FER AYANE! DON'T LET 'EM TOUCH HER!
KLANG
AND HOW EXACTLY WOULD YOU LIKE ME TO DO THAT?!
YE SAID YER ALL SPECIAL AN' SHITE.
TIME TA PROVE IT!

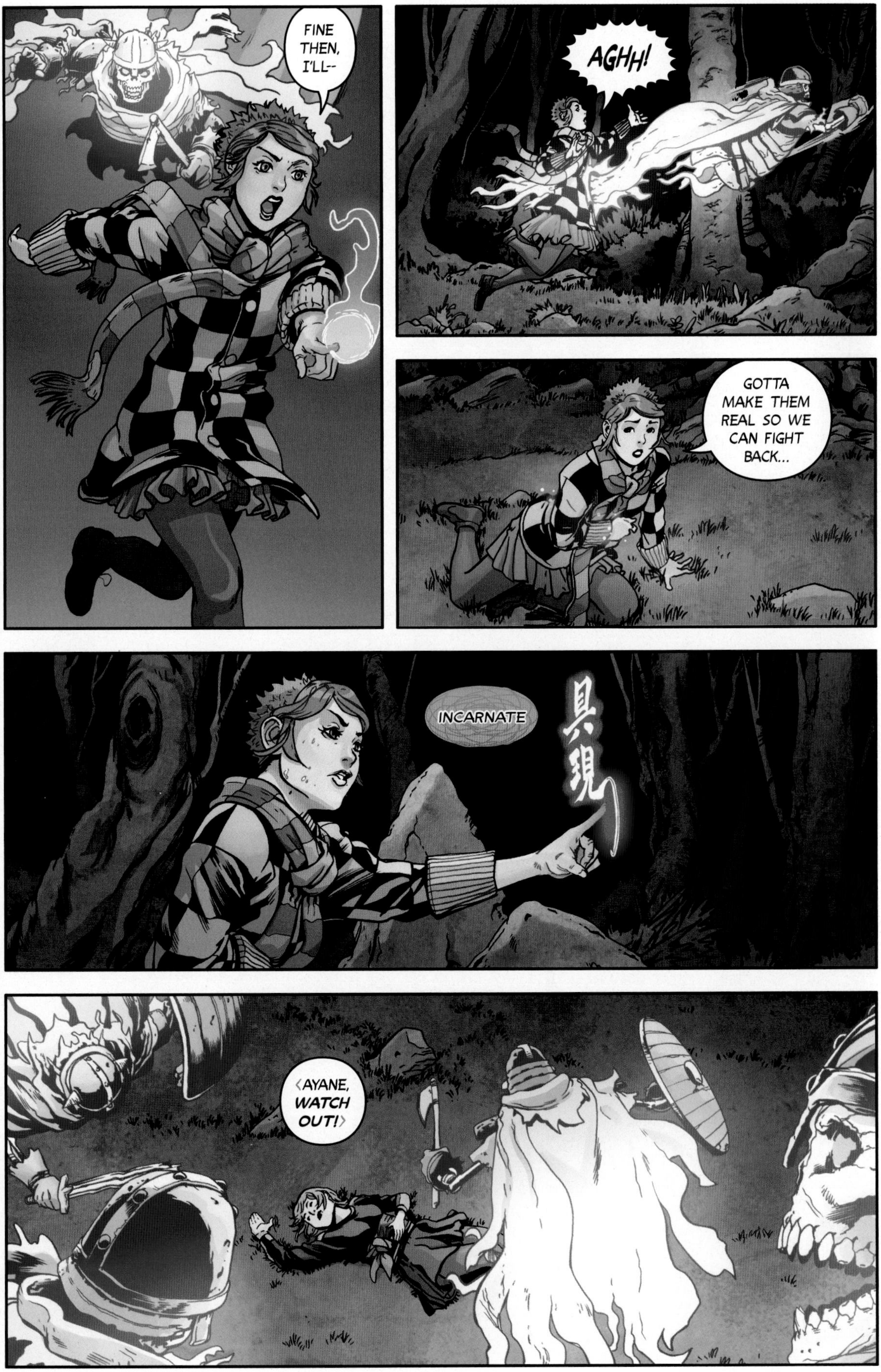
FINE THEN, I'LL--
AGHH!
GOTTA MAKE THEM REAL SO WE CAN FIGHT BACK...
INCARNATE
具現
‹AYANE, WATCH OUT!›

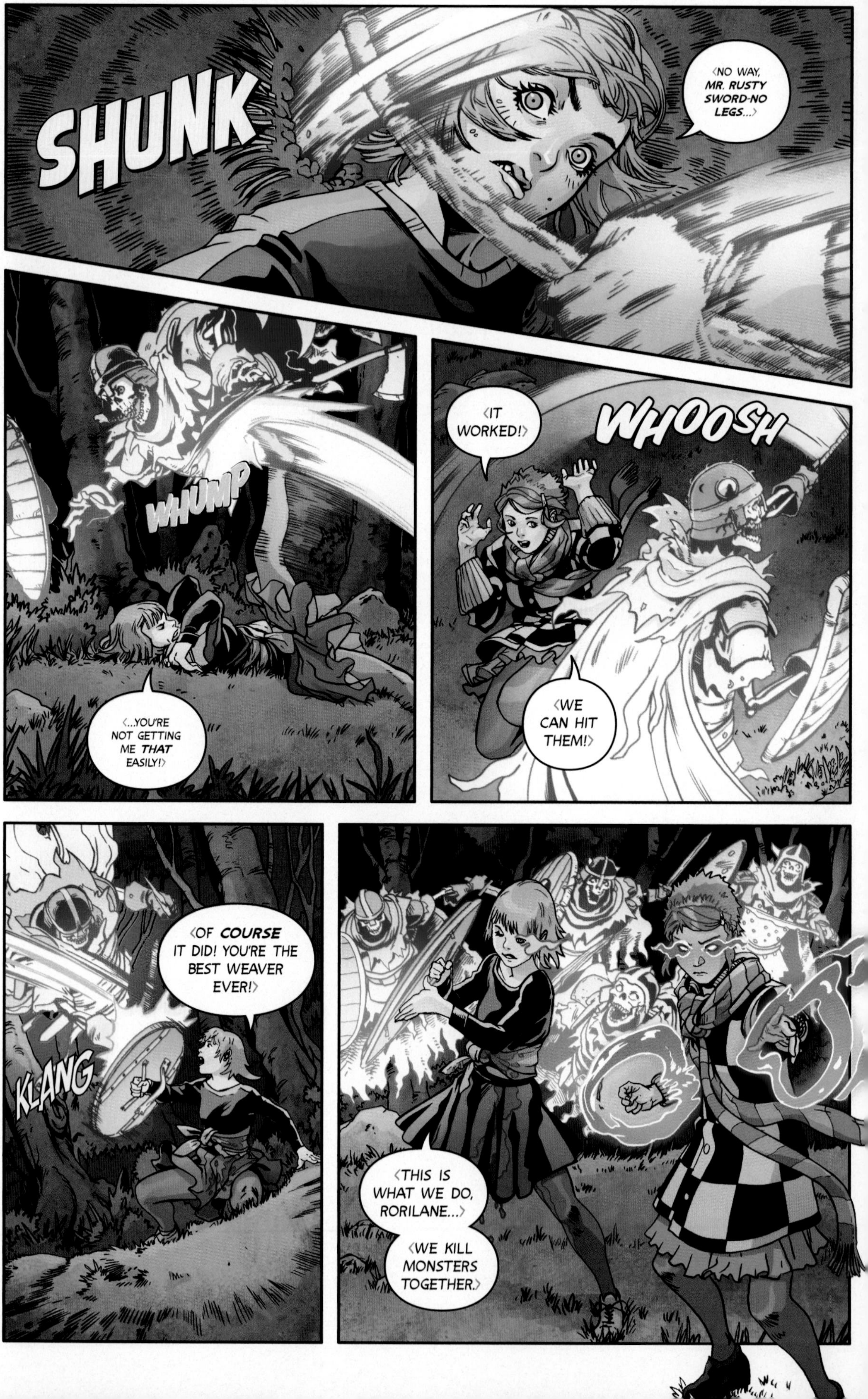
SHUNK
‹NO WAY, MR. RUSTY SWORD-NO LEGS...›
WHUMP
‹...YOU'RE NOT GETTING ME THAT EASILY!›
‹IT WORKED!›
WHOOSH
‹WE CAN HIT THEM!›
‹OF COURSE IT DID! YOU'RE THE BEST WEAVER EVER!›
KLANG
‹THIS IS WHAT WE DO, RORILANE...›
‹WE KILL MONSTERS TOGETHER.›

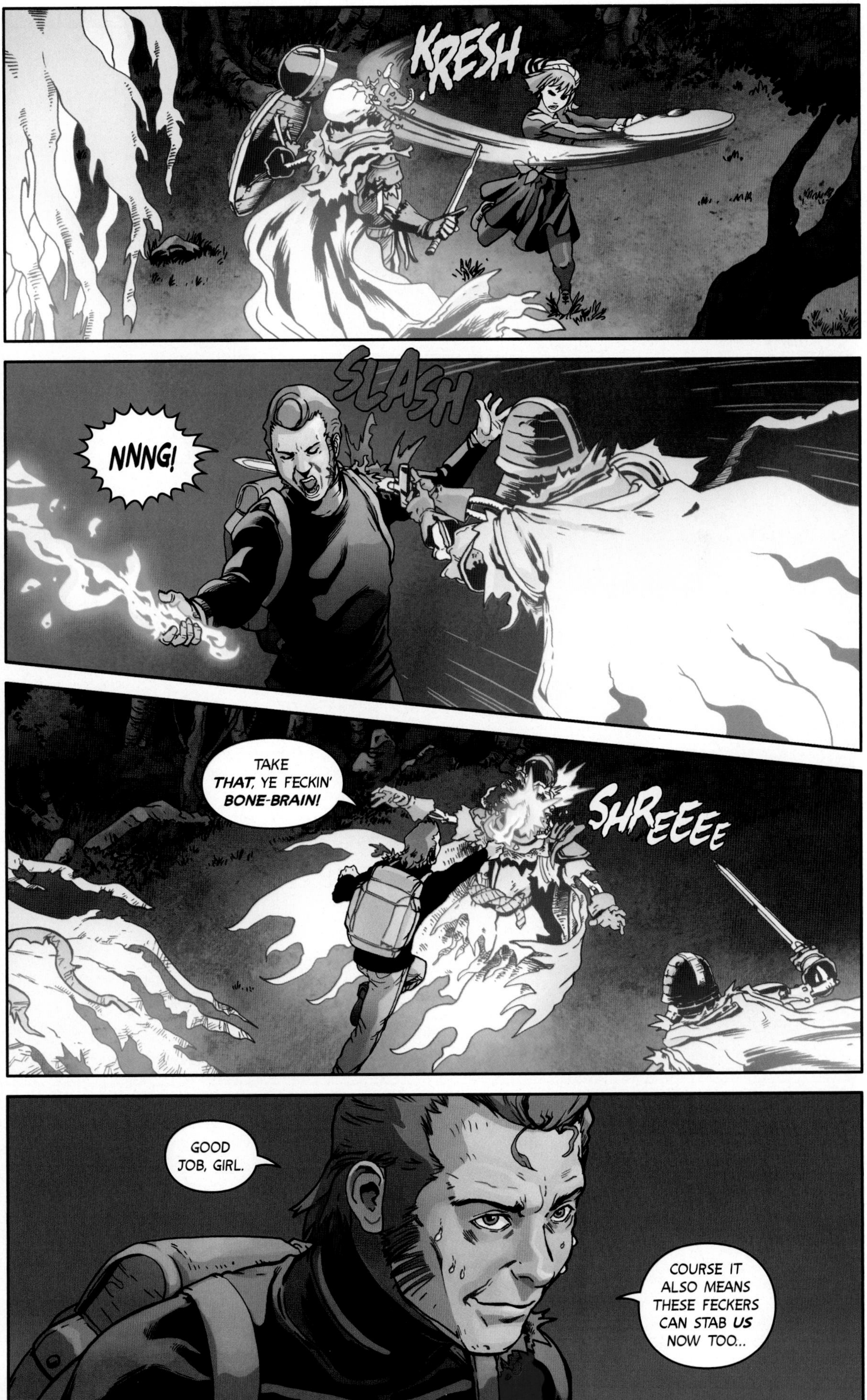
KRESH
SLASH
NNNG!
TAKE *THAT*, YE FECKIN' *BONE-BRAIN!*
SHREEEEE
GOOD JOB, GIRL.
COURSE IT ALSO MEANS THESE FECKERS CAN STAB *US* NOW TOO...

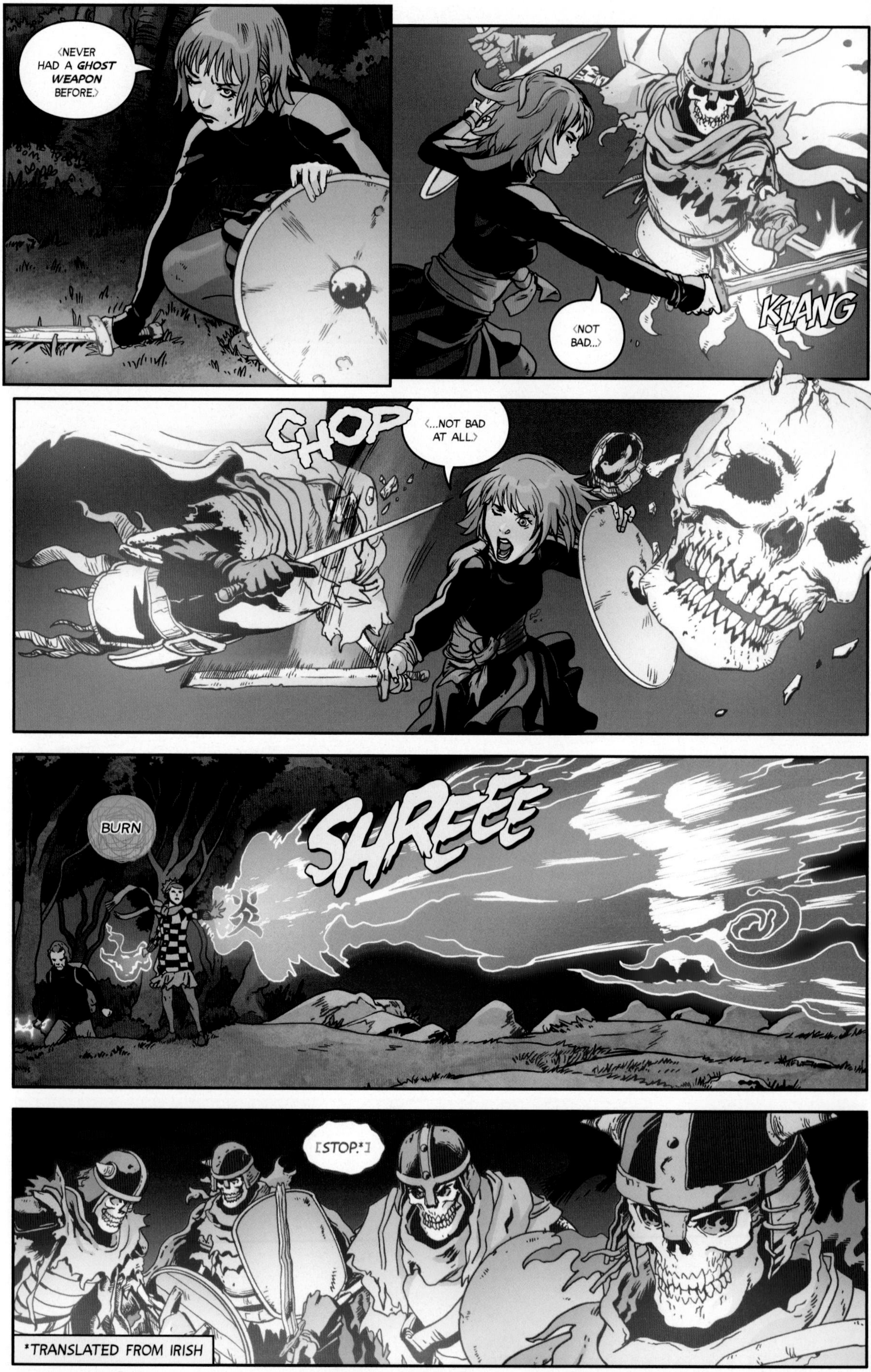

⟨NEVER HAD A **GHOST WEAPON** BEFORE.⟩
⟨NOT BAD...⟩
KLANG
CHOP
⟨...NOT BAD AT ALL.⟩
BURN
SHREEE
[STOP.*]
*TRANSLATED FROM IRISH

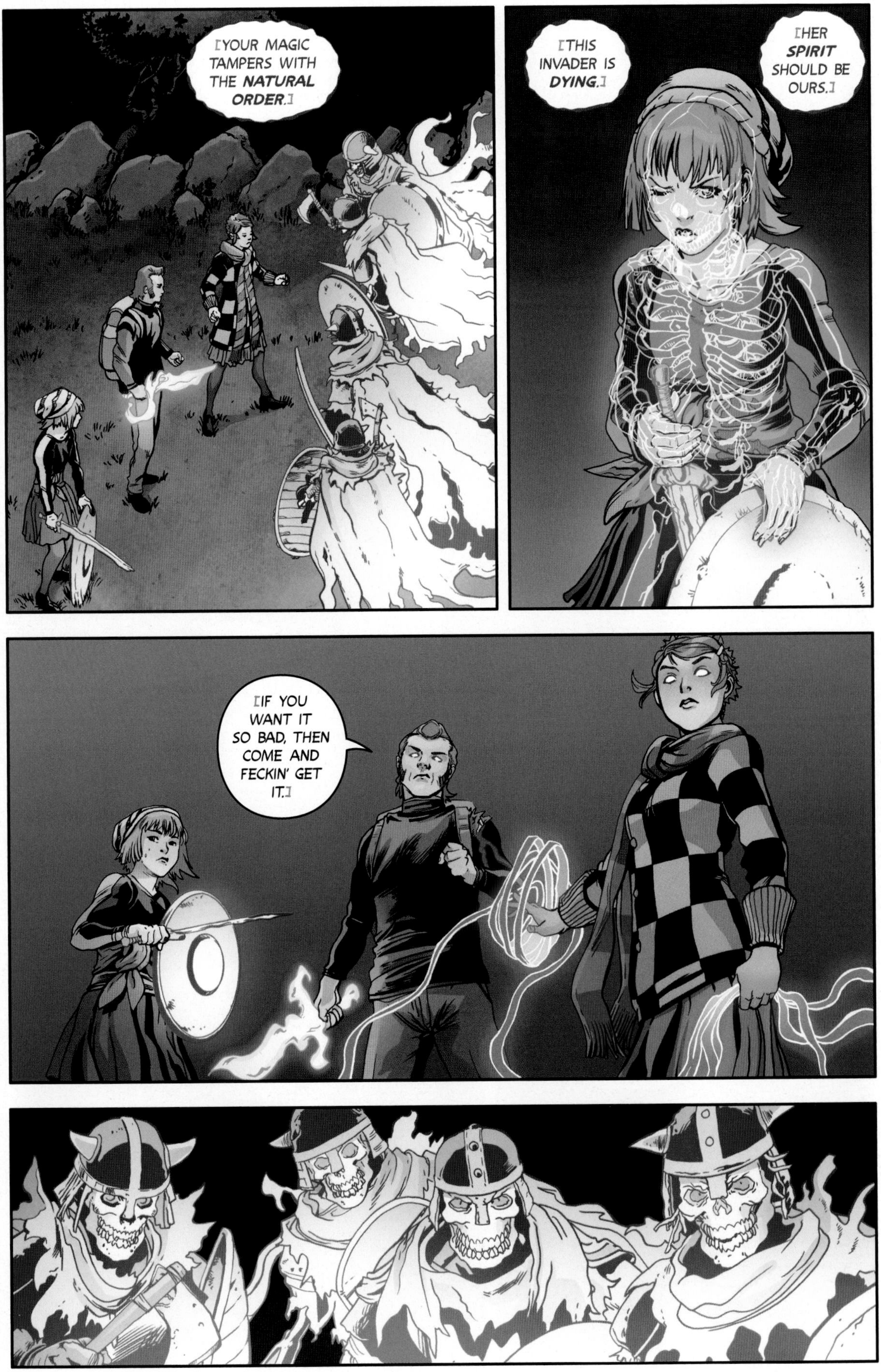
[YOUR MAGIC TAMPERS WITH THE NATURAL ORDER.]
[THIS INVADER IS DYING.]
[HER SPIRIT SHOULD BE OURS.]
[IF YOU WANT IT SO BAD, THEN COME AND FECKIN' GET IT.]

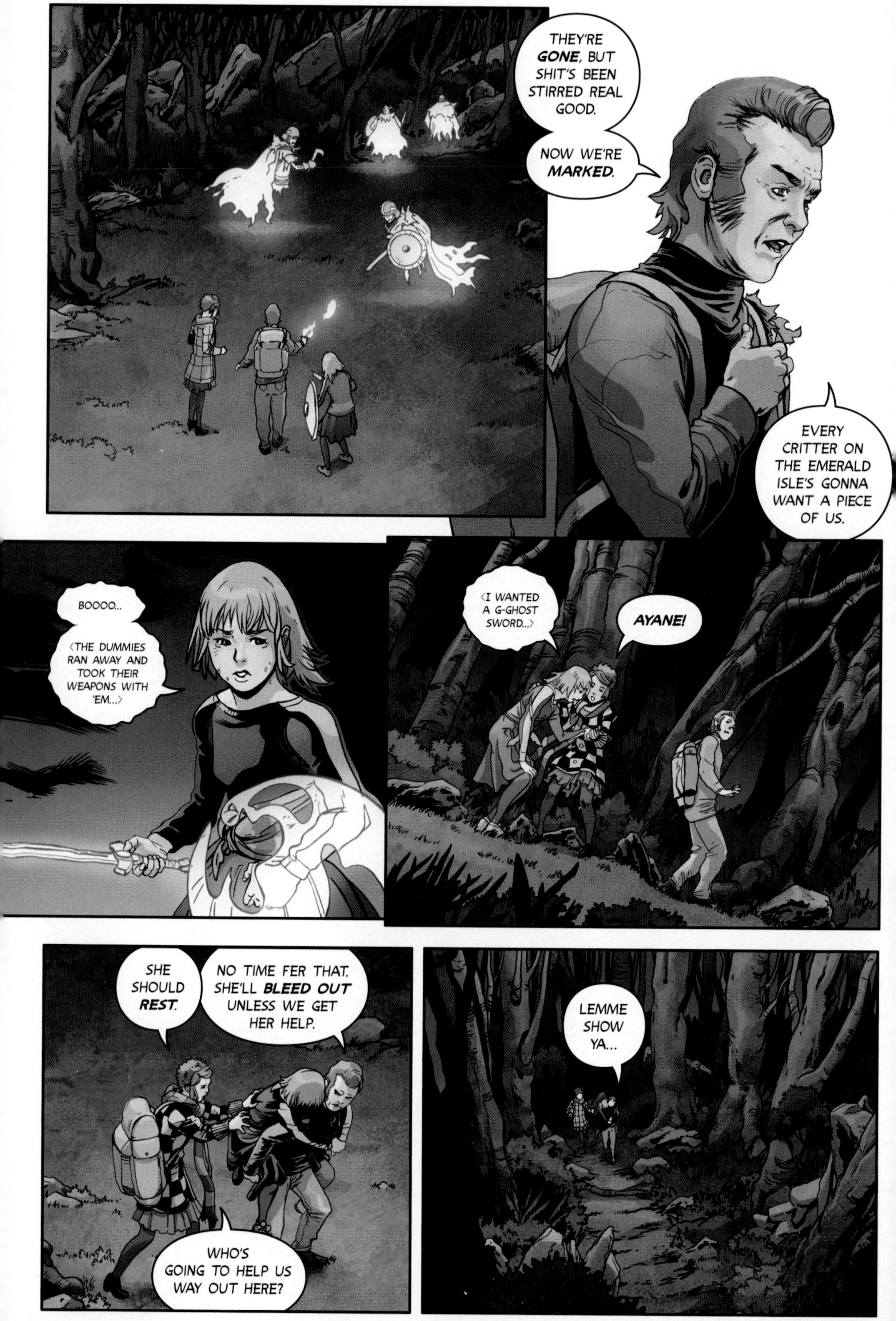
THEY'RE GONE, BUT SHIT'S BEEN STIRRED REAL GOOD.
NOW WE'RE MARKED.
EVERY CRITTER ON THE EMERALD ISLE'S GONNA WANT A PIECE OF US.
BOOOO...
<THE DUMMIES RAN AWAY AND TOOK THEIR WEAPONS WITH 'EM...>
<I WANTED A G-GHOST SWORD...>
AYANE!
SHE SHOULD REST.
NO TIME FER THAT. SHE'LL BLEED OUT UNLESS WE GET HER HELP.
WHO'S GOING TO HELP US WAY OUT HERE?
LEMME SHOW YA...

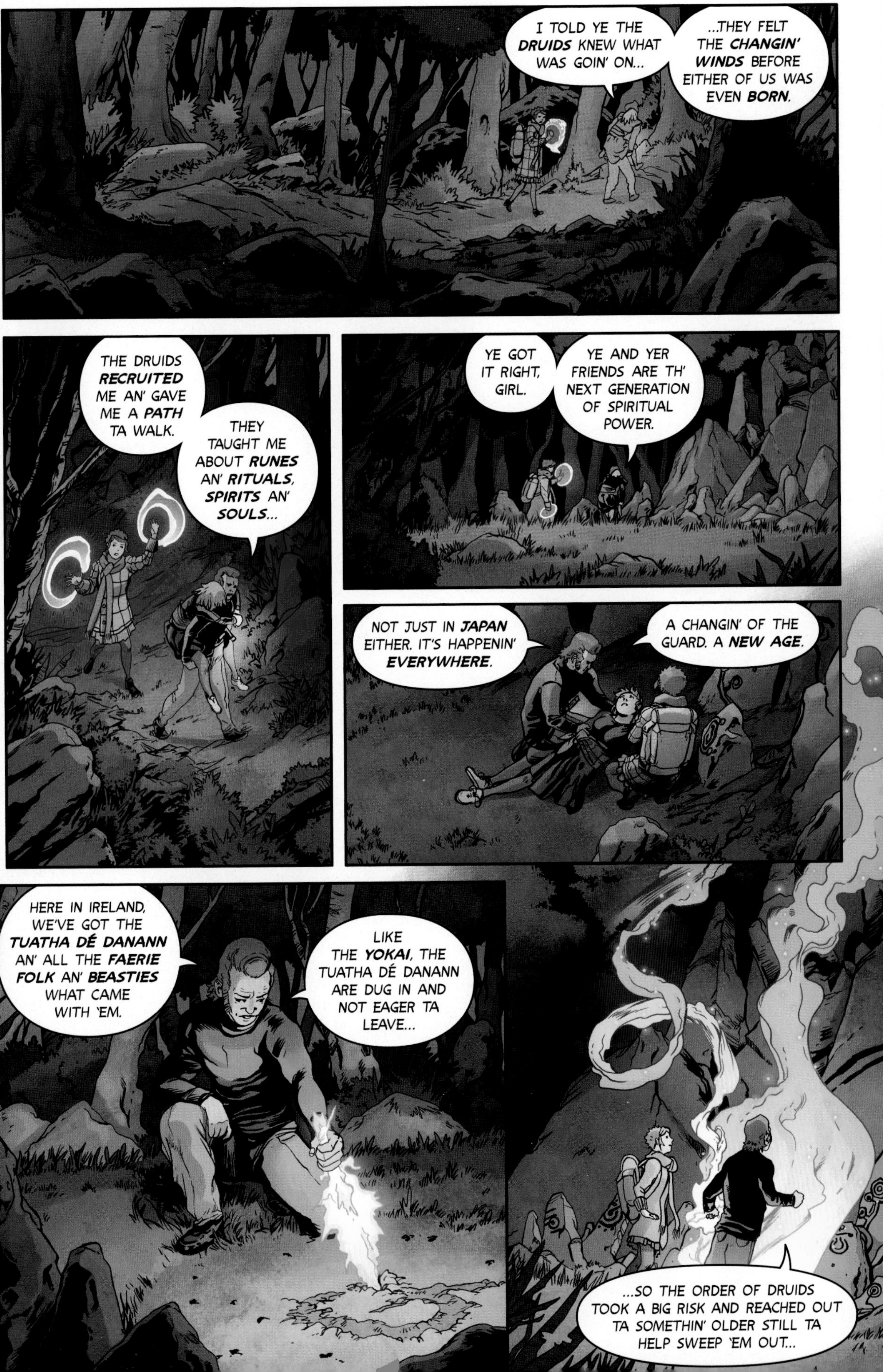
I TOLD YE THE DRUIDS KNEW WHAT WAS GOIN' ON...
...THEY FELT THE CHANGIN' WINDS BEFORE EITHER OF US WAS EVEN BORN.
THE DRUIDS RECRUITED ME AN' GAVE ME A PATH TA WALK.
THEY TAUGHT ME ABOUT RUNES AN' RITUALS, SPIRITS AN' SOULS...
YE GOT IT RIGHT, GIRL.
YE AND YER FRIENDS ARE TH' NEXT GENERATION OF SPIRITUAL POWER.
NOT JUST IN JAPAN EITHER. IT'S HAPPENIN' EVERYWHERE.
A CHANGIN' OF THE GUARD. A NEW AGE.
HERE IN IRELAND, WE'VE GOT THE TUATHA DÉ DANANN AN' ALL THE FAERIE FOLK AN' BEASTIES WHAT CAME WITH 'EM.
LIKE THE YOKAI, THE TUATHA DÉ DANANN ARE DUG IN AND NOT EAGER TA LEAVE...
...SO THE ORDER OF DRUIDS TOOK A BIG RISK AND REACHED OUT TA SOMETHIN' OLDER STILL TA HELP SWEEP 'EM OUT...

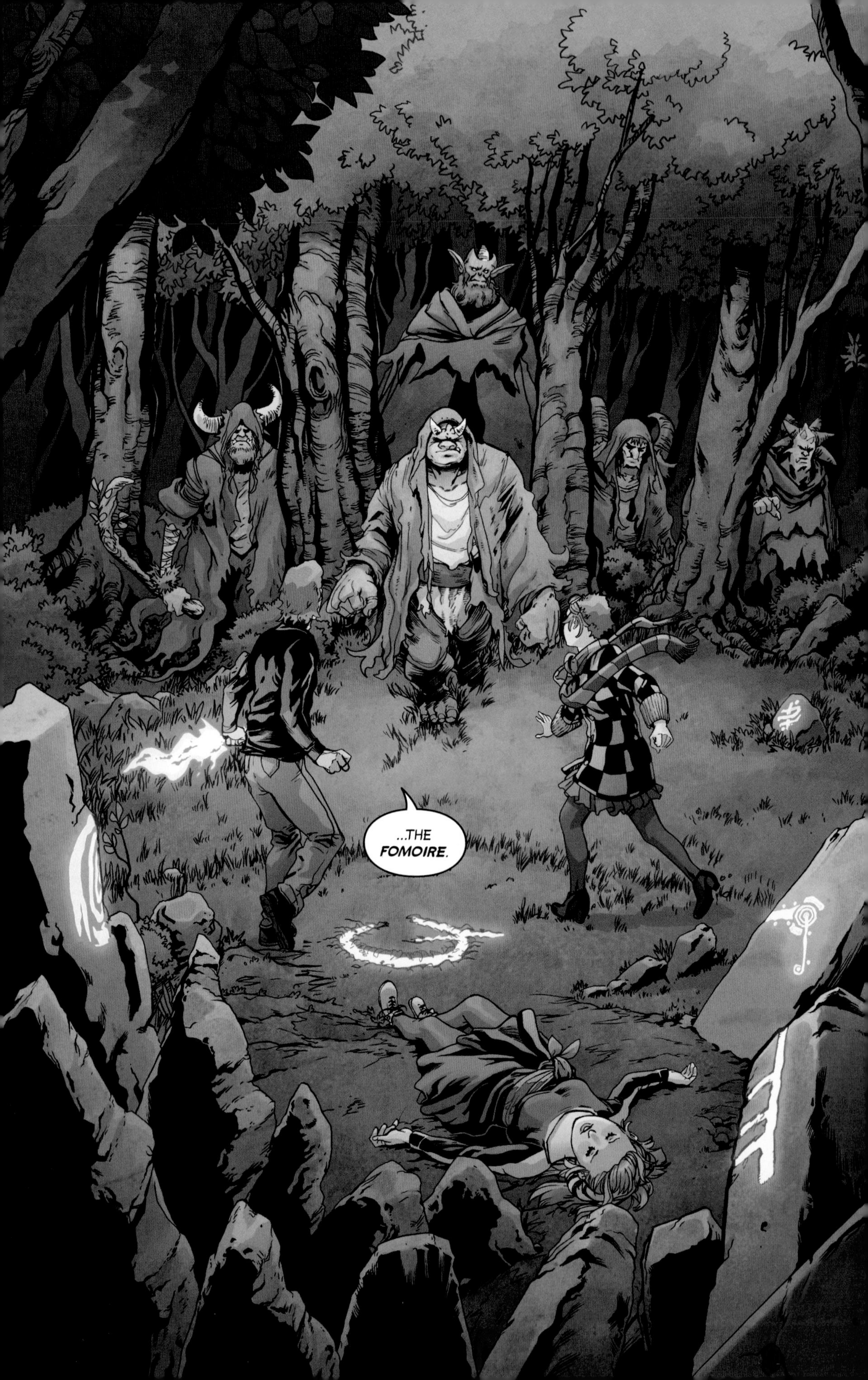
...THE *FOMOIRE*.

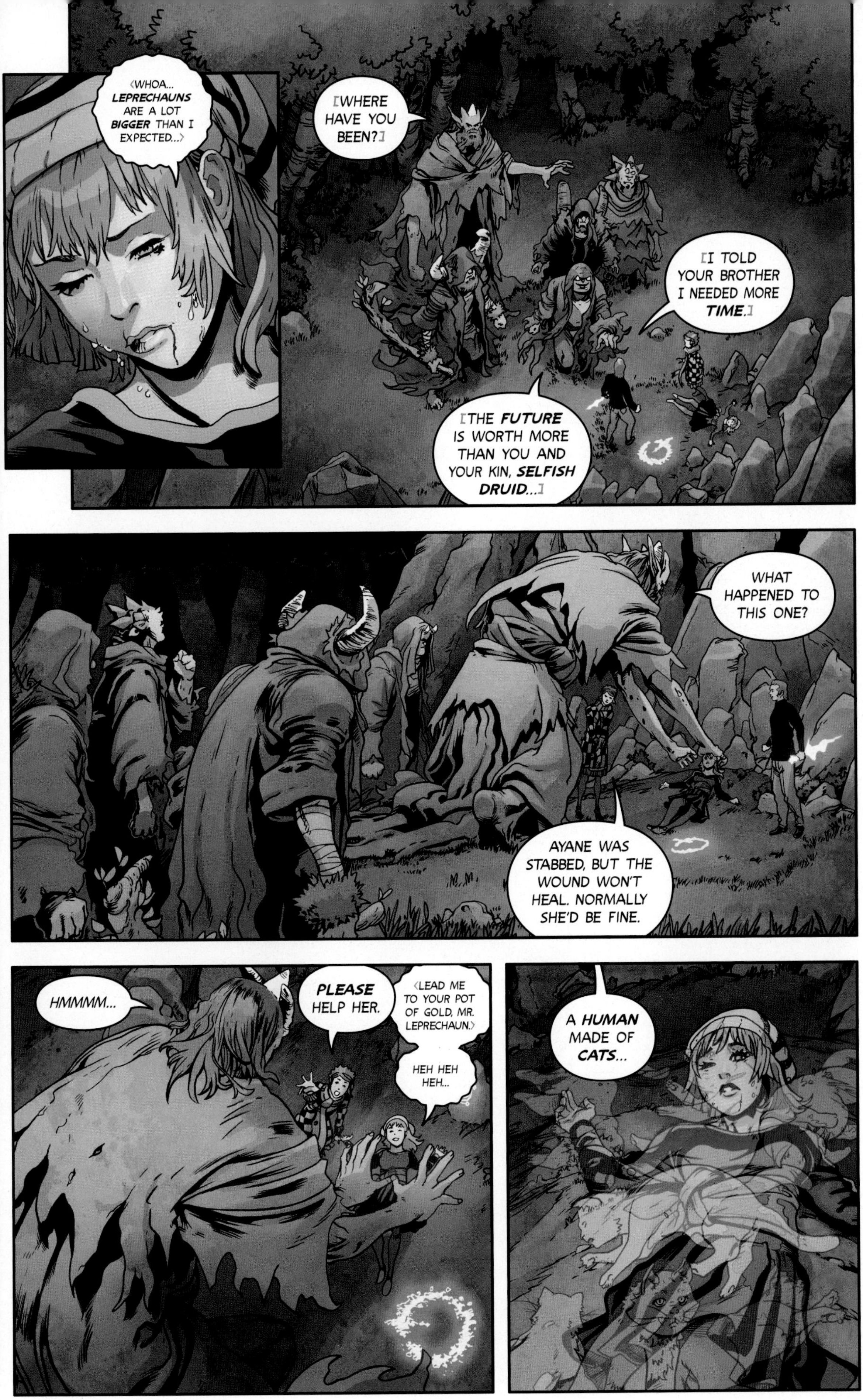
⟨WHOA... LEPRECHAUNS ARE A LOT BIGGER THAN I EXPECTED...⟩
[WHERE HAVE YOU BEEN?]
[I TOLD YOUR BROTHER I NEEDED MORE TIME.]
[THE FUTURE IS WORTH MORE THAN YOU AND YOUR KIN, SELFISH DRUID...]
WHAT HAPPENED TO THIS ONE?
AYANE WAS STABBED, BUT THE WOUND WON'T HEAL. NORMALLY SHE'D BE FINE.
HMMMM...
PLEASE HELP HER.
⟨LEAD ME TO YOUR POT OF GOLD, MR. LEPRECHAUN.⟩
HEH HEH HEH...
A HUMAN MADE OF CATS...

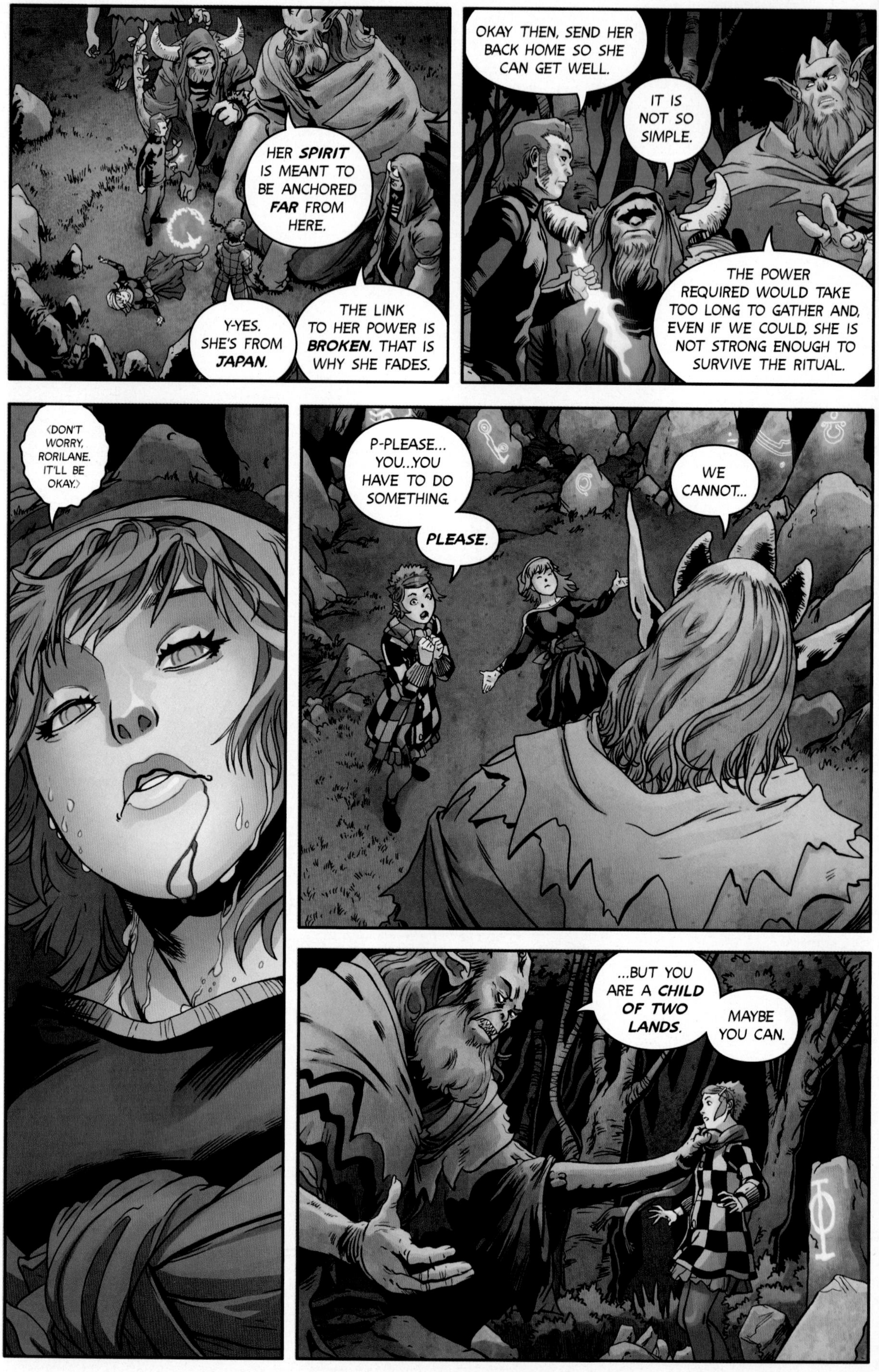
HER **SPIRIT** IS MEANT TO BE ANCHORED **FAR** FROM HERE.
Y-YES. SHE'S FROM **JAPAN**.
THE LINK TO HER POWER IS **BROKEN**. THAT IS WHY SHE FADES.
OKAY THEN, SEND HER BACK HOME SO SHE CAN GET WELL.
IT IS NOT SO SIMPLE.
THE POWER REQUIRED WOULD TAKE TOO LONG TO GATHER AND, EVEN IF WE COULD, SHE IS NOT STRONG ENOUGH TO SURVIVE THE RITUAL.
‹DON'T WORRY, RORILANE. IT'LL BE OKAY.›
P-PLEASE... YOU...YOU HAVE TO DO SOMETHING.
PLEASE.
WE CANNOT...
...BUT YOU ARE A **CHILD OF TWO LANDS**.
MAYBE YOU CAN.

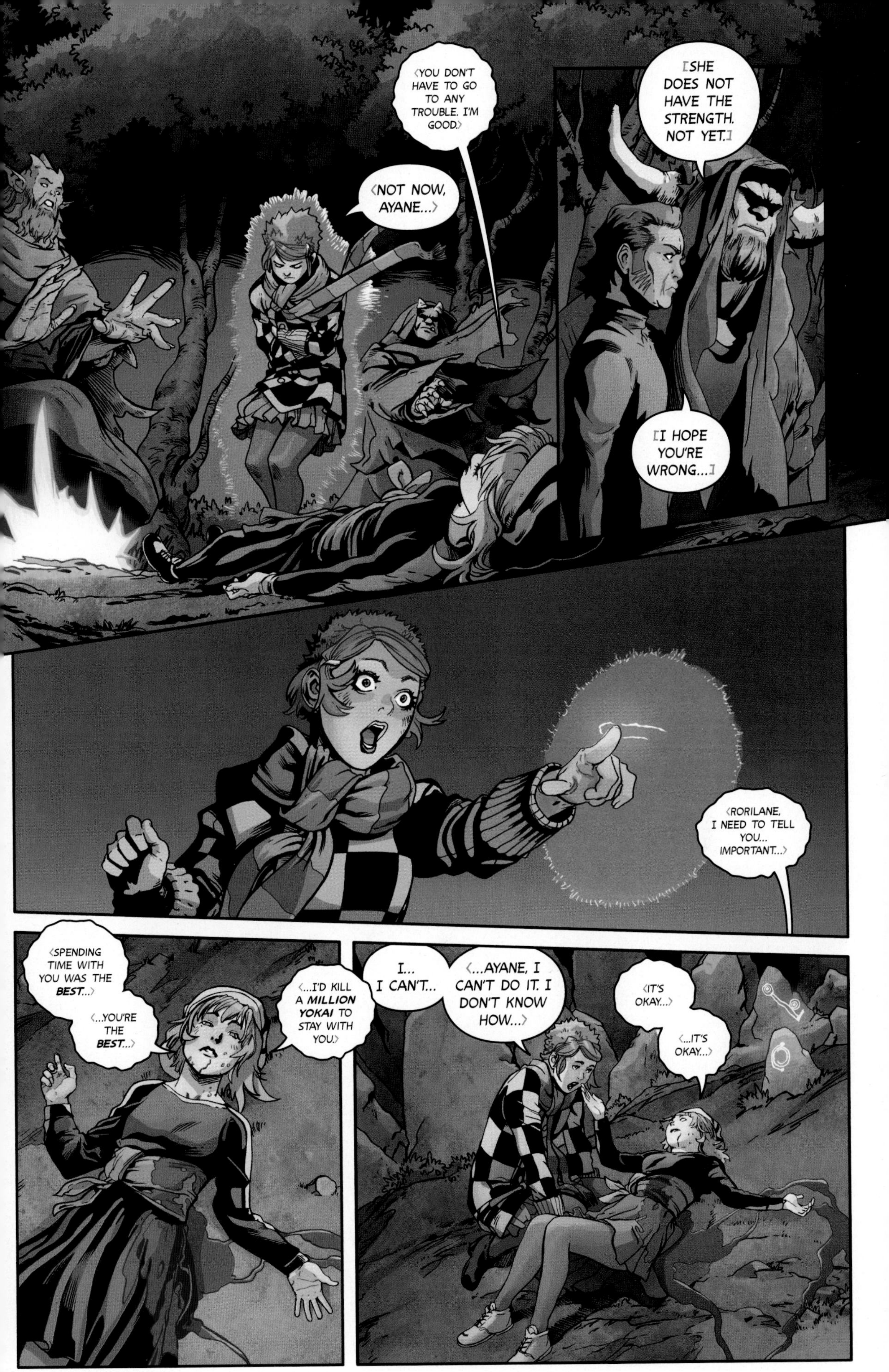

‹YOU DON'T HAVE TO GO TO ANY TROUBLE. I'M GOOD.›
‹NOT NOW, AYANE...›
[SHE DOES NOT HAVE THE STRENGTH. NOT YET.]
[I HOPE YOU'RE WRONG...]
‹RORILANE, I NEED TO TELL YOU... IMPORTANT...›
‹SPENDING TIME WITH YOU WAS THE BEST...›
‹...YOU'RE THE BEST...›
‹...I'D KILL A MILLION YOKAI TO STAY WITH YOU.›
I... I CAN'T...
‹...AYANE, I CAN'T DO IT. I DON'T KNOW HOW...›
‹IT'S OKAY...›
‹...IT'S OKAY...›

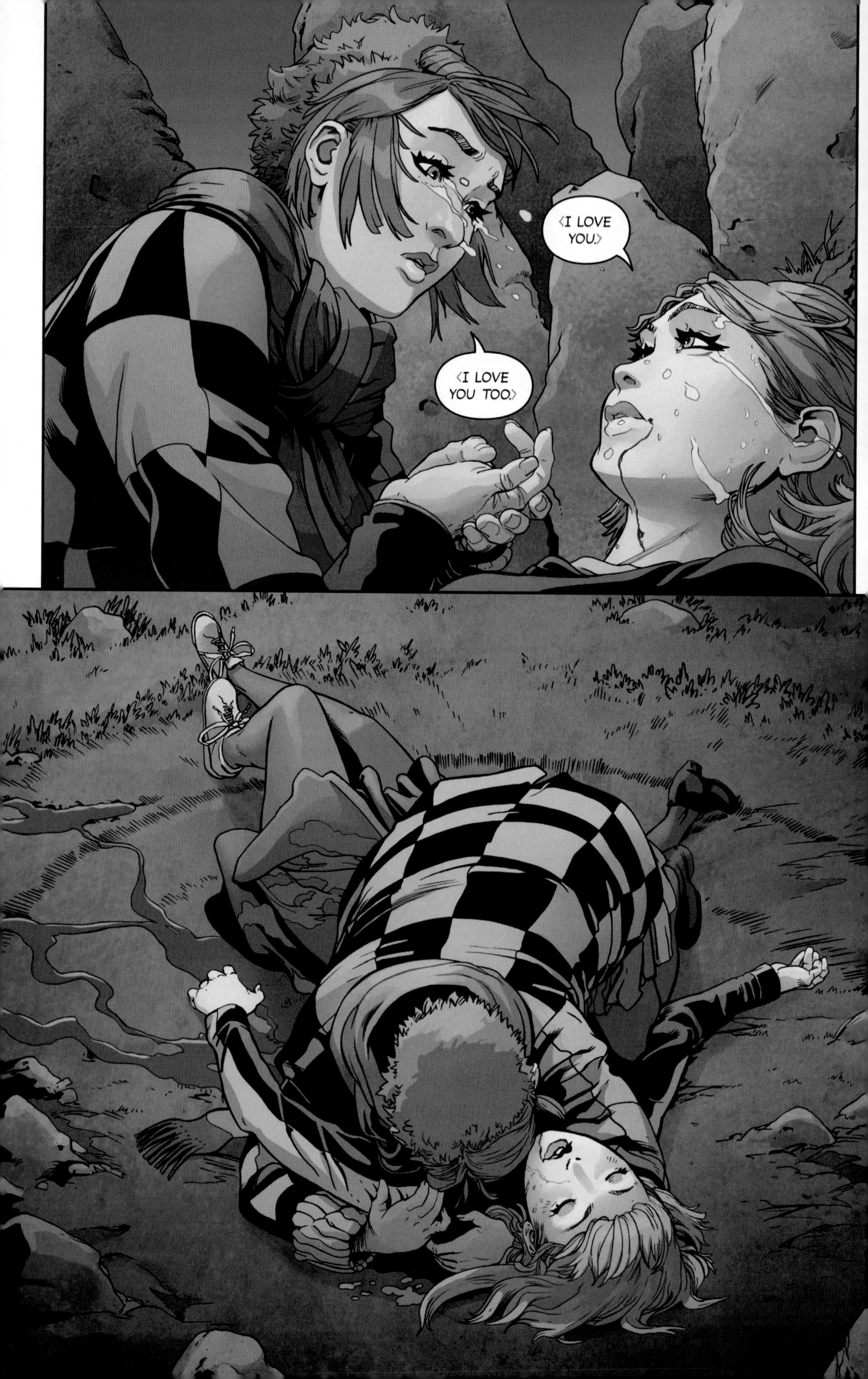
〈I LOVE YOU.〉
〈I LOVE YOU TOO.〉

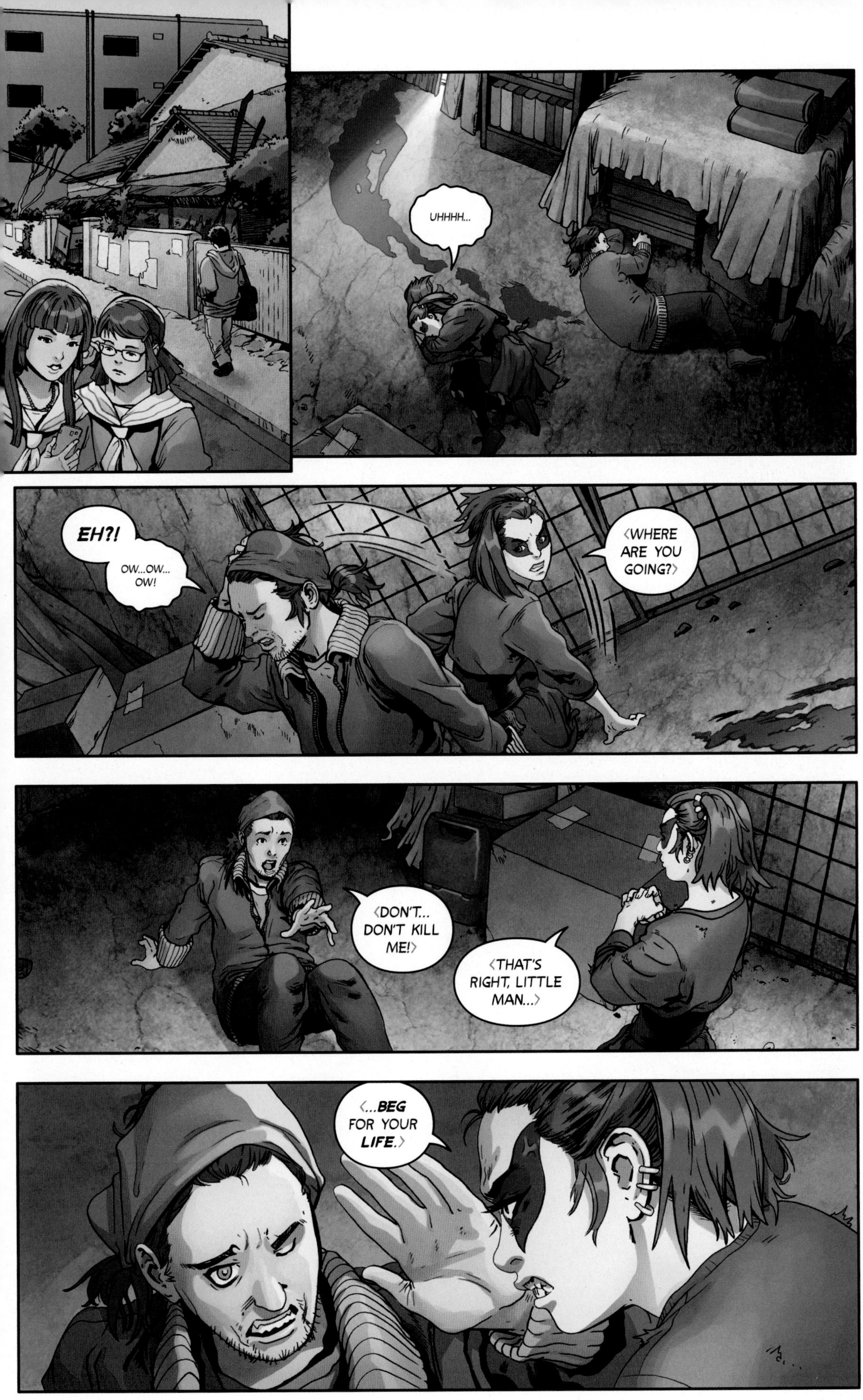
UHHHH...
EH?!
OW...OW... OW!
⟨WHERE ARE YOU GOING?⟩
⟨DON'T... DON'T KILL ME!⟩
⟨THAT'S RIGHT, LITTLE MAN...⟩
⟨...BEG FOR YOUR LIFE.⟩

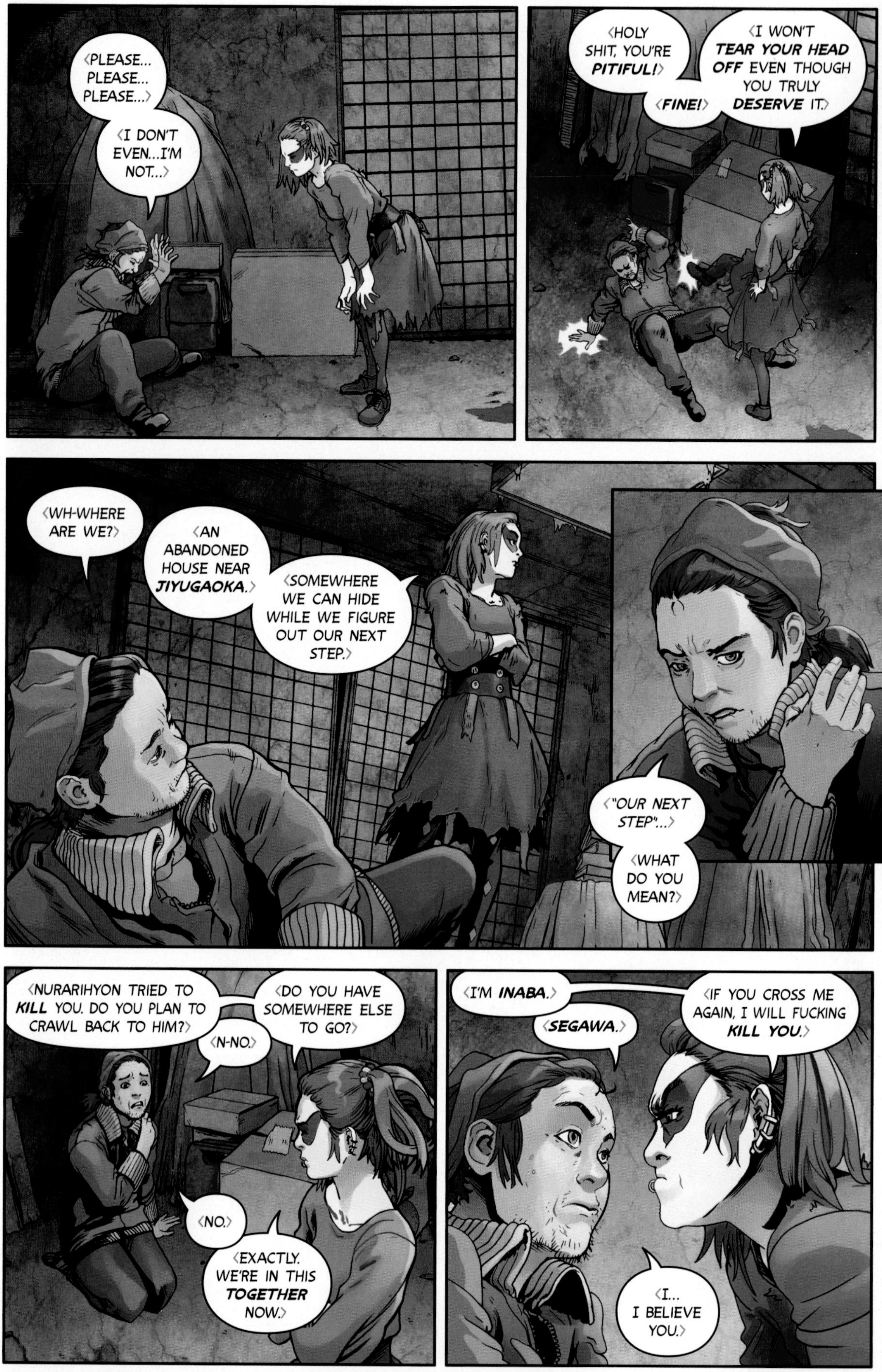

‹PLEASE... PLEASE... PLEASE...›
‹I DON'T EVEN...I'M NOT...›
‹HOLY SHIT, YOU'RE **PITIFUL!**›
‹**FINE!**›
‹I WON'T **TEAR YOUR HEAD OFF** EVEN THOUGH YOU TRULY **DESERVE** IT.›
‹WH-WHERE ARE WE?›
‹AN ABANDONED HOUSE NEAR **JIYUGAOKA.**›
‹SOMEWHERE WE CAN HIDE WHILE WE FIGURE OUT OUR NEXT STEP.›
‹"OUR NEXT STEP"...›
‹WHAT DO YOU MEAN?›
‹NURARIHYON TRIED TO **KILL** YOU. DO YOU PLAN TO CRAWL BACK TO HIM?›
‹N-NO.›
‹DO YOU HAVE SOMEWHERE ELSE TO GO?›
‹NO.›
‹EXACTLY. WE'RE IN THIS **TOGETHER** NOW.›
‹I'M **INABA.**›
‹**SEGAWA.**›
‹IF YOU CROSS ME AGAIN, I WILL FUCKING **KILL YOU.**›
‹I... I BELIEVE YOU.›

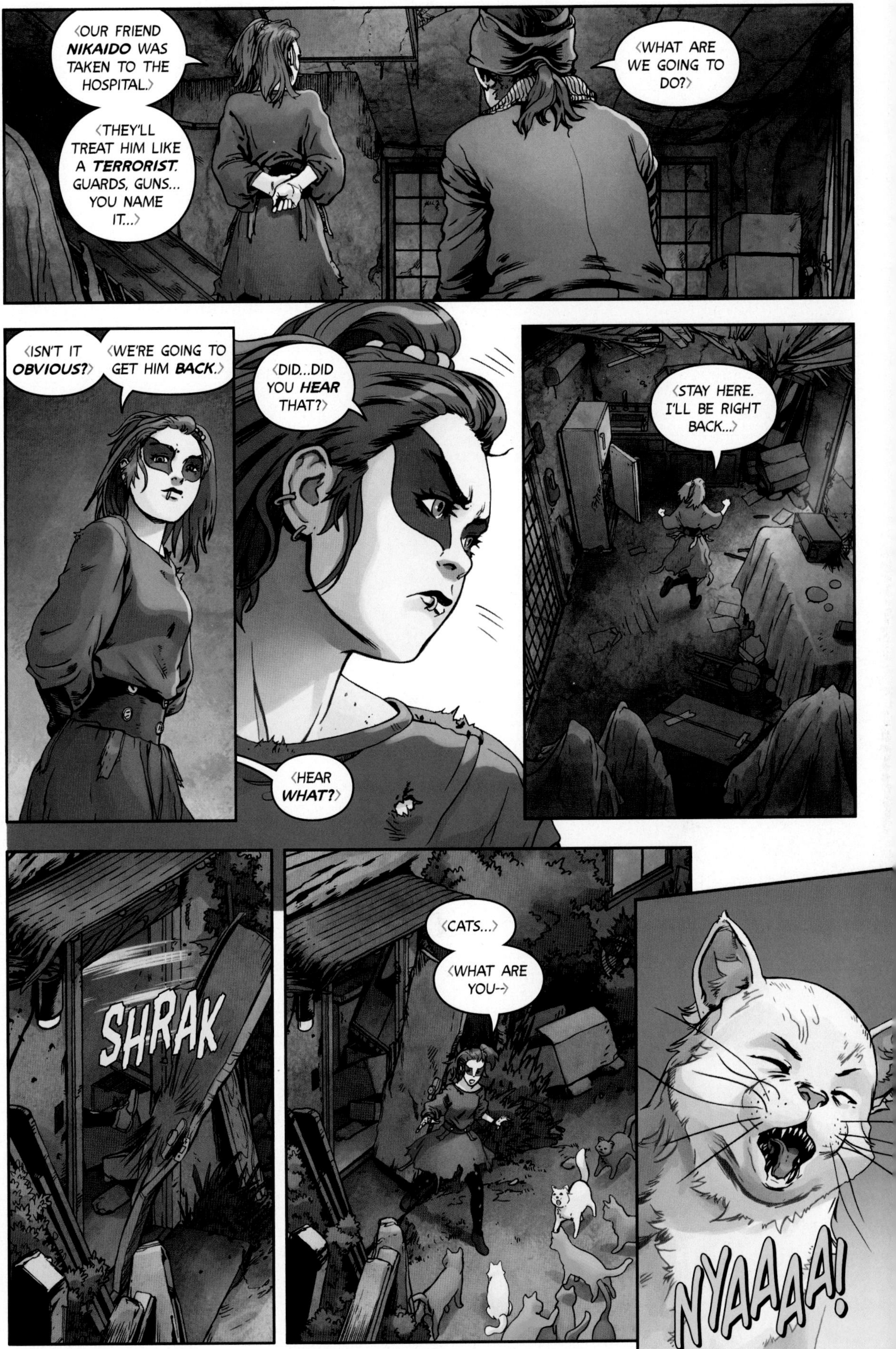
‹OUR FRIEND NIKAIDO WAS TAKEN TO THE HOSPITAL.›
‹THEY'LL TREAT HIM LIKE A TERRORIST. GUARDS, GUNS... YOU NAME IT...›
‹WHAT ARE WE GOING TO DO?›
‹ISN'T IT OBVIOUS?›
‹WE'RE GOING TO GET HIM BACK.›
‹DID...DID YOU HEAR THAT?›
‹HEAR WHAT?›
‹STAY HERE. I'LL BE RIGHT BACK...›
SHRAK
‹CATS...›
‹WHAT ARE YOU--›
NYAAAA!

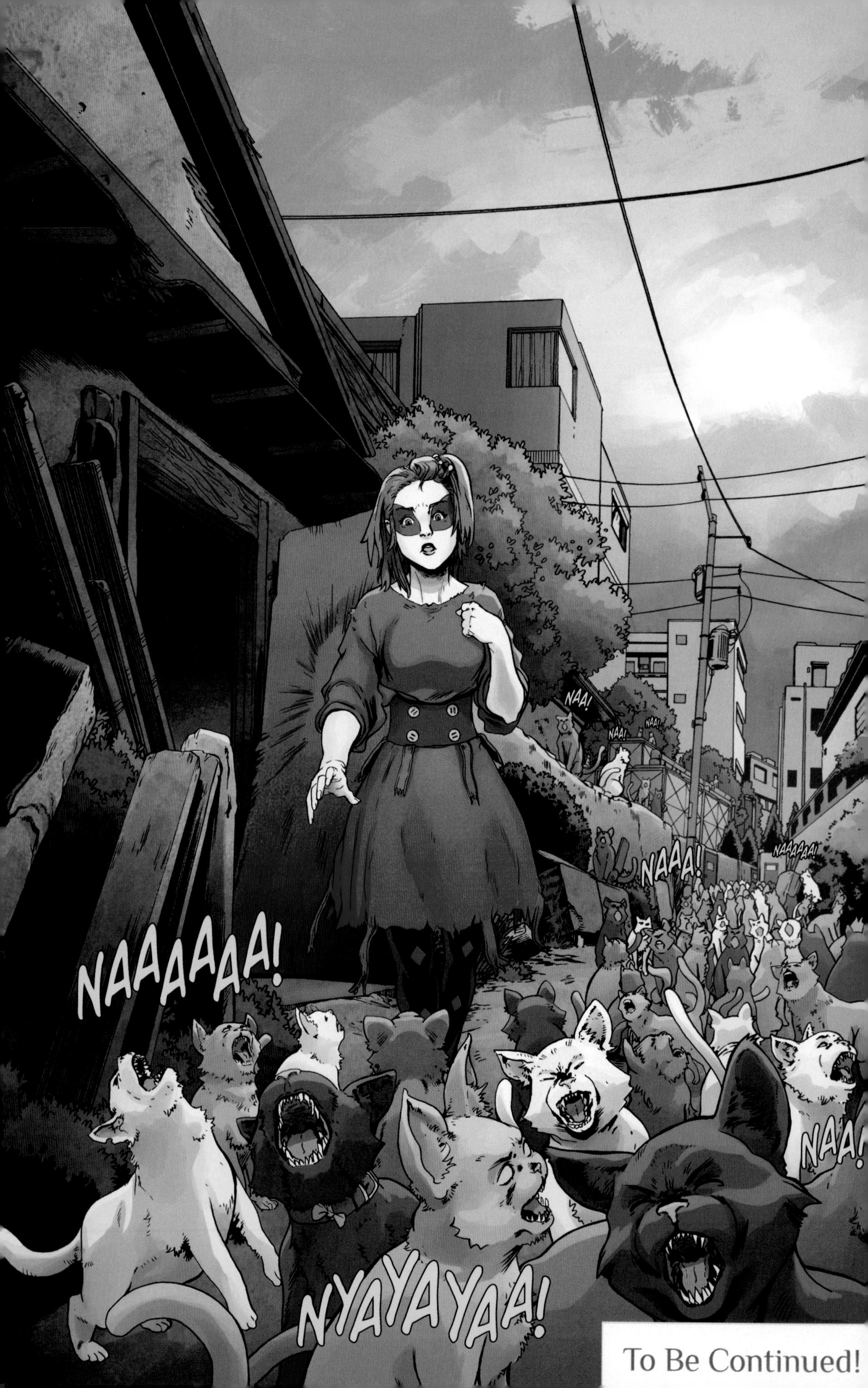
NAA!
NAA!
NAA!
NAAA!
NAAAAAA!
NAA!
NYAYAYAA!
To Be Continued!

Wayward's Kanji Spells

When Rori casts one of her powerful kanji spells, our friend Nishi Makoto is the one using traditional brush and ink to make the sweeping strokes you see incorporated into the comic page art. Here are some of the ones he's done so far:

Chapter #9: "Clothes"

Chapter #9: "Forget"

Chapter #20: "Incarnate"

Chapter #13: "Fly"

Chapter #20: "Burn"

Gods, Myths and Mortals of the Emerald Isle

When it comes to Irish history, there is a point where 'fact' takes a backseat and tales of legendary heroes and villains take centre stage. What did you expect? We are a nation of storytellers!

While the races of the Tuatha Dé Danann and the Fomorians are known worldwide, many forget that the Fir Bolg, or *Men of the Bog,* were long settled on the desolate Irish landscape. Do not let the translation of the name fool you—it simply means they were able to turn rocky, barren fields into fertile, arable lands. These literal and figurative ground-breaking men also established the sacred Hill of Tara and were the first of the High Kings of Ireland.

It is little wonder, therefore, that a race of demi-gods, descendants of the goddess Dana, mother of the land, would take an interest in conquering a domain of such opportunity. So it was that several decades after the Fir Bolg were settled, the Tuatha Dé Danann rode on the wind and came down from the sky and set foot in the Emerald Isle.

The number four is paramount throughout any documented accounts of the Tuatha Dé Danann. They created four cities: Falias, Gorias, Finias and Marias. They had four wise men to teach their youth both skills and knowledge, for without both they could not know wisdom. Each city had its own treasure, the keystones of the Tuatha Dé Danann—the Stone of Virtue which called to the King of Ireland, the Sword from which no man could escape once drawn, the Spear of Victory and the Magic Cauldron which left no appetite unsated.

Nuada was the King of the Tuatha Dé Danann. Around him he had great men such as Ogma, teacher of the written word, Dian Cecht, an incredible physician, Goibniu the Smith and Credenus the ultimate Craftsman. Also on the great warrior's team were his own gods—Neit, the god of battle and *The Morrigan,* triple goddess of war, fertility and sovereignty.

It is said that the mighty Tuatha Dé Danann arrived in the Province of Connaught on the first day of the feast of Beltaine. The Ancient Druids told the King of the Fir Bolg, Eochaid, that his dreams foretold of a powerful enemy approaching. He sent his Champion, Sreng, to meet with the emissary of the Tuatha Dé Danann known as Bres (an interesting sidebar is that Bres was of mixed race, Tuatha Dé Danann and Fomorian, a fact that will become of much relevance soon).

Sreng informed Bres that the weapon he carried was called *Craisech.* It could cut through flesh and bone, no shield could defend against it and the wounds it inflicted would never heal. An offer was made to the Fir Bolg that they could settle in one part of Ireland and leave the rest to the mighty Tuatha Dé Danann, an offer that was refused. And so began the First Battle of Magh Tuireadh.

The Fir Bolg were strong, led by their hurlers, spearmen of immense strength and agility. They were pitted against the triple goddess Morrigan, who rained down fire and cast great mists and clouds of the darkest night.

Despite the demi-god status of the Tuatha Dé Danann, they were driven back by the Fir Bolg; however, their king fell and the indigenous race conceded defeat and took Connaught for their home, leaving the Tuatha Dé Danann the rest of Ireland.

Now around this time, the King of the Tuatha Dé Danann, Nuada, lost an arm. Under the doctrine of the Tuatha Dé Danann, no incomplete man was able to reign. Nuada lost not only a limb but his crown, which went to Bres, foster son to the Tuatha Dé Danann but his father a Fomorian. Bres was a poor leader and showed none of the hospitality and social skills required of a king. While Bres began his reign, Nuada was gifted a silver arm from his physician, Dian Cecht. The son of the healer was impressed by the gift of alchemy shown by his father and studied harder and reached into darker magic. It was the son of Dian Cecht who created living tissue over the silver arm of Nuada, thus enabling him to be restored to power. Was Miach the creator of the first Cyborg? Regardless, his work drove his father to jealous rage and filicide.

Incensed by his deposition, Bres sought sanctuary and assistance with retribution from his paternal family, the Fomorians. His grandfather, Balor of the Evil Eye, agreed. Balor was so called because he has one eye that would cause death upon his penetrative stare. I often wonder if Balor was the inspiration for the Eye of Sauron, but I digress—the great battle of Magh Tuireadh had begun.

Bres went to war against his former kinsmen, his power in the form of his grandfather. Balor slayed his opponent Nuada with a single gaze from his evil eye. Undeterred at the loss of their king, the Tuatha Dé Danann were unrelenting in their attack and intent on winning the battle.

The new leader of the Tuatha Dé Danann was brought forth. Lugh, who like Bres, was of Tuatha Dé Danann and Fomorian birth. His loyalties were firm, however, and he killed his grandfather Balor with a single slingshot into his eye of poison.

Lugh found his half-brother Bres unprotected on the battlefield. Weak and defenseless, Bres begged for both mercy and his very life. In a moment of pity for his kin, Lugh agreed in exchange for Bres teaching the Fomorian people agriculture.

It is interesting to note that King Nuada had previously rejected Lugh, who had travelled far to the Court of Tara to be accepted as one of the Tuatha Dé Danann. When Lugh had asked for a place as either a blacksmith, wheelwright, swordsman, king's champion, druid, magician, craftsman or wordsmith he was refused. It was only because he excelled at all that he was accepted.

Lugh's power and influence went on to the creation of the festival of *Lughnasadh*, a Druid celebration held on the first of August every year. Such were his strengths and abilities that a test in the form of games was set up in his mother's name and became known as the Tailteann Games. These have progressed over recent centuries to become known as the Gaelic Games, played throughout Ireland to this day, growing stronger in popularity every year.

So what became of the Fomorians, the Tuatha Dé Danann and even the Fir Bolg? Well, we are talking demi-gods, supernatural races and magic—they may have been driven underground, back to the ethereal world of the Sidhe; however, they are not truly gone. Maybe there will be a third battle and the wars of Magh Tuireadh are not yet over. We will just have to wait and see...

Many a conversation in Ireland starts with 'do you know who's dead?' Death is a normal topic of discussion any self-respecting *Seanchái* (Irish Storyteller) will include death and haunting in his tale. In modern day Ireland, the customs of old still remain and the event is treated with weighted respect and tradition. We seem to have a fascination and fear of our own mortal demise that stems back to our ancient roots and the safeguarding of the soul.

For the majority, it isn't so much the dread of death itself, but what happens to the spirit and where it goes afterwards. There have always been the takers of souls in the form of demons, fairies, spirits and other ethereal beings. Over the centuries, the Irish have gotten wise and found different ways to repel or hide from those looking to reap the soul and cast it to eternal damnation – or worse.

In order to find the right protection from these creatures of darkness, you have to know who they are and what they want. Some are merely harbingers; others seek to harvest your very essence of being. Those such as the *Banshee* will (mostly) just warn you that death is imminent, however, there are two terrifying beings you should avoid at all costs.

SLUAGH

Once thought to be Angels that have tumbled from the grace of God, the *Sluagh Sidhe* actually have a far more sinister origin and purpose. Can you imagine how evil you have to be for your soul to be deemed too tainted for the fires of Hades and rejected by Satan himself? Well that is who the Sluagh are— souls of sinners not wanted by Heaven or Hell, destined to roam the Earth and take the departed for no reason other than the thrill of the hunt and to add to their ever-growing number.

Unlike other *Sidhe* (fairies), the Sluagh are unable to walk this mortal coil. They ride on the wind as a host, unable to touch the ground. They travel as a flock and, for all intents and purposes, look like a conspiracy of ravens, which is probably one of the reasons the raven is seen as a portent of death. As the howling wind and darkening sky take hold, they close in, and it becomes quite clear they are not bird like at all. With wizened, leathery wings and gnarled, skeletal frames, these twisted creatures fly in from the west and seek out the homes of the dying. This is why one of the traditions that still holds today is to close any westerly facing windows when a loved one is taking a last breath.

Sadly, not every innocent (or indeed not-so-innocent) soul escapes the clutches of the evil Sluagh, and these misfortunes are caught up in the host of the soul hunters, not to touch the Earth again or reach Heaven or Hell for all eternity.

THE DULLAHAN

The *Dullahan* and before him *Crom Dubh*, are descended from the god Crom Cruaich and are synonymous with dark rituals, death and folklore.

Crom Cruaich was first introduced to Ireland some time before the arrival of the *Tuatha Dé Danann*. Tigernmas was one of the first High Kings of Ireland, and, as a Milesian, brought the worship of this deathly idol to Ireland, building a shrine at the top of Magh Slécht in County Cavan in order to win favour from his god.

King Tigernmas and most of his troops mysteriously died on Magh Slécht on the night of Samhain, now known as Halloween, as they worshipped their dark, sacrificial deity. As the centuries passed, Crom Dubh evolved from Crom Cruaich and became a worshipped figure in his own right. He is still left 'offerings' in rural parts of Ireland today on Crom Dubh Sunday.

The darkest incarnation of the sacrificial god, however, is the Dullahan, also known as *Gan Ceann*, meaning 'without a head'. Crom Dubh did not want to be denied human souls following the introduction of Christianity and so disguised himself as the one without a head, a tribute to the sacrifices by beheading that gave Crom Cruaich/Dubh his power.

For centuries, the Celts have believed the head to be incredibly powerful as both the sacred and physical resting place of the soul. Warriors would decapitate their foes and keep their heads to ward off evil and gain more power. Those believed to have died as deviants would have stones placed in their mouths to stop the evil soul escaping. It is no surprise therefore, that one of Ireland's most feared unearthly beings incorporates all of these Celtic beliefs over the ages.

Gan Ceann is a part of the 'Unseelie Court' of the fairy realm, filled with the nastiest and darkest of the Sidhe, and his job is to reap souls. He carries his head in the crook of his arm, black eyes darting from the mottled, decaying flesh stretched thinly across his skull, searching for his prey.

The Dullahan carries a whip made from the spine of a human corpse as he stands on his wagon. The wheel spokes are made of thigh bones and covered with dried human skin, and the coach is pulled by a jet black horse with eyes of glowing embers.

The headless horseman has supernatural vision, and when he senses a soul for the taking, he holds his head high, seeing across landscapes, through windows and into the darkest corners of the most remote homes.

The soul taker does not stop for anyone and all locks swing open, no one is safe. If you get in his way, at best your eyes will be lashed out with his whip or the Dullahan will throw a bowl of human blood upon you. The stain cannot be removed and you are marked as his next target.

Certain festivals increase the power of The Dullahan and this is a time to stay in and draw your curtains tightly. If you are out in the still of night, there is no protection from this agent of death. He does however fear one thing – gold. Throwing a piece in his path may make him back off for a while and may be the only thing that will save you.

The Dullahan is only permitted to speak once on each ride and that is to utter the name of the person who is going to die. When he finds his quarry and speaks their name aloud, their spirit is brought forth to be devoured.

So we closed our west-facing windows and turned mirrors so our souls would not be trapped. We paid Sin Eaters to take our transgressions and clear a path to Heaven. We left food as offerings to the Sidhe and the departed that they may look favorably upon us. We hired Keeners to cry at wakes so as not to invoke the Hounds of Hell, sent to collect the dead and take them to eternal torment. All in the name of saving our souls.

The fate of the spirit is of more concern to the Irish than death itself, and, over the centuries, protection of the soul has taken precedence over anything else. Sometimes it doesn't matter what protections are put in place however, as the malevolent search for souls by the Dullahan and the Sluagh is too powerful and relentless. All we can do is the best we can in this life, maybe close the odd window at the right time, oh, and carry a bit of gold in our pockets – just in case!

Tsukimono – Yokai and Spirit Possession

There are eight million gods and monsters in Japan, and more than a few of them ride around in human bodies on occasion. Yūrei, kappa, tanuki, tengu, and kitsune. Snakes, cats, horses, and spiders. Almost any yokai can possess a human. When they do, they are known by a single name—*tsukimono*.

The concept of spirit possession is an ancient and ubiquitous belief in Japan. In his 1894 book *Occult Japan*, Percival Lowell wrote:

The number of possessing spirits in Japan is something enormous. It is safe to say that no other nation of forty million people has ever produced its parallel...

Spirit possession alone is nothing unique. Cultures with a history of ghosts or supernatural beings (that is to say, all cultures that have ever existed) have near identical traditions: mediums enter a trance, clear their minds, and willfully draw spirits into their bodies to serve as oracles. In Japan, these mediums tap the power of kami or ancestor spirits in a process called *kamigakari* (神懸り; divine possession). The kami can be singular or plural, ancestor spirits or a merger of deities. Because of the obscure nature of kami, it can be difficult to tell exactly who is speaking from the medium's mouth. But they all know it is a voice from beyond.

Where Japan really gets wacky—where it takes a giant leap sideways from most supernatural traditions—is tsukimono, yokai possession. If it gets pissed off enough or is willful enough, pretty much anything can take control of your body. As Lowell wrote:

...there are a surprising number of forms. There is, in short, possession by pretty much every kind of creature, except by other living men.

Tsukimono are rarely a spontaneous event. Often the yokai possesses as an act of revenge—perhaps a human killed one of the yokai's children, or destroyed their home. Or it could be simple greed: a fox wants to eat a delicious treat that it otherwise can't get its paws on. The reasons are as innumerable as yokai themselves. But as opposed to kamigakari, it is always involuntary. No one invites tsukimono into their body.

Tsukimono effects come in various forms. In most cases, the victim takes on the attributes of the yokai or animal. All you have to do is take a yokai, add *–tsuki* (possession) to the end of it, and let your imagination go wild.

A victim of *tanuki-tsuki* (tanuki possession) is said to voraciously overeat until their belly swells up like a tanuki, causing death unless exorcized. *Uma-tsuki* (horse possession) can cause people to become ill-mannered, huffing at everything and sticking their face into their food to eat like a horse. *Kappa-tsuki* (kappa possession) overwhelms people with the need to be in water and develop an appetite for cucumbers. *Yūrei-tsuki* (ghost possession) leaves people to wither away and die as their life force is slowly snuffed out. Almost any bad or unusual behavior could be blamed away as possession by some yokai. A very convenient bit of folklore.

In general, the only way to free someone from a tsukimono is through an exorcist. Usually these were the wandering Shugendo priests called *yamabushi*. They were the great sorcerers and exorcists of pre-modern Japan, roaming through the mountains and coming down when called to perform sacred services and spiritual battles.

Not all forms of tsukimono follow those same rules. *Kitsune-tsuki* (fox possession)—by far the most common type of tsukimono—is unique in that it resembles classic demonic possession in Western culture. Instead of the possessed taking on fox attributes, kitsune-tsuki feels like a bodily attack. The victim experiences shortness of breath, phantom pains, speaking in strange voices, and epileptic fits.

Up until WWII, kitsune-tsuki was treated with deadly seriousness by both mystics and scientists. In his 1913 book *Myths and Legends of Japan*, F. Hadland Davis wrote:

Demonical possession is frequently said to be due to the evil influence of foxes. This form of

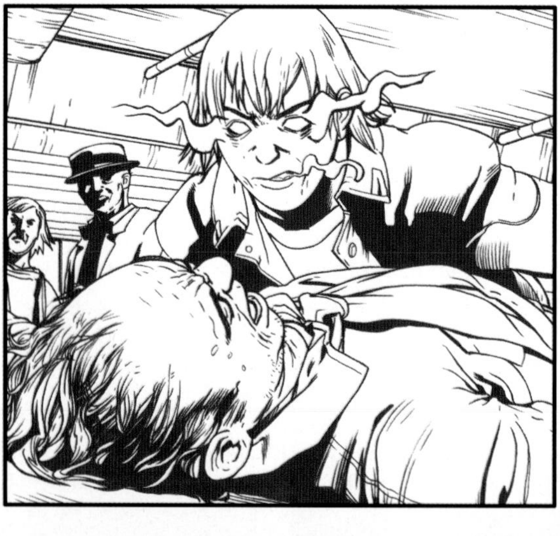

possession is known as kitsune-tsuki. The sufferer is usually a woman of the poorer classes, one who is highly sensitive and open to believe in all manner of superstitions. The question of demoniacal possession is still an unsolved problem, and the studies of Dr. Baelz of the Imperial University of Japan seem to point to the fact that animal possession in human beings is a very real and terrible truth after all. He remarks that a fox usually enters a woman either through the breast or between the fingernails, and that the fox lives a separate life of its own, frequently speaking in a voice totally different from the human's.

Another unusual type of possession was by *inugami* (犬神), the god dogs that moved throughout the Shikoku and Chugoku districts. Inugami possession was less direct than other forms of tsukimono—it was a hereditary taint that affected an entire family line. Inugami-possessed families were called *tsukimono-tsuji*, meaning something like a witch clan. The invisible dogs acted more as familiars than invading spirits. Tsukimono-tsuji families were able to command inugami to spiritually attack others.

Victims of kitsune-tsuki and tsukimono-tsuji were actively discriminated against. Possession was a stain that lasted forever. People carefully checked the family backgrounds of potential marriage or business partners to ensure they had no hint of yokai lineage. To bind your family to a possessed family was disastrous—you and all your heirs would now carry the taint. During the Edo period in particular, people were vigilant against possession. Accused families would be burned out of their homes and banished.

With no surprise, tsukimono discrimination is often linked to the untouchable caste known as *burakumin*. These were the outcasts of traditional Japanese society: undertakers, butchers, tanners, and the like, those who worked with blood and corpses. Many burakumin families were accused of being tsukimono-tsuji; people said that when you walked through a burakumin village, you could sense the invisible foxes and dogs, waiting for their master's commands.

Of course, in modern, more enlightened Japan, no one believes a word of it. Or do they? While you can probably no longer get away with blaming your expanding waistline on being possessed by a tanuki who is forcing you to overeat, there are still rumors of inugami families and those with kitsune-tainted bloodlines. Folk beliefs die hard. Like the tsukimono themselves, they never completely go away.

When it comes to Fairy beasts, there is much debate as to whether they should be categorized as animals or just transfigurations of other fairy creatures. Regardless they are mysterious, powerful and, in many cases, deadly.

The Cat Sidhe (cawt-shee) or Cat Sith is one of these very beings and is one of the most enigmatic and little known of the fairy realm. Although more widely recognized in tales of folklore from the Scottish Highlands, as with much of Celtic lore it also appears in the traditional tales of the Emerald Isle.

The size of a dog, the Cat Sith is jet black except for a white spot upon its breast. Synonymous with death, the feline fairy is feared around the bodies of the deceased as it is a taker of souls. Traditions include putting out fires so as not to entice the Cat Sith with warmth and distracting it from the corpse with

games of jumping and tussling or setting riddles and not solving them.

On the feast of Samhain, many homesteads would leave out a saucer of milk so that the Cat Sith would bless the home for the coming year. Those who didn't would be cursed and the milk from their cows would run dry.

One of the most interesting theories is that the Cat Sith is, in fact, a witch. It is said that certain witches have the ability to transform into a cat shape up to eight times while retaining the ability to change back. Should the witch decide to change a ninth time, she is destined to stay in cat form forever. Could this be the source behind the legend of a cat having nine lives?

Regardless of its origin, the Cat Sith is a formidable creature with all the tricky attributes of its feral cat counterpart. Add in the fact this beast can steal your soul, and I imagine it would be very bad luck indeed for you to cross the path of this particular black fairy feline.

The Fomoire or Formorians were a race of demi-gods who arrived in Ireland from across the seas and were some of the very first settlers on the shores of the Emerald Isle. In fact, the name is sometimes believed to derive from the sea, however it is more likely it relates to being of the Underworld.

Unlike their supernatural counterparts, the Tuatha Dé Danann, the Fomoire were wild forces of nature, embracing chaos and shunning order. Some believe the ways of the Fomoire were so feral and dark that they bordered on the demonic, which reflected in their appearance and references to the Underworld. This could be misconstrued as a reaction to their unsightly form. They were generally ugly creatures, some part-man, part-animal, others with limbs missing or with one dominant eye, such as the King of the Fomoire know as Balor of the Evil Eye.

In *Leabhar Gabhala Eireann* (The Book of Conquests of Ireland) dating back to the 11th Century, the Fomoire were described as '*crowds of abominable giants and monsters*'. The women of the Fomoire were no exception to this rule. There were some Formorians, such as Elatha, who was looked upon as a human-shaped creature of beauty.

Fomoire were beings of the land. Farming and breeding were their specialty. These skills were unknown to the Tuatha Dé Danann and they were desperate to get their hands on them. That talent for working with the earth may have been because the Fomoire had been a part of Ireland since long before their rivals and were spiritually one with the land and sea in ways other settlers could only dream of.

In truth, the Fomoire are an enigma. No one quite knows from where or when they came. They dipped in and out of history and the annals of Ireland and never decisively left. Nobody can tell if they were good or evil and no one knows for sure their ultimate goal. Perhaps they slipped quietly into the shadows, watching, biding their time, waiting to rise once more...

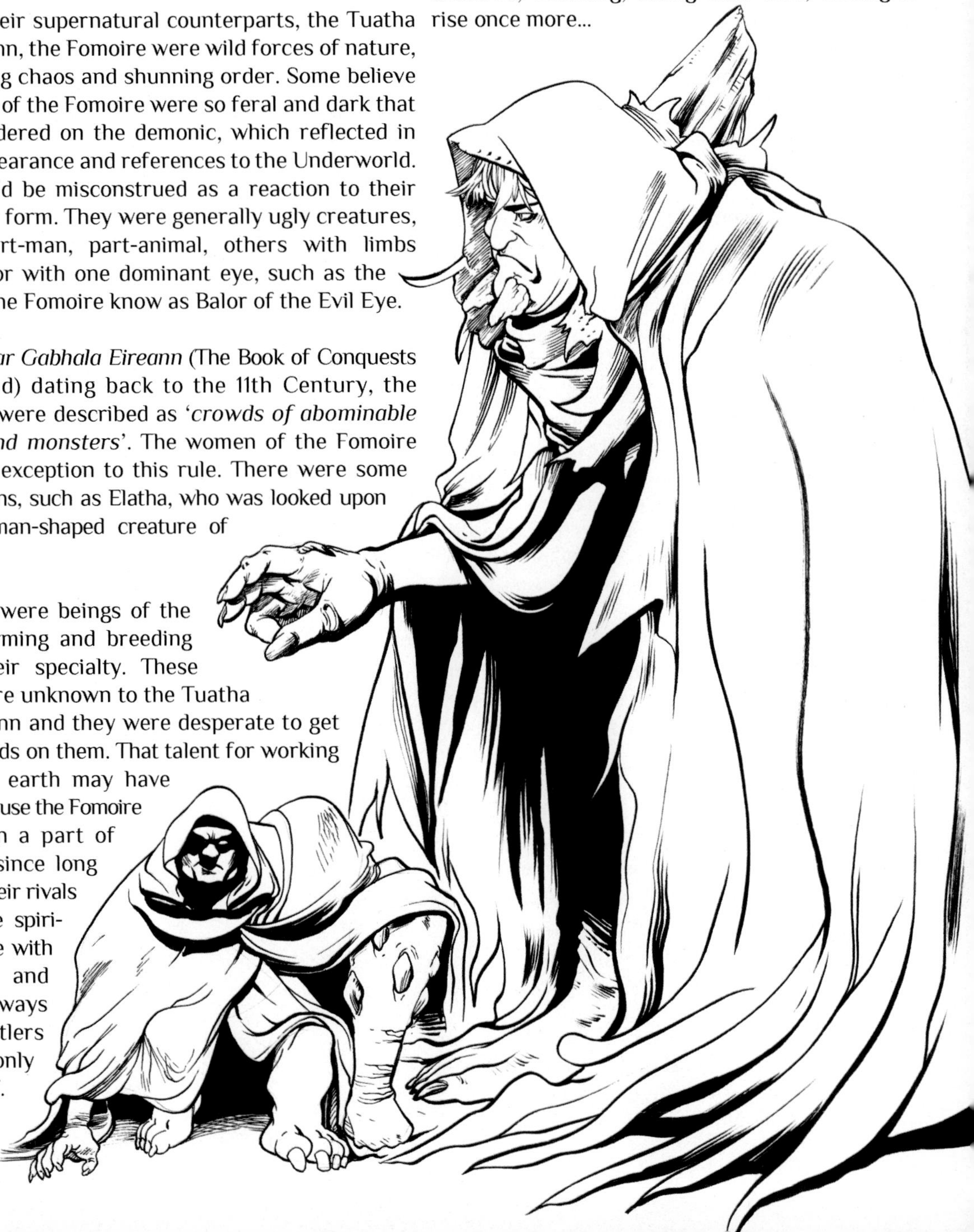

If you wondered why Irish males have a reputation for being smooth talking, tall, dark and handsome strangers, then you need look no further than the Gancanagh (Gawn-canack). The name has a literal translation of '*Love Talker*' and the title is no word of a lie!

One of the solitary fairy folk, the Gancanagh is part of the leprechaun family, although you wouldn't think it to look at him. Tall, wiry and very easy on the eye, women are drawn helplessly to this ethereal being before he even begins to weave his intoxicating magic.

Tales of this mystery man stealing hearts and sanity date back over millennia. Likened to the Incubus, the Gancanagh is more subtle and much more deadly. Traditionally, his target would be the women of rural areas such as milkmaids, devouring their chastity and casting shame on the family, but he moves on with the times as much as he does with locations.

He is dressed stylishly and oozes charm with his distinguished pipe or 'dudeen' pressed between his lips. The Gancanagh is nonchalant on the surface and appears lazy, but don't be fooled. He will charm, lie and ultimately seduce his target - once that happens, their deadly fate is sealed.

I may have misled you by painting a romantic picture of this fairy. Trust me, this is just a façade. He isn't looking for love, he seeks complete control using his intoxicating touch and, when his prey is completely dependent upon him, he callously withdraws his affection and leaves. The victims of the Gancanagh fall into a lovesick frenzy, and, like any drug addiction, it takes over their minds and bodies with disastrous consequences. Isolated from family and friends, pining for the touch of the Gancanagh, they spiral into madness until death becomes a welcome release.

There is one way to protect yourself from this seductive creature. An amulet made from the twigs of rowan and mistletoe, pinned together with an iron nail and bound with a blood-soaked thread.

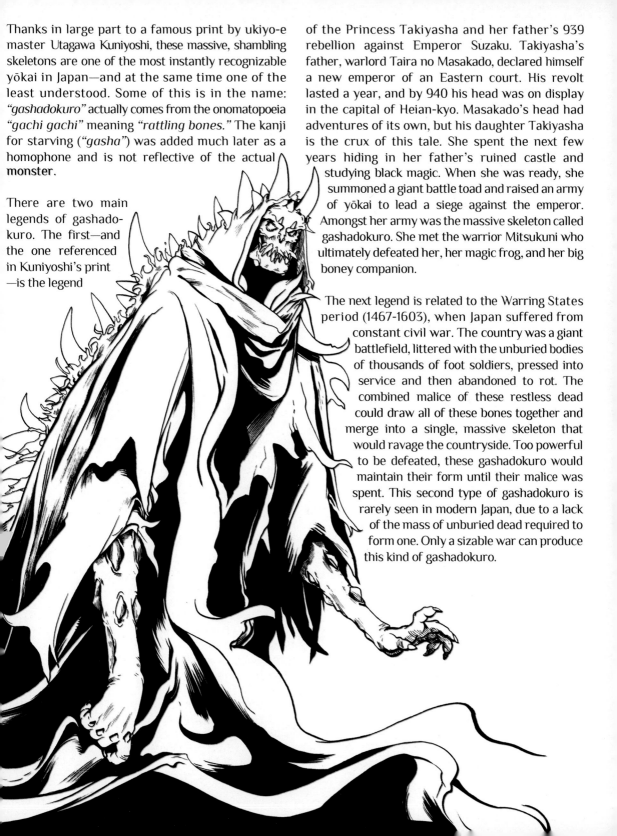

Thanks in large part to a famous print by ukiyo-e master Utagawa Kuniyoshi, these massive, shambling skeletons are one of the most instantly recognizable yōkai in Japan—and at the same time one of the least understood. Some of this is in the name: *"gashadokuro"* actually comes from the onomatopoeia *"gachi gachi"* meaning *"rattling bones."* The kanji for starving (*"gasha"*) was added much later as a homophone and is not reflective of the actual monster.

There are two main legends of gashado-kuro. The first—and the one referenced in Kuniyoshi's print —is the legend of the Princess Takiyasha and her father's 939 rebellion against Emperor Suzaku. Takiyasha's father, warlord Taira no Masakado, declared himself a new emperor of an Eastern court. His revolt lasted a year, and by 940 his head was on display in the capital of Heian-kyo. Masakado's head had adventures of its own, but his daughter Takiyasha is the crux of this tale. She spent the next few years hiding in her father's ruined castle and studying black magic. When she was ready, she summoned a giant battle toad and raised an army of yōkai to lead a siege against the emperor. Amongst her army was the massive skeleton called gashadokuro. She met the warrior Mitsukuni who ultimately defeated her, her magic frog, and her big boney companion.

The next legend is related to the Warring States period (1467-1603), when Japan suffered from constant civil war. The country was a giant battlefield, littered with the unburied bodies of thousands of foot soldiers, pressed into service and then abandoned to rot. The combined malice of these restless dead could draw all of these bones together and merge into a single, massive skeleton that would ravage the countryside. Too powerful to be defeated, these gashadokuro would maintain their form until their malice was spent. This second type of gashadokuro is rarely seen in modern Japan, due to a lack of the mass of unburied dead required to form one. Only a sizable war can produce this kind of gashadokuro.

Irish forms part of the group of Celtic languages and is also known as Gaelic. There are several languages including Scottish, Manx and Welsh. Irish is most closely associated with Scottish Gaelic and originated more than 2500 years ago.

Although English is the predominant language, Irish or Gaelic is the official language of Ireland and you cannot become a police officer or 'Garda' (pronounced 'Guard-ah') in Ireland without having passed Irish language exams. It is tied into our culture, history and folklore in such a way it can never die and the language itself is being revived and taken to new levels through the arts, music and literature. There are also still several parts of the Emerald Isle where Irish is widely spoken day to day such as areas of Connemara, the Aran Islands and Kerry.

Although Irish follows the same alphabet as English and many European languages, we have our own unique traits such as our accent known as the 'fada' which changes the pronunciation of words by elongating the vowel. As an example the name Séan. Without the fada it would simply be pronounced 'Seen', however the fada changes the pronunciation to 'Shawn.'

There are some set rules and order to speech and pronunciation, however with regional dialects changing sounds and spellings, it can all be a bit of a challenge!

The Races and Warriors
Cú Chulainn – Coo Cullen
Fionn Mac Cumhaill – Finn Mac-Cool
Fir Bolg – Fear Bowlg
Fomoire – For-mora
Partholóin – Par-ho-lowen
Tuatha Dé Danann – Tooha Day Dan-ann

Feasts, Battles and Fairy Curses
Bealtaine – Bell-ta-na
Imbolc – Im-bol-cha
Lughnasa – Loo-nas-sa
Magh Tuireadh – Mog Tiera
Piseóg – Pish-owg
Samhain – Sow-ann
Tailteann – Tell-ten

Fairy Folk (good and bad!)
Aes Sidhe – Ass Shee
Crom Dubh – Chrome Dove
Dullahan – Doo-la-han
Fear Dearg – Far Darrig
Gan Ceann – Gone Ki-oun
Ganacanagh – Gone-canack
Púca – Poo-ka
Sidhe – Shee
Sluagh – Sloo-ah

As you can see, we rarely spell a word in Irish the way it actually sounds! My advice? Have a bit of craic trying and, after a bit of practice and a drop of fine Irish whiskey to loosen your vocal cords, you'll be a natural! *Sláinte!*

Runes, Protections and Ogham, the Ancient Language of the Druids

Ogham is the ancient language at the heart of Pagan Ireland and is shrouded in mystery and magic. Believed to have been created by the Druids, it was a cipher designed to confuse those unfamiliar with the ways of the Pagan.

The language is based on the Druid beliefs associated with trees, which is why it's also known as the '*Tree Alphabet*'. From these tree meanings, the Druid spells, protections and 'runes' were created and they've stood the test of time.

Ogham Stones are markers discovered all over Ireland, with Ogham carved into the stone itself. Believed to be everything from gravestones of warriors to warnings, they are most prevalent in Munster, with one being found on the Mountain of Truth, portal to the Fairy Realm.

Although runes are associated with Norse mythology and magic, the Druids created their own protections using Ogham and borrowed more than one symbol from their Germanic counterparts. Runes tend to be positive energy, divination and magic as opposed to a symbol of strife.

For example, the yew represents being solitary, standing alone but the mark itself means accepting the inevitable, destiny, new beginnings and contact with the past.

The Ogham symbol for the Rowan tree (Irish word '*Caorthann*') represents Strength, Healing, Health, Protection, especially against enchantment and Psychic Energy. Delicate enough for baby Rori's forehead!

For extra strength and protection, it was very common to combine the symbols for extra potency such as a combination of the Elder and Holly Runes. The Elder is an overall tree of protection casting a great shadow of protection over those in its shade. The Holly is very much used in Paganism even now as it survives even the harshest and cruellest of winters and thus is a symbol of hope and protection against evil.

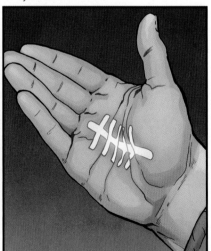

Letter	Name	Tree		Letter	Name	Tree
B	Beith	Birch		M	Muin	Vine
L	Luis	Rowan		G	Gort	Ivy
F	Fearn	Alder		NG	nGéatal	Reed
S	Sail	Willow		Z (st)	Straif	Blackthorn
N	Nion	Ash		R	Ruis	Elder
H	hÚath	Hawthorn		A	Ailm	Silver Fir
D	Dair	Oak		O	Onn	Gorse
T	Tinne	Holly		U	Úr	Heather
C	Coll	Hazel		E	Eadha	Poplar
Q	Quert	Apple		I	Iodhadh	Yew

Wayward Pronunciation Guide – Japanese

While grammar and vocabulary can be a twisting, winding, endless staircase—especially the Chinese characters called *kanji*—one of the ways the Japanese language is much easier than English is in pronunciation. There is no coarticulation, elision, intrusion, or aspiration. What you see is what you get—with a few exceptions. Most Japanese words use consonant/vowel pairs, so pronunciation is simple. Just toss a hyphen after every vowel and you are good to go!

Oh, and remember that every vowel gets its own beat, even when next to another vowel. Take a word like "yokai." In English, you blend the last two vowels together into a single sound, pronouncing it "Yo–Kai." In Japanese, it is a 3–syllable word. "Yo–Ka–I" (Yoh–Kah–Ee). See? Easy!

The Wayward
Ayane – A–Ya–Ne (Ah–Yah–Neh)
Emi Ohara – E–Mi O–Ha–Ra (Eh–Me Oh–Hah–Rah)
Inaba – I–Na–Ba (Ee–Nah–Bah)
Nikaido – Ni–Ka–I–Do (Nee–Kah–Ee–Doh)
Rori Lane – Ro–Ri (Roar–Ree) * *Lane is pronounced...*
   "Lane." And I'm not going to get into the R/L
   pronunciation thing. Consider that the advanced class.
Segawa – Se–Ga–Wa (Say–Gah–Wah)
Shirai – Shi–Ra–I (She–Rah–Ee)

The Yokai
Akaname – A–Ka–Na–Me (Ah–Kah–Nah–May)
Gashadokuro – Ga–Sha–Do–Ku–Ro (Gah–Sha–Doh–Ku–Roh)
Hitodama – Hi–To–Da–Ma (He–Toh–Dah–Mah)
Hyakume – Hya–Ku–Me (Hyah–Ku–May)
Jorogumo – Jo–Ro–Gu–Mo (Joh–Roh–Gu–Moh)
Kage Onna – Ka–Ge O–N–Na (Kah–Geh Oh–N–Nah)
Kappa – Ka–Ppa (Kah–Pah) * *Another oddity, the double*
   consonant. You have to kind of pop your lips for this
   one to do it right. Like a glottal stop, but with your lips.
Kitsune – Ki–Tsu–Ne (Kee–Tsu–Neh) * *Note that "tsu"*
   is a single sound in Japanese. Try saying "su" with
   your tongue in the "t" position and you will get near the
   target.
Kyokotsu – Kyo–Ko–Tsu (Kyoh–Koh–Tsu) * *All the*
   tricky bits in one name. If you can say this one, you can
   say any of them.
Neko Musume – Ne–Ko Mu–Su–Me (Neh–Koh Mue–Sue–May)
Nopperabo – No–Pper–A–Bo (Noh–Peh–Rah–Boh)
   * *The same double–consonant as kappa.*
Nurarihyon – Nu–Rah–Ri–Hyon (New–Rah–Ri–Hyon)
   * *Did I say "no coarticulation?" Sorry, a bit of a lie.*
   There is "some" coarticulation, like the H and Y here
   that make up "hyon."
Suiko – Su–I–Ko (Sue–Ee–Koh)
Taka Onna – Ta–Ka O–N–Na (Tah–Kah Oh–N–Nah)
   * *Same again with the "n." It's the only free–standing*
   consonant in the Japanese language. "N" never comes
   at the start of a word, only the middle or end.

Tengu – Te–N–Gu (Te–En–Gu) * *That one's weird,*
   right? But yeah, the "n" in the middle totally gets
   its own syllabic beat. It's pronounced..."n". Think of
   how an "N" sounds without a vowel, and you got it.

Sorry...I lied a little about that "easy to pronounce" thing at the beginning....I also skipped over long vowels to make things a little easier. So this guide isn't 100% accurate, but should give you enough to approximate the accurate pronunciation!